PRETTY LITTLE WIFE

PRETTY LITTLE WIFE

PRETTY LITTLE WIFE

A Novel

Darby Kane

WILLIAM MORROW
An Imprint of HarperCollinsPublishers

PRETTY LITTLE WIFE. Copyright © 2020 by Helen Kay Dimon. All rights reserved. No part of this book may be used or reproduced in any manner whatsoever without written permission except in the case of brief quotations embodied in critical articles and reviews. For information, address HarperCollins Publishers, 195 Broadway, New York, NY 10007. Printed and bound by CPI Group (UK) Ltd, Croydon, CR0 4YY

HarperCollins books may be purchased for educational, business, or sales promotional use. For information, please email the Special Markets Department at SPsales@harpercollins.com.

FIRST EDITION

Designed by Diahann Sturge

Library of Congress Cataloging-in-Publication Data has been applied for.

ISBN 978-0-06-301640-8 (paperback)
ISBN 978-0-06-308013-3 (international edition)

21 22 23 24   CPI   10 9 8

To my mom, Joan Dimon, who passed down her love of thrillers and suspense to me, who never said no to buying me a book, and who gave birth to me (admittedly, I should probably lead with that one).

PRETTY LITTLE WIFE

PRETTY LITTLE WIFE

Chapter One

A MONSTER.

She missed the signs before. Maybe ignored them without fully realizing it. Now she couldn't unsee them.

Adrenaline raced through her as she tore their bedroom apart. Overturned the laundry basket and scattered the contents. Shoved the bed, banging her shin on the metal bed frame before pushing the mattress to check underneath. Crawled on her knees across the floor, ignoring the shooting pain as bone struck hardwood. She even checked behind the heavy curtains he insisted they use because light in the morning gave him a headache.

The revulsion festering inside her, carefully tucked away for years so as not to spill over and contaminate their tenuous peace, exploded. A wave of scalding heat ran through her, poisoning and erasing every good memory.

The stupid blackout curtains. She'd searched for weeks for the combination of the right color and the perfect dark liner he'd barked at her to find. Never mind that she preferred waking up to the light pouring in or that the heavy material gave the room a suffocating sense of darkness.

His rules and *his* needs.

All of her energy—all of that pent-up hate—built and concentrated until it boiled. The recent string of slights and snide comments she'd ignored. The frustration she'd choked back. The disappointment that she'd let her need to feel normal, to mimic everyone around her, lead her here. To him.

Throwing all her weight into it, she tugged and yanked on those precious curtains. Pulled as a scream rumbled up her throat. A ripping sound screeched through the room, and her balance faltered. The stiff material she'd pulled painfully taut at last gave. The left side shredded on the rod, and the pressure holding her up released in a whoosh.

Her feet tangled and she fell. She landed in a hard sprawl near the end of the bed then stayed there, staring at a blank space on the white wall, wishing she'd made better choices.

There in the quiet, she heard the snap. That barrier deep inside her, walled off and hollow, that allowed her to stumble along and ignore what she needed to ignore, crashed down. Anger and distaste, disappointment and guilt. The emotions tumbled and mixed, spilling through her, flooding every cell.

As soon as the rush of flaming heat arrived, it evaporated. Dried up and disappeared in the space between breaths.

She felt nothing.

Chapter Two

AN HOUR HAD PASSED SINCE THE INITIAL FRENZY. SHE'D MAN-
aged to sit up, but not much more. She balanced on the edge
of their bed buried in a pile of clothing. Dirty and clean mixed
until one merged into the other. Jeans and sweatshirts lay scattered around, thrown in her haste to dig to the back of every
drawer and search through every hidden nook.

Random thoughts slipped into her mind then whipped
right back out again. She couldn't hold on to an idea or manu-
facture an explanation for what she'd found. None that made
sense or matched the stories he told. Not one.

The truth bombarded her, but her brain refused to focus.
Every time she tried to fit the pieces together, to decipher,
something inside her misfired.

Such an ordinary thing landed her here, in this upended
state. Clothing. She'd been searching for the T-shirt he
blamed her for misplacing while doing the laundry. As if that
were even possible.

"Lila?"

She jerked at the sound of her name. He shouldn't be home

for hours. Of course he picked today to slip away early. To surprise her.

What do you want now?

"Where are you?" he shouted to her as he stomped through the house.

Her muscles refused to move. They'd clamped down, locking her in a haze of blurry vision and fogged thinking.

The damn videos. She'd punished herself by watching the first one. Then the next. That's as far as she got before the breath left her body.

Minutes ticked by while she stared at the cell screen. Her fingers clenched around the phone she'd never seen before. The one he hid from her in the chest of drawers he insisted she leave alone because she didn't fold clothing the way he wanted it folded. Stored behind stacks of thin and faded T-shirts he kept promising to weed out and throw away. So many promises . . . gone.

Didn't take a genius to guess why he'd been so territorial over a piece of furniture. It was his hiding place. The phone clearly meant something to him or she would have known about it before now. No one hid meaningless things.

The screen, now dark, the battery having blinked off, tormented her. Somewhere in minute two or three of listening to those female voices spin in her head, her brain clicked off. All those years of pushing the dark back, of denying and pretending she'd locked this type of horror out of her life, of wallowing in guilt until it threatened to suck her under, jammed up on her. The memories. They flooded her now. All the yelling and name-calling. The questions. So many questions.

This couldn't be happening again.

"Lila? Where the hell are you?"

The house was big but not that big. He'd find her soon in the massive bedroom at the far end of the hall, lost in a pile of his precious belongings.

"Hey . . ." His voice faded as he stalked into the middle of the wardrobe bloodbath and stopped. "What the hell happened in here? Why did you touch my stuff?"

His stuff. He viewed everything, even her, as his property.

For a few seconds, she stared at him and wondered why she'd ever agreed to that first date. He'd been charming, sure. All guy-next-door with his light brown hair and bright blue eyes. He was tall, but not threateningly so. Attractive in his confidence. His smile had won her over. He seemed . . . harmless. That's what she'd craved. The benign.

Now she wanted to punch that mouth and keep hitting until silence blanketed her.

"Why are you just sitting there? What's wrong with you?" he asked as he turned in a slow circle, taking in every inch of her rampage.

"I was looking for your shirt." Her voice came out steady, amazing even her.

"The one you lost." He said it as if that were a fact. "I appreciate the effort but you should have asked before you went rifling through my things."

"I live here, too."

"Okay, but you have to admit that this looks . . ."

"What?" She had no idea how he would twist his way out of this one.

"Unhinged."

Oh, right. Of course he would say that. Blame her.

This time—this time only—he wasn't wrong. She felt unwound. Held together by a thin thread of sheer will and nothing more.

"I found this." She held up the new-to-her phone.

His expression didn't change. His mouth didn't so much as twitch. "What is it?"

As if he didn't know. The lying asshole.

"Don't do that. It's yours, and we both know it."

He let out a long breath. It came out as an exhausted sigh, as if he'd been stuck with her for too long and had grown weary. "Now, don't get hysterical."

Gaslighting. She heard it in the fake soothing cadence of his voice. In every syllable.

"I haven't moved." She forced her voice to stay flat. Sucked all of the emotion out of the words to prevent him from throwing them back at her.

He glanced at the phone then to her face. "But you've let your imagination run wild. I know you."

He didn't, but leave it to him to find a way to make himself the wronged party in this. "That's not true."

"Look at this mess." He motioned toward the empty dresser drawers.

She tightened her grip on the phone. "You didn't even use a different pin."

"That's enough." The deeper they waded into the emotional morass, the more in control he sounded. That placating voice. He even held up his hands in mock surrender as if he needed to calm *her* down. "Listen to me."

"Go ahead. Try to explain."

"I shouldn't have to." He stopped the sentence there and held her gaze for a few seconds with an unwavering glare. "But the reality is it's nothing. A practical joke by a couple of students that went sideways. Nothing to worry about."

He thought she was an idiot. That was the only explanation.

Her muscles shook, but she forced her body up. Somehow managed to get to her feet and stay there. "I know what I saw."

He sighed at her again, full of indignation and unsteady tolerance. "What you *think* you saw. Because I promise you're wrong."

More gaslighting.

The trick jumped out at her now. He formed sentences and revised history to make her think she was the unreasonable one. Turned and twisted the facts until she questioned her brain and her eyes. Dumped her in a place where she doubted everything except him.

Not this time. He'd done the one thing she couldn't slap an explanation on, or let him weasel out of, or chisel down into nothing.

Her fingers clenched around the phone until the plastic dug into her palm. "Get out."

All that fake civility vanished as his mouth curled in a snarl. "It's my fucking house."

He had never hit her, but maybe that had been a matter of good timing and a bit of luck. The right push and this could be it.

Every cell inside her screamed to move, but she refused to back down. She took a step closer, challenging him on the most basic level. Questioning what he insisted belonged solely to him. She lifted her chin higher. "The house is ours."

His hand whipped out and caught her around the throat. "Say that again."

She tried to swallow but couldn't. Said his name, but it came out as a harsh whisper. Her spirit refused to break. "It's ours. Mine as much as yours."

Those fingers flexed against her skin. His palm pressed against her windpipe, daring her to push him past the brink. He didn't squeeze, but the hatred pulsing off him told her he could and would never regret it. Pure disdain. There was no other way to describe it. As if he wouldn't blink if she disappeared.

He leaned in until his mouth hovered over her ear. "Did you pay for the house, Lila? One mortgage payment? One tax payment? A water bill?"

He'd put her name on the title, but he viewed the property as his. He deposited money into the joint account to cover bills. Not a penny more. He let her write the actual checks, but he controlled every dime, every month, then looked like he expected her to thank him for being a great provider.

"You never gave me that choice." She wanted them to be equals. That's what she'd signed up for when they got married. It's what they'd agreed to. But with each year he took more control and lessened her role. Turned her into some sort of dress-up doll he paraded around town.

She silently fought back by going out to dinner less and never attending his events. He'd sweet-talk and push, and now she recognized every move as manipulation. Nothing more than a long con that she'd fallen for until he'd gone one step too far.

"I run this household," he said.

His money. His house. He made the decisions, even the ones that impacted her job and where they lived. Him, him, him.

She'd conceded so much ground to him. She had no idea when it'd happened or why she'd let her life get so small.

No more. The unspoken declaration vibrated through her.

"Do it or let go." Her voice strained against his hand.

He frowned at her. "What?"

"Kill me. That's where this is heading, right?" Every move and the dragging anger in his voice pointed there.

Despite his need for control, his mood had always been pretty even. But she had something on him now. Something that could break him and ruin that shiny reputation he stoked with neighborly good deeds and a fake smile. It was as if her breaking point this afternoon tipped off his.

He shook his head but didn't let go of her neck.

Her hand covered his. She tried to pry his fingers off, to put an inch of distance between them, as the panic constricted her throat.

That quickly, he dropped his arm to his side. The swift move had her tipping forward when all she wanted to do was run away.

After a few seconds of her stumbling, he put his hands on her forearms to steady her. "I'm not the kind of man who hits."

"Because that's the bar? You don't beat me, so you're a great husband."

"You're pushing me, Lila. I advise you to stop." He never blinked as he watched her. "This thing with the phone really is nothing. Don't let your imagination fill in gaps that don't exist."

"The videos—"

He made a tut-tutting sound. "I told you. Silly girls doing silly things. That's all."

Liar.

It was as if he'd forgotten about her previous life. She'd played verbal gymnastics with people much more cunning than him. The kind who would be smart enough not to use the same password on their secret phone as they used on their usual one. "If that's true, then why did you save them? And why hide the phone?"

"For insurance."

"How? Even if the videos were a prank, they could be used to ruin you. I heard your voice on one." She feared she would never forget what she'd heard. "Explain how you've protected yourself. Us."

"I don't appreciate your tone." When she started to respond to that, he held up a hand and talked over her. "This discussion is over. I've told you what you need to know, and now you can stop worrying about this. There's more to it than the videos. I have the whole matter handled."

She knew that was a lie. All of this was one big lie. She didn't ask anything else, because the responses would be more of the same. Nonsense and bullshit.

He smiled in a way that made her feel more like prey than a wife. "Now that we've resolved that . . ."

He leaned in and kissed her on the forehead. She fought off a flinch but just barely. Maybe that's where he wanted her energy focused, because he swooped in and pried the phone out of her hand before she realized what was happening.

"Clean this room up. I came home early to take you to dinner, but I can't do that with this mess." Then he walked out, cell phone in hand.

To him, that was it. He actually thought his comments and weak assurances ended the conversation. That she would slink back into her life, forget what she'd seen, and move on. That she was too stupid to have forwarded some of the videos to her email before the battery on his top secret phone died.

She would review them all and tease out every detail. And no, she would not let him turn this around and make it her fault. He'd always known the one thing she could not live through again . . . and he'd crashed their marriage right into it.

She'd *handle* it. She didn't before, but she would this time.

She would be the one to stop him.

Chapter Three

Six Weeks Later
End of September

A NORMAL TUESDAY.

The relatively boring nature of the usual morning schedule would tumble through Lila Ridgefield's mind every time she thought back on this day. Nothing different. Nothing to see here.

She walked around all morning, groggy and unsettled. Nursed a cup of coffee as it morphed from piping hot, to lukewarm, to sour and cold. By a little after ten, she slipped out of her comfortable pajamas and put on long, flowy black dress pants and a green silk blouse. The kind of outfit worn by ladies who enjoyed a fancy lunch out at the club but didn't do much else with their time.

The temptation to find sweats or yoga pants tugged at her, but she didn't give in. She maintained the image Aaron wanted, even this morning. Casual clothes would be out of character. People would notice. Today needed to look like a normal day. Blend in so nothing stuck out as unusual or, worse, memorable.

The wardrobe specifications had been a request from Aaron early in their marriage. After suffering through a difficult childhood, complete with the loss of both parents, he insisted a family look a certain way to the outside world. For his wife—if only on the exterior and to others—to come off as put together and project a certain image at all times. For them to have a weekly housekeeping service and meal delivery for the times when neither of them wanted to cook. For anyone watching to see success.

She chalked up the request to his idealized view of family. One different from what he'd known. It was as if he believed if he had all the outside trappings, from the big house to the perfect wife, the rest would fall in line. No one could question or destroy it. She understood because she'd maneuvered her way through a dysfunctional upbringing and knew the things you grabbed on to to survive weren't always rational.

At the beginning of their marriage the Aaron-imposed public dress code, while sometimes annoying, wasn't a problem. It blended in with what she needed to wear to the office. That changed when they moved and she left her job, but his requirements for that dream of perfection never dimmed.

Now he couldn't play that game. Thanks to her.

Today she complied on her terms. She picked the perfect outfit to stand outside on the long driveway that twisted its way up to her sprawling ranch house at the top of the hill. Hair styled and a light touch of makeup. Ready to fake mourn.

The gardeners deserved the credit for the pristine lawn and intricately shaped bushes. Her contribution amounted to writing a check for their services every month. Growing up, her father viewed mowing as a man's job, convinced she'd hurt herself. The lectures about what was and wasn't her place blurred into a humming sound in her head. His stern and disapproving voice. The way he screamed *Jesus* at her mother so often that Lila didn't realize it wasn't part of her mother's actual name until she got older. Right around the time the whispering about her parents started.

A buzzing vibrated in her brain now. The memories itched and scratched, desperate to break through the invisible barrier she slammed into place to shut them out. She did what she always did to survive. Blocked and refocused, this time on the warm sun. It beamed down, breaking through the lingering chill.

She touched the top button of the silk cardigan draped over her shoulders and looked at the straight edge where the grass met the pavement. The line, too perfect, called out for flowers. A splash of color amid the sea of brown. Brown house siding on top of brown stone. Brown shutters with a darker brown front door.

Aaron had bought the property without her input about four years ago. She'd stayed behind in North Carolina to clean up before their move north. He'd gone up for a quick meeting about his new teaching job and called her, shouting about a bargain. One with old plumbing and wiring so unpredictable that it prevented them from plugging in more than two lights in the living room at the same time during the first few months they lived there.

He'd already signed the offer by the time he called. Of course he had. Still in those earlier days, flush with a sense of hopefulness and a naïve optimism about how they could do better than their parents and forge a path, she didn't recognize his move for what it was—a complete dismissal of her opinion. Treating her as an afterthought.

She was wiser now. More jaded but open to the truth about the minimal role she played in his thinking and in his life.

She refocused again, this time on that razor edge of green, and thought about pink. Aaron would hate the change. He viewed pink as a direct blow to his masculinity. So pink flowers in spring it would be.

After a quick scan of the quiet suburban cul-de-sac, she took the cell phone out of her pocket and checked for messages. Nothing waited for her.

Unexpected, but it was still early.

She wandered down to the mailbox. After Aaron ran over the last one during a bad ice storm in March, he'd picked out one shaped like a duck as the replacement. He joked about how great it would be if it made a noise. Spent the afternoon he bought it walking around the house and scaring the crap out of her by yelling, "Quack!" She had no idea why he found that funny or what the duck meant to him, but then many things Aaron did and said were a mystery to her.

A sign hung off the duck's belly, taunting her. THE PAYNE'S. Block letters of a name she never informally or formally agreed to take. Ridgefield was the last piece of who she'd been before. She clung to it even as she said yes to a marriage to someone as broken as she was.

Her refusal to capitulate on this one thing dropped a wedge in the center of her marriage. Her last stand led to the spousal fight that refused to die over the years.

Then there was the apostrophe. She'd dared to question if one should be there and he'd kicked the sign, shattering the bolt. The force of the blow knocked the left side from its hook and sent it swinging with a screeching sound of metal scraping against metal.

She'd left the unwanted sign hanging there ever since. Crooked. Half-broken and off center. It struck her as the perfect metaphor for their marriage.

"Lila?"

The singsongy voice made Lila cringe. She managed to plaster on a smile by the time she turned to face her seemingly ever-present neighbor. "Hello."

Cassie Zimmer. Every sentence she uttered ended on a tonal upswing as if she were asking an unending series of questions instead of just talking. She smiled without ceasing. That alone made Lila want to slap her. She didn't, of course, but the temptation hovered *right there.*

From the day they moved in, Cassie had been *that* neighbor. She brought cookies on her *welcome to the neighborhood* visit then overstayed by walking around the living room, asking an endless line of personal questions disguised as get-to-know-you talk while she peeked at every unpacked possession.

Lila had mentally put Cassie on the *intolerable* list she kept in her head, and Cassie had never worked her way off it again.

She was a one-woman neighborhood watch. Never mind that no one asked her to step up and take the position. Worse, it was as if Cassie sensed those rare occasions when Lila stepped outside for a moment of fresh air during the day and pounced, mindless chirpy greeting ready.

To be fair, Cassie likely was fine. Probably not all that offensive. Maybe even a decent neighbor because she'd be the first one to jump on 911 if she spied someone walking down the street whom she didn't know. But Lila valued privacy and personal space, and Cassie had only a passing acquaintance with either.

"Are you thinking about doing some gardening?" Cassie winced. "Maybe not the best idea. You're a bit out of season."

Small talk. Lila's least favorite thing.

"We need some color out here." "We" meaning her. She liked color. What Aaron wanted didn't really matter anymore.

Cassie fidgeted with the broken sign under the mailbox, as if simply rehanging it would fix the household's problems.

"The bolt is cracked."

"Hmm?" Cassie's head shot up. "What?"

Lila refused to find a more descriptive way to say it. "No bolt."

Cassie's eyes widened. "Oh. I wonder what happened to it."

Aaron had. But enough chatting. "I should head back inside."

Lila didn't get two steps before Cassie wound up again. "You look nice. Are you working today?"

"Today and every day." Last week one of Aaron's fellow teachers dropped something off at the house and joked about her barely working and then tried to cover with some drivel about her not *needing* to work. His grating nasal voice still rang in her ears. Her employment was one of those pressure points that made Lila grind her back teeth together. Leave it to Cassie to locate the exposed nerve then jump up and down on it. "But yes, I need to do some research."

"It must be so interesting to check out all those different houses. Peek inside and see what's really happening in there."

She had to feel the conversation drag, right? Lila couldn't imagine Cassie didn't hear it . . . or see the attempt to escape back up the driveway and into the house.

The anxiety Lila wrestled with for decades trickled in. Her control skimmed along the far edge, but soon it would crack. Then the race and swirl would begin inside her. That need to be away from people. To speak, but only on her terms.

When she decided to be "on," that was fine. She'd practiced the skill of pretending to be comfortable while the flight instinct kicked into high gear inside of her. She'd lower her voice, slow it down to sound more in control. Concentrate so that her hands wouldn't shake.

But now was not one of the times for which she could win an acting award. Stress after stress piled up. She no longer had the reserves to act like everyone expected her to act.

She pulled the cell out of her pocket to stare at it again. Avoidance often helped, but still no calls. No viable excuse to transport her to somewhere else.

Why hadn't the call come yet? What was taking so long?

"I guess you're on the phone all the time." Cassie let the comment sit there, but when Lila didn't respond, Cassie rushed to fill the quiet. "Being a real estate agent, I mean. You're usually on call, right?"

"It does feel that way."

She *got* to work as much as she wanted. *He* gave that to her . . . or so Aaron claimed. He went to work, taught math to hormonal high schoolers who viewed calculus as a punishment, and she stayed home.

Some women in town once cornered her while getting coffee, those who enjoyed small talk and big gossip, told her in their voices, dripping with jealousy, how lucky she was to have a husband like Aaron. As if playing the role of pretty little wife were a gift and not a life sentence of boredom.

"Do you want to come over—"

The crunching sound of tires on gravel drowned out what sounded like an unwanted invitation for coffee. Lila had never been so happy for visitors. Never been happy about guests— period—until now.

She recognized the black sedan that said *all of my self-esteem is bundled up in an inflated monthly car payment.* Brent Little, Aaron's golfing buddy, best friend, and the principal of the high school, slipped out. He wore a navy suit, looking every inch the guy who was on the hunt to find a girlfriend to re-place the wife who'd left him after sixteen bumpy years of unhappy marriage.

He'd sported that put-together, exercised-to-exhaustion, fake-tanned outer shell for the last two years. Girlfriends would come and go, impressed by the flash and then, Lila assumed, horrified by the single-digit bank balance of a man paying alimony and child support under court order for a family living two states away.

Lila smiled, this time a genuine one because Brent trumped Cassie as the preferred companion. "Shouldn't you be send-ing kids to detention and hiding in the faculty lounge at this time of day?"

Despite her light tone, Brent's expression didn't change. Eyebrows drawn together and mouth flattened into a thin line. His usual sunny smile gone and his steps halting instead of the rushing gait that carried him down the school hallways.

Finally. This was it. She'd been waiting all morning for a visit. She hadn't expected it to be from him, but whatever.

He stopped in front of Lila, sparing only a glance in Cassie's direction before he spoke. "Is Aaron home?"

Lila felt something inside her fall. That wasn't right. That's not what he should be saying. "Why would he be home?"

"He didn't come to work. I've looked everywhere. He didn't call in sick, and when I didn't hear from you . . ."

Not possible.

"Wait a second." She took a deep breath as she tried to maneuver through the questions bombarding her brain. "I got up and he was gone, as usual. He's at the school."

Because that's what they did. She stayed up at night to read or watch television. He went for a run in the early morning and fixed his breakfast, all without having to dodge her, because she only got up when he was about to walk out the door. The system worked for them. That was the schedule . . . until today.

"Look for his car." She couldn't believe she had to be so specific to get this part done, but fine.

A strangled sound escaped Brent's throat. "I've been calling him for almost two hours without success."

"His car is there." Lila *knew* that was true.

Brent shook his head. "Where?"

By the field behind the football stadium where he coached field hockey. That's exactly where it had to be because that's where she put it a few hours ago while their part of the world still was plunged in darkness.

She forced her brain to stay focused. "At school."

She understood some confusion. That was to be expected. He usually parked the SUV in an assigned spot by the school's back door. Far right. First row. Aaron viewed the close-in spot as some sort of badge of honor. But that's not where they'd find it today, and they *should* have found it by now.

"Lila, listen to me." Brent put a hand on her forearm and gave it a gentle squeeze. "He's not there. He never came to school today."

This was ridiculous. How hard could it be to find a vehicle with a body in it?

"I don't get it." She choked the words out over the unexpected ball of anxiety clogging her throat.

"It's probably nothing. A minor accident." Cassie's voice didn't go up at the end of that sentence. "I can call . . ."

Cassie's panicked voice faded until all Lila heard was the rush of blood as it drained from her body.

"There's an explanation." She said the line, hoping to mentally grab on and believe it, but no.

"Yes." Cassie nodded in full helpful-neighbor mode. "Of course."

"He might have needed a day off from the kids." Brent let out a fake laugh that sounded more nervous than sincere. "I'm tempted some days."

All the words and reassurances blended in Lila's head. Brent alternated between rubbing her arm and patting it. Cassie's voice finally registered as she talked on that call. Lila heard a few whispered words. "Police" and "missing" popped out.

Missing. Missing. Missing.

The truth body slammed her, leaving her chest heaving as she struggled for breath. The call she'd been waiting for would never come because Aaron's car wasn't in the lot or by the field. There wasn't a car to find. Despite all her careful planning, he was gone.

She had to find Aaron before he found her.

Chapter Four

AT THIS TIME OF YEAR, THE WEATHER IN THE AREA IN AND around Ithaca balanced the thin line between fall and early winter. Temperatures dropped. Sweaters and sturdier shoes made an appearance. This part of New York, surrounded by the Finger Lakes and shoved right up against Cayuga Lake, defined "bucolic." Trees awash in vibrant color. Waterfalls and hiking trails. Lush gardens and lots of places with "gorge" in the name.

A city with a small town buzz that expanded and contracted when the area's three schools—Cornell University, Ithaca College, and Tompkins Cortland Community College—filled and emptied as the seasons turned. A place where people enjoyed a mix of the outdoors and scholarly discussions. The favorite local pastimes included boating, coffee, and insisting no intelligent person would live in New York City for more than a few years without bolting.

Lila transplanted to a neighborhood outside of Ithaca after meeting Aaron in North Carolina eight years ago and beginning their marriage less than a year later. For Aaron, the move north was a welcome return home, or near it. He'd grown up a bit farther to the east, in Central New York.

The area looked and felt the same to Lila, but the good people of New York knew the geographical boundary puzzle like a secret handshake. Central New York was not Upstate New York. Neither had much in common other than a shared state government with downstate.

Lila stood in Aaron's empty school parking space and stared at the crowd of tress surrounding the one-story red-brick building and the athletic fields in the distance. Her gaze skipped over the vehicles, most some shade of blue or red, to the far end of the lot. She scanned the fields and saw kids out running and playing some sort of sports. Not one sign of Aaron's SUV or a hint of screams as someone peeked inside the window at his still body.

Trying to end this mess, she'd insisted Brent come in by the back entrance to the school grounds. That he drive around, just in case Aaron was outside for an impromptu practice or getting some air. That was the excuse. It gave her a few minutes of silence as she traced a finger down the inside of the car window and tried to make this morning's events make sense.

She focused on the exact spot where she'd parked his SUV hours ago. Lights off, drifting over divots and bumpy grass at less than five miles per hour. Well before sunrise. Maneuvering around security cameras.

She'd planned it all, and somehow it still failed.

Leave it to Aaron to piss her off even in death.

Bells rang inside the building. A second later, the chaotic

burst of talking and laughter seeped through the school walls and floated out to them. Lila focused on the faded white lines and the number twenty-seven printed in the parking spot. Aaron's number.

"Lila?"

Brent's voice broke through the clanging silence in her head. Cassie had volunteered to stay behind to watch in case Aaron wandered home. Brent mentioned the police and questions. Lila heard the words, but they bounced off her, refusing to settle in.

"Are you okay?" he asked.

No. Absolutely not. "Where's his car?" The question flipped over in her head until it slipped out.

"He's probably out on a ride somewhere, clearing his head or laughing at us for not trusting he'd be fine. Just enjoying the day, and then he'll come back and apologize."

Wrong answer. Brent didn't know how wrong that was. He couldn't know, but she did. If Aaron showed up—if that bastard was alive—his anger would destroy everything in its path, especially her.

She took out her cell and hit the app Aaron had set up in case she lost her phone. She'd added his on there, and she tried to locate it now.

Nothing.

"Does an unexplained joyride fit with his personality?" The voice followed the slam of a car door.

Lila's attention shifted, but then that was clearly the goal. A woman. Average height and weight. Curvy. A round, striking face with big dark eyes. Short black hair and a brisk walk. Lila didn't recognize her at all. "Excuse me?"

"Ginny Davis." She held out her card. "Senior investigator."

Lila turned the card over in her hand, too on edge to see anything but a smudge of black lettering. "For what?"

"C.I.D."

Lila looked at the woman but didn't say anything.

The woman explained anyway. "The Criminal Investigation Division of the Tompkins County Sheriff's Office."

Law enforcement . . . already? Lila tried to take a deep breath. Everything was moving too fast and in the wrong direction. "How did you get here so quickly?"

"I called her." Brent grumbled something under his breath. "Well, my secretary did. And your neighbor called someone."

The investigator nodded. "My office. We've received three calls this morning about a missing teacher. I was wrapping up another matter and agreed to swing by and see what exactly the issue was."

She'd stepped in too fast. Hell, they didn't even have a body. And Lila had trouble thinking about anything else.

"So you believe Aaron really is in trouble?" Brent asked.

The investigator shrugged. "I have no way of knowing right now."

That sounded like the right answer to Lila. Smart and effective. It didn't overpromise. It also matched the woman standing in front of Lila in a navy pantsuit. Not cheap but not expensive. The kind that mostly fit except for the slightly too long pants and a waistband that required a belt.

She didn't make any attempt to hide her visual once-over of the area, or of Brent and Lila. "Are you Mrs. Payne?"

The name ripped across Lila's senses, blocking out everything else. "Lila Ridgefield."

"Aaron's wife." Brent said the words in a rush, as if the women needed his guidance through the conversation.

Ginny, because that's how Lila already started to think of her rather than as some faceless, nameless investigator, didn't even blink. "Several people seem concerned about your husband and his whereabouts. We likely don't have anything to worry about. Most people show up within a day or two and have an explanation."

Yeah, that better not happen. "Your response really didn't answer my question. Why are you here *now*?"

"I'm doing a courtesy check only. Right now there's nothing to investigate." Ginny focused on Brent. "Mr. Little?"

"Yes." After a quick handshake, Brent returned to his position slightly behind Lila. "Aren't you supposed to wait forty-eight hours before you start investigating?"

"That's a bit of a Hollywood myth based on the idea that grown-ups sometimes wander but usually come back. We don't want to waste resources, but we don't want to lose precious search time either." Ginny's eyebrow lifted as she looked from Brent to Lila. "Unless you want us to hold off for some reason."

"No." Brent shuffled his feet and stammered for a solid minute before kicking out an answer. "No, of course not."

"If someone truly is missing, we'd rather know immediately

and start working." Ginny's gaze switched to Lila. "Before the trail goes cold."

"Right." Brent nodded as he regained his composure. "When Aaron didn't show up today, I went over to their house and broke the news to Lila."

Ginny frowned again. "What news?"

"That my husband isn't where he should be."

Brent nodded. "She wanted to come to the school to see for herself."

The conversation struck Lila as obvious and not half as interesting as Ginny's intense stare suggested.

"When did you last see your husband, Ms. Ridgefield?"

Now the questions would start. The need for explanations. The digging into her marriage. Taking apart every sentence, every choice, every piece of her life with Aaron. He'd gone missing, and the spotlight would shine on her, casting shadows everywhere. He wasn't where he was supposed to be, and she would pay.

She'd prepared for so many contingencies, but not this one. All of them depended on Aaron being found.

Lila took a long breath. "Last night."

"Not this morning?"

The verbal dance annoyed Lila. The detective or whatever she was had a job to do. Lila needed to find her husband and didn't believe someone who didn't know him, who might get sucked in by his outward charm, could find him faster than she could. "No, which is why I said last night."

Ginny's gaze bounced from Brent to Lila. "Is Aaron the type to take a day off without warning?"

That question was easy to answer because it was a point of pride to Aaron, which Lila found ridiculous. "Not at all."

"He's had perfect attendance for the almost four years he's been here," Brent said as he shook his head. "Hasn't missed a day. Even comes in when he's sick, which is against the rules, but we make an exception. His record and personality are why we called your office immediately rather than waiting to see if he showed up."

"That's who he is." Lila wasn't sure if that fact helped her or not, but she wanted the lead role in shaping that vision for any and all law enforcement who stumbled into the case.

"Okay." Ginny's gaze lingered on Lila before she turned to Brent again. "I understand what you're both saying, but is there anywhere—?"

"On a weekday during the school year he goes to work. That's the point." The thumping in Lila's head kicked up, threatening to swallow the last of her attention.

Ginny's gaze snapped right back to Lila. "Except today."

The noise from inside the school spilled out. Two boys yelled with hands raised as they stumbled outside and stepped in and out of each other's personal space. No one crowded in or joined them in their amateur fight, but faces appeared in the door's glass and a rapt audience formed.

Brent's focus shot to the door. "If you'll excuse me."

He was off, with those long legs chewing up the feet

between them and the brewing fight. The second he stepped in, the shouts of juvenile retribution cut off. After some finger-pointing, the chaos moved back inside the building.

"May I call you Lila?" Ginny asked.

If this were a game, then Lila would play, too. "May I call you Ginny?"

"Sure." The older woman dropped the clipped response before launching into a new topic. "Is there anyone you can think of who might want to hurt your husband?"

Yeah, her.

At any other time, under any other situation, Lila might admire Ginny's style. She verbally zigged and zagged. Asked what she needed to ask, the usual initial questions, most likely, but Lila sensed Ginny didn't care much about the answers. Fact-finding was not the purpose of this trip, at least not in the sense of hearing the one thing that might explain how a thirty-seven-year-old man vanished on his way to work.

No, this back-and-forth was about sizing her up. Ginny's gaze assessed every stray move and every swallow. She pinned Lila under an unseen microscope and gently poked around.

Lila's senses screamed at her to be careful. To cut this short before the anxiety crawling through her burst out of her like a bad horror movie. "He's a high school math teacher."

"Teachers have enemies."

Lila refused to take the bait.

"I'm trying to understand what we're looking at here." Ginny's soothing voice, deep and calm, had a hypnotizing effect. "There were no car accidents in the area this morning with his make of car. No John Doe fitting his description at any local hospitals."

"Aren't you thorough?"

A tiny smile broke over Ginny's lips. "Always."

Lila forced the sensation rushing through her back—the one that shouted to pick flight over fight—as she watched the woman who might feign friendship and support but would likely become her adversary. And a worthy one.

Ginny took out a small notebook and scribbled a few things down. She handled the situation with the confidence of a person who'd fought and clawed her way into the position she held and refused to relinquish it. As a black woman high up in law enforcement, she likely both earned respect and spent most of her day demanding it from men who would prefer to ignore her.

"May I go home?" Lila asked, because the house would ground her as she tried to reason out what happened this morning.

Ginny nodded. "If Aaron doesn't show up by this time tomorrow, I'd like you to come to my office and—"

"You can come to my house and ask whatever you want. Now or later, doesn't matter to me." When Ginny didn't jump on the offer, Lila fell back on reason. "Isn't that better? I'm inviting you in. You can walk through and look around. No need for probable cause or a warrant." Lila found her first smile of the day. "Did I forget to mention I'm a lawyer?"

She had to drop that piece of intel sooner or later. Now worked.

Ginny's eyes narrowed. "One of the people who called mentioned that you were a real estate agent."

Huh. Interesting. "Why does my career matter?" Not that this was a sensitive subject for her, but it was.

"Technically, you mentioned it first." A small smile came and went on Ginny's mouth. "But if you're asking *why* I know, the fact is in my notes. The person calling likely volunteered."

The tension snapping between them subsided. The air shifted, as if they'd reached more even footing. The gun and badge and whatever else Ginny carried in or under that suit might win most battles, but Lila had a few weapons of her own.

"Anything else I should know about you?" Ginny asked.

"I expect you to find Aaron. If you can't do that, I'll hire someone who can." As soon as the words left her mouth, Lila realized she'd spoken her first lie of the day.

"That's not how it works."

"I know Aaron is not the only missing person in the area." Lila had been following along on the news and listening to a weekly true crime podcast that highlighted the case.

She'd done her homework before she launched her plan. The horrible backdrop of a missing woman might help blur the picture of what happened to her husband . . . of course, that all depended on Aaron staying dead.

Ginny didn't so much as twitch at being thrust in the heated spotlight for questioning. "Do you think the cases are related?"

"I hope not, since you haven't found her yet."

Chapter Five

Three Weeks Earlier

AARON SET THE PLATE IN FRONT OF HER. GRILLED CHICKEN and a salad. It was his go-to meal on his night to make dinner. They took turns when they ate in, but he took more food shifts than she did. Probably because her cooking skills extended to grilled cheese and pasta and not one inch further.

Pasta. That's what she really wanted tonight. She'd watched a cooking show this morning and now craved cacio e pepe. She'd never had it, but the idea of noodles with cheese and pepper sounded so simple and delicious that it made her despise the chicken without tasting it.

Aaron stood there, looming over his side of the square table instead of sitting down. "You're staring at the plate."

"It looks good." Sitting there, moving the food around on her plate, all she could think about was how she'd folded her life into his. Her needs grew smaller and smaller, less important and less of a priority, until only broken pieces of what she thought marriage would be remained.

The relationship didn't start that way. He'd been a regular at the sandwich place across from her office where she went to pick up lunch and sometimes dinner. She'd see him and catch him glancing her way. They eventually met when he dropped a full travel coffee mug right in front of her. Stunned and stammering, he apologized and shot her a sweet smile.

He was attractive in a nonthreatening way. A little quiet with a tough background she would learn rivaled her own on the pain scale. So she let him in. Let him as far in as she let anyone, which to be fair was not far.

From the beginning neither demanded much of the other. They built a relationship based on companionship and understanding. He didn't balk at her need for alone time. He liked to fish and was fine to do that without her. He provided stability and safety. When she thought about family, she thought about a home and dinner at the table and the absence of yelling. With him she had all those things.

She'd never looked at Aaron and felt a breathy rush of desire or the need to strip off his clothes and have sex against a wall. They'd done that, but the zing she was supposed to feel never hit her. But it wasn't just Aaron.

For most of her life, she hadn't felt the thrumming sensation. A few twinges of attraction, but the idea of purposely seeking out something fleeting, based on hormones and body parts that could disappear with the wrong haircut or by gaining twenty pounds, seemed like a waste of time.

In reality, she'd spent her entire life running from that out-of-control dynamic in search of safety and would only base a marriage on the latter. Her fear sent her spinning into the arms of the very thing she sought to escape.

"Jim told me a funny story today."

She couldn't call up any interest in what Aaron had to say, let alone some boring story from a random guy. "Jim?"

The chair legs scraped against the floor as Aaron pulled it out and sat down. "Biology teacher from Maine. The one with the thick accent."

She pretended to care as she moved the lettuce around on her plate. "Oh, right."

"He slept in his car last night."

They hadn't gotten to that point, but Aaron did use the guest bedroom right now. Lila refused to feel guilty about that. He deserved to be banished. She'd wanted to pummel him, slap him—something that ended with a crack of skin against skin. Anything to break through the frozen mush of disdain she felt for him.

But she had to wait. Plan. Make her move at the right time.

"Why?" She put down the fork, abandoning any pretense of interest in the food.

"He and the wife argued about money."

"I once read that money is the issue couples fight about the most." Not them, not usually, but other couples. They had enough issues without adding stressed economics to the pile.

"Well, it happened with Jim and . . ." Aaron flipped his fork around in the air. "I can't remember her name."

Of course he didn't. Aaron sucked at names. Not guy names. No, he knew the mailman's name and the guy who worked at the coffee place he stopped at after his Saturday-morning run. Even the guy who'd sold them that overly bright blue paint for the bathroom last year. But someone's wife or girlfriend, or a female colleague? He stumbled every single time. It was as if all women registered in his mind only in connection to some guy he knew.

"Let's make this easier. Call her Anne." Lila reached for a roll. "Go on with the story."

"Right." Aaron pushed the butter closer to her before talking again. "Anne . . . you know, that might actually be her name."

"I doubt it." Her knife scraped across the plate as she scooped the butter up.

"What?"

She preferred the uncomfortable silence of the last few weeks to actual conversation. "You were saying?"

At least once a week during their marriage he accused her of not listening or showing any signs of caring about his work, so she pretended. So much pretending.

"Anne is a vet. She works at that animal hospital around the corner from that taqueria we like near Ithaca Commons." Aaron stared at her for a few beats of silence before continuing. "She makes something like three times what he takes home as a high school teacher, and it's killing him."

Aaron had her attention now. The way he sat forward in his seat with his elbows balanced on the edge of the table. The excitement in his eyes and that insipid smile. It was as if he were internally cheering at the idea of a guy's marriage crumbling thanks to a dented ego.

"He tried to tell her that she made him feel inferior, and she told him he was."

Lila felt a sudden kinship with the nameless woman. "Maybe he is."

"Yeah, right." Aaron laughed as he reached over and tore off a piece from one of the rolls in the basket. Didn't grab the whole thing because he tried to limit his carb intake. He insisted *only a bite* was enough to satisfy him. "Then she kicked him out."

"Sounds fair."

He had the nerve to frown at her. "You're not serious."

"I actually am."

"You take her side even though you don't know her?" He popped the piece of bread in his mouth.

"Neither do you, apparently."

He shook his head. "I can't talk to you when you're like this."

"Let's examine the fact scenario you laid out. Why does he care how much she earns? I assume they both benefit from her paycheck. The money goes into an account, or they're like us, multiple accounts, and then the bills get paid." She shrugged. "He should thank her for doing more than her share and be grateful. Then shut up."

"Look at you sticking up for Jim's wife." Aaron sat back in his chair, causing the wood to groan under the strain of his weight.

"Sounds like someone should."

"At least you're finally talking to me." He sounded unhappy about that. "Aren't I lucky?"

Yeah, she'd screwed up and let her indifference slip, but what the hell. Defending the woman they'd renamed Anne made her happier than anything else in the house had for months. "I can stop."

"You're too busy judging Jim and Anne to be quiet."

She snorted and liked the sound so much she did it again. "Don't pretend you know her name."

"What the fuck is wrong with you? I'm trying to have a normal conversation."

Her fault. He always made everything her fault. Shifted the burden and played the victim. "You get ticked off when we don't talk about your work. Now that we are, you're ticked off about that, too. It's hard to make you happy."

He let his hand fall against the tabletop with a hard slap. "Married couples talk, Lila."

She could barely tolerate being in the same room with him. Not after those videos. "Did you read that somewhere?"

"This shit is you, not me." He stood up and thudded across the kitchen the refrigerator to grab another lite beer. His second. "It's not normal. You're closed off. Go stone-cold. You don't care about anyone." His words tripped over one another as he rushed to list her flaws. "We barely talk. You don't even go outside all that much."

"I show houses."

He held up both hands as if he'd stepped into an impromptu religious revival meeting. "Ah yes. Your precious fucking job."

She shoved her plate toward the middle of the table. "Is this still about Jim and whatever-her-name-is or are you really upset about my career choice?"

He snorted. "The one you barely do?"

"At your insistence!"

"Don't blame me for your choices."

"So now I don't work enough? Your usual argument is that you prefer for me not to work because you don't want all your little school and coaching friends to think you can't support us." She forced her fingers to unclench around the knife and set it down when she really wanted to throw it. "Make up your mind, Aaron."

He leaned against the sink with his hands balanced on the counter on either side of him. "You are so hard to love."

The shot bounced off her.

As if he knew what the word even meant. As if she cared if he got enough pampering and cuddling. He'd screwed up this pathetic excuse of a marriage, not her.

"So you've said." She hit him with an eye roll because she knew the gesture battered his control. If he wanted to fight, then they should really fight. Scream and accuse. Dump all their personal garbage right on the floor and sort through it with a chain saw.

"Don't do that. Fight back without the passive-aggressive bullshit. Show me you care at least a little."

His anger bubbled and churned right below the surface.

Another push or two should do it. "My personality hasn't changed from the day we met. I'm not the problem in this marriage, *darling*."

"How many times do I have to apologize for what happened?"

"Try doing it once. Just one lousy time." The asshole got caught and lied. Insisted the videos on his phone from his damn students—intimate videos—meant nothing when they really could ruin him. She was saving him, but he conveniently ignored that fact, which was smart because she didn't plan on doing it for much longer. "You've never taken one ounce of responsibility for your shitty choices."

His mouth thinned, and a tiny muscle in his cheek twitched. He watched her, looking ready to spring, then took a sharp turn away and stared out the window above the sink, out into the darkness. "We had this fight weeks ago. I told you it was a prank gone wrong. I'm not reliving this nonsense again. Let it go."

"Wait, was that your apology?"

"You're blameless, I suppose. You kicked me out of our bed. You barely speak to me. Have you left the damn house in three weeks? Because to me it looks like you're sulking rather than trying to put this marriage back together."

She would not let him spin this back on her. He was lucky she let him in the house at all. "Still waiting for that apology."

He turned and faced her again, breathing heavy and grabbing the counter in a white-knuckled grip as if he could no longer hold the icy edge of dislike from spilling out. "Over something minor? Something a bunch of stupid kids did? Not going to happen."

She pressed her hand against her chest in mock surprise. "Right. How dare I suggest you've ever done anything wrong in your life. Silly me. It's always the rest of us who are wrong."

"Tell me your theory about the video." His mouth twisted in a hateful scowl. "Say. It."

Videos. Plural. "You're a pitiful excuse for a man."

He snorted. "You wouldn't know what to do with a man."

Every word he uttered breathed more life into her hatred. Gave it legs and a beating heart. Fueled it until it sucked all of the air out of the room. "I'm not the one who messed up."

"I didn't either."

He was delusional. "How can you say that?"

He shook his head as he left the room. "Fuck you, Lila."

Chapter Six

Present Day

This is Nia Simms and Gone Missing, *the true crime podcast that discusses cases—big and small—in your neighborhood and around the country. While we usually delve into cold cases, pick apart the clues, and talk about other possibilities, and we will get back to that, we're switching gears today. Just like last week, we're focusing on the case everyone is talking about.*

We usually don't jump in and review an active case for fear of getting in the way, but this one is happening right in our backyard, and it's possible one of our listeners saw or heard something that might be helpful.

We're talking, of course, about Karen Blue, the SUNY Cortland sophomore. Campus video shows she got in her car about eight weeks ago and left school to visit her parents for their anniversary weekend, and was never seen again.

We know this case is all over the news. This is a multiagency investigation. There's a task force. Local and state police are on it. The sheriff's office weighed in, and now the FBI is stepping in. That's a lot of resources with no resolution.

We've all seen the grainy video of Karen putting a bag in her trunk before getting in and driving away. That was sixty-one days ago. Since then? Not a word from Karen. Law enforcement have ruled out the idea of her voluntarily leaving or hurting herself. This is a case of foul play.

Her parents are frantic. The police have searched her boyfriend's house twice. One of Karen's friends gave an interview talking about the boyfriend's temper. This was looking like a relationship turned violent. A horrible but not unheard-of story. But notice I said "was" . . .

Let's think about this case another way. What if Karen wasn't the first woman to go missing in the area without any explanation over the last few years? We've spent weeks looking into this question and believe something bigger, more malicious, might be happening in this part of New York. We actually have a trio of missing women, and we're going to talk about the one question the police have refused to answer: What if the disappearances are related . . .

"Lila?"

She hit pause on her tablet. The voice cut off midsentence through the all-house speakers as her brother-in-law shut the front door and walked down the hall toward her.

He leaned over the kitchen island and kissed her on the cheek. "What the hell are you listening to?"

"I was trying to keep my mind busy." Which wasn't a lie. It

wasn't easy to have a nice lunch when her dead husband might not be dead.

"Uh-huh."

"You know, background noise." When he continued to stare at her, she tried again. "It's that true crime podcast that's been all over the news."

Jared's expression went blank. "What?"

"The one started by the Syracuse University graduate student as part of a class project." When Jared didn't move, Lila tried again. "Her name is Nia. She's on once or twice a week and sometimes does interim videos with updates of the cases she and her followers are reviewing. She's been interviewed on the news."

Still not one bit of recognition on her brother-in-law's face, so she tried again. "She's very determined, which is great because from what I can tell she has a big following of armchair detectives who are experts at using the internet. She's using those minions to keep pressure on law enforcement, the media, and this task force about Karen Blue's case."

Jared shook his head. "You lost me at 'podcast.'"

Really? The guy needed to step out of his office now and then. "Karen Blue? Straight brown hair. Athletic. Really pretty."

"Do I know her?"

"Forget it." Lila eased the seat around and jumped off the stool. "Coffee?"

She didn't wait for an answer. Jared always said yes to coffee. If she offered water, he said yes. A cookie, he took it. He was the most agreeable person she'd ever met.

"Brent called." He took the seat she'd just vacated and reached for the mug when she offered it. "Have you heard anything? What are the police saying about Aaron?"

The slight tremor in his voice had her glancing up. Where lately Aaron's mood bounced around, Jared's hummed along nice and even. He was the older Payne brother by fourteen months. Slightly shorter at six foot with a young-looking face. Perfect nose and soft blue eyes. Women in town whispered about him being the objectively more attractive brother, but not as good of a catch as Aaron. Aaron was husband material. The one they praised for grocery shopping and running errands . . . or so the town gossip went.

Little did they know.

Lila viewed Jared as stable and with a seemingly bottomless well of kindness. He'd welcomed her into the family and the community, using his contacts to help launch her real estate career.

Jared's work ethic was the problem. It ran at 100 percent all the time. He spent so many hours in the office that no woman could compete. He'd dated a few in more than a casual way during the almost four years Lila had lived there and watched the ritual unravel. None lasted for long. They'd meet, have couples' dinners, and then Tara would be traded in for Dawn and then Linda. Jared's bedroom door tended to be a revolving one.

One girlfriend also shared that he liked sex pretty wild. Lila went out of her way not to think about Jared and his bedroom preferences.

She wrapped her fingers around her mug and let the warmth of the liquid seep through the ceramic and into her hands. "I expect Ginny any minute."

He frowned. "Who's Ginny?"

"The investigator."

"There's already one assigned to look for Aaron?" Jared dumped a second packet of fake sugar into his coffee. "Shit, this is happening too fast. Where the fuck is he? It's not like him to disappear."

"Not at all." Aaron left a note when he went outside. It was one of the little things she'd found endearing at the beginning of their marriage. Since she'd found the videos, everything he did filled her with rage.

"So . . ." Jared winced. "Did you guys fight?"

She started to reach her hand across the counter in comfort then stopped. A foot separated their fingertips, and she didn't want to bridge that yawning abyss. "Why would you ask that?"

"Because after two days of him sleeping in my guest room weeks ago I sent him back here to work it out with you." He lifted the mug to his mouth but didn't take a sip. "Did you two settle whatever that was?"

Six weeks. It had been just over six weeks since they'd gone from a tenuous peace to a showdown.

An unexpected coolness washed through her. "He didn't come back to your house again, did he?"

Jared started to talk then stopped. It was a full minute before he tried again. "Aaron refused to give me any details. I got the sense he wasn't over it."

Her fault. Jared didn't use the words, but she heard them as if he'd screamed right into her ear.

She stood up and went over to the long table stretching across the back of the sofa and separating the kitchen from the living area. She grabbed her laptop then returned to the bar. Took the open seat next to Jared. "I was going to look at our bank accounts and his credit cards to see if that would give us a hint where he went."

"Hey." Jared put his hand on top of the computer to keep her from lifting the lid. "You can't think he walked out on you. He would never do that."

Her gaze shifted from his long fingers to that sleek black watch that cost more than most people paid for six months of mortgage. Jared's one nod to the mix of money he'd inherited, earned, and stockpiled.

After a few seconds, they fell back on comfortable, unflinching eye contact.

"He should be at school. I don't understand why he's not." And that was the truth. The SUV should be where she'd parked it. He should be in it. Dead but there.

She'd turned the mystery over in her head. Spun it around, flipped it over. Nothing she did, no matter how much she reasoned it out, led to a comprehensible answer. Was he alive? Injured? Playing with her?

"I called everywhere I could think he might go if he needed to clear his head," Jared said.

That stopped her from fidgeting. She rubbed her hands together under the safety of the bar overhang. "What *did* Aaron tell you about the fight?"

"That you both said some things. I know he regretted however it rolled out. I'm sure he told you that." Jared started to say something else but stopped when his cell buzzed. He pulled it out of his jacket pocket and read the text on the screen. "Brent wants to take the afternoon off and drive around."

"Doing what?" She'd assumed Brent would be the kind to fade into the background if things got tough. That's how he'd mismanaged his marriage until it finally sputtered to a halt. He'd put more into his friendship with Aaron in five hours than he had with caring about his ex-wife's obvious unhappiness and spiraling depression during the last two years of their marriage. Lila knew because she'd had a front-row seat to that disaster.

"Looking for Aaron." Jared shrugged. "Brent thinks he might have driven to the lake. There are places he likes to go there, like that one hiking trail."

Her mind blanked for a second. "You think that instead of going to work Aaron took off on a drive and went hiking?"

"I don't know, Lila." Jared pushed the mug away from him and shifted until he faced her. "Look, you can talk to me."

She could hear the thread of concern in his voice. See it in his eyes. "About what?"

"Anything. I know Aaron can be tough. People think he's outgoing, but we both know he's not emotionally very open." Jared hesitated for a few more seconds before sitting up straight again and leaning away from her. "Are you going to be okay with the detective on your own?"

"Investigator."

Jared snorted. "Is there a difference?"

"I guess we'll see." She'd gone out of her way not to know anything about the intricacies of New York law enforcement, both because she didn't plan to take another bar exam and because she didn't intend to ever return to a courtroom.

"Okay." He stood up and adjusted the waistband of his dress pants on his waist, trim from hours of running each morning. "I'll do a quick drive with Brent then circle back here to help out and make some calls. I'll have my cell. Text if you hear anything."

The second kiss landed in her hair. It was quick and brotherly and comforting in a way she never expected. She wasn't exactly one to relax and let someone else share the load, but from the moment she'd met Jared they'd clicked. They understood each other and never needed to verbally vomit their life details to each other.

They were reluctant survivors. Angry and unwilling to open up and invite more pain. Aaron bonded them, but most days—and especially recently—she preferred spending time with Jared over Aaron.

She glanced at the tablet and the podcast site. "Jared?"

He turned around in the doorway to the hall and stopped. "Yeah?"

The hopeful expression, all wide-eyed and waiting, pulled at her, but she let it go. She wasn't even sure what she intended to say when she'd called out to him. It wasn't as if she had anything encouraging to offer. No hope. No empty words about finding Aaron safe.

She shook her head. "Nothing."

Aaron wasn't coming back. But if he did, she'd finish what she started.

Chapter Seven

GINNY CALLED TO SAY SHE'D LEFT THE OFFICE AND WOULD BE there soon. That was thirty minutes ago. She showed up with a younger man. No uniform on him either. Just dark pants and a bright white shirt. When he asked to use the bathroom, she directed him to the one down the hall and told him to do whatever he needed to do. She had nothing to hide. There was no reason to pretend she did.

"This is a big house. No kids?" Ginny ran her finger along the fireplace mantel, hesitating only when it landed on the frame of the one photo sitting there.

Lila standing between Aaron and Jared. The picture was a little more than a year old and captured a rare moment in time when all three of them looked genuinely happy. It was taken only a few minutes before they headed out on a boat on Cayuga Lake. The bright blue sky and late-summer sun had them looking tan and rested.

"No." Kids or no kids was the one marital decision she and Aaron had made together.

Ginny set the photo back on the mantel and turned to face Lila. "Walk me through this morning again."

This was a game. Lila didn't feel like playing. She sat down in the middle of the couch and opened the laptop she'd carried into the room after Jared left. "I got up, and he was already gone. That's normal, by the way."

"Normal?"

She didn't look up. Just kept typing. "Do you object to the word?"

"What are you doing?"

"Checking Aaron's bank accounts."

Ginny sat down next to her, leaving only a sliver of space between them. As far as pressure moves went, it had its benefits. It likely worked on some. Lila appreciated the intimidation tactics, but she'd learned in her old legal life when to jump and when to ignore.

"Joint or individual accounts?" Ginny asked as she took a pair of glasses out of her jacket pocket and put them on.

"Both." Lila glanced over. "You should wear them. They look good."

"I'd fall on my face. They're just for reading." Ginny never broke eye contact with the screen. "And what are you finding?"

"Nothing. He last took cash out two days ago."

"How much?"

"Sixty dollars." Lila shifted the screen toward Ginny. "He's not a big spender."

"Your house suggests otherwise."

Lila closed the laptop and sat it back on the table in front of her. "He bought this as a fixer-upper. We updated it a little at a time."

With the computer gone, the closeness of their positions became tough to ignore. Lila protected her personal space. She didn't like to be crowded or hugged. Hated shopping and anywhere bunches of people gathered, walked and stumbled around.

She forced her body to still. Mentally counted down from ten then did it again to fend off the inevitable punch of anxiety she sensed lingering but coming fast.

"Are you handy?" Ginny asked the question in a calm voice, ignoring that they practically sat on top of each other.

Lila rested her hands on her lap and concentrated on not shifting around or rubbing her hands together. "I learned how to put down tile. Hang crown molding. Paint with a finish that looks professional."

"And Aaron?"

Lila barely heard the words over the whooshing sound in her head. She diverted all of her energy into keeping her voice even. "He preferred to knock things down."

"Excuse me?"

It took Lila a second to remember what she'd said. Right . . . "Demolition. He excelled at that and then got pretty good at drywall."

"There's no one here with you. I met a neighbor on my way in, but she didn't follow me inside." Ginny stood up and took off her glasses. They disappeared back into her pocket as she continued her walk around the living room.

Lila's chest ached. The force of keeping her relieved exhale trapped inside had her shoulders slumping. "I didn't think you'd want an audience for our meeting."

"Do you have family in the area?"

The thumping anxiety subsided. That question proved how little homework the investigator had done. "Other than Aaron's brother, no."

Ginny froze and stared down at Lila again. "Does that mean they live in another state or . . . ?"

"What does my family have to do with Aaron?"

"This could get difficult, Lila." Ginny let out a sigh. "Press. Questions. Search parties. Unless your husband walks in that door soon or calls, that sort of intrusion lies ahead of you, and you might need some support."

Lila hadn't associated family with support or peace in a very long time. "I can call my friend."

"Singular."

"Nothing on his credit cards either." The comment came out as a blurt, but if Ginny could leap from topic to topic, so could she.

Ginny hummed. "He could have some you don't know about."

"Possible, but since I pay all the bills from a joint account it would be a surprise. I'm not sure he even knows where I keep the checkbook." She leaned back into the couch cushions, more comfortable and back in control as she crossed one leg over another. "I have a question for you."

"Go ahead."

"There's a woman missing. Disappeared about thirty minutes from here." It was time to start poisoning the well. Not that it would be hard since the details were all over the news and the headline on that damn podcast. "Brunette. Young and pretty. What we all need to be if we ever go missing because those seem to be the only victims the public cares about."

Ginny didn't even blink. "Karen Blue. What about her?"

Lila dropped her foot back to the floor and leaned forward with her elbows balanced on her knees. "If you're the lead investigator, why aren't you working on that case?"

Ginny made a face, almost a wince, but quickly schooled her features again. "Maybe I am."

"You think the same person who took Karen, a female college student, also took Aaron, a thirtysomething male teacher?"

"Despite what television suggests, we work on more than one case at a time."

"You're not on the task force?"

"There are also jurisdictional issues. Her case is outside of mine. It's a different county." Ginny crossed her arms in front of her. "How were things between you and Aaron last night?"

Look at that topic pivot. *Blow landed.* Now Lila knew where to hit next time. "The usual."

"Be more specific."

"He talked about work. We watched television. He went to bed early."

More humming from the investigator. "Does he always?"

"Earlier than I do, yes."

"Why did you leave law?" Ginny's eyebrow lifted. "Or maybe you never practiced."

The response wouldn't lead to answers about Aaron, but let her dig. "I never practiced in New York. I'm not licensed here. I was a partner in a small firm in Greensboro, North Carolina."

"And?"

"And a few years ago I grew tired of the work and the lying, and Aaron wanted to move back to New York, where he grew up, so we did."

She'd repeated the lines so many times that she almost believed them. The truth was much more complicated than the glossy version she tried to sell. The criminal practice annoyed her, yes, and she'd craved a break, but she expected any leave of absence to be temporary. The relocation and need to take another bar exam, plus Aaron's pleas that she switch to a less time intensive area of law, convinced her to abandon her path on a test basis . . . and that test had sputtered along for more than three years.

She left out the part about how unhappy Aaron had been in Greensboro. Not at first. When she'd met him, he loved his job and helped out after school with the debate team. He spoke with pride about his students and their achievements, which she found appealing.

She also appreciated his close bond with Jared. They visited each other often. Aaron would spend a chunk of the summer in New York with Jared and come back talking about how he wished they lived closer together. By the time the fall semester started, Aaron usually would move on and be back in the North Carolina groove . . . until that final year.

He generally got along well with coworkers. He turned on the charm and then came home and blasted them to her. The friction with another teacher who shifted to administration arose out of nowhere, and Aaron became obsessed with everything the guy did and said.

Looking back, seeing Aaron through a different lens, she wondered what that North Carolina school administrator knew that she didn't know. What secrets he'd stumbled over.

"I didn't love dealing with clients." Lila didn't like to give anything away, to let people have a peek inside her and steal it for themselves, to think they knew her when they didn't, so she would bob and weave during conversations. Give away some, shade it a bit, but not all.

"Divorce work?" Ginny asked.

"Criminal defense." Lila held up her hand. "And before you ask, felonies. Murder. Kidnapping. I was a trial attorney."

"So you know how the system works."

"Depends on what system you're talking about."

She could almost hear Ginny's mind race. To a novice, it might sound like she spun around in circles, but Lila could see the bigger plan. Dodge in and out of topics, pepper personal questions with general ones. Jump from here to there. While that might be interesting to toy with on one level, Lila had no intention of having her life become the step someone with the smarts and drive might use to further their own career.

"Thanks for letting me look around." The younger partner . . . or whatever he was . . . reentered the room.

He'd taken a long time in the bathroom, which Lila hoped meant he'd been experienced enough to search the place when she gave him the opening. She tried to remember his name. Paul . . . no, not that.

She made nonsense conversation while she mentally scrambled to recall the name on the card on the kitchen counter. "Nothing to see."

He threw her a half smile. "Right."

Pete Ryker. That was it.

She rushed to categorize him. Once she did that, she wouldn't forget anything about him again. It was a memory trick and one she'd depended on forever. They'd spent only minutes in the same room, but she had a few thoughts. Thirty-something and a mass of muscles that suggested he spent all of his off time in a gym. Expensive shoes. For some reason, that struck her as odd for a guy who likely walked through crime scenes.

"Unless we hear from Aaron, I'll need you to come to my office tomorrow." Ginny scanned the floor and the furniture as she stepped out of the living area and walked over to Pete. "Answer some questions. Look at some photos."

"Of what?"

"People." Ginny nodded. "Maybe seeing a face will help you remember something that doesn't seem important right now."

Spoken like someone who didn't know her at all. "That's hard to imagine."

"Where are your husband's wallet and keys?" Pete asked.

"Gone." Lila shrugged. "With him, I'd guess."

They both stared at her after that answer. Lila reran the sentences in her head but didn't find a problem.

Ginny nodded in the direction of the coffee table. "Do you and Aaron share that laptop?"

"We each have one, plus we share a desktop." She had their attention now. "I need them for work."

"All three?" Pete asked.

"Yes."

Ginny cleared her throat before talking again. "We'll discuss that later. For now, does your husband's car have GPS?"

"He said it was a waste of money. He uses the one on his phone, but even that is unusual. He's one of those people who goes to a place one time and remembers the directions forever, unlike me."

"And his cell phone is gone as well, I take it." Pete glanced at Ginny after he delivered that statement. "That's inconvenient."

Lila gave them a push in another direction. "While you're checking, you should talk with Aaron's brother, Jared. He has access to the one bank account that I don't."

Ginny's eyes narrowed. "What are you talking about?"

"Jared and Aaron inherited money, though I don't think that's the right word for what happened. Either way, it's in trust."

"How much money are we talking about?" Pete asked.

"A few million each."

Ginny didn't show any outward reaction to the amount. Pete wasn't quite as careful. His eyes widened. "If anything happens to Aaron, then that money goes to . . . ?"

"Jared. It's not mine." Lila almost smiled as she watched the excitement on Pete's face vanish.

He looked doubtful. "Your husband has millions of dollars and yet he works as a high school teacher?"

"He likes the students." And she left it at that.

Ginny took over. "Who did he inherit the money from?"

"Freak accident. A group of hunters shot his mother. She was outside, they didn't see her when they fired, and they killed her." Lila recited the version she'd heard almost verbatim from both brothers. "The hunters were drunk and rich, and Aaron was only eleven, so Jared would have been not quite thirteen. Part of the settlement—the one their father signed to buy the entire Payne family's silence and the court signed off on—included sizable accounts for Jared and Aaron."

"What about their father?"

"The money he received? I have no idea. I never met him." From what she'd heard about him, that was not a loss. According to family lore, he'd grown up in a minimalist environment with a father who didn't believe in government or electricity or any comforts.

Even as Aaron's father grew up and moved out of the charged environment, the drumbeat of disillusionment and violence didn't leave him. He preached his antisociety beliefs to Aaron and Jared. On those rare occasions when Aaron talked about his father at all, he credited Jared with getting them out of childhood intact and surviving a father he described as practical but brutally mean. The man ruled the house and his wife as a despot and used his hand and belt to drive home lessons.

Lila rarely spared a thought for her father-in-law, except to curse him now and then for being poison and passing a portion of his *I'm in charge* way of thinking on to his son.

When it came to paternity, neither she nor Aaron had won the jackpot.

"Why haven't you met you husband's father?" Ginny asked.

"Seven or eight years after losing his wife, he was walking on the side of the road and got hit by a car. Died after spending days in a coma."

Pete whistled. "That's a lot of tragic accidents for one family."

Exactly. "Yeah, you're not the first one to think so."

"Who else did?" Ginny asked.

Lila smiled. "Me."

Chapter Eight

GINNY WAITED UNTIL THEY WERE OUTSIDE, STANDING AT THE bottom of the long driveway next to her car, before talking again. She wasn't sure what to make of Lila's last comment. Pointing the finger at Jared and Aaron . . . but about what?

Pete followed her lead on the silence but beat her to the first comment now that they were alone. That's what he did. Raced to be the first. He lacked discipline and experience, but you'd never know that, because he wasn't afraid to speak up. "She's weird, right? It's not just me."

"It's not."

"Like, emotionless or something. But very attractive."

Ginny fought back a groan. Pete didn't possess an internal filter that signaled when he should just shut up. She used to give her son "the look" when he spouted off the wrong thing at the wrong time. It worked because he generally knew what was okay to say and when. Late into his twenties, Pete had yet to learn those skills.

He started yammering, like he often did. "Look, that face and those stylish clothes. She's like Old Hollywood. All buttoned-up but yet not really. Reddish hair, sort of . . . it's a hot look."

Working with him was exhausting. "Her hair is brown. Circle around to your point, please."

"She looks like she could break a man in two, if you know what I mean." When Ginny didn't show any reaction, Pete shrugged and kept going. "But there's a bit of a Stepford wife, trophy thing happening. I bet Aaron enjoys showing her off."

"Do you know how annoying any of what you just spouted off is?" She doubted it.

Ginny had her own assessment. Lila came off as capable and determined. Strong and fully in control. She'd been blessed with a striking face. Pale, perfect skin highlighted by the right shade of red lipstick. A body honed by exercise or surgery or something that worked for her.

She possessed the perfect mix of pretty with a whiff of mystery. Ginny could imagine men at the yacht club falling over themselves to flirt with her, and her not reacting at all. A hard-to-get-and-hard-to-please vibe pulsed around her.

"She doesn't seem . . ."

Ginny rolled her eyes. "I dread however you're going to finish that sentence."

"Real." He made a humming sound. "Not at all like the cuddle-in-bed type."

"Are you done?"

"You told me I need to learn to assess people. What I got from her was pretty but really chilly."

"Possibly." If Aaron didn't walk in the door soon, she'd

need more time with Lila. Stockpile more questions. Engage in extended observation and try to gather insight from those who knew her. Right now the picture was blurry and confusing. Ginny sensed Lila made it look that way on purpose.

"She could be a hell of an actress," Pete said.

That's exactly what she was and why Ginny found her so intriguing and so damn dangerous. "She's a former trial lawyer and a current real estate agent. She can play the game when she needs to. Don't be fooled."

Pete leaned against the side of her car and folded his arms across his stomach. "But what game is she playing? Certainly not grieving wife. She's not weepy or worried."

Pete earned his spot on the investigative team. He'd done some great work on a series of thefts that ended in a murder. He'd spied the bit of video footage that tied it all together. The move fast-tracked his career. Jumped him ahead of others, which didn't exactly make him the office favorite.

She tolerated him. His know-it-all attitude grated, but she wanted to believe he meant well. He wanted to succeed, and she could understand that.

She took him on because her boss ordered her to. She'd gotten on the sheriff's bad side, through no fault of her own, and now she stepped carefully. But she demanded respect, and lucky for Pete, he gave it to her . . . usually.

He had a pretty serious blind spot and no self-awareness about his weaknesses. He faltered when it came to some basic human interactions, as people who hadn't experienced that much living tended to do. He saw people as one thing or another. He lacked nuance. He hadn't seen the worst and didn't appreciate the dense fog of gray he was about to wander into.

"She doesn't give much away." When Pete just stared at her after the comment, Ginny listed off a few of the things she noticed during her short meetings with Lila Ridgefield. "She's skilled. Dodges questions. Half answers. Pivots away from difficult topics. Feeds me information I didn't ask for."

"Is she socially awkward or is this something else?"

"This feels practiced. Careful." The question was whether the games came from a general survival instinct or were part of a ruse to keep them guessing about her missing husband. "Tell me about what you saw in the house."

They got a rare glimpse inside. This early into an investigation—barely having started—they didn't normally poke around in the potential victim's possessions. When Lila offered, Ginny didn't think she could say no. Now she wondered if the early look was meant to throw them off.

"I took some photos." Pete took his cell out of his pocket and held it up.

"Any surprises?" Lila had invited them in and basically told Pete to go hunting, so Ginny doubted it.

"All of the husband's clothes are in the extra bedroom. Looks like he's been sleeping there." Pete smiled. "That could mean something."

Or nothing. "You're so single."

"What?" He sounded offended by the comment.

"I love my husband, but when we go on vacation we get a room with two double beds." She loved the man and had since she saw him walking across the quad at Howard University her freshman year, but he sprawled and snored, and she craved a night or two of quiet.

Pete laughed. "How sexy."

"A good night's sleep can be better than sex."

"That's the kind of comment that will keep me single."

Ginny swallowed her smile. "Back to Lila."

"The house? Not too messy. Not too picked up. The bedrooms looked lived-in but sterile."

So, just right. Nothing to raise suspicion. "I guess bloodstains would have been too much to ask for."

Pete stepped away from the car. "You think she did it?"

"We don't even know what 'it' is yet. I basically stopped to do a wellness check on the way back from another incident and now we're off and running. We need to give Aaron time to wise up and come home." He hadn't been missing even twenty-four hours yet, so Pete needed to slow down a bit. "People who cared about him called in—"

"But not his wife."

"We only have her word he left this morning. If this doesn't get resolved, we'll have to verify that." The open questions would let Ginny poke around, but right now she was waiting for a little time to pass.

Aaron could have a girlfriend on the side or be sick of his life, or it could be nothing. She half expected him to walk through the door while they were there. In most cases he would. Despite what televisions suggested, these issues rarely spun up and into actual cases.

The immediate concerned calls and all that talk about how *Aaron would never* and *he was never even late* had Ginny thinking something was wrong here. The picture everyone painted showed Aaron as a guy who wouldn't just run, but then it was amazing how often what people thought was going on was very different from what actually was.

"We now know Aaron Payne's got millions. So, just divorce and go live on a beach with some hot thing if he's done with his marriage," Pete said.

If only people who made bad decisions picked common sense instead. "He wouldn't be the first guy to think divorce would kick his ass. He could have worried that his former lawyer wife would figure out a way to take part of his money or that a judge would stick him with a big alimony payment."

Pete groaned.

"If this blows up, I'll need to know everything. Money. History. Family. Why she really left her law practice. Who her friends are. What people in and around the school and this neighborhood think about this couple. Security camera footage. Phone records."

"I want to take a peek at that trust fund." Pete shook his head. "That was weird."

Ginny guessed that was the point. "Notice how she switched the focus off her and onto her brother-in-law."

"It was subtle." Pete glanced at his watch. "By this time to-morrow, her husband's face is going to hit the news. The press will descend on her front lawn. Every inch of her life, every movement, will be dissected."

Exactly. "Then we'll see how chilly she really is."

Chapter Nine

Two Weeks Earlier

THE ALARM SCREAMED THROUGH THE QUIET HOUSE FOR THE second time that night. The first came around two. Now, barely an hour later, it wailed again.

Lila heard footsteps and swearing. Lights flicked on as the house scrambled to life.

She kept watch from the kitchen window. Wearing pajamas and slippers, she stood on tiptoes and leaned over the sink to peer into the backyard. Nothing moved out there.

"See anything?" Aaron stumbled out of the guest bedroom where he'd been banished to sleep ever since the fight over the videos and came bounding down the hall. He swore as he lost his balance, trying to pull on a pair of faded jeans and running sneakers, jumping on one leg before slamming into the side of the refrigerator. "I should have kept my clothes on after last time."

She ignored the uncoordinated display. Her focus went

right to the bat in his hand and stayed there. "What are you doing with that?"

"Turn off the alarm."

He ignored her question. Not a surprise. He'd been hostile since she found out about the videos. Turned the whole thing around on her and acted like the tension between them was her fault because she didn't believe the crap excuse he offered. "The intruder could have a gun."

He zipped up his sweatshirt. "It's probably nothing. Some stupid animal."

She watched as he headed for the French doors to the patio. "You don't know that. Someone could be out there."

"I know you want to fight about everything right now, but please take a break and handle the alarm." He swore under his breath as the phone rang. "I don't want to get charged by the police for a false alarm, so get that call and give the code."

"That's your concern?" A fifty-dollar fee. Only Aaron would cast losing that amount of money as a bigger horror than getting shot in the head and bleeding out on the grass.

"Lila, get the phone."

She picked up the receiver and said the safe word. Their alarm snapped off right after.

He opened the door and a second alarm screeched through the house. This one came from outside and had more than one neighbor's house sputtering awake in the darkness.

The Filmores lived next door. Other people on the street whispered "pharmaceutical money" when they referred to Pat and Kitty. Theirs was the first house on the corner when someone turned onto the street. Set back in a tunnel of trees with only the third floor and the hint of a driveway peeking out from the branches.

With their kids in college, they no longer invested in private high school and swanky family vacations. Instead, they redesigned their backyard with a spa and gardens. They had an outdoor kitchen and family room, complete with a huge television where they watched movies in the summer while lounging in the pool.

The bottom floor was a playroom for grown-ups and kids. It housed old-school video games and a pool table. A media room with oversize couches. A lot of shiny, expensive things that required an intricate alarm system and video equipment to protect them.

When the Filmores' alarm turned on, their outside lights also flipped on. The place lit up like a carnival. Any intruder should have been pinned in a spotlight and caught on video. Pat bragged about that enhancement. Now they would see if the system delivered.

When she heard familiar male voices around the corner of the house, she followed Aaron's path outside. He stood on their side of the tall trees that marked the boundary between properties, bat in hand. Pat paced along the hedge shaking his head.

Just as she reached them, she saw Kitty running out a side door toward them. She'd wrapped an oversize robe around her and wore it with what looked like snow boots. Pat was a bit better, having slipped on sweats and a jacket that was inside out.

"Well?" Pat shouted to his wife over the din of the alarm.

That fast, the noise cut off. Silence descended, and the yard folded into darkness as the emergency lights clicked off.

"The police are coming to do a quick check, but I looked at the videos." Kitty sounded out of breath. "There's nothing."

"You sure?" Aaron asked.

Kitty reached out for Pat to help her down the slight slope between the properties. The consoling gesture seemed to be automatic, as if he'd spent his life protecting her and didn't plan to stop now.

That type of coddling didn't really register with Lila. She'd never experienced it and didn't go looking for it.

To outsiders, Pat and Kitty looked a bit mismatched. He possessed that spends-Fridays-on-a-golf-course look. Tan and lean. Pure businessman, ready to charm and make a buck. A little gruff when he thought people didn't treat him as he deserved to be treated, but a good neighbor. Quiet and not one for nosiness.

Lila wasn't all that familiar with what defined a motherly type. Probably a mom who went to kids' practices and made sure the family had dinner together most nights. Kitty gave off that vibe. She was always cooking or redecorating the house. She was a good foot shorter than her husband, and the years and having children had rounded out her figure a bit.

Aaron joked about how Pat likely would come home from a business trip one day with the future, and much younger, second wife on his arm. That showed Aaron's priorities, not

Pat's. Lila didn't buy into the concept of happily ever after, but Pat and Kitty made her believe some people might.

Pat nodded as he pulled Kitty tight against his side. "I'll do a more in-depth check, and we'll look back on the video, just in case this is some sort of ongoing review of the alarms in the neighborhood."

"Look back?" Lila asked.

"Five days. That's how long before the video recycles." Kitty glanced up at her husband. "At least only one sensor went off this time. The one by our nursery shed. In the video you can see things blowing around."

Pat frowned. "It's not the damn wind doing this. The system better not be that sensitive."

"Not possible, really." Aaron said as he tapped the tip of the bat against the ground. "The wind wouldn't have set off our inside alarm at the same time as yours went off outside."

Pat's frown only deepened. "That sounds coordinated."

Lila offered one possibility . . . the one she hoped they'd grab on to. "We used your alarm company. Could it be a bug in the system?"

"We pay too damn much to lose sleep over nothing."

Kitty patted her husband's arm in a way that suggested she'd calmed him down using the gesture before. "Pat, it's okay."

"It's not." But some of the anger left his voice.

Lila wasn't ready to abandon her theory. "Does anyone else on the street use the same company?"

Aaron waved off some neighbors who were milling around out front before his gaze shot to Lila. "What?"

"Well, if it's only alarms from one company I do think it's a bug. Tomorrow we could see if anyone else's system is going off or malfunctioning. If not—"

"The alarm company can come out here and rip this one out." As soon as Pat's voice rose, he brought it under control again. "Sorry. I just don't get it. It worked fine for two years."

"We'll check the video tomorrow and see where we are." Kitty shot Lila a warm smile. "Come over for coffee and we'll review the alarm data together."

"Perfect." Because that's exactly what Lila needed.

Chapter Ten

Present Day

GINNY SAT AT THE OVERSIZE DESK THAT TOOK UP HALF OF THE space in her home office. Really, *their* home office. She shared it with her husband, Roland. Ever since he'd been promoted to dean of admission at Ithaca College he spent more time in the office and less at the desk his father had made when Roland graduated from college.

The job required long hours and carried a lot of stress. Whining parents. Whining students. Grumpy professors.

They both suffered from career frustrations and rounds of thoughtless comments from coworkers, and they shared the burden in private. They'd been together through every loss and success since they'd met as undergrads at Howard University. The deaths of both sets of parents. A miscarriage. Her injury at work. His promotion. Her promotion. Four moves. Their beautiful son.

She'd told Roland about the new case of the missing teacher.

As expected, he rolled his eyes and mumbled something about "pathetic men" not living up to their responsibilities. Roland stood firmly in the Aaron-Payne-went-for-a-joyride-and-is-afraid-to-come-home-now camp. She still wasn't convinced.

Her fingers moved over the keys as she searched for more background on the Payne family. The clicking sound of typing filled the still room. She ignored the shiver spinning through her but tightened the thick robe around her to help fight off the chill.

The door creaked open, and Roland peeked in. He let out a dramatic exhale, as if she didn't know his position on the concept of too much work and not enough sleep.

"You've been on the computer for two hours." He crouched down next to her chair and balanced his cheek on her arm, right near her exposed wrist.

The rough edge of his scruff against her bare skin had her smiling. "Maybe I was in the mood for porn."

"If so, you should share." He straightened up until he was on his knees, half leaning into her side and the chair as he stared at her computer screen. "But what's really going . . . ah, okay. I see you decided not to let this case go tonight."

Her fingers dropped from the keyboard and she turned to him. "This guy's mom died in an accident. Then his dad died. Now he's gone missing."

Roland frowned as he pushed her reading glasses up for her. "You think it's all linked?"

"No."

He kissed the sleeve of her robe. "Then I don't understand why I'm sleeping alone."

"Can one person be that unlucky?"

"I thought you said he could be out with a girlfriend or driving to Vegas or doing something fun."

Without thinking, her fingers went to his hair. Heat thrummed off him, wrapping around her. "It feels like the wrong answer."

"Boring high school teacher gone wild doesn't work for you?" He lifted his head and watched her. The amusement in his voice faded by the end of the question, as if he started to doubt his original assessment of Aaron. "I mean, it's not as if your gut is ever wrong."

"He's a millionaire, or so his wife says. He's had the chance to take the money and live it up and hasn't."

From the first call that came in, people spoke of Aaron's disappearance with a sense of urgency. No one thought he'd slept in or driven away without warning. All three people who called insisted he would be at school unless he couldn't be. That's who he was. A grown man who showed up. Add in the money and resources he had and how long he'd had them without acting out, and she doubted he was a man overstaying his lounging time.

Roland hummed as he nodded. "Midlife crisis?"

"He's not even forty."

His fingers slipped through hers, and she squeezed his hand. "Is that the age for it?"

"If so, you missed it." *Thank God.* "The idea of having a useless husband sounds like a nightmare."

She had friends who put up with that nonsense. Not her. She wanted a partner, not another child in a grown-up body.

He'd always been steady. Present. Supportive. Driven. A little too set in his ways, but a loving dad and husband. As a child of divorce, he fought hard for their marriage. They'd hit rough patches and lived through a painful year filled with yelling and disappointment when they both hated their jobs and their expenses didn't allow for a change.

"I don't need anything but what I've got right here." He lifted their joined hands and kissed the back of hers.

"Sweet-talker." She loved them now. How they fit together. They'd settled into this spot where they connected and listened to each other. Probably had something to do with Kingston turning sixteen and already shifting out of the horrors of being fifteen and thinking he knew everything. She did not enjoy that stage and was happy to see it go.

Roland stood up, never letting go of her hand. "Any chance I can sweet-talk you into coming to bed?"

"I want to be ready when I speak with Lila again tomorrow."

"You sound like you're sparring with this woman."

The visual imagine struck her as right. "I have a feeling every conversation with Lila Ridgefield will demand I be at the top of my game."

He kissed her forehead. "You always are."

No, she'd made mistakes. Not listened to her gut. Let protocol and red tape stop her. Gotten into battles with her boss and lost her way.

Not this time.

LILA CRAVED SLEEP, but her body fought it even harder than usual.

The day's chaos gave way to an eerily quiet night. After all the calls and running around, the hours lapsed into a foreboding silence as if she were on the edge of something so menacing, so unexpected, that she could not afford the vulnerability of sleep.

Brent and Jared had brought dinner. They hovered for hours. Talked about kicking Aaron's ass when he showed up from a few days away fishing. Cassie came over with pound cake but only lasted a half hour when no one picked up any of the inane conversation starters she kept dropping.

Lots of mindless chatter but no answers. No movement.

Now, with everyone gone, her mind filled with what-ifs and a list of should-have-done tactics. Thinking about all of that time and work being wasted, about him walking the streets, ratcheted up the pounding inside her. Panic hummed in her ears. Tension swept over her and through the house. The walls practically thumped with it.

She focused all of her control on keeping her body moving, on ready. Aaron could creep back. Walk in. Break a window. Go to the police. The endless possibilities swirled in her brain, making the breath hiccup in her chest.

They'd disconnected the house alarm a few weeks ago. Now she needed it.

Standing in front of the living room's oversize windows made her a target. The position also let her keep watch. The houses around her were mostly protected by tall hedges with blind spots perfect to hide a stalker. She could see a light on here and there. The house directly across from her stood in shadowed darkness, a vague outline of a two-story colonial with only the soft yellow porch light to suggest someone lived there.

The Johnsons. Daniel commuted from Ithaca to Albany every Monday and came home late Thursday. Sherri, likely exhausted from bundling up and dragging three kids under five everywhere on her own, turned off the lights and shut out the world by nine. Now, well after eleven, she'd been out for hours.

Lila envied her. Both of them, really. Her for being too tired to move and him for being anywhere but here.

With one hand clenched on her cell and the other resting on her stomach over the soft cotton of her pajama top, Lila continued to watch, forcing her eyes to stay open until fatigued by the strain, tears pooled at the edges. Still, she stood in the darkness of her quiet house and scanned every inch of sidewalk. Studied every tree and every branch, looking for movement.

She wasn't sure how much time had passed since she'd started her impromptu sentry duty. Five minutes . . . an hour. Seconds blurred even though she felt a loud ticking deep inside. A sort of countdown to the inevitable end.

Her mind heard sounds. Aaron's voice. His footsteps. Him haunting her in his supposed death as he had in life.

Cradling her cell in both hands, she backed away from the window and the desperate scene she provided to anyone watching. Inch by inch, never breaking her surveillance, she moved. She only stopped when her heel slammed into the far wall. She'd slid from one side of the room to the other, so sure a shadow would spring to life and attack her.

Aaron and his games had reduced her to this.

With her back against the wall, she lifted the phone and dialed. It rang once.

Before she heard a voice, she jumped in. "I'm in trouble. I need to see you."

Chapter Eleven

PETE RUSHED INTO GINNY'S OFFICE THE NEXT MORNING BE-
fore she had a chance to take her jacket off and sit down. She
knew she should have shut the door behind her. She might
have if he hadn't been closing in on her from across the busy
floor at the time. Only his wise decision to bring her coffee
saved him from getting a door slammed in his face.

"You're awfully energetic this morning." She dropped into
her chair and turned on her computer. "For the record, I hate
that about young people."

"I'm not that young."

She peeked up at him as she signed in, not bothering to
look at the keys as she typed in her password. "Uh-huh."

"I do have news on our most recent case." He slipped a thin
file from under his arm and waved it in the air.

"Your youthful energy level just got less annoying." She
leaned back in her chair and gestured for him to take a seat
across from her.

"First, no sighting of Aaron or his car. No hits on his credit cards or bank accounts. No calls. No pings to hunt down." He smiled. "You know what that means."

"You're too excited." She had to admit the haze was clearing in an unfortunate way. With each new piece of information, Aaron Payne looked less like a runner and more like a victim.

"I'm enthusiastic about my job."

It was too early for this disagreement. "I see it's going to be that kind of day. The news?"

"Before we get to that, I checked with the principal and the brother." He words sped up as if they were trying to catch up to the eagerness in his voice. "Nothing. Aaron never checked in or showed up. He's missed work for a second day, which the way the principal made it sound bordered on apocalyptic."

"What did Lila say? Did she hear from him last night?"

He winced. "I figured she was the least likely to give me a straight answer about her husband's whereabouts."

"She's not a step you can skip."

Loud shouts from the outer room grabbed their attention. From the two sheriffs making the noise, she guessed the cheers were sports related, likely college football—the office's favorite pastime.

"I had a car go by the house this morning. All quiet." He dropped the file on his lap. "Because I was curious, I drove by as well, and no sign of him or his car at the house."

The move didn't surprise her. They'd already started

collecting information and picking through the couple's lives. "But clearly you're keeping an open mind as to his wife."

"Of course."

Possibly the least convincing response she'd ever received from a partner. "This easily could be a guy needing space. Don't jump to conclusions. That will just keep you from seeing what you need to see."

Ginny stumbled trying to sell the line. It rang hollow in her head and sounded even worse when it came out.

Pete snorted. "Doubt it."

No need to argue since she felt the same way and sucked at hiding it. Save the lectures. They had a case, and it promised to be messy. Which led to her biggest concern. "Any sign this has spilled out into the media?"

Once word got out, the phone lines would light up with neighbors tattling on neighbors, conspiracy theories, and fake sightings. That was nothing compared to the wrath that would fall on Lila. The press would stake out her house and rip apart her life.

"Not yet, but he works at a school as a teacher and coach. Kids know him. Parents know him. There will be talk. There's no way to keep a lid on it and . . ." Pete exhaled. "Should we? The louder this gets, the more likely we'll find something."

That theory backfired in the biggest case of her career so far. The one that didn't resolve clean with a jury finding, despite the battle she waged and all it cost her. "I find that the more people involved, the more likely we'll all trip over one another. So we need to get moving before the good citizens of this county descend with their theories. But you mentioned news. I'm still waiting to hear it."

Pete looked down at his file but didn't hand it over. "I think I know what your first line of questions to Lila will be about."

Yeah, he looked far too pleased with himself. "You have something big in that file and you didn't lead with it? I've been in here for twenty minutes. What's wrong with you?"

He put up a hand. "I was drawing it out for maximum dramatic impact."

She felt her eyes bulge. "What is it?"

"I found one very big piece of the puzzle." His smile fell a bit. "Even though I'm not sure what it means."

Her patience expired. "Tell me before I fire you."

"Fine. Ruin the moment." He leaned forward and dropped the file in front of Ginny. "Lila Ridgefield is a hard woman to track."

"Meaning?" Ginny grabbed the cover and flipped it open.

Before she could read more than a few sentences, Pete started the explanation. "She appeared out of nowhere thirteen years ago at age twenty-one."

Ginny glanced up. "And before then?"

"Before then, Lila Ridgefield didn't exist."

Chapter Twelve

A MIX OF EXHAUSTION AND SUFFOCATING WARINESS WOUND around Lila as she sat at her kitchen island the next morning. She'd turned the coffeemaker temperature to scalding. Anything to revive her. To force her brain to restart and work through the very real problem in front of her.

A curl of steam rose from her coffee mug. She watched it twirl then vanish. In her sleep-deprived state, the puff of heat hypnotized her. Seemed much more interesting than it probably was.

She hadn't managed an hour of sleep. Common sense told her to stay in all night when she really wanted to leave this house. Get out. She settled for a few stolen minutes on the phone. Those weren't enough to settle her restless brain.

For the hundredth time, the possibility of Aaron being very much alive skittered through her mind.

Impossible. Had to be. She had killed him. She'd checked. Waited until his breathing stopped before dumping him in his SUV. A guy couldn't just come back from that.

Still, she half expected him to walk through the door in a

storm of outrage, dragging chaos behind him. Blaming. Calling the police. Kicking her out. But then, that would be risky, because she had something on him. Something that could destroy everything he'd carefully built, lie by disgusting lie.

She set the mug down and mentally ran through the last few days. Backtracked and relived every moment. She needed answers, and she couldn't exactly ask someone . . . or could she? There had to be a stray piece of paper, a note—something that told her where he was and how he'd escaped.

She slid off the bar stool and walked around the kitchen. Paced without any discernible pattern. Walked from the kitchen, down the hall. Stopped at the doorway to Aaron's office. She knew from previous missions to uncover answers that he didn't keep anything of value in here.

The empty safe mocked her. The blank calendar with page after page of blocks devoid of any notes. She had no idea why he'd bought it if he didn't intend to fill it with a record of his activities. Just one more way for him to be secretive as he pretended to be like everyone else.

Now she knew better.

She gave the room one last look before backing into the hallway. She had the door halfway closed and was thinking about where else to look when the shadow cleared in her head. There, in one of the panes of the double French doors to the outside patio, she saw the reflection of a square . . . or what looked like one.

"What the hell?" She whispered the question to the empty room.

Forgetting the exhaustion and the threat closing in around her, she stepped across the oriental carpet he'd insisted on buying from the antiques shop on their way back from a long weekend in Vermont.

The crisscross panes rose from the inside of the glass. The straight edges of the flier or whatever it was were slipped into a space on the outside. It hadn't been there yesterday, but it was now. That meant someone had walked through her backyard. The idea of anyone getting that close to her sphere of privacy sent her stomach plummeting.

She unlocked the door and opened it. What looked like an unlined index card, folded in half, lay tucked into the edge of the door. The wind whipped it around, but it held.

The thick paper felt heavy under her fingers as she slipped it out of its hiding place. A typed message in block letters.

THAT DIDN'T GO AS PLANNED, DID IT?

Not specific, but she understood. Enough to make her heart stop.

This person knew what she'd done . . . or tried to do. That could only mean one thing.

Aaron was alive.

Chapter Thirteen

ON THE THIRD MORNING AFTER AARON PAYNE VANISHED, HIS boss and best friend visited the sheriff's office. Brent came without being asked. Sat and waited, insisting he speak to someone handling the investigation.

That level of interest raised a flag. Put the spotlight on him. Ginny assumed he didn't know, and she didn't bother cluing him in. She also didn't rush around and jump to do his bidding.

She finished her call with Aaron's brother, Jared, becoming more and more convinced that something bad had happened to Aaron. No one had seen him. He wasn't touching his money. Everything—his car, his wallet, and his phone—seemed to be missing.

None of that sounded good.

Neither did Lila's name change. Pete had dug around and not found anything. He was extending the search, and Ginny wanted to talk with Lila, surprise her with the information they did know, but she wasn't answering her phone. Next stop, a home visit. But Ginny had to get through another talk with Brent first.

Twenty minutes after he showed up unannounced, Ginny walked into the interrogation room with a blank notepad in her hand and the video running. The office recorder cataloged everything that happened except when a conversation occurred between a person and their attorney or when someone from the department turned the equipment off. Today it was up and running.

She slipped into the seat across from the principal and watched him fidget and squirm in the metal chair. "Did you need to tell me something, Brent?"

He put his joined hands on the table then lowered them to his lap again. "Any word on Aaron?"

She bit back a sigh. "We're investigating."

"What does that mean?" The chair scraped across the cement floor as he leaned forward, elbows on the table now. "Look, you have to know this isn't normal. There's no need for delay . . . or whatever is happening."

She knew how he felt about the investigation needing to move very quickly because he'd told her. He'd also told Pete when he went to visit the school to ask follow-up questions yesterday. He made it clear one last time when he called the office for a status check earlier that morning. The one thing that Brent had done was make his point.

She leaned back in her chair, taking on a more relaxed stance as Brent's frustration ratcheted up. "What do you think is happening?"

"I don't . . . it's just . . ." He sat up again, mirroring her position, then slammed his back against the chair.

So many jerky movements. An air of nervousness. Every twinge highlighted how uncomfortable he felt.

Some people got twitchy around officials with a badge. She got that, but she found it hard to believe this guy could handle a lecture hall full of teens without falling apart, but not her. "It feels like there's something specific you want us to know."

"You've met Lila."

Ah. This could get interesting.

"I really like her. She's very nice." He was speed-talking now. "I mean, not nice in the usual sense. More like . . . do you know what I mean?"

"No." There was no way she was helping him through this babbling.

He returned to shifting and moving and generally making her dizzy. He lifted his cell phone out of his pocket and checked the screen. Whatever he saw there had him frowning.

She could hardly wait to analyze the video from this meeting. "Brent?"

"Okay." He put the cell facedown on the table. "She's . . . attractive. She has this thing about her."

"What thing?" Ginny thought Lila had a *thing*, but who knew if they were talking about the same *thing*.

"Aaron liked to show her off."

Creepy but okay.

"Like she was some sort of prize." Brent stopped and gulped in a big breath. "He never said, *look what I snagged,* but you could feel the pride. He liked that people saw them a certain way. She's beautiful, apparently really smart, but aloof. It gives her this almost larger-than-life feel."

"What are you trying to tell me?"

He gave her full-on eye contact. "It all stopped."

Ginny slipped her pen out of her pocket. She wasn't sure what to write, so she waited. "What did?"

"Them. They stopped working."

"That's a big statement." The kind that could matter and provide motive. "When?"

"More than a month ago." He rubbed his palm with the thumb of his other hand. "Something happened."

"What?"

Brent shrugged. "Who knows? They're super private."

Not helpful. She tried again, crossing one leg over the other, aiming for calm. She hoped that would ease some of the tension he sent jumping around the room. "What makes you think there was a problem?"

"Again, I just want to be clear. He didn't say there was. He actually insisted everything was okay, but it wasn't."

One more time. "How do you know that?"

"He stopped mentioning her." He cut her off before she could ask for clarification. "I know that sounds ridiculous."

"Confusing, yes."

"Being married to her matters to him. It's part of his persona. He has this mysterious, glamorous wife who rarely comes to anything school-related, but he'd drop references about her. Something she said or somewhere they went. It was kind of a teacher's lounge joke that no one would believe she existed except we had met her or seen her around town."

"Okay, but—"

"He didn't tell bad stories about Lila. Ever. If they fought, you'd never really know, because he never mentioned a negative thing."

"Brent." She held up her hand to get him to stop talking at record speed. "I don't think I'm getting your point."

"Starting a few weeks ago, he acted as if she no longer existed. Not a word about her or anything that's happening away from work since then." Brent stopped moving. "And now he's missing."

"Do you think Lila did something to Aaron?" That sounded to her more like Aaron had done something to Lila, but that wouldn't explain the missing husband.

Brent frowned. "I think something happened that changed everything between them. Figure out what it was and you'll find Aaron."

Chapter Fourteen

GINNY AND PETE WALKED INTO LILA'S REAL ESTATE OFFICE IN downtown Ithaca the next morning. She didn't own the place or run it, but she worked out of the brokerage firm. Had a desk there, which was empty.

They'd tried her house first and no one answered, so they'd come here as the logical second choice. Finding her empty desk took two seconds. The lack of personal photos and a nameplate gave it away.

Ginny waited until the woman at the big desk in the office in the back got off the phone. The badge didn't impress the woman into cutting short the conversation about some lake property with a strange smell in the back bedroom. Neither did Pete's dramatic sighing.

When the woman finally hung up, Ginny shot her a *you can't out-attitude me* glare. "Are you ready now or do you need to get coffee or make lunch plans first?"

The woman took her time meeting Ginny's gaze. "Don't tempt me."

Pete sighed one last time before nodding in the direction

of Lila's unoccupied desk chair just outside of the glassed-off office they all stood in. "She's not here?"

"Lila?" The woman shrugged. "Should she be?"

"Tell me your name." Because Ginny was done with this bullshit.

"Christina Torres." She straightened her nameplate. "This is my firm and Lila works here." She hesitated before providing the rest of the information. "But she's not here now."

Clear, concise, and totally not useful. Ginny couldn't help but be a little impressed.

She sized up the business owner. Fortysomething, possibly fifty, and wearing a white silk blouse. She had that put-together vibe that suggested she could go all day without getting a stray pen mark on the damn thing. Ginny appreciated the skill and the perfectly styled black hair that fell just above her shoulders. The lack of helpful information? Not so much.

She swallowed the edge in her voice and tried one more time. "Has Lila checked in with you today, Ms. Torres?"

"She came in this morning."

Ginny felt her patience slip. "And?"

"She said Aaron didn't come home or go to work for a few days." Christina leaned back in her oversize black leather chair. "I told her to take whatever time she needs."

"To do what?" Pete asked.

Christina's eyes narrowed as if she were trying to hide her exasperation and failing miserably. "Excuse me?"

Enough of this. Ginny put her body right in front of the desk. When Christina shifted to get a better look at the outer office,

Ginny stepped sideways and blocked the view. The move said *listen to me*, which is exactly what Ginny intended. "Do you know Aaron?"

"He stops in sometimes when she's working late. But generally, no. And before you ask, I haven't seen him in a few weeks."

Pete glanced at Ginny before turning back to Christina. "Your grip on the armrests and the tightness in your voice make it sound like you're not a fan of his."

Christina let go of the chair and flexed her fingers a few times. "Lila's marriage is not my business."

The woman didn't care that a man was missing, and Ginny knew that meant something. Having to drag it out of Christina only added to the tension pounding through the room. "Pretend it is."

Phones rang in the outer office. A man walked in and dumped his keys on a desk at the front. He picked up the phone, all without looking at the people standing at the back of the room.

With the interruption handled, Ginny stared at Christina again. "Well?"

Silence descended. No one said anything until Christina finally started talking. "Aaron doesn't support her career."

"Did she tell you that or did he?" Pete asked.

"I have eyes." Christina rolled them as if for added impact.

Ginny wasn't in the mood to play. "Elaborate on that."

"I see him here, how he talks with her. It's very different from how he acts out in public and on the field." Christina glanced up from the pen she was holding. She must have seen the question on their faces, because she answered before they could ask. "Both of my daughters play field hockey. Aaron is the assistant coach."

Information they knew. A fact they'd learned early from Brent and others at the school and filed away to assess later. "Different how?"

"He's charming. People love him." Christina picked up the pen again and spun it between her fingers. "But in here, talking to Lila, especially in the last few weeks I saw him, he was in a hurry to leave and to get her home."

That might fit with Brent's comments. Ginny had trouble imagining Lila ever was the touchy-feely type, but Aaron being inappropriate in public didn't fit with anything they'd heard about him so far either. "And before the last few weeks?"

"Dismissive but much better at hiding it."

"Do you think that he treats her poorly? Is he demanding, abusive—what are we talking about here?"

Christina made a face, as if she was mulling over Pete's question and deciding how to answer. "Aaron is one of those guys. All shiny and charming on the outside. Probably, though this is a guess, a condescending asshole at home."

Knowing that not saying anything was the best way to keep people talking, Ginny remained quiet. She used a small shake of her head to telegraph to Pete to do the same.

"So, I guess not abuse." Christina sighed. "More like he had this sort of *how dare my wife have a job and not need me?* aura to him."

Not abuse. Whenever Ginny heard that phrase she wanted to explain how the definition encompassed more than hitting.

Ginny stepped out of the office and put her hand on the chair at the nearby desk. "Does Lila sit here?"

"Usually. She mostly uses the conference room for signings, but she reviews listings there."

Pete walked around to the far side of the desk. Using the end of a pen, he moved a file and uncovered a pile underneath . . . and one more important thing. "Is this laptop hers?"

"Wait a second." Christina came out of her seat and followed them into the outer office. She motioned for the man in the office to step outside before continuing. "I'd appreciate it if you didn't dig around there. That computer belongs to the office."

They were waiting on the phone records to come in. Ginny wanted to move on a search of Lila and Aaron's home, including grabbing the computers for analysis. She didn't want to miss one. "Is this the computer she works on while doing business?"

Christina shook her head. "It's an office laptop. She uses it sometimes. As do other people."

"Does she ever take it home with her?" Pete asked.

Christina didn't break eye contact with Ginny. "She's an independent contractor. I don't watch every move she makes."

Pete touched the closed computer. "Then we can take it with us."

"Absolutely not."

"Ms. Torres, it feels like you're fighting us when all we're trying to do is figure out if Aaron is missing or if he chose to leave."

Christina opened her mouth then shut it again. She shifted her weight from one foot to another. Ginny could almost see the battle waging in her head. How much to say? What to disclose? She got it, but she needed help, and right now Christina was one of the people with easy access to Lila, and almost no one else enjoyed that.

After all the fidgeting, Christina shook her head. "I don't want you to twist anything I say and use it against Lila."

Friendship. Admiration. Maybe a mix of both. Whatever the feeling, it snuck in and got in the way. "What do you have to say?"

"Nothing."

Each question took them further away from an answer. Christina could have a natural distrust of people asking questions, but Ginny couldn't tell if that's what was ticking off the alarm ringing in her head. "Let me try this again. Do you *know* where she went?"

"No."

"Would you say if you did?" Pete asked.

Christina's eyes narrowed and her body stilled as she clicked right back into defensive mode. "Are we done here?"

Sensing they'd need to get answers elsewhere, Ginny offered her card and the usual spiel about calling if Christina saw Lila. A quick goodbye and she retreated with Pete to the street.

She abandoned her planned lecture, the one where she

questioned Pete's bedside manner, when she saw his confused expression. "What is it?"

"I interviewed people at the school today and a few neighbors. Christina is the first person who seems to like Lila more than Aaron. The school people were pretty lukewarm on her. Everyone talked about how she dressed and how put together she was. Nothing personal."

"I don't think we can draw any conclusions from that. Could just be that they see him more." Made sense to Ginny. "Christina and Lila have the connection. Aaron is the *spouse of* and probably not much more."

"Possibly. I wonder if Christina knows what Lila's real name is and why she changed it." Pete glanced at the people going in and out of the downtown coffeehouse before looking at Ginny again.

"She's not the right person to ask, but I agree that Lila's behavior continues to be odd." Ginny couldn't use the word "suspicious" because Pete would leap on it.

"With her husband missing, you'd think she'd be on top of us. She's not checking in or asking about Aaron."

Ginny had an easy answer for that one. "She wouldn't be waiting around and worried if she knew he wasn't alive anymore."

Pete shot her a wide grin. "Now who's jumping to conclusions?"

"Just stating the obvious."

Chapter Fifteen

LILA STARED AT THE NEW NOTE.

YOU'VE BEEN VERY NAUGHTY.

She found this one slipped under the wiper on her windshield this morning. Almost missed it until she put the car in reverse and started moving down the driveway. The paper flapped in the breeze and she slammed on the brakes.

Same as last time, it was typed on a white unlined index card. Blank back and no other words or writing on it. Nothing to give away the identity of its creator but the kind of paper that could be found in a school supply closet. A full sentence with a period, like a teacher or principal might write.

The tone was taunting but in a weird, somewhat playful kind of way. Condescending, which reminded her of Aaron, but the rest didn't sound like him. But since he should be dead, she had no idea what the sentence structure meant, if anything.

She sat in the driver's seat now and stared at the black ink.

Turned the thick piece of paper over in her hands and tried to figure out her next move. If Aaron drafted it, it was only a matter of time before he sprang a trap on her or broke into the house and attacked or had her arrested.

If her new stalker was someone else, she expected some sort of blackmail request. Some end to this game. But with her luck, the one person who knew her secret valued creating chaos over getting cash.

Her mind drifted back to those damn videos. It tried to inch back further, to their years in North Carolina. She'd spent an hour last night wondering why they'd really had to move during the school year. Wondering what games Aaron had played with his students there.

"These are ugly and really thick," the pretty blonde said as she tugged on the bedroom curtain. "Weird since your wife always looks so nice."

"Let's not talk about her."

The young girl smiled as she got up on her knees in the middle of the bed and started to undo the buttons on her shirt. "We can talk about the things I can do for you that she can't."

"Crawl over here and show me what you learned from watching that video link I sent you."

Lila closed her eyes, but the image refused to vanish.

Aaron had used their house to have sex with students. The bastard filmed this girl stripping down and talking about how he liked to take her on her hands and knees.

He insisted the video was just a joke. As if she didn't know his voice, her own bedroom, or how he liked to have sex.

Fucking asshole.

A horn sounded behind her, and she got pulled right back to the present. She also dropped the card.

"Shit."

She looked in her rearview mirror and motioned for the car to pass her. With one hand balanced on the wheel and the other on the front seat cushion, she felt around under the seat and mat trying to locate the newest threat. The last thing she needed was someone seeing it.

She sat up and bit back a scream when a shadow moved outside the driver's window. A body. Male. He caught her off guard. So did the tapping against the glass and his motion for her to lower it.

The jumpiness moved into her chest. She prided herself on being unshakable, on being able to crush any emotion and not let fear or pain show. Ever since Aaron's stupid car unexpectedly disappeared, she'd lost that gift. Now her mind bounced from thought to thought, and the perpetual shakiness in her hands seemed like it could be permanent.

She crushed the card in her palm and felt the rigid corner dig into her skin as she smiled up at the man in uniform. "Yes, sir?"

He barely spared her a glance as he gestured with what looked like a flashlight to tell other cars to pass them. Then he looked down, scanning her face and the inside of the car in one swoop. "You can't park here."

Airport security.

She glanced up at the sign next to the curb. Saw a few people exit the double glass doors, loaded down with luggage. "I'll only be a few—"

"Move or I'll tow you." The security guard issued his command and headed for the car behind her.

The vehicles sat with engines running, all lined up near the front doors of Ithaca Tompkins International Airport. She could fly direct to exactly four cities, and none of them was outside of the United States, so she didn't get the "international" part. But right now she needed quick access, so the name didn't much matter.

A missing husband. Threatening notes. A detective of some sort shadowing her.

She'd ignored Ginny's calls and the not-so-subtle suggestion she be home when Ginny got there to question her this morning. Traffic didn't matter. The weather didn't matter. Even that damn note scraping the skin off her hand didn't matter.

This was where she needed to be, waiting for the one person she trusted to help her.

Chapter Sixteen

FOURTH MORNING WITHOUT AN AARON SIGHTING. TODAY they'd hit Aaron's disappearance head-on. Interviews. Document dumps. Search warrants. Lila might be ignoring her phone, but Aaron's brother and best friend Brent checked in nonstop about the status of the case. Brent kept dropping hints about Aaron not being very happy in his marriage.

Pete looked up from the mountain of paperwork on Ginny's desk. "Do we need to put out a—"

"Wait . . ." Ginny's answer changed just that second, as two people appeared in her doorway. "You're here."

Pete spun around. "Who?"

"Your message suggested I get here or you'd send half of New York's law enforcement officers after me." Lila delivered her explanation from her side of the doorway.

"Not half." Ginny got up and held out her hand to the man with Lila. "I'm Ginny Davis."

He wore a navy-blue suit on his lean frame. Tall with a bright smile. Very much in charge and holding a suitcase. Looked like he was made for desk work and not for outside labor, or any labor. The kind of guy who oozed charm but probably couldn't rewire a ceiling fan.

A lawyer. Had to be.

"The investigator. Right. I've heard." He took a few steps forward, leaving Lila at the door, and extended his hand. "Tobias Maddow."

He had one of those voices. Low and soothing. She'd bet he could sell anything to anyone with the combination of that pretty face and the inviting tone. "And you are who, Mr. Maddow?"

"Tobias. Please," he said in that smooth *we can be friends* voice. "I'm Lila's lawyer."

Yep, lawyer. Ginny could spot them a mile away. The slovenly type. The put-together type. Didn't matter. They all had a look that, to her, said, *I'm going to bullshit you now.*

She waited until Pete and Tobias exchanged greetings then glanced over Tobias's shoulder toward Lila. "You hired a lawyer? That was fast."

Tobias shifted. The move was so subtle Ginny almost missed it. The perfect lean, just enough to block her view of Lila. To cut off the chance to read Lila's gaze.

"I'm her former law partner and her current lawyer, if that's actually needed. I'm hopeful Aaron will walk in the door soon and the rest of this nonsense can be forgotten." Tobias glanced at Lila without losing one spark from his high-wattage smile. "Does she know about your past life in the law?"

Lila nodded. "I'm sure she's been studying up on me for the last few days."

Very true, but still. "My main concern is your husband."

Tobias finally dropped his hand and took a step back. "Ours, too."

"Really?" Pete asked.

The two men could play whatever testosterone-laden games they wished. This was her case, and she was not about to let anyone interview Lila but her. "We went to your office to speak with you."

"For the record, I mostly work from home."

Tobias shot Lila a quick side glance before smiling at Ginny again. "She likely was at the airport, picking me up."

Lila held up both hands. "See? No big conspiracy to avoid you, though I can see why people might."

Ginny ignored the glass walls and the audience both inside and outside of the small tension-filled room and kept her focus on Lila. Keeping with her usual people skills, Lila didn't attempt to put on a show or make a good impression. There was nothing warm and fuzzy about her, and that intrigued Ginny. A lawyer, someone trained who had worked in criminal law, should know how to play this game better. The fact Lila didn't even try felt purposeful. Like a challenge.

"No, you were busy out there, finding a lawyer. And one from out of state. Interesting choice."

Once again Tobias responded for Lila. "I'm licensed to practice in New York as well as North Carolina. Call me an overachiever."

Lila never broke eye contact with Ginny, and that continued as she spoke. "You had questions for me?"

"I'm excited to hear your answers."

Tobias nodded. "Let's get this over with so Lila can get back to finding her husband."

They filed into the small interrogation room down the hall from her office. She and Pete sat on one side of the desk. Lila and Tobias were on the other.

This would be informal. Not too daunting.

Before Ginny could lay any groundwork, Lila broke into the silence. "What have you been doing to find Aaron?"

An attempt to throw her off, maybe? If so, she failed. Ginny had been playing this game long enough to not let the potential suspect take over. "I'm assuming he's still not home."

"He's not anywhere."

"We expect the news to catch on to Aaron's absence today. I've been to the school, and the kids and teachers are talking." Pete shifted in his seat, causing it to creak and moan beneath him. "Brent says he can't keep anyone's focus on class, including his own."

The words just sat there for a few seconds. No one said anything until Lila finally shrugged. "Okay."

Stone-cold. If someone asked Ginny to describe Lila, that would be the first thing she'd say. But there was more to her. A heat that simmered beneath the surface. She didn't fidget or panic. In so many ways she seemed dead inside, but Ginny didn't miss the other pieces. The intelligence in Lila's eyes. The pain that sometimes flashed across her face before she spoke. The way she would stare as if she were looking deep inside you.

Still, she didn't get how Lila ignored the load of scrutiny headed straight for her. "You're not concerned?"

Lila's eyes narrowed. "Should I be?"

Tobias cleared his throat. "Have you heard anything? Done a search? Located his car?"

Pete started to talk, but Ginny stopped him with a small shake of her head. She needed to take this one. "We've put out a BOLO on Aaron, asking all of the local police departments—state, county, municipal, and university—to look for the car. We've talked with your neighbors, people at the school, and a few friends. His brother will be coming in soon."

"I've driven in and around your neighborhood looking for signs of Aaron or the car. Some of the sheriffs have taken shifts looking in and around Cayuga Lake." Pete leaned back in his chair with his arms folded over his chest. "Started the process to get some records we'll need and registered Aaron with a national database of missing persons, NamUs. I'd like a recent photo so we can make fliers."

Tobias nodded. "Sounds thorough."

"As your client pointed out, it's as if Aaron disappeared without a trace." Ginny looked at the pair across the table until her gaze landed on Lila. "Which leads us back to you, Lila."

"You're investigating me." Lila's tone remained flat as she said the words.

"Is that a surprise?" Pete asked.

"No."

Ginny bit back her usual explanation about the spouse and looking at him or her first. The two people sitting across from her knew the drill. They didn't need to be baby-stepped through Investigation 101. "Then you had to know we'd find out about your past."

For the first time since they'd met, Lila looked genuinely stumped. "What about it?"

Ginny pounced. "You don't have one."

Chapter Seventeen

THEY MISSED THE POINT. SHE HAD A PAST. MAYBE NOT AS LILA Ridgefield, but changing her name hadn't wiped out the years of confusion and self-loathing that had come before.

"What's your real name?" Pete asked.

"Lila Ridgefield." She wasn't playing games. She went to court, paid, testified about her reasons, and changed it. Forget shortcuts. She'd followed the rules because she didn't want to mess up her chance of letting go of a life that sucked her down into darkness and left her bloodied and wallowing.

"You legally changed it."

Of course Ginny would be the one to guess the right answer. From the interaction she'd had with the two investigators, Pete was by far the less experienced. He didn't hold a poker face and would often spout off with a question she knew Ginny wouldn't ask.

No, Ginny was the pro. The one who knew how to verbally bob and weave. The one who assessed every word and shook Lila into being extra careful.

There was no need to hide this part, so Lila didn't try. "Yes, I did. The court sealed the case at my request."

"Why?"

"Let's put the brakes on for a second." Tobias leaned forward, resting his elbows on the edge of the table. "How is any of this relevant? It happened more than a decade ago, before she and Aaron even met, let alone got married."

Pete met Tobias's smile with one of his own. "An overachiever would know the answer to that question."

As usual, Ginny took a more reasoned approach. "Right now the motive for the name change seems to be a secret, and all secrets are suspect when someone is missing."

Tobias scoffed. "That's kind of a broad rationale, isn't it?"

The question seemed to put a ticking clock on Ginny's patience. Her neutral expression morphed into exasperation. Everything about her demeanor said she'd sooner throw them both in a cell than continue with the questioning.

"She changed her name as an adult. Is she running from a juvenile crime? I don't know, but I sort of doubt it. And the point is I can ask that the records be unsealed." Ginny looked at Lila now. "It will take longer, but maybe that's the goal. Put distance between the question and Aaron going missing. Make the investigation that much harder."

Tobias shifted as if he wanted to answer for her, but Lila put a hand on his arm and went first. This was her part to tell. Her life. Her shame. "When I graduated from college I wanted a new start."

"Okay." Ginny blew out a long breath. "From what?"

"Life. My background. The family I left behind."

"Be more specific."

Lila understood the frustration in Ginny's voice, but she actually wasn't trying to evade the other woman's questions this round. Everything inside her clenched in a desperate need to bat the words back. The topic chipped away at the life she'd made, at the progress she'd fought so hard to achieve. The urge to get in her car and not look back hit her so strong that it shook her.

You should be more like your friend, Carina. Look at Amelia in her pretty dress. Dance for me, sweetie.

Lila tipped her head back and stared at the ceiling to keep from throwing up. The memory of her father's deep voice echoing in her head always touched off a roiling in her stomach. He'd make excuses to see Amelia. It happened for years. The way he would hover in the doorway whenever Amelia came over. He'd hug her and run a hand through her hair.

As a kid she'd been jealous. *Why doesn't Daddy like me as much as he likes Amelia?* Now she knew the answer and it made her physically sick.

For a few minutes, no one said anything. The only sound in the room came from the air vent on the far wall. The slight whistle breaking through the silence.

"My . . . father . . ." She stumbled over the word. She hadn't said his name in years or thought of him as a father for even longer. "He's in prison. His name is Grant Fields."

Ginny looked at Pete until she made eye contact. She then nodded toward the door. The chair legs screeched across the floor as he got up and silently left the room.

Lila got it. Pete would now race around and find the information about what happened. Every hideous detail.

She debated waiting for him to return and let him divulge the facts. The computer search couldn't take that long, and maybe a few extra minutes would make the telling easier, though she doubted it.

When he didn't immediately return, she started explaining. "It happened when I was fourteen. Though, really, I think the touching and leering had been happening for years. My father waited to make his big move."

Pete eased the door open and stepped inside just as Lila finished the sentence. He held a handful of papers and placed a few in front of Ginny before sitting down.

"My father became obsessed with a girl named Amelia. He'd watch her. Acted like a father figure to her and claimed he needed to because her parents were divorced and her dad lived out of state. My father would go to Amelia's events. I didn't know that then, but found out later when I looked at the trial transcript as an adult."

She stopped long enough to catch her breath. To see the concern on Tobias's face and the resigned, knowing look on Ginny's.

"My father was deluded, or so his attorney said. He talked about how once he figured out I'd had my period that Amelia likely had hers, which meant she was ready for him." Lila blew out a long breath, trying to hold steady and get through this. "He said he was in love with Amelia and was convinced she felt the same about him."

"I assume he acted on his sick feelings," Ginny said in a quiet voice.

"He kidnapped her. Picked her up from school and, of course, she got in the car like she had a thousand times before." The police said he admitted he told Amelia they were going for an early dinner. She was his secret weapon in teasing Amelia along. He promised they were going to get her then eat. "He owned a construction company and brought a trailer to sites. He kept her hidden in the back of one of the older trailers at the lot. Raped her repeatedly."

Tobias put a hand on her arm and squeezed. "He put her through some sort of fake marriage ceremony first, which he took photos of. Had her dressed up as a bride."

He'd actually tried to explain to the prosecutor that the fact he waited to force her to have sex until after his bizarre wedding ritual made him the good guy. Lila could never forget that part of reading the testimony. Any part of it.

"After eleven days, all while he was out with the search teams pretending to try to find Amelia, she tried to escape. When he got back, she was screaming. He panicked and hit her with a crowbar to get her to stop. The hit killed her." It was all an accident, he claimed. He loved her and would never hurt her. He totally ignored the horrible things he did to her, how he'd hurt her and scared her.

Tobias cleared his throat before offering the rest. "He dug

a hole to bury Amelia. He was found a day later, lying in the hole and holding her body, saying he couldn't let her go."

"To this day, when he tells people his wife died, he's not talking about my mother. He's talking about Amelia." That was the horrific punch line to the sordid tale.

"Amelia . . . She was your friend," Pete added in a soft voice.

The word whipped through Lila. Best friend, but that fact only made what happened next worse. "She lived on our street. She'd been to my house a million times. We'd played together since kindergarten."

Ginny never looked at the papers or the wall. Not anywhere but at Lila as she talked.

Now Lila returned the stare. "Wouldn't you want to change your name and forget it all?"

Chapter Eighteen

THE INTERVIEW WENT ON FOR ANOTHER FIFTEEN MINUTES, BUT the emotional drain from the father-as-murderer reveal made progress tough. They all sat there thinking about the crime back then, assessing what it meant now. Ginny watched a shadow envelop the room and knew the others saw it as well.

Charles Gan, the elected sheriff and Pete and Ginny's boss, stepped out of his office and watched Lila and Tobias leave the building. In his late fifties, his face showed every year of his time on the job. The omnipresent frown and wrinkled forehead were so familiar to Ginny that she got thrown off stride when Charles actually smiled, which was almost never.

He had weathered tough election cycles and one devastating year when a traffic call ended up with him working his son's death scene. He never talked about family. Never drank. He lived for the job and didn't tolerate mistakes on his watch.

He also wanted a "win" because the Karen Blue disappearance and the resulting bad press, questioning missed leads, had every law enforcement officer in New York on edge. "Where are we?"

Pete shrugged as he handed his gathered paperwork on Lila's father's past over to Charles. "With the missing husband? Nowhere, but we do have a better handle on the wife."

Charles hummed as he read. The noises of the room, the phones ringing and officers moving in and out, faded into the background when he lifted his head. "Looks like she testified against her father. That sort of thing has to mess a kid up."

"So does having your father rape and murder your best friend." But Ginny knew there was way more they hadn't talked about. She doubted that Lila and her mother got support from many sources. They likely were ostracized, made to feel like freaks and criminals.

She didn't have to read the case specifics to know Lila shouldered the blame, took it on, at least in part, herself. Ginny heard it in every word, how they sounded ripped out of Lila when she talked about this one issue. Saw the thumping pain in Lila's eyes as she relayed the bit of information she shared.

Charles nodded. "Is this father still alive?"

"In prison in Colorado, where Lila—then known as Carina Fields—grew up." Pete flipped to the next page and pointed at a line there. "Only child. Went to live with a relative in Florida after her mom died."

Ginny hadn't gotten that far because she hadn't wanted to show that much interest in the information while in front of Lila. "Died how?"

"Uh . . ." He skimmed down the page then shook his head. "Doesn't say, but it happened after the trial when her father was awaiting sentencing."

Ginny couldn't imagine, but she couldn't afford to get lost in sympathy either. "Devastating and awful, but none of this gets us closer to finding Aaron. I'd hoped the name change related to something *she* did, not her father."

"Right." Charles handed the papers back to Pete.

"Pete has been checking video from around Lila's house around the time of the disappearance." They'd only started the process, but Ginny remained hopeful they would get more.

"No video from their street yet, but I'm checking the alarm videos from every house. I got one from the florist shop across the street from the entry to their development. You can see Aaron's SUV turns left at the light out of their neighborhood before four in the morning on the day he went missing, which was way earlier than Lila said he usually heads out," Pete said. "We pick the vehicle up again going through some lights and then see it heading toward the school and around to the back entrance, but that's where we lose it."

"We can't actually verify where it went at the school, but we don't see it again, which is odd since it's not there." Ginny knew "odd" was an understatement, but she used the word anyway.

"Check again." Charles made a sound that didn't give away what he was thinking. "Do we know Aaron was the one driving around that morning?"

Ginny had reviewed the video with that in mind. "No. You can't tell, but it does look like only one person in the car. The shadowed outline suggests someone wearing a tie."

"Good work. Keep on it." Charles nodded. "Also, do some

digging into the father's case and make sure it's unrelated. I want us all to agree that what happened back then didn't spin into something now."

"Like revenge?" Pete asked.

"Possibly." Charles turned to Ginny. "Also, the Ithaca Police Department offered us assistance on this, and so did the state police. Everyone is busy with the Karen Blue task force, but we can get reinforcements."

"I appreciate it—"

He laughed, this hollow sound that lacked any sort of amusement. "No, you don't."

"—but everyone is spread thin enough already." It was a good argument. Ginny refused to believe her stance had anything to do with Lila or wanting to win. For a safe area of the country, law enforcement was crawling all over the place. Fighting off public dissatisfaction only added to the load.

"Ever since the video of the police bringing in Karen's ex-boyfriend for questioning got out, that podcaster has been digging up information," Pete said.

The line between public and private information grew blurrier each day. Ginny did not want private citizens getting in the way in Aaron's case. "There's huge pressure on everyone to find her before the podcast blows up into a vigilante mess."

Charles swore under his breath. "Armchair investigators."

"They're not all bad." She believed that. Sometimes a person sitting in their living room held that one piece of information that tied everything together. She didn't care if they came forward as a result of police pleading or a podcast, so long as they came forward . . . and didn't mess up her case. "But as to bringing in the state police or FBI or whatever, I'd prefer to handle this in-house until we know more. Lila and Aaron lived outside of Ithaca, which makes this our case."

"For now, but get something, and do it fast. I don't want to get into a jurisdictional pissing match over a high school teacher."

"Yes, sir." She responded to an empty space because Charles had already headed back to his office and closed the door.

Pete stared after him. "Does he want us to make up evidence?"

"He wants us to find some, which means it's time to put a lot of pressure on Lila." Phone records and search warrants. Pick her life apart. Inadvertently, or maybe on purpose, put a target on her back.

"Sounds like she's used to being under the microscope."

Ginny remembered Lila's blank expression and emotionless stare as she talked about her friend from childhood. "That doesn't mean she welcomes it."

Chapter Nineteen

GINNY USHERED JARED INTO THE EXAMINATION ROOM HOURS after Lila and her lawyer left. Pete followed a second later with coffee for everyone.

This was the informal talk. The getting-to-know-you part where she tended to shake loose information that would lead her where she needed to go. Her boss had given her the green-light to press hard and demanded she make progress.

They'd started putting together profiles and timelines. Collecting security videos and records. But Jared was the brother, the one with the most intimate details about Aaron and, hopefully, some insight into Lila. He was a commercial real estate developer with a pristine reputation. No criminal record. No debts or addictions that anyone could tell.

Bottom line, he knew people, and none of them offered a negative word about him, except to suggest the man had an obsessive streak when it came to work. That likely also explained his lack of a meaningful personal life outside of his brother and sister-in-law.

He was also the one to benefit financially from Aaron's death, though Jared seemed to have enough money without needing to stockpile more from his brother. Still, it was a possible motive she couldn't ignore.

She smiled at Jared across the table as Pete sat down. "Thanks for coming in."

Jared cradled the coffee cup in his hands. "Have you found anything?"

"Honestly, it's as if Aaron walked out of his house and disappeared."

He shook his head. "That doesn't make any sense."

"Not his style?" Pete asked.

"Not remotely." Jared's attention flipped back to Ginny. "Do the security videos show when he left the house? Can you see if he was okay?"

"We'll check those." They'd run into a bit of a roadblock when the closest neighbor admitted that he'd turned off his alarm weeks ago due to a malfunction and hadn't used it again. Lila and Aaron had done the same.

There were transcripts of calls between both couples and the alarm company. A technician visited both houses. Nothing turned up, which made the malfunction convenient and suspicious.

Jared stared into his black coffee. "This is unbelievable."

After only a few minutes, Jared had shown more emotion than Lila had in all of their meetings. Lila was exactly the topic Ginny wanted to discuss. "Let me ask you a few questions.

I need to start with an obvious one we ask everyone. Where were you between four and seven in the morning on the day Aaron went missing?"

"Four?"

"Yes." She wasn't about to go into a detailed explanation of the video intel they'd found. Not yet.

"At a conference in Rochester. It was about discount pricing for companies who improve properties." He took a sip of coffee. "In other words, mortgage strategies for property flippers. I left two days before Aaron went missing and was there until about ten in the morning on that day. I came home as soon as Brent called me."

"I'll need the hotel information and any names of people who can confirm you were there." Ginny waited until Jared nodded to continue. "Did Lila get in touch with you that morning as well as Brent?"

"She didn't do this."

That was quick and adamant. His voice still rang off the walls when Ginny started poking around in his response. "What exactly?"

"Anything to my brother." Jared sat back, taking the cup with him. Holding it in a tight grip that suggested he needed it to keep from fidgeting or flailing. "Look, I know she's different, but so is he. They've both had these horrible things happen to them. They're . . . I don't know, careful."

"Broken?"

"Not really. They both function fine." He took a long sip. "She had a successful legal career. Now she sets her own schedule and sells houses without trouble. I've been told people like her no-bullshit style as an agent."

Pete nodded. "I can see that."

"My brother has exactly the job he's always wanted. He loves kids. Always talked about being a coach." Jared smiled as he played with the handle on the mug. "I thought he'd go on and teach at the college level, but that wasn't his thing. He wanted to mentor kids through the teen years. The tough years."

"Why did they move to New York from North Carolina?" That question stuck out in Ginny's mind as an area to pursue. Pete had made some calls, but no one offered much.

Jared shrugged. "Aaron wanted to coach but couldn't there. He and the guy in charge of the athletic programs argued about it, so when a position came open here, near where we grew up and where I live, Aaron grabbed it."

Sounded reasonable. Ginny still wanted another opinion before she'd drop it, but for now that explanation worked. "You and your brother are close."

"We are. Some kids who are close together in age fight. Some are close. We're lucky to be the latter."

He had a smooth style. Didn't offer too much or too little. Smiled when it was appropriate to smile. Ginny tried to read deeper and hit a roadblock. But the way he described his brother and Lila made them sound pretty normal. He seemed to be alone in thinking that. Brent suggested, at least recently, they tolerated each other more than they loved each other.

"Are you . . . What was the word you used to describe your brother and his wife? Different?"

"Yes, and careful. I haven't dated a woman for more than a month my entire life, so yeah, I'd say I have some issues. It's hard not to." His fingers tightened on the mug. The clench lasted for a second, then he relaxed again. Not fully relaxed, but his shoulders slumped and he blew out a long breath. "I should probably explain a bit about our upbringing."

She had the basics. The kind of stuff that's included in an official file, which she knew from experience was never the full story. By the time he'd finished talking about his mother's death and the accident that took his father, Ginny hadn't learned one new piece of information. "Lila told me the same thing."

It was almost like listening to a tape. Mom shot by accident by hunters. Dad killed in an unsolved hit-and-run. A nearly word-for-word description that mirrored Lila's telling of the same events.

Where Jared was warm and smiling when talking about Aaron and Lila, his voice remained flat when walking through his parents' deaths. Could be some sort of post-trauma issue. Since those deaths were long ago handled by other law enforcements officials, she didn't bother digging too deep. They needed to stay focused on Aaron, the possible third catastrophe for this family.

"Do you know about her parents?" Jared asked.

Ginny wasn't sure if she was being tested, so she played along. "Her father is in prison. Does she ever talk about him?"

"Never. Would you? He sounds like a psychopath."

Probably not a surprise. Ginny couldn't imagine having

that man as a father or the destruction he'd unleashed on Lila's life. But there was one more player. "And her mother?"

Jared's eyes narrowed. "She died."

"How?"

This time he drained the cup before speaking. "The official story is she fell off the rooftop of her office building. People went up there to smoke, and she smoked. It was one of those misty, rainy days, and she fell."

Pete stopped taking notes. "What's the unofficial story?"

"She killed herself." Jared let out a long breath. "Lila thinks she jumped. The pressure of having a pedophile for a husband was too much. The trial was all over the news. Someone tried to burn down their house. Lila couldn't go to school because she was getting beaten up and threatened."

Pete whistled. "That's pretty awful."

"Unimaginable, actually."

The words sounded defensive. Rough, as if he wanted to do battle for her. An interesting idea, since Lila struck Ginny as a pretty self-reliant and tough woman. The kind that didn't need a savior. "You're fond of your sister-in-law."

"Not sure what you're saying there, but yes, in a sister kind of way only."

Very defensive. Ginny saw Pete freeze at the sound of Jared's voice that time.

"That's what I meant," Ginny said.

"She's perfect for Aaron." Jared sat forward in his chair again with his elbows resting on the table. "She doesn't demand much from him. Neither wanted children. She's quieter, prefers being at home, but she's friendly. Smart. I enjoy talking to her about things."

"She very attractive," Pete said. "It's one of the first things people say about her when you ask them."

"Sure, she's pretty." When no one jumped in, Jared added on to his explanation. "A lot of women are pretty. I think what people are reacting to is her affect. She's confident. Very self-aware. Then there's the fact she always looks perfect."

It sounded to Ginny like he was describing a mannequin, not a woman. "But you've seen her in sweatpants and workout gear, right?"

"Honestly? Rarely." A smile came and went. "She looks pretty amazing just sitting around the house, too."

Ginny wasn't sure what to do with that tidbit of information. She stored it away, thinking Jared might have a bit of a crush. Harmless, but there.

"You've spent a lot of time together." Ginny held up her hand before he could launch into another denial. "With them as a couple, I mean."

Jared's shoulders unbunched as he nodded. "Yes, and a lot of fishing and hiking time with Aaron."

"What about their relationship? Do they fight?" Pete asked.

"They're human."

Ginny tried to imagine how fair of a fight Lila would engage in. "Anything that concerned you? That you considered out of the norm for them?"

"No." He winced. "Well . . . It's not a big thing, but they had a fight and Aaron ended up at my house for a few nights, but he went home and apologized. They were working it out."

Ginny thought about that interview with Brent. "When was this?"

Jared picked at the mug handle again. "Six or seven weeks ago."

Ginny felt Pete glance in her direction before he took over. He'd watched her interview with Brent. He knew about the odd comments. "They still hadn't made up?"

"They did. He went back home, but things could still get tense." Jared made a strangled sound. "I'm not married, but I assume it's a normal marital thing."

This matched the timing Brent had mentioned, so Ginny wasn't quite ready to let it go. "What was the fight about?"

"I have no idea. Neither of them volunteered a lot of information. Again, they're very private."

No . . . that sounded wrong. She had a sister. She would ask. Poke and wait it out, but she'd give her every chance to talk about it. "Did he normally run to your house when they fought?"

"The way you're saying it sounds like you're attaching some sort of judgment, but no. This was the first time." He hesitated for a few seconds. "I don't think she kicked him out. It was more like he was giving her space."

"Some guys need that." Pete leaned in. Did a sort of man-to-man, just-us-talking thing with Jared. "Do you think your brother needed an escape and left for a while? A too-much-yelling-at-home sort of thing?"

"We had plans to go fishing this weekend. He rented a boat. I can get you the information, but it's the same one we've used before. Just the two of us. Why do that if he was going to run?" Jared smacked the side of his hand on the table as he made each point. "And he's not the type. Not without talking about it or formally separating from Lila, which I can't really see him doing anyway."

It sounded like they'd reached the end of his tolerance for talking about his brother's marriage. Ginny didn't see an opportunity for breaking through on that point, so she circled and tried a different tack. "Do you know anyone who would want to hurt your brother?"

"He's a teacher. It's pretty safe stuff."

Pete snorted. "Have you been to a school lately?"

"Good point." Jared's mood lightened a bit. "Some of his stories were wild, but none of them were about safety or threats. They were more like *you'll never believe what this kid said today* stuff."

That matched what the other teachers said. "Other than Brent, does your brother have a lot of friends?"

"Some. Mostly through school and coaching. I can give you a list."

"What about Lila?"

Jared's mood slammed closed again. He became almost guarded, as if he knew he needed to weigh each word to protect her. "She has some anxiety issues, so she sticks close to home except when she's working."

"What about . . ." Ginny made a show of leaning over and

looking at the file in front of Pete, even though there was nothing spur-of-the-moment in the question she was about to ask. "Ryan?"

Jared's expression went blank. "Who?"

"Ryan Horita."

He looked at the table and the file. Even spun his mug around in between his palms once before answering. "Who's that?"

"Someone close to Lila." She chose every word for a reason.

Jared shook his head. "That's not possible. I've never heard of him."

That's exactly what Ginny wanted to hear.

Chapter Twenty

Welcome back. This is Nia Simms and Gone Missing, *the true crime podcast that discusses cases—big and small—in your neighborhood and around the country. Even before we started focusing on Karen Blue, every week I hoped to come on here with the good news that she's been found or, at least, that there has been a break in the case. She's officially been missing nine weeks, and the news remains bleak. Karen's ex, the one who allegedly shoved her into a wall and claims to have been out with friends the night Karen disappeared, still looks like the lead suspect . . .*

"Listening to that sort of thing is not going to lessen your anxiety." Tobias made the assessment while sprawled on Lila's sectional sofa, scanning through the emails on his phone.

She slipped back into the family room with a bottle of water for her and a glass of red wine for him. She handed the crystal she almost never used to him. At home, away from prying eyes, she was the wine-in-a-mug type—no need for anything fancy—but Tobias strenuously disagreed.

"The podcast works as background noise."

He stared at her over the rim of the glass. "It's a true crime podcast. About death and murder."

"Nia, the person who runs this one, said Karen's disappearance was fading from the news. Nia is semilocal and so is the missing woman, so now the *where is she?* talk is nonstop." She shot her workaholic friend a smile. "Honestly, true crime podcasts are all the rage right now."

"Yeah, I know." He took a sip of wine then set the glass down on the stack of magazines on the table in front of him. "We have podcasts in North Carolina, too."

They were casual and comfortable together. Nothing had changed on that score despite her move to New York. Their friendship had started back in law school. They'd launched their careers in different ways. Hers in a boutique criminal defense firm. His in the prosecutor's office. It didn't take long for their interests to merge again and the need to be their own bosses to take over.

They'd been colleagues and friends, and now she would be the client. She didn't like the change.

He shifted his leg until his knee touched hers. "You okay?"

"Haven't you heard? My husband is missing."

"I'm going to ignore how flippant that sounded and ask you lawyer questions now."

She ignored the fine tremble in her fingers and focused on the opportunity to practice. "Fire away."

"Where were you when he disappeared?"

The real answer—planting video evidence in his car showing

the sick bastard liked young girls—seemed wrong, so she evaded. "Where do you think I was in the morning?"

"Asleep and without an alibi." He let out a dramatic sigh. "Thanks for that."

"Anytime."

"Did you guys fight?"

She fiddled with the top on the water bottle. "I think all couples fight."

"Do not tell an engaged man that." He held out a hand. "Here, let me try."

He opened the top and handed the bottle back to her. He was smart enough not to call her weak. She was horrified that she couldn't get her body to work with her. Waves of anxiety crashed over her, pressing her down, making her doubt every sentence and every thought. She wanted to get in the car and drive away. To mimic what some thought Aaron had done to get out of a loveless marriage.

She'd heard the whispers. They would only grow louder and angrier. Those who knew about Aaron's disappearance pointed. Once the news went out wider, her life would turn to shit. Every time she'd ever put her head down in the grocery store rather than say hello to someone would be brought up, twisted, and dissected.

She needed to think of something happier, even if only for a second. "How's Cade?"

Tobias's smile was so big, so genuine. "He's great, despite his ridiculous family."

She loved hearing about the preparations for the wedding

of infamous playboy Cade Linden and hot lawyer Tobias Maddow. She was pretty sure one email he'd sent had talked about having doves at the reception. Another said something about horses and hinted at a huge argument about guests being ferried to a private island by yacht.

"That's what you get for marrying into Southern money." Like, stupid money. Tobias's in-laws-to-be owned most of South Carolina, or so it seemed. "There are how many retired politicians, big law firm partners, and business owners in the family?"

"I stopped counting." Tobias picked up his glass again. "And you need to stop changing the subject."

He was the one person she couldn't fool. He'd known about her feelings on marriage and love from the beginning. She'd been looking for a home and exchanged that with a marriage.

She knew it. Tobias knew it. Hell, she thought Aaron knew it.

"You've hung around Aaron. He's solid and stubborn. Dependable and frustrating."

Tobias barked out a laugh. "It's like you're describing an annoying puppy."

Sort of. Maybe a feral one.

She twisted the bottle cap back and forth. "Not all of us get a grand love story."

"You could."

"I wanted simple and clean. A guy with his own paycheck who didn't depend on mine." The more she added, the lamer it sounded. "Company and comfort."

Tobias toasted the air. "Very romantic." Some of Tobias's

amusement faded. "But really, I can't see him leaving you without a word."

"Me either." And he didn't. Not on purpose, but the leaving was not her concern right now. She was far more invested in learning about his current location. She imagined him sitting somewhere, writing those damn notes as he plotted his revenge.

"So, what does that mean? Where do you think he is?" Tobias asked.

She didn't know what to say. Make up something, maybe? Nia Simms's voice saved her from having to do that.

. . . but let me suggest another possibility. What if Karen wasn't the first college student to go missing in the area? There's Yara James. Her cousin contacted us and reminded us of this cold case. It hasn't gotten as much attention as Karen's case, but Yara is still missing. She was thinking about transferring and visited Cornell, and no one has seen her since. We know she was on campus and that she checked out of the hotel she was staying in. That disappearance happened two and a half years ago, and she hasn't been seen or heard from in all that time.

Yara's cousin mentioned another missing woman. Julie Levin. She went hiking with her boyfriend in Treman State Park near Lucifer Falls and disappeared. That happened about a year ago. Her boyfriend has been arrested but he insists he's innocent. What if he is and we don't have one missing woman . . . we have three? Three women, all college-aged. All with long brown hair. All with a certain look and body type—athletic build, fit, pretty, *and around five foot seven. Does that description fit a lot of women? Sure, but these women are all missing from the same general area. Is it possible one person is responsible for all three disappearances?*

Tobias made a face. "Can we turn the podcast down? It's distracting . . . and now I want to know about these women."

"That's how these podcasts lure you in, but sure." She reached for the remote control and froze.

And then there's the case of Aaron Payne. This one is just breaking, and there's not much information yet. It involves a man, yes, but a respected one. A high school teacher and coach gone missing. It's unlikely his disappearance is related to that of three college-aged women, but his addition to the growing list of missing individuals raises one very big question: Are our neighborhoods, our roads, and our beautiful parks as safe as we think they are?

Lila tried to say something, but babble filled her brain. She couldn't think or function. She fell back into her seat on the couch and stayed there.

The podcast. Aaron was on the podcast.

"Lila?"

The announcement could change everything. She sparred with Ginny. She could ignore neighbors and people from school. She already planned to drive out of town to get anything she needed, just to avoid a confrontation. But the fans from this podcast? All those amateur detectives aimed directly at her. That was too much.

Tobias put his hand on her arm. "Is there anything you need to tell me?"

The videos. The fact she knew about them before Aaron disappeared could incriminate her, but they really incriminated Aaron. What the girls said. His voice in the background. Using their bedroom in one of them. Once released they might make it impossible for him to slink back into town.

The front door opened, and Jared's voice floated through the now-quiet house. "Lila?"

"In here," Tobias said as he stood up.

Jared stalked into the family room in an uncharacteristic rush. He wore a dark gray suit, but he'd loosened his tie. His wrinkled jacket bunched up on one side. His hair stood straight up, as if he'd been combing his fingers through it. She'd say his state was not quite disheveled, but he came as close as she'd ever seen him.

The ruffled look shook her. "Have you heard something?"

"No." Jared looked from Lila to Tobias and back again. "I didn't know you were in town."

The "no" didn't convince her. "I called him and asked for help."

The men shook hands, but Jared's focus stayed on Lila. "In searching for Aaron?"

"The ultimate goal is to keep the police focused on Aaron and not get sidetracked." Tobias offered Jared a glass of wine.

Jared shook his head as he sat down across from Lila. "Speaking of that, who is Ryan Horita?"

The name vibrated through her. She called up every ounce of control to hold her expression and keep her body still. Energy pounded through her as she struggled to keep her voice steady. "He's a client. I sold him a house."

"Why do you ask?" Tobias asked.

Jared's gaze wandered over her face. "The investigator asked about him."

Tobias picked up his glass again. "Okay. I'll try again, why?"

Jared shrugged. "That's what I was wondering."

Lila knew exactly why, and having a possibly alive husband was no longer her biggest problem.

Chapter Twenty-one

Seven Months Earlier

MARCH ON CAYUGA LAKE. THE TEMPERATURE STILL HOVERED in the midforties. The snow had cleared . . . for now. With the sun out and the bright blue sky calling, Lila and Aaron headed out for a hike. Lila insisted it be a short one because even at a brisk pace and with the best gloves on the planet, the chill coming off the water seeped right into her bones.

They stuck to the southern end of the lake. The muddy ground slushed beneath her boots. With most of the leaves gone, she had a good view of Cornell University in the distance. The clock tower loomed. In the fall, the area would be awash in color and the population would almost double in size due to student and tourist traffic.

Bright oranges and reds. She missed living in the South, but nothing compared to those few weeks of fiery colors breaking through a blanket of green and blue.

They moved back from the shoreline now, following a path

that led them to a series of boulders stacked at the bottom of a scaling hill. Aaron hit the incline, grabbing on to tree limbs to boost him up.

She wasn't ready to leave the quiet lapping of the water. She sat down, startled when the coldness from the rock passed right through her jeans to her bare skin.

Aaron looked over his shoulder then stopped walking. "What are you doing?"

Instead of answering, she lifted her head and let the warm sun beat down on her skin for the first time since winter set in last October. "Enjoying the scenery."

"That's not a bad idea. I think I'll join you." He slid back over the rough terrain and plunked down next to her.

She smiled but kept her eyes closed. "It also helps that I have the car keys."

"Then I'll definitely sit with you." Not really one to stay still for long, he picked up two sticks and rubbed them together.

The breeze whipped around her. She inhaled, letting the fresh air fuel her. Out here in the quiet, while other hikers nodded and walked around them, ideas popped into her mind. Questions she'd never bothered to ask. But life kept racing past them, and with her jacket warming her, lulling her into a false sense of security, she asked a question that had been dancing in her head.

"Do you ever wonder if there's more?"

"To the lake?" He pointed over to their right. "We've driven—"

"No, I mean to us. To life."

"That's a pretty heavy question for a Sunday afternoon hike."

She could hear the amusement in his voice. She got it. This was not the sort of topic she usually used to waste time. "I'm serious. Do you ever wonder if we settled?"

She didn't wonder, she knew. Aaron wasn't the problem. She was. She'd never felt that anticipation. Sexual attraction, yes. Desire. But not the deep bonding that allowed her to let someone else steer for a while.

She'd become convinced all of that hearts-and-flowers nonsense was illusory. What counted was staying power. Determination. A will to get along. They had that. A shared commitment that arose from upbringings that told them the wrong way to do things.

She glanced over at him, expecting to see anger. Like he sometimes did, though not often, he surprised her. His forehead wrinkled as if he were actually considering the question. "Was I your safety net?"

Sort of, but not really, because she never felt truly safe and calm. "Neither of us demands that much from the other. We fell in together, decided to start dating without ever having a discussion about it. We rolled from one relationship stage to the other and now sort of bump along."

He shifted until he faced her. One of his hands slipped to her knee. "I married you because from the minute I met you I thought I'd found someone who understood me."

"That's actually very lovely."

"The way you look, how put together and sure you are—it's all such a departure from how I grew up. My dad believed in the land. He hunted and fished and didn't trust anyone. Life was about simplicity and strain." He whistled. "You blew into that deli, and I couldn't see anything else."

She put her hand over his knee. Not something she usually did in public, but it felt right. "From what I can tell, your dad was—"

"A complete asshole." They both laughed at the topic even though it wasn't funny. "He taught through shame and by wielding his belt. Nothing I ever did was good enough. Jared was the star. The one who listened and learned. I just wanted out."

He rarely talked about his upbringing. She knew bits and pieces but not specifics. He didn't share details. "Neither of us had it easy, but I'm happy Jared was there for you."

"You experienced shock and horror growing up. You understand an adult's life isn't about rainbows and romance."

She smiled at him because they really were the worst at those sorts of lovey-dovey things. She'd only remembered his birthday last year because Jared called and asked if he could bring over Aaron's present. Without that call, she would have zipped right over it, and she didn't think he would have cared. They weren't celebration people.

"We give each other the stability we missed." She swallowed as she said the words, both grateful that they never strayed from being on the same page and wistful for what might have been if she were a different person.

"Right." He reached over and squeezed her hand. "We have expectations."

Something about that word struck her the wrong way. "Are we broken?"

"We're more like . . . bent." They both laughed at that, but he kept going. "With you I can be imperfect. I can retreat, and you understand. We both need time by ourselves. Who else would get us?"

"I guess that means we're stuck with each other."

Her mind went to her new client and the kick of need that moved through her when he smiled at her last week. She hadn't felt that sort of longing to get to know someone in, well, almost forever. Heat, interest, need. The unexpected sensations had pumped through her and had her questioning her neat, boxed-up little life with Aaron.

But nothing could happen. That client would want normal. She'd never been normal.

Chapter Twenty-two

Present Day

IT WAS LATE AFTERNOON THE NEXT DAY BEFORE THEY TRACKED down Ryan Horita. The Ithaca College professor's office and home phones went direct to voicemail. Then he had classes and office hours. Now he sat at his desk, across from Ginny and Pete in his cramped, dark office, and frowned. "I'm a little confused about why you're here."

Ginny studied the man for a few seconds before answering. Unlike many people, his photos on social media and in the school records matched the live version. Black hair and attractive. Very fit with an open friendliness about him. He looked about thirty but actually was in his midforties.

The rest of the personal stuff she knew—smart, from a family of academics, divorced twice but close enough to both women to still go on vacations together and take photos, active in the local music scene. None of it mattered much except that some of his habits, like attending book signings and open mic nights, made him seem far more outgoing than the woman with whom he'd been spending so much time lately.

Speaking of . . . "We're here about Lila Ridgefield."

A small smile came and went on his lips. No other sign of familiarity, but that was good enough to grab Ginny's attention.

He nodded. "My real estate agent."

They'd uncovered that piece of information as well. For Ginny, a deeper dive was in order. "Her husband is missing."

His eyes widened. "Missing?"

That look . . . Ginny wasn't convinced he sold it. "The disappearance has been all over the news."

"I must have missed it."

"He failed to show up to work five days ago. No one has seen him since." Pete studied the books on the shelves next to him. He stopped scanning long enough to stare at Ryan. "It's unclear if he's taken an unexpected trip, if something happened to him on the way to work, or . . ."

Ryan shrugged. "Or what?"

Pete shrugged right back. "We're not sure."

"Okay, but what does this have to do with me?" Ryan shifted to the front of his chair with his fingers linked and hands resting on the desk.

Ginny looked for signs of fidgeting or discomfort but couldn't pick up anything. Ryan handled the conversation in the dispassionate way someone might if they only knew their real estate agent as their real estate agent.

She wasn't convinced. "How did you pick Lila?"

"She was recommended by another professor."

"Are the two of you close?" Pete asked.

He frowned. "She sold me a house. One of the new builds on Crescent Way."

"That's it?" Pete asked.

"I've never met her husband."

The words fell with a plunk. He offered them fast, and it wasn't the expected response to anything he'd been asked. To keep him talking, and potentially trip him up again, Ginny shifted to information she knew and didn't care much about. "When did you buy the house?"

"About four months ago. We had a quick closing because the sellers needed to get into a new school district before the year started." He rubbed his hands together. "We looked for houses on and off for a few months prior to that."

"You started working together about seven months ago, according to the brokerage files." The start date wasn't Ginny's main concern, though it did give them a timeline to trace back and see how, and if, Aaron and Lila's marriage changed since then.

"The timing fits. That's probably right."

Pete made a strangled sound. "It took you that long to find a house?"

"Is that a lot of time?" Ryan's gaze switched from Pete to Ginny. "I didn't want to jump on the first one. I only plan to move once, so I wanted to get it right."

She didn't answer.

Pete made another noise but didn't actually say anything.

"The home office mattered to me," Ryan continued. "The whole mix of right size, right price, and office tripped us up for some time. She kept looking, and I kept calling."

Ginny swallowed a smile. Silence and a lack of reaction almost always got people to continue talking. They chattered away to fill the quiet, convinced the silence was more damning. That assumption was almost always wrong.

Ryan leaned in closer. "I still don't get why you're here. Lila must have a lot of clients—"

"The two of you met for coffee." Not news by itself, but there was more.

Ryan hesitated before responding. "Sure. To go over listings."

"And you met for lunch," Pete added. "Several times."

"Maybe a few times." The tempo of Ryan's hand rubbing increased. "Honestly, I was probably a pretty needy client."

"We're talking about the lunches and coffee dates during the last two months." Those were the ones Ginny cared about. The ones people at the deli and coffee cart near Stewart Park noticed. All the phone calls. What looked like constant contact even after the business ended. "Which, according to you and your property records, was months *after* you bought your house."

Ryan didn't blink, but his hands had stopped moving. He sat there, watching his interrogators with his gaze skipping between them.

Maybe she needed to reassess her thoughts about witness blathering, because this silence proved pretty damning. The charming, otherwise accessible professor appeared to be at a loss for words.

"You got really quiet," she pointed out.

"Water issues."

She hadn't expected the blurt. From the *what the hell?* look on Pete's face, he hadn't either.

"Excuse me?" she asked.

"The house had water damage not found in the inspection." As soon as Ryan started talking, his cadence went right back to what it had been before—smooth and consistent. Not a hint of floundering. "Lila has been working with me to get reimbursed without having to sue the inspector or the previous owner for nondisclosure."

As comebacks went, this was a good one. Ginny had to admit he sold the lines. If he could prove them was another question. "And you can verify this?"

"She can. She has all the paperwork. I was too angry to deal with the couple myself." He leaned back in his chair, fully in control and smiling now. "I wanted move-in-ready, and, instead, my house is under construction."

"You're saying you don't have a relationship with Lila?" Pete asked.

The delivery made Ginny wince. Too amateur to get the right reaction.

Ryan nodded. "I do. I just told you. She's been working on my behalf."

"Are you sleeping together?"

Ryan's smile widened. "That's an odd question. No."

Direct hits like that wouldn't work. Ryan was too smart to step in shit. He needed to be led around it then fall in. Ginny tried to steer them in that direction. "You teach sociology?"

Obvious, maybe, since they were in the sociology department, but getting him to talk about his work might trigger something. She knew from her husband that Ryan was considered a bit of a folk hero on campus. Roland didn't know him, but he knew of him. Said Ryan taught one of the must-take classes on campus.

"Yes. I analyze crimes, some unsolved cold cases. The goal is to break down preconceived notions of—"

"You also write true crime." Pete nodded toward the bookshelves. "Your name is on a few of these."

"I teach about crime and write about it, yes."

For some reason Ryan found that distinction important, and Ginny wanted to know if it was a case of professorial snobbery or something else. "What classes do you teach?"

"The most popular one is The Sociology of Violence."

There it was. Ginny felt the heat of Pete's stare and ignored it.

"I'm guessing you're well aware of my teaching and research background." Ryan leaned back in his chair and crossed one leg over the other, calm as could be. "Are you looking for assistance on this case?"

A memory hit her. She'd seen him on television, offering bits of wisdom about Karen Blue. "Do you consider yourself an expert on crime?"

"Not on committing it, no. But analyzing motivations and backgrounds, looking for patterns. Yes."

He probably thought that was funny. Ginny didn't. "Did you talk with Lila about your work?"

"In passing." He flicked a hand in the air as if to say *no big deal*.

"What does that mean?" Pete asked.

This time Ryan concentrated instead of answering right away, picking a piece of nearly nonexistent lint off his dress pants. "Small talk."

The big show didn't impress Ginny. "You engaged in small talk about violence during your real estate lunches?"

Ryan lifted his head and stared at her. "We all have our interests."

And now he had her attention.

Chapter Twenty-three

SHE HAD TO BE MISSING SOMETHING. SOMETHING OBVIOUS.

Aaron had hidden a phone and those videos. Once she found those, she didn't go hunting because she couldn't handle finding one more thing. But now Lila was convinced another piece of evidence existed somewhere in the stupid house that would point to where Aaron waited right now. A place he could crawl away to, hole up and plan. Because if he didn't have that special location set aside, that meant he absolutely had an accomplice. The list of possible suspects for that was too short, and the people too close to her, for peace of mind.

Part of her still believed at least one other person at the school knew about Aaron's sick games. Teen girls weren't exactly known for being quiet. One might view him as a conquest and brag. A teacher might have seen a glance that lasted too long or struck them the wrong way. The possibilities kept her from disclosing everything right away. The conspiracy grew in her head. Brent could be in on it. Other teachers. Maybe even some of the dads.

*"Peel that shirt off nice and slow. Let your hair down . . .
that's good. Just how I taught you."*

"Do you like what you see?"

*"I'm rock hard for you. Sometimes it happens during last
period while I'm sitting there, thinking about how good you look
stripped bare. How you smell on my fingers . . . and I can't wait
until that bell rings so I can take you somewhere."*

The stray memory punched into her chest. She could go
days without thinking about the videos, but then a line or a
stray image would pop into her head and push her back.

Last period. He had a seminar last period. Juniors. Sixteen,
seventeen. Kids. Too damn young to be making dirty videos
and having sex with him.

Inhaling, drawing in one slow breath then another, she kept
the anxiety percolating inside her from growing into a dark
ball of self-hatred that would double her over. She needed to
think. Concentrate.

She'd searched every inch of the house while Tobias was out
or asleep in her renewed belief that Aaron had a secret place
to hide. This was the last stop. She reached up and tugged
on the cord hanging from the ceiling. One pull and the ladder to the attic unfolded in front of her. The only access was
through this removable square piece in the hallway ceiling
by the bathroom. She never went up there. Aaron sometimes
did, if he was looking for something from when he was a kid,
which was almost never.

The last time he ventured up there that she could pinpoint

was almost six months ago. But if he were going to squirrel something away, it would make sense to do it out in the open and where she rarely went. The most likely spot for that—the dingy attic.

Her sneakers thumped on the rungs as she climbed. The second she stuck her head into the dark space, a wave of heat hit her. She blinked into the darkness and choked on the still air. Another step, and she ended up on her knees on the wooden flooring, which creaked and dipped under her weight.

She aimed the thin beam of the flashlight around the cramped space. The ceiling height barely measured seven feet, adding to the suffocating feel. It took a few seconds to find the light switch. She flicked it and bathed the room in harsh yellow. A thin layer of dust covered everything. She could make out lines on the floor where it looked as if Aaron had dragged boxes or furniture from one stack to another.

An old rocking chair that had belonged to Aaron's dad sat in the middle of the space, set off from the blankets and boxes. Aaron had told her once that his dad kept it on the front porch of their house growing up. Aaron remembered him sitting out there, rocking as he waited for dinner each night. Six o'clock sharp. Aaron's mother was expected to have it served at that time every day, and not one minute later.

She looked at the handmade rocker now. At the broken spindle on the left side. The wood reflected the years of hard use. Long gashes here. A divot taken out of the arm there. Someone had carved a tiny circle on the left armrest, right where Aaron's dad likely rested his hand before curling his fingers over the edge. The marks inside the circle were small and hard to make out.

She picked up the flashlight and shined it straight on the carving. A bear. Not a great depiction of one, but a bear standing on its back legs with its front paws in the air. Possibly something carved to entertain the boys, even though their dad didn't seem like the type. All irrelevant to her task now.

She turned to the boxes. Most were taped shut except for a few tops, and most of those had the word KITCHEN written on the side. Others had been ripped open, and random items like a lamp and a rusted screwdriver stuck out of one. Digging, she found old pamphlets for campgrounds up and down the East Coast, likely long closed. Papers that looked like old report cards for Aaron. As expected, he'd aced math.

Not one photograph anywhere.

What felt like hours later, her back ached from bending over, and the pounding in her head would not stop. If there was something here to find, she'd lost the ability to see it. Her eyes refused to focus, and a cup of coffee called to her.

She turned off the light and shimmied back down the ladder. As her foot hit the hallway floor again, she heard a noise. She spun around, flashlight raised as a weapon as a scream raced up her throat.

"Stop!"

Lila blinked at the sound of a female voice, trying to figure out what she was seeing. "What the hell?"

But she knew. Cassie. Her nosy neighbor stood in the

hallway with her hands raised in panic. One held a plastic-wrapped bundle that looked like banana bread.

"It's me." Cassie repeated the phrase over and over.

"Get out!" Lila knew there were other things she should have and could have said, but that came out first.

"I . . . you . . ."

"What?" Lila finally let the arm with the flashlight drop to her side. "What could possibly explain your breaking into my house and scaring the shit out of me?"

"I knocked and—"

"I did not answer." Tension and frustration whipped up into a full, frothing fury now. "That is the universal way of saying *you're not welcome*."

"I knew you were home and tried to call first." Cassie bit her bottom lip. "I was worried."

She had to be kidding. "Worried?"

"Your husband is missing. Your lawyer friend is out."

Lila stared because she honestly had no idea what to say. The sheer bullshit this woman was spewing to justify coming into her house uninvited had Lila sputtering. She couldn't think of a single coherent sentence that wasn't a profanity-laced tirade.

"Lila?"

"Get out."

More lip crunching. "I know I should have—"

"Now, Cassie." Lila found her voice and was fully prepared to use it.

"You don't—"

"You know what, Cassie?" Lila started walking, which forced Cassie to back her way down the hallway or get mowed over. "I'm sick of people walking all over my life, thinking they can do whatever they want, when they want."

"I get that. I really do." Cassie glanced behind her as she headed for the door.

All the years of Cassie peeking in the windows and showing up unexpectedly backed up on Lila. At least before this Cassie honored the sanctity of the door and didn't walk inside unannounced. This time she'd gone too far. Her nosiness butted up against Lila's need for privacy in the worst possible way.

"Hear me, Cassie. You aren't welcome in my house." When Cassie held up the bundle in her hand and started to say something, Lila talked over her. "No. You may not speak or explain. You may not come inside my house unless I escort you. I don't even want your feet to touch my driveway unless I call and ask you to come over."

Cassie's back hit the front door. "I can help you."

"I don't want your help." Lila reached around Cassie and tugged on the doorknob until the door opened a bit. "Ever."

"Okay. I'm sorry. I'm leaving."

Lila let Cassie scurry out with the bundle before slamming the door in her face. "Damn right you are."

Chapter Twenty-four

GINNY SHUFFLED THE PAPERWORK PILED IN FRONT OF HER ON the desk. She looked through bank statements and phone records. Reread the statements from Brent and Jared, the neighbors and the people at school. They all echoed the same refrain—Aaron was not a guy who would run away from his responsibilities. And Lila, well, she was different, but Aaron never complained.

She glanced up at Pete on the other side of her desk. "Did you get through to anyone from Aaron's last job?"

He shuffled his notes. "The good people of North Carolina aren't being very forthcoming. All my calls to the school were rerouted to the school district's attorney, who gave me a one-liner about Aaron being a highly regarded teacher, but they understood his preference to be closer to family."

She sat back in her chair. "That's interesting."

"Something is wrong there, and no one is talking." Pete flipped the page in his notebook. "I talked with a Greensboro neighbor who said they were quiet but fine. Aaron more friendly than Lila. So, the usual."

"Nothing helpful or new." It had only been a few days, and Ginny had hit a wall of frustration. "There's no sign of a girl-friend or someone he might have run off with in the credit card or bank records."

"No motive for anyone to kill him." Pete shrugged. "Money, I guess. That would point toward Jared, not Lila."

"And that ticks you off because you think the answer is Lila?" She understood but she also knew that jumping to con-clusions was a huge job danger and Pete needed to learn that before a career-ending disaster happened.

"Don't you? She's the only one who doesn't seem to care that he's gone."

She couldn't argue with that, so she didn't try. "Her being odd isn't evidence."

"You sure?"

"We have Jared, who was at a conference when his brother went missing." She closed a file in front of her containing Lila's cell phone records. "But he could have left or come in and out, so it's not airtight. Do some more digging on that."

"Okay." He leaned back and folded his hands behind his head. "Lila was at home sleeping. Brent was alone at his place doing the same. Those are pretty shaky alibis, too."

"But we have video from the neighborhood, and there's no sign of Lila's car going in or out. All we have is Aaron's car leaving, hours before his usual time, driving to school, and vanishing."

"So what does that mean?"

"We need a deeper look around Lila's house."

JARED WASN'T AT home. Lila had called, and he told her to let herself in. He'd given her the code for emergencies years ago and to help out when people came to do work in and around the house. A few weeks ago she was there to make sure the guys cutting down a dying tree didn't crash it into the house.

His willingness to give her open access to his most private space was exactly what she wanted, but taking advantage felt wrong. She knew Jared wasn't hiding Aaron, but maybe Aaron had stashed something here, where it would be out of her reach.

She typed in the security code on the number pad and opened Jared's back door. While Aaron had insisted on owning a big, fancy house, Jared didn't. His needs were more understated.

If he was trying for a swanky modern bachelor pad, he'd missed by a mile, but the place was very him. A gray midcentury modern one-story house on a hill. Surrounded by trees and very few neighbors, it had a carport, a small stone patio in the back, and a distant view of Cayuga Lake out the front.

The furniture inside matched the outside aesthetic. Simple with clean lines. A little sparse and impersonal for her taste, but the décor fit Jared. He'd picked out every piece himself and declared the place his refuge. It also had a separate building on the other side of the carport that the previous owner had used as an art studio. Jared used it as a home office.

She walked past the kitchen and down the hall to the extra bedroom. Aaron slept here for a short time after the fight that started all of this. If he hid something this might be where. But the furniture in the room consisted of a bed, a chair, and a dresser. The search took all of five minutes. She even stomped on floorboards and looked under the mattress, thinking those might be places Aaron thought Jared wouldn't look.

Anxiety bubbled up inside of her as soon as she finished digging. She could hold the churning sensation off for long periods of time and get through the day, but another night without knowing where Aaron was or what game he was playing pushed on her reserves. Every time the sun went down, her nerves unraveled. The only thing that saved her was having Tobias in the house.

She peeked through the curtains. Her gaze bounced around before landing on the studio office. If she were Aaron, she'd hide whatever he needed hidden in the one place he knew she viewed as off-limits—Jared's private space.

She bit on her bottom lip as the urge to peek built inside her. Without thinking, she shot down the hall and out the side door in the kitchen. A few minutes later, she stood at the entrance to the office and engaged in an internal debate over whether it was okay to invade her brother-in-law's privacy. Her patience snapped, and she typed in the code, surprised when it worked here, too, and the lock clicked open.

She stood there, taking her time looking inside the open room. She had no idea what made her so hesitant to breach this one last space. It wasn't as if she'd been playing nice and following the unspoken rules in the weeks since she'd found Aaron's secret cell phone. But this was Jared, and he wasn't her target.

"Screw it." She forced her legs to move.

Once inside, a new sense of dread filled her. The drumbeat of her heart in her ears muffled all other sounds. She felt achy and a little nauseated. A voice in her head screamed at her to turn back. Blocking it proved impossible, so she tried to ignore it, letting it morph into a steady beat in her head.

The desk chair creaked as she sat down. She tried not to notice the shake in her hands as she opened one desk drawer after another and rifled through the contents. The task didn't take long. Jared had everything organized. A place for every paper clip and pen. Labeled bins and files. The only thing without their own bin or drawer were a few stray coins. He had a jar of coins across the room on top of a cabinet. She thought about combining the ones in the desk with them, then decided she shouldn't move anything.

She scanned the bookshelves and sighed at the file cabinets, unwilling to go through every bit of paper. Chalking this up to a bad idea, she shifted to stand and kicked something. Shoving back in the chair, she looked down and saw a small fireproof lockbox—the kind she had at home and used for things like passports and important papers.

Jared had a built-in safe in the closet. She knew because he told her that's where she should look if anything ever happened to him. So . . . this? She scooted back and reached for the handle. She maneuvered the heavy box to the desktop just as she saw a flash as a car turned into the driveaway.

"Come on. Come on." She begged the box to open, but it was locked. She rummaged through the top desk drawer but didn't see a small key.

Jared's car eased to a stop, and he turned away from the house, reaching into the back seat for something.

She had only seconds. She grabbed a paper clip and unbent it.

Jared's car door shut.

Right as she put the end of the open clip into the lock and started wiggling it around, a wave of guilt hit her. Her hand dropped to the desk. "What the hell am I doing?"

She stood up and quickly sat back down again, debating what to do next. After she dumped the box on the floor, she slammed the desk drawer shut. She was up and out of the chair as Jared passed by the carport, heading for the front door.

After a few deep breaths, she opened the door to the outside office and put on her best smile. "Hi."

Jared spun around to face her. Between his look of surprise and the way her heart slammed against her rib cage, she was not far from losing it.

One swallow then a second. "I thought maybe we got our signals confused and you were in this office, waiting for me."

His gaze toured her face, and his expression went blank. "No."

"Sorry."

He walked over to her. Stopped right in front of her, still wearing his suit and tie and holding his briefcase. "Are you okay?"

She was a mess. Not her style at all, and she didn't like it. This whole lost-body thing had her rattled and making mistakes. Maybe that was Aaron's plan. His way of letting her expose herself.

Jared slipped past her and into his office. He scanned the room until his gaze landed on the desk. A second later, he looked at her with a question in his eyes.

She realized she'd never answered him. "Not really. Okay, I mean. I'm not."

Not her smoothest moment, but at the sound of her voice his expression changed. Now he looked like the Jared she knew. Open and welcoming. A little wistful as he watched her.

"What can I do to help?"

Guilt pummeled her. "Find Aaron before the entire county comes after me."

He stared at her for a few extra beats then put down his briefcase. "You should be at home, out of the fray, until we figure this out."

"It's hard to stay still."

"You know I'm here for whatever you need."

Typical Jared. She could depend on him. "A few minutes of quiet where I don't have to think about any of this?"

He just smiled. "Done. Let's go inside and I'll make you dinner."

Chapter Twenty-five

Seven Months Earlier

LILA APPRECIATED AN ATTRACTIVE MAN AS MUCH AS THE NEXT person. This one had deep brown eyes that seemed to watch everyone around him. He sat in the coffee shop on the edge of campus, right by the window. The position gave him a view of the sidewalk and almost every table inside.

A coffee cup sat in front of him, but he hadn't taken a drink from it in the ten minutes Lila stood there, waiting in line for her turn to grab a cup of tea. He focused mostly on the small notepad in front of him. Jotting down notes then watching and writing again.

When she was much younger, like eight or so, she'd spin wild stories in her head about the people around her. Neighbors. The mailman who lingered on the porch and talked to her mom. The teacher she saw out of context with friends, trying on a lacy dress at the mall. It was the first time she'd realized teachers had friends and gossiped, and her mind danced on that one for days.

All that creativity and fanciful thinking died the day the police came and took her father away. Teams of uniformed men marched through their house, opening everything. Touching her things.

The brutal violation of her privacy didn't compare to what came next. The taunting and hitting. The woman who yelled at her as she got off the bus.

Lila stopped dreaming. Her mind no longer had the freedom to wander. She had to be on the lookout for anyone who might be lurking, ready to hurt her. She didn't have time for kid things.

The daydreaming had just started to come back, decades later. At first she quashed it, not wanting to get entangled in unreal things. Survivors stayed awake and ready. Falling into fantasy invited trouble, and she'd had enough of that.

But something about him had her staring and thinking. The dark hair, smooth and straight. The intelligent eyes that were always searching. That pronounced chin and inviting face. She'd seen plenty of pretty people, known some who other people found attractive, and probably were on some objective scale, but their blowhard personalities killed it for her.

He sat quietly. His gaze slipped to a dog sitting on the floor, and he smiled. She waited for him to visually stalk some younger woman so she could write him off as a loser, but it never happened. The watching never shifted to anything prurient.

"Here you go."

She nodded as she took her tea from the barista and walked

across the room. After a few steps, the man's gaze shifted to her. When she got to the side of his table, he stood up.

"Lila Ridgefield?" He extended his hand. "The woman who will help me get out of my condo and into a house. I was hoping that was you. I'm Ryan Horita."

Not knowing where to look, she glanced around him and saw the notes on the pad. A rough sketch of what looked like a floor plan. When she glanced up again, he was staring at her.

He smiled. "It's nice to finally put a face with a name."

That's exactly what she was thinking.

Chapter Twenty-six

Present Day

THEY MET AT THEIR USUAL SPOT. CORNELL'S BIRD SANCTUARY.
It had a more official name, Sapsucker Woods Sanctuary, but
that wasn't the point. They'd picked it because it was away
from his campus and her job and provided over two hundred
acres of trails and swamps and trees for privacy.

Over the last few months, they'd walked through the area
and talked. Lila would listen to his ideas for future books.
Ryan would laugh as he heard the complaints people made
when looking at houses.

Today they met because they had to. They'd had a brief
talk after Aaron first went missing. She'd called him from a
phone she asked to use at the bank and given him a heads-up.
But today was in person, as Ryan had insisted. He'd sent an
email from a dummy account and used their emergency code,
which they'd picked specifically because it looked like spam.

The overcast skies and threat of early snow had more visitors staying inside, doing behind-the-scenes tours. She rarely

welcomed cold, but today she did. They needed time alone to talk, and this was as close as they could get.

She spied him sitting on a bench near a clump of trees and speeded up her walk. She sat down next to him without glancing his way or acknowledging his attempt to move closer.

"This is risky." She hadn't meant to blurt that out. She'd honed her control, her ability not to show any response or react, but having Aaron's body disappear messed with her hard work to never panic.

"I had to see you."

She picked up on the pleading in his voice and pretended to ignore it. She couldn't afford to have him unravel. "This is not the right time."

"Tough." He turned to face her, making it clear to anyone who might be watching that they were together. "Investigators came to my office yesterday."

"Who?" She waited as he dug the business cards out of his pocket and flashed them at her. Ginny and Pete. No surprise there. At least the investigation hadn't expanded to state and federal law enforcement, both of whom were crawling all over the county as part of that task force searching for Karen Blue. "That's what I thought."

He frowned as he tucked the cards back in his pocket. "You know them?"

"We've spent too much time together lately."

"What the hell is going on?" He stretched an arm across the back of the bench, leaning in and casual.

His hand hovered. Part of her wanted to shove him away,

but another sensation, a slight thrum that ran through her, called out for him to come closer. The collision between craving comfort and being ready to flee left her breathless. "What did they ask you?"

"How I knew you. If we went out. If we had sex."

The final sentence screeched across her brain. *Sex.* "They asked about sex?"

He exhaled, tipping his head up and showing off that pronounced Adam's apple that intrigued her so much the first time they went to bed. "Danced around it for about fifteen minutes but eventually got there."

Her thoughts scattered as memories mixed with fears of getting caught. Panic rose in her chest until it clogged her throat. She coughed the questions out over the invading lump. "What did you say? How did you answer?"

"Thanks for being concerned enough to warn me, by the way."

The words sent the crescendo of sensations crashing down, and her mind went blissfully blank. The absolute last thing she needed in her life was one more man who worried about his life and his safety as he discarded hers. "They're checking my phone records. How do you think they got to you?"

"We usually stuck to coded texts that sounded house-related."

"There were other times I called. Times when I used my cell or contacted you from work." He was right that as his real estate agent contact made sense. She'd figured the few stray calls would get lost in a series of other ones. "They have all of those records and are likely following me, so I couldn't exactly stop by your house to warn you."

He glanced over her shoulder. "Following you?"

"No one did today." She'd doubled back and took random turns. "And it's not my car."

"I didn't admit to the affair." His fingertips brushed against her shoulder then off again.

"Maybe not the best move. They already suspect, Ryan." She wanted to grab his hand and shake it, make him understand. "If they talked with you, called you in, then they've figured it out or are close to doing so."

"Witnesses told them about us having coffee. They didn't mention us meeting at my house or about that hotel in Syracuse, but we both know we used both." He shrugged. "Paid cash at the hotel, thank God."

He might think they were home free. She knew better. Ginny would pick and poke. She'd get it in her head there was something to find then hunt it down. Lila knew because that's exactly what she'd do if she were Ginny.

Lila fell against the back of the bench. "Discovering that, or most of it, is likely coming."

"To throw them off I told them about the ongoing water issue." He played with the ends of her hair. Wound it around his finger. "Made it clear there was a perfectly good reason for us to keep meeting."

So sure. Real or not, only a man would find solace in such flimsy excuses at a time like this. Women were programmed to fight to be believed.

She sat up straight again as she batted his hand away. "That investigator, Ginny? She's smart."

"I'm smarter."

So much ego. She hadn't seen that in him until the end.

He understood violence and familial destruction. He listened and seemed to get it. Didn't judge. She could keep him over *there*, away from her daily and mundane life and just enjoy. Then she ruined it.

As her plan to deal with Aaron came together a few weeks ago, she merged the pieces of her life. Ryan had priceless intel she needed, so she began asking questions. Going deeper. When the topic dipped into his expertise, his ego flared. It was all about him and how he "got" things his contemporaries didn't.

The hubris burned through the zing, leaving her bored and itching to get out. What she'd felt for him flickered and died. For the last month, she'd been going through the motions. With him. With Aaron.

She was not good with men.

Despite how important he thought he was, she needed him to let her lead now. There were things he didn't know. Things that could get them in trouble if he shared because he thought they were innocent instead of her calculated attempt to remove Aaron from her life.

She poured every ounce of concern and anxiety into her voice, silently begging for him to get it. "Please listen to me."

"Where's Aaron?"

"I have no idea. Honestly. None." That pissed her off, but it was true.

"Did he find out about us and take off?"

"No." There was no way Aaron could have hidden his fury at being replaced in the bedroom, even temporarily. "I mean, not the 'us' part. Could he have left for some other reason? I guess, but I can't imagine."

"You can't know he didn't figure it out."

"He would have mentioned stumbling over my adultery. Trust me." He'd choked her for finding the videos. The punishment for embarrassing him would have been a campaign of destruction that burned through every part of her life.

"Did you talk about being unhappy in the marriage, maybe give a hint that you might leave him?"

Interesting how he assumed she'd messed up, as if she were lost in some sort of romantic stupor and let the incriminating information slip. "Never."

"Wait." Ryan's head shot back as if he'd been slapped. "Never?"

Not this. Not now. "That wasn't the plan. You know that. We agreed on no commitment."

He moved back, putting a few more inches of space between them. "Seven months, Lila. That's a long time to have sex and meals together and meet and not have some feelings for more develop."

Not for her. Not ever for her. "Stop talking like that."

With him, at the beginning, for these amazingly bright

flashes, she hoped it would be different. Better. That she could be normal and seek what other people sought. The sex was exciting, not just a set of moves she'd done for years.

Then their differences, once faded in the background, pulsed to life. He liked people and going out. He bought tickets to events and dragged her to see live music. Being trapped in swaying rooms that reeked of liquor and dripped with the sweat of a heated audience ignited her anxiety. Even if she weren't married and in a frenzy of panic about being seen, his constant need to be fed by a sea of people would have drained her.

At least with Aaron she had hiking and a mutual respect for quiet. Ryan tried to coax her "out of her shell." She was married and dating and dreaded both. It was the ultimate nightmare.

Ryan's arm dropped to the bench. Without moving, the chasm between them expanded. "You're unbelievable."

Did he really not get it? This was not the time to talk about seeing each other more or bigger feelings. "I'm trying to save both of us."

He stood up. "Try harder."

Chapter Twenty-seven

BEING IGNORED PISSED GINNY OFF. SHE'D TRIED CALLING LILA, but she didn't answer. With a squad waiting around the block and the forensic team ready to go, she stood on Lila's front porch and verbally wrangled with her attorney and friend. Probably her only friend.

"Where is she?" Ginny asked in a tone that suggested this was not the time to play.

Tobias closed the door behind him and stepped out into the cold, wearing black pants and a sweater but no shoes. "She had errands."

Ginny nodded in the direction of the driveway. "Her car is here."

"She has mine."

This guy had an answer for everything. He was smooth, but Lila hid her constant assessing better than this guy did.

"So she made sure to take the car that's not being followed by my office. That suggests she has something to hide." Ginny made a mental note to pull more records.

"Or that she needed a minute of peace."

"You're in a rental. We'll track the GPS on it." They'd find out where she went. Check cameras in the area. See if she had the suspected check-in with her supposed not-boyfriend.

Tobias crossed his arms across his chest and leaned back against the front door. "It sounds like you're convinced Lila has done something wrong."

"She's not exactly an open book."

"She's not that hard to figure out either."

From what Ginny could tell, no one in town agreed. Literally, no one. They all described Lila as pretty but pointed out how she didn't seem to support Aaron's career. That was her big sin in many people's eyes. "You're alone in that assessment."

"When we were in practice together and would have a case involving a felony, like drugs or murder or whatever, Lila would give this speech. She'd talk to clients and their families and sometimes their friends about how she didn't have any ethical responsibility to tell law enforcement where to go find evidence, but if someone moved the evidence and gave it to her so that the police couldn't find it, then there was a problem."

"Sounds like a criminal defense attorney way of rationalizing the law." And she didn't mean that as a compliment. "I'd argue she'd have a moral responsibility to do the right thing in either case, but okay."

"One day a man comes in with a gun. He's not our client. He's our client's brother, and he's heard the speech, but the police were closing in and he couldn't hide the weapon his brother used to kill his wife for fear of being exposed."

"He sounds lovely."

Tobias flashed a smile. "You don't always get to pick who you defend."

She didn't think that was true in a private firm, but she let it go. "So, he brought it in to you . . . and?"

"Lila left the room and called the police." His arms fell to his sides, and he smiled. "Cost us our case. The client and his brother had to plead. They tried to sue us, but Lila had followed the rules."

He acted like he'd shared some big morality lesson with her. "I'm not clear on the point of this story."

"A lot of other attorneys would have reminded the person about their earlier speech and made a big deal of going to the bathroom or taking a call, giving the person the chance to fix their mess."

Lawyers. "I don't know how you do what you do."

"Criminal defense is more interesting than probate work. Trust me." He waved a hand as if to dismiss the moment of amusement in his voice. "But my point is that you're dealing with the same Lila. She follows the rules. She does not flinch."

That last part they agreed on . . . so far. But Ginny believed everyone had a flinching point. "Is that really the moral of your story?"

"You think it says something else about her?"

"Maybe she doesn't like men who break the law. Or maybe

she likes being in control. Or, like me, she hates when people don't listen to her." Ginny understood all of those. She also thought they fit Lila, either due to her father or in spite of him.

"Like I said, doesn't flinch." He pointed to the street. "And here she is."

Lila turned into the driveway in the big SUV rental. She didn't look surprised or scared. She didn't look like a woman who was worried about her husband either. No, her blank expression didn't give away much at all.

"Where have you been?" Ginny asked before Lila got to the porch.

"Are you my babysitter now?"

"Lila," Tobias said, the warning obvious.

"Fine." Lila rolled her eyes. "I needed a drive to clear my head."

"From what?"

"Her husband is missing," Tobias said in a dry tone.

"Right. That reminds me." Ginny reached into her inside jacket pocket and pulled out the official document. "This is a search warrant. In about a minute, a whole lot of forensic types will descend on your house and start looking around. Anything you want to tell me first?"

Tobias swore under his breath. "Interesting how you saved that bit of information to spring now and didn't tell me while we were waiting for her to come home."

Ginny couldn't help but smile. "I don't flinch either."

Chapter Twenty-eight

THE NEXT MORNING ABOUT A HUNDRED PEOPLE GATHERED AT the southern end of Cayuga Lake. Members of the sheriff's office and a few police from some of the smaller communities in the area circled before handing out instructions. Two local television stations sent camera crews out.

Ginny shut her car door and walked through the packed parking lot, searching for Pete. He came bounding away from the crowd and headed for her. "Looks like we got some extra law enforcement help. I heard the Ithaca Police Department is sending a few officers as well."

"They volunteered, and Charles said we couldn't say no." Ginny didn't agree, but whatever.

Pete watched Charles pick up a megaphone. "But when did he give the okay for a public search?"

"He decided it was a win-win. Get the public looking and talking and make it clear the case is a priority."

Pete rolled his eyes. "You'd never know he's about a year out from the next election."

"He's always running. Pleasing people is nonstop." It was a

requirement of the job, which was part of the reason Ginny did not want that desk. "He's also getting some pressure. Brent's been calling in and getting the press to ask questions."

"Yeah, he stopped by the office twice yesterday."

"He's panicked that Aaron is hurt somewhere and we're not looking for him." Little did Brent know they'd been poking into his background. The man had significant debt, but unless Aaron promised to give him money, that debt likely wasn't relevant to the disappearance.

Pete looked out over the trees and toward the lake. "We've driven all over this area looking for Aaron's car."

"The hope is to find a body, not a car." Ginny scanned the crowd. She recognized some faces of teachers who had been interviewed. A few other from business owners of places that either Aaron or Lila frequented. A bunch of kids, likely his students or from his team, showed up as well. She counted only one obvious absence. "I don't see Lila."

"Unless I missed her, she's not here." He snorted. "Big surprise."

For Ginny, it was. Lila didn't make mistakes, and missing this event and the chance to cry on camera counted as a misstep. "That's going to cause problems for her."

"People are already talking. I've heard about her not supporting Aaron's coaching a million times." Pete ticked off her list of supposed sins. "Not having people over to the house to celebrate wins or the end of the season."

As a parent who had to drag her tired butt to sporting events to cheer on her son, she could understand why someone who didn't have to attend would skip. "Which, of course, means she killed her husband."

"You know how people gossip. If they thought she was quirky before, now they'll think she's a dangerous psychopath."

Ginny remembered Brent's pleading yesterday. His not-so-subtle jabs at Lila and her lack of urgency in getting answers about Aaron. "And Aaron has been elevated to near saint status by some."

"I somehow doubt he's earned that. Even Jared seems to recognize his brother's faults. But let's not forget that Lila's attitude toward Aaron being missing can be described as lukewarm, at best."

She watched as Charles, with the help of the road patrol and police officers who didn't even work for him, organized the volunteers into groups. People stood around, some playing on phones. But they'd showed up and she admired that.

Outcry and theories were fine for others. She followed evidence. Unfortunately, there wasn't much of that. All they didn't have ran through her brain. "She doesn't financially benefit from him being gone. As to happiness or urgency, Jared and Lila describe the marriage as—"

"'Not a great love affair,' which sounds like an understatement."

She didn't comment on the state of the marriage. She wasn't convinced the way Lila approached it now was any different from how she discussed it before Aaron went missing. "The only impressive thing is the lack of evidence. The forensics team didn't pick up any signs of blood or cleaning solutions in the house or her car. Both of their prints were everywhere, as you'd expect, but that means Lila didn't have a need to clean those up either. She doesn't have an alibi for that morning, but being asleep at four in the morning seems logical, and her phone was at the house. No pinging off cell towers."

Pete nodded. "I showed the video the forensic team made as they walked through the house to Jared and he didn't see anything missing or out of order in the house."

Whether he'd know or not about missing items wasn't clear, but the point was nothing jumped out. Nothing soaked Lila in a spotlight or pointed to another explanation for his absence.

"The home computers checked out. No signs of troubling searches or attempts to dump programs and documents. Every number on her cell phone and office phone records is accounted for." That one frustrated Ginny. With all those computers she'd hoped to find something interesting.

Pete smiled. "But . . . Ryan Horita."

"She has a logical explanation." Then again, she had an explanation for everything. It wasn't that she'd scrubbed her records clean. It was more that she was careful not to create troubling records in the first place.

"You think there's really nothing happening with Lila and Ryan?" Pete asked.

"I think they're having an affair." Ginny smiled at Pete's stunned expression. "But does Lila strike you as a woman who would have trouble divorcing a husband to run off with a boyfriend? No kids. She has money of her own. She doesn't stand to inherit much from him."

"But Aaron is still gone."

"Which means we're missing something." The reality of that kicked around in her gut, keeping her up at night.

"Her father?"

"It's not her fault he's a killer."

The volunteers started to spread out in a line through the park. "I wonder if this crowd will agree once they find out Daddy is in prison for killing a young girl."

Ginny knew people, so she knew the answer. "Not likely."

Chapter Twenty-nine

LILA STOOD AT HER KITCHEN COUNTER, DEBATING WHAT TO DO next. She'd searched the area around the lake. Every place Aaron had gone fishing. Every open field and secluded street. Before the police came with the search warrant, she'd turned the house inside out, even looking in air-conditioning vents and under loose floorboards. There wasn't a single stray piece of paper or evidence in this house that pointed to where Aaron might be now.

She even forced herself to watch those damn videos again, hoping she'd see something in the background, that maybe the girls were sitting there, filming in a location she could identify. And nothing. He'd brought one young girl to their bedroom and the others to what looked like a cheap motel. The stingy asshole.

She refused to sit around, waiting for Aaron to stumble back in and upend everything. Being reactive was the wrong strategy. Proactive. She was done letting life happen to her.

The front door slammed, making her jump. She shifted

and stared down the hall, ready to yell at Tobias for scaring the crap out of her on his way back from the coffee run.

Not Tobias.

Jared shouted as he stomped toward her. "What the hell are you doing?"

Anger deepened his voice. Fury pulsed off him and into the area around him. The air went still, and a red haze filled the room.

She'd never seen him like this and didn't like it. "What are you talking about?"

"There was a search for Aaron today." He tugged down his coat zipper and tore at the material until he had it off and threw it over one of the bar stools.

The whole time, he watched her. Concern gone. Distrust and disappointment floating through every word.

She sat down on the stool closest to him but didn't touch him. "Brent got a bunch of people together to walk around the lake. That's not a search. It's not even a thing."

He paced next to the stool. "He's missing, Lila. Aaron. Your husband is gone and no one has heard from him. You have to admit that's terrifying."

In ways he couldn't possibly imagine, but she couldn't say that. "If I thought he fell down while jogging around the lake, I would have been there. It's busywork. Not real. He went to school that morning."

"We don't know that!" His yell vibrated against the walls.

For a few seconds, she didn't say anything, hoping the silence would calm him. "Do you think he left me?"

"No." He shot the answer right back, but his voice sounded more like his usual tone.

She debated the best way to say the pieces she knew were true. "He's missing. His car is missing. His phone is missing. His wallet is missing. Something happened between our house and the start of school."

"Please . . ." He braced a hand against the kitchen island. "Just tell me if you know something."

"I have no idea where he is." She stretched her hand out. So close to his on the counter but still not touching. "That's the absolute truth."

It took another minute of silence before his shoulders fell. "Okay."

She watched the anger drain out of him. The fight left him in inches. His whole body relaxed as he slumped onto the stool next to hers.

His eyes remained closed, but her gaze searched his face. "People are going to say things. Ask questions about our marriage. Draw conclusions."

He slowly opened his eyes and stared at her. "Are you worried I'll believe them?"

Stark pain lingered there. It was almost as if he'd been emotionally running and had finally fallen. His worry. His doubts. They all floated to the surface and seemed to overwhelm him, pushing him down and sucking the life out of him.

She'd heard the whispers. Some were far louder than that. People knew Aaron had left in the morning and disappeared, and they'd started talking. All of it was about her and how she couldn't be trusted.

She'd expected this, but she'd expected cover. The incriminating evidence she'd planted in the car should have been the main focus after finding his body. Without his body, the spotlight fell on her. Burned right through her.

"We're not a warm and publicly affectionate couple." She'd planned but not for that long or far back. "Hell, if I'd known that was some sort of test I would have faked it."

Jared's hand covered hers. "That's all bullshit. If that's the test, then everyone should be whispering about me. You're married. I'm perpetually not and don't see it ever happening."

She thought about all he'd lost. He'd known so much pain, and this time she'd caused it. "That's not—"

"I feel nothing." He shook his head. "I like seeing someone and feeling that ping. I love the chase. The initial being together. But after that . . ."

She'd never heard him talk about his romantic life in depth. In passing, or in response to jokes from Aaron, sure, but the words now, so simple and plain, sounded like they were being ripped out of him. A lack of connection. Loneliness.

Understanding wasn't the same thing as offering hope, but she tried. "At least you feel a ping."

He laughed, but there was no lightness in the sound. "God, maybe we are broken."

"That's a big word." She turned it over in her head. She wanted to deny it. A survivor. That's how she saw herself.

He gave her hand a final squeeze then let go. "Ginny used it when she asked about you."

No shock there. Lila could almost hear her say it. To be fair, Lila had thought about Ginny's life, too. About what happened when she put down the gun and went home. "I imagine she has a nice house and nice husband and they have nice dinners together."

Jared made a choking noise as he stood up and headed for the refrigerator. "That makes me want to walk into traffic."

"Oh, hell. Same." The last bit of tension left the room. She welcomed back the ease. Fighting with Jared, hurting him, made her sick. She didn't need many people, but her life would be so much sadder without him. The significance of how much he meant to her compared to his brother was not something she wanted to assess right now.

Jared stood across the island from her and slid a water bottle in her direction. "I get you."

"I get you, too."

He looked at her right before he took a drink. "I'll take care of you."

"I can take care of myself, but it's sweet you want to."

He froze before slowly lowering the bottle to the counter. "He's not coming back, is he?"

God, she hoped not. "I don't think so. No."

Chapter Thirty

THE NEXT MORNING LILA CALLED TO RECONNECT THE SECU-
rity alarm and changed the code. She gave the new one to
Jared and Tobias, but no one else. It would be up and running
this afternoon. If Aaron breezed back into her life, he'd have
to ring the bell or break down the door to do it.

Good luck, asshole.

Maybe she'd sleep again, but she doubted it. The calls had
started. Threats and yelling. With the public search splashed
all over the news and the podcast, her private life ripped open
to expose a malformed core. People who claimed to be horrified by violence and what she might have done to Aaron promised to hurt her. She guessed they didn't get the irony.

She turned the alarm system back on for one reason. The
cameras. The person leaving the notes—getting close enough
to make sure she knew she wasn't safe—had to be Aaron.
Maybe with some help, but Aaron. All she needed was for him
to shift one inch too far and show himself. Then she would
unleash Armageddon on his reputation. Too soon and he

might not reappear, and then the focus would stay on her, not the pedophile.

No, she needed to wait. Hold on. Bide her time, just as she'd done through her entire marriage.

She mentally ran through the possibilities of who could be helping Aaron, keeping him hidden and quiet, which had to be tough, as she ran to her car. Ginny and her team had shown up at the real estate office with a search warrant, and she wanted to be there to keep Christina calm. Getting wound up and defensive wouldn't be helpful, and those were Christina's two go-to moves.

Lila got within five feet of the car and stopped. The telltale corner of white paper peeked out from under her windshield wiper.

She'd park in the garage from now on. Let him come up to the house and risk being seen.

Without bothering to look around and see which neighbors were watching, she swiped the card off the glass. For a second she held it, refusing to read the taunting message.

The temptation to scream Aaron's name, to challenge him to come get her, swamped her. She fought against the tide, but the waiting was killing her. She'd bet that was his goal.

She turned the paper over and looked at the message.

YOUR TIME IS ALMOST UP.

"Lila."

She jumped at the sound of Brent's voice. She'd been so

lost in her head that she'd missed him driving up behind her, blocking her easy exit.

The visit likely meant bad news. He hadn't been to the house since that first morning, but he called numerous times each day. He'd been interviewed on television. Very busy.

She met him as he got out of his car. "What's going on?"

"That's my question." He slammed the door.

More anger. His rage didn't reach Jared levels, but close.

His hands balled into tight fists at his sides. "Where is he?"

He'd turned some sort of mental corner and blamed her now. She could see it in the rigid line of his body and in the frown dimpling his forehead. "I don't know."

"You do." He leaned in. His gaze held hers as his mouth twisted in hate. "You did something to him."

He sounded so sure that it threw her off. She mentally searched through every conversation she'd had with Aaron about Brent. Remembered the number of times they'd gone off fishing, staying out all day. When Brent's marriage collapsed, he'd leaned on Aaron for support. They spent a lot of time sitting on the couch, watching football and bitching about his wife.

Now it was her turn to deal with him. "What are you talking about?"

"You had that fight a few weeks back. He was devastated."

She refused to let that nonsense stand. "He wasn't."

If he was devastated about anything, it was about being caught for being a piece of garbage, and even if that did bother him, he hid it well. But he was still garbage, and even though she had to fake-worry about him being gone, she had a limit. Brent pressed right up against it.

"He said you wouldn't let it go. He tried to reason with you." Brent's eyes narrowed. "What was it about?"

She came so close to spilling the truth about his great buddy, Aaron. The timing was wrong, or she'd have him in a puddle from screaming the facts at him. "That's none of your business."

"Tell that to the investigator."

"She knows all about it!" The minute she raised her voice, she fought to bring it back down again. Cassie was already out on her porch, pretending to water plants. "It was a fight, Brent. He wouldn't listen, and I got angry. Typical marriage stuff."

"Bullshit."

True, but that wasn't the point right now. "Did you and your ex get along fine all the time? Now things are supposedly settled. But does that mean you never argue or disagree?" It was a low blow, and she saw when it landed. "Don't pretend, because I know better."

"Meaning?"

"I was here for the end of your marriage. Your wife spent every day in tears, and you don't hear me making accusations and blaming you for her misery."

He grabbed her arm. She felt the bruising grip through her coat. "Be careful what you say next and who you say it to."

The surge surprised her. She'd always thought of him as weak and easy to run over.

She put her face close to his, not backing down. "Let go of me or I will call the police."

"Do it."

With her free hand, she slipped her cell out of her pocket, careful not to dislodge the note tucked in there. She didn't want to come up with a fake explanation for that. Not when Brent was in a heightened state she'd never seen before. Just as she started dialing, he let go.

"That's right. And for the record, you do not have my permission to touch me." She funneled her anxiety into fury and aimed it right at him. "Do you hear me?"

He blinked a few times, as if he just realized how much control he'd lost. "That was . . . not right."

She wasn't ready to let it go. "Ever."

"Look, I'm worried about Aaron. Come on. He wouldn't just disappear without a word. He'd at least tell me or Jared, probably both."

No apology. So many men who wandered in and out of her life sucked. "None of what is happening right now makes sense, but turning on me isn't the answer."

"You know more than you're saying about Aaron." He blew out a long breath. "I can feel it."

"What you feel is impotent." She hurled that word at him on purpose. Aaron had shared a bit about that part of Brent's marriage. At the time she'd told him to stop because he sounded almost gleeful about his friend's bedroom failures, but now she used the information to her benefit. "You want to find Aaron but can't."

"Why weren't you at the search?" Confusion showed on every inch of his face. "Really. It would have been so easy to do that one thing. To stop people from talking."

Jared asked. Men on the nasty phone calls asked. Now Brent. It was as if the men in this town thought it was her job to go out and cry and wail on cue.

Never going to happen.

"Because we both know he didn't go missing while hiking." She knew Ginny saw the car leave the neighborhood because she'd followed up to ask why Aaron took off so early that day. It added a level of intrigue and confusion to the search. Lila wished it would point the spotlight elsewhere, but she knew it didn't.

Brent leaned his back against the side of his car. "Your presence would have made people feel . . ."

"Better? That's not my job." Neither was this conversation, and her patience for it waned.

He sighed. "The kids are scared."

The parents should be. Brent acted like he cared about their welfare, and she knew he did on one level. But if he were paying attention and less worried about being Aaron's buddy, he might have noticed the problem. He might have been able to protect those girls from Aaron's lies and grooming.

Unless he knew and didn't care. The thought whizzed into her head and right back out again.

"You should get them a counselor. Let the kids talk about Aaron." Maybe one of the girls would reveal some of what was on those sickening videos. "They need it."

Brent took a deep inhale as his gaze wandered over the neighbors' houses. It took a few seconds before it landed on her again. "The investigator isn't going to let this go. You know this is just the beginning, right?"

He still viewed her as the only suspect. Probably not a surprise, but not comfortable for her either. He could work on the press and on Ginny. On Jared. "I should hope not."

"I want to believe you didn't do something . . ."

She looked at him, really looked. The dark circles under his eyes spoke to his exhaustion. He came off as deflated. The steam he'd built up on the way here had all but disappeared. Under it all she looked for something more. Brent had a reason to go to the school early each day. He was the principal. He had access to the grounds and the parking lot by the field. And he would have saved Aaron.

He'd been pushing her, and she wanted to shove back. "I'd think I'd earned your trust by now. The things I know about your marriage . . . I've never shared them. All those times when you hid out at our house, or spent the weekend with Aaron instead of with the kids, as promised."

He stood up straight again. "Are you threatening me with something?"

"I'm trying to make a point." One conversation kept spinning in her mind. She and Aaron agreed on how he should handle a certain uncomfortable request Brent had made, but

Brent didn't know that. "If the investigators are going to look at people with motive, they might talk to you."

His mouth dropped open. "What the hell are you talking about?"

"You asked Aaron for a loan. He said no."

The last of that fiery anger vanished. His skin took on a chalky white hue.

"Why do you think we fought?" It wasn't true, but all she needed was for him to think it was. To get him twitchy and panicked. To make him mess up.

"I don't believe you."

She had his attention now. "Ginny will."

Chapter Thirty-one

THE LONGEST DAY OF LILA'S LIFE GOT LONGER WHEN SHE pulled up to her house a few hours later after a drive to calm down. She saw the message. White paint splashed across the brown garage door in a scrawl.

WHERE IS HE?

MURDERER

STUPID BITCH

The words crisscrossed one another. Looked like two different sets of handwriting. Not that she was an expert on such things.

Cassie stood in front of the doors with her hands on her hips. Seeing her there smashed through the last of Lila's energy. She didn't have the strength to argue with one more person today about how much she sucked.

She really needed Cassie to shove her nose into someone else's life and leave her alone.

A mental debate started as she turned off the engine and

sat there. She could unload on her busybody neighbor and possibly end the unscheduled visits for good. The idea of walking right past her, ignoring her, sounded even better.

When Cassie turned around and waved, Lila didn't wave back. But then she saw the bucket in Cassie's hand and noticed how some of the words looked faded. Her mind refused to take in the visuals and come up with a reasonable explanation.

Forcing her legs to move, she got out and walked toward Cassie. Each step brought her closer to reality. The bucket with soapy water. A scrub brush in Cassie's hand. A can of what looked like unopened paint.

Tobias was out talking with local defense attorneys, trying to get a sense of how Ginny operated and what they were looking at going forward. He'd teamed up with one, in case the worst thing happened and Ginny arrested her without a body or evidence.

That left Lila and Cassie. Here, with the hate-filled graffiti.

"What are you doing?" Lila heard the confusion in her voice.

"Cleaning up."

"Why?" Because it's not as if she'd been all that nice to Cassie. She'd ignored half of what she said. Made excuses not to spend time with her.

Cassie pointed at the doors. "This is not okay."

"Are you worried about property values?" It was a shitty thing to say, and she didn't put much heat behind the words, but Cassie standing there struck her as so odd that Lila came out swinging.

Cassie dropped the brush in the bucket and ignored the small splash and water dripping off her pants. Her fingers were red, likely from the cold and from clenching the brush.

"I know you think I'm nosy." She held up her hand as if to quiet Lila even though she hadn't rushed in and said a thing. "But I watch over you, visit unannounced, and walk by because I've been there."

"I don't understand."

"You go for these long walks on your own, even more so lately. You spend weekends alone. When Aaron is here, he's often outside with his brother or friends."

"That's a lot of surveillance." Which made Lila nervous. She couldn't afford to have Cassie know her secrets.

"My first husband spent seven years convincing me I was worthless and unlovable. That I didn't deserve friends and couldn't handle money. He took everything from me, including my self-respect. Then the hitting started."

A rush of regret pummeled Lila. "Cassie, I didn't—"

"Of course you didn't. You didn't know him. You didn't know me back then." She glanced away. The pained expression came and went, coupled with a quick gnaw on her bottom lip before talking again. "That's how they win. They destroy you in silence until you're afraid of speaking out. They attack you in your own damn house, where you should be safe."

The words tumbled and spun in Lila's head. She'd spent so much of her marriage mentally insisting Aaron wasn't abusive. He was different and a loner. A guy who needed validation but not a lot of attention. None of which was surprising in light of how much he'd lost as a kid. Lila understood. She wasn't easy either, so they made sense together.

Then she found the videos. He came out fighting. Gaslighting her with ease, as if he'd been using it against her their whole marriage, and she realized now that he had. So much lying and subterfuge.

Looking back, she wondered how much of his behavior she forgave and explained away. She viewed their marriage through a clouded lens and didn't see abuse, but she was beginning to question if what she saw and accepted as truth was real.

His first instinct when she became a threat to him was to wrap his hand around her throat and squeeze. The clench of his fingers against her skin—so vicious and primal—slashed through her feelings for him, leaving them shredded and forgotten.

The right word abandoned her, but "abusive" might not be so far off as she once thought. He had abused those girls. He'd preyed on them. Her knowing that changed everything. It broke something inside her.

"Look, you don't have to talk about what life is like in your house." Cassie wrapped her jacket tighter around her body. "I'm just saying I saw how he looked at you sometimes, how he treated you. There was this whiff of superiority about him even though you're the lawyer and clearly smarter."

Cassie saw through him. Most people who knew them both would praise him, but Cassie praised *her*. The unconditional support left Lila stumbling and a bit breathless. "I don't know what to say."

"He did this thing where he played up his hero image at the school and around town." Cassie clamped her mouth shut as her eyes filled. She swallowed a few times before starting again. "It all was so familiar."

Lila's gaze went back to the garage door. The accusations, those words . . . weren't totally wrong. Not in her case. She deserved to be called out and ridiculed. She had killed her husband . . . or at least tried to. If she had to do it again, the only thing she would do differently was make sure the bastard was truly dead. She had no remorse.

Cassie followed her gaze. "So, no. You don't deserve to be put under a microscope and dissected. He did."

Past tense. Because she knew.

Lila wanted to ask how Cassie got away and what she'd lived through. Lila never viewed the other woman as a survivor. She had a quiet husband, clearly her second, who seemed nice enough and didn't get into people's business. The relationship made more sense with the new information. Lila had thought of Cassie's husband as plain, but now she wondered if he was safe. Kind and nonthreatening. Things that should be automatic in a spouse but weren't.

"And if what people say and what they think about you is true, that's your business." Cassie reached for the brush again. "That investigator won't hear anything different from me."

A free pass for murder. God. Lila spent every hour thinking she was alone, but maybe not. "Cassie."

"After I tone this down, you'll need another coat of paint to get a clean line." Cassie nodded at the can. "I took a paint chip to the hardware store, and they matched the color."

"Cassie." This time Lila touched the other woman's shoulder as she said her name.

"Yes?"

Cassie didn't demand the details or have to be convinced. Lila had a support system, but the circle was small and tight, and she didn't share the truth with them. She wouldn't with Cassie either, but she sensed, for the first time, that if she did Cassie might get it.

Lila wasn't sure what to say, so she said the first thing that popped into her head. "Come in for tea."

Chapter Thirty-two

Five Weeks Ago

NOW THAT SHE HAD A PLAN, SHE NEEDED TO FILL IN THE DE-
tails. There was no good way to do this. Every minute of research made Lila heave. The first day, she choked and swore
and broke two mugs before getting a bit more control.

All told, it took her four days of looking through high
school yearbooks and studying social media to find the girls
she'd seen in the videos. And those were only the girls she
saw . . . she knew there were more. She suspected this went
back to North Carolina, probably before.

Of the faces she recognized, one girl was still in school. A
senior and not in Aaron's class. She'd dropped out of field
hockey, and Lila feared Aaron was the cause.

The other two women graduated from high school last
year. One went to college out of state. She kept the photos
from her time on the team and in Aaron's class in her history
online. Smiling photos, seemingly innocent. Whatever time
Aaron stole from her appeared not to be problematic because

she even referenced him in comments. All positive, with perky little emojis.

The third woman went to the community college nearby. Eighteen. That put her at seventeen when she made the video, maybe younger. Lila remembered being that age and not being nearly as savvy and wise as she thought she was.

This young woman recorded every moment of her life in photos and videos. Up until the month before, she showed off products she bought and modeled new clothes. She had big group photos and some with her and a few friends. None of her older high school photos or information suggested she was on the field hockey team. She never mentioned Aaron or popped up in photos with him.

There were comments on some of the clothing photos about going out with her "secret" boyfriend. She would have been a senior at the time. Last year. In her world, likely the equivalent of decades away from where she was now.

Over the last few weeks, the photo subjects changed. She posted inspirational quotes almost daily, along with pictures of her school apartment and complaints about the cost of textbooks.

Regardless of when the posts were dated, in every photo she wore her straight blond hair down, flowing over her shoulders. The realization made Lila wince. She could hear Aaron's voice talking about how women should have long hair, not short. They should let it grow . . . as if their hair were for his pleasure only.

Lila tried to ignore that as she sat in the driver's seat of her car with her hair pulled up in a bun. The college had a few visitor spots close to the admissions building, and she parked in one. The position gave her a front-row seat to watch.

Lila knew from the other woman's posts that she often came here and sat by this tree. Today the surveillance worked. Sitting this far away, Lila couldn't really make out her face. Not when she was looking down, reading or studying but definitely not paying attention to the two guys behind her who kept glancing her way. But it was her. Blond and very pretty. Big brown eyes and a round face that Lila knew could light up with a smile.

The live version seemed more serious, more involved in school. This was the second time Lila had come looking for her, and both times the woman had sat alone. Gone were the big crowds and high school T-shirts.

Lila debated talking with her. Going up and introducing herself and assuring the woman none of what had happened was her fault. Because this wasn't about adultery or making Aaron pay in a divorce. This was about ensuring he took responsibility for hurting this woman, for playing with her emotions and taking advantage of her.

On some level, Lila also needed to know the younger woman was okay. That she hadn't been too late to notice something terrible happening from inside her house like she had been all those years ago with her father and Amelia.

She opened her car door but then shut it again. The woman

could be angry or, worse, think she was actually in love with Aaron . . . or vice versa. She might not want help or revenge. There were so many "ifs" and worries and things that could go wrong.

Aaron would pay. Lila just had to figure out if she needed this woman to make that happen.

Chapter Thirty-three

Present Day

BY THE NEXT MORNING, TELEVISION TRUCKS AND REPORTERS
had camped out at the end of Lila's driveway. She was surprised it had taken them this long.

She could see her neighbors scurry away from the fray if
she watched out her front window, so she closed the curtains
and didn't look. Instead, she sat at her kitchen island and
tried to think of a new plan. The not knowing what came next
plagued her. She had allies she'd never expected, like Cassie,
and doubters that took her by surprise, like Brent.

Through it all, Aaron hovered in the background, waiting
to pounce. She didn't understand the delay. Even if he weren't
close enough to watch every moment, the notes suggested he
was nearby. He had to know she was under siege. He'd relish
that. Seeing her squirm and panic.

Tobias stayed with her. He grabbed groceries to save her
from a potential battle with the public. Jared came by, but

now, seven days out from disappearance day, she'd become a shut-in with the alarm set, the news permanently off, and a makeshift weapon nearby at all times.

If Aaron's goal was to slowly make her unravel, that she could understand. Only by force of sheer will did that not happen. She focused all of her energy on staying up and moving. Anxiety crashed over her, sending her to the floor of her closet last night, but she rode through it. He would not win by pounding her mentally and physically into the ground.

If he wanted to pop up and insist she tried to kill him, she'd bring out the videos. The extra set sat in a safety deposit box at a bank thirty miles away in an institution she otherwise didn't use for banking. She had made arrangements for them to automatically be released to the police and press if anything happened to her.

Mutually assured destruction. That was the plan. It might not be perfect, but if she was going down, then people would know why. After every single piece of dirty laundry got aired, they could decide if her vigilante justice was so wrong after all.

What she really wanted was for his body to turn up and for the games to stop. She'd planned this to give herself an out, and she wanted to take it. Running without answers would leave everything undone. But a part of her thought it might be time to hand over the videos and tell the truth.

She glanced over at Tobias. He lounged on the couch with a mountain of paperwork around him. He'd suffered through meetings with other lawyers in the area about strategy. He'd met with Jared. Tobias had even managed to sweet-talk Brent into admitting Aaron had never said anything that would suggest Lila did something to him.

His meeting with Ginny was, as he described it, bumpy. Lila would have been disappointed in Ginny if Tobias had any other reaction.

"The police aren't telling us what, if anything, they've found." Worries about Aaron getting in the house and planting something incriminating swam in her head from day one.

Tobias snorted. "You haven't been arrested. Take that as your answer."

Lila could see him winding up to ask a series of questions. She couldn't blame him. If this spun out, he'd need as much information as possible to defend her. There was a limit on what she would say. She refused to drag anyone deeper into her decisions, but she could divulge the things that had put her on her current course.

"Ryan Horita's name came up more than once in my meeting with Ginny." Tobias flipped the pages of his notepad and seemed to be silently reading from it.

"She's had him in for questioning."

"You know what I'm saying, Lila." Tobias glanced up at her. "What do I need to know about this guy?"

In every way, Ryan had been irrelevant to her thinking on Aaron. She didn't start her plan because she wanted out of her marriage or a divorce. She'd plotted and researched because she wanted to stop Aaron. It was that simple.

She thought about the affair and the videos. Tobias needed to know about the existence of both. What he did with the information or how he spun it in her defense would be part of the legal dance they'd do later. Hopefully never, but she suspected later.

"I need to tell you about Ryan and about some evidence I found."

"When?"

"The evidence? Weeks ago. Before Aaron went missing." She knew the explanation sounded ridiculous. "They're unrelated, but together might make it look like I did something to Aaron."

He stared at her for a few seconds before saying anything. "Do you know where he is right now?"

"No." She needed him to believe her on that. "I really don't."

"Okay, good." He nodded. "I was going to tell you not to tell me, if you did."

She couldn't help but smile at his practical way of dealing with this case stress. He rarely judged, not even clients. Other lawyers would trade stories once the trials ended or talk in hypotheticals. Tobias never did. He insisted good people could be driven to do horrible things, which was why he was the first person she called.

"Tell me the worst." He flipped his notepad to a blank page. "So we can plan."

He intended to protect her just like he did with the secrets about her past. But this time, she'd tell only part of the story.

She'd made her decision about Aaron, and she'd face the consequences alone.

Chapter Thirty-four

Five Weeks Earlier

LILA DID NOT SNOOP. SHE DIDN'T GO THROUGH HIS JACKET AND pants pockets. She never listened in when he talked on the cell or when he hung out with a visiting friend. She'd never so much as stumbled over a hidden Christmas present, because she never went to places in the house where someone might hide something.

That all changed after she found the videos. With the trust shattered, any and all violations of Aaron's privacy seemed like fair game. If he didn't like the intrusion, he never should have acted like a piece of shit.

If he'd kept his bastard tendencies from her, they'd be in the same place, stuck in a revolving cycle where their marriage switched from mundane to tolerable and never reached higher. He'd pushed them into a new cycle.

But now she had a purpose. There were things about Aaron she needed to know. Her plan to expose who and what he really was depended on her gathering as much intel as possible. He'd lied and cheated his entire life. When slammed against the wall and hanging on the edge of being outed for what he'd done, he'd come out swinging. She needed to lessen his leverage. Take away part of that arcing swing.

That was the only reason for her being up before six and in a car on an overcast Saturday morning. He mentioned checking out a field. Field hockey session started early in the school year and ended with the state championship in November. He suggested the team had a chance this year, at least at playoffs, but that he needed more information on the opposition.

In other years, his excitement would have made her smile. Coaching gave him somewhere to go and guaranteed her some alone time. But this year his schedule filled her with dread. Road games. Time after and before school. Coach and player training sessions. Every aspect of the game sounded suspect to her now.

She rubbed her eyes, sorry she hadn't managed to drift off to sleep last night. The steady thump of the tires against the road lulled her into a calming sense of exhaustion. The miles passed as she followed Aaron's car. Him in his SUV. Her in a rental he wouldn't recognize. She hoped the baseball cap she wore hid her face but decided the slight distance between the vehicles and Aaron's own ego that reassured him he was getting away with it all would protect her from being found out.

But where the hell was he going?

The double yellow line passed by as they drove around Cayuga Lake and kept going north. They drove deeper into the trees and away from residential areas. Cars passed them, and a refrigerated truck separated their vehicles right now, giving her a slight buffer.

After two hours, her mind wandered to more sinister options for this trip. They skirted Canada and drove north, then east. Through wooded areas and near streams. Objectively picturesque, but knowing what she now knew about his needs, she found the remote area scary and obscene. A place to take someone when you didn't want to be seen.

The idea that he could be out here, where no one knew him, scouting other girls, ran through her head. This spot, so far away from where they lived and worked, might provide enough distance for him not to worry about being found out.

She was so lost in her thoughts that she almost missed him turning off the main highway. He cut to the right, onto a side road that dipped deep into a wooded area. She slowed just on the other side of the entrance then stopped. She could see the top of the sedan as he drove into the distance.

She looked around for signs in a desperate attempt to spy buildings or something familiar. Frustrated, she checked the map on her phone for landmarks or schools. Nothing pointed to the existence of an athletic field nearby. She saw trees and greenery. Not another car or person, except for the few that passed by on the main road.

She toyed with the idea of following him down what looked like a quiet two-lane road. The type where it would be impossible for her to hold back far enough to hide the fact she was tailing him.

He'd see her and know. He'd stop and she'd never figure out why he'd done this drive on this day.

Concern ran both ways. Part of her feared what she'd see. The reality was she knew enough. She'd plotted the points for this drive as she went. She could lead the police back here. Let them see if there was anything to find.

She had a murder to plan.

Chapter Thirty-five

Present Day

GINNY DREADED MORNING MEETINGS WITH THE BOSS. CHARLES, always "on," shaking hands. He wore a big smile outside of the office that fell into a flat line every morning when he walked in the door.

She got it. He had political pressures and community pressures. That damn podcast tying three open cases of missing women together—something the police hadn't announced publicly—added a crushing weight to all of their backs. The sheriff's office only tangentially helped on those cases, but the outcry shot a bolt of electricity through the local law enforcement community.

Locals in charge fought not to lose control. All of that meant Charles was crankier than usual.

He stared at her over the top of his glasses from his oversize leather desk chair. "You're telling me we have nothing on Aaron Payne."

The file sat in front of him. Closed. That meant he'd read it and got ticked off . . . then ordered her to come in and give a verbal status report instead. He wasn't paging through, picking apart the pieces. He silently fumed at the lack of anything he wanted to see in terms of progress.

"If Aaron or Lila were hiding something they didn't use computers to do it." As smart people would refrain from doing. Calls from Lila to the boyfriend, yes, but not an extreme amount, and none on the days leading up to the disappearance. Nothing at all during the time Aaron's car left the house. Her phone appeared to have been at home, on, and not in use.

Charles shook his head. "It was too much to hope she'd have searches on how to dispose of a body."

"Not just a body. A car and a phone, too." Ginny stood with her hands linked together in front of her. "All missing."

"She's been busy covering her tracks, or she planned all this out, which is pretty devious shit."

"Maybe." Ginny wanted to jump there, too. Grab that conclusion and run with it, but not one piece of evidence supported that. What they had was circumstantial and supposition.

"Ginny." He sighed at her. Something he excelled at. "We both know she's in this. Add in the boyfriend and it's looking like Lila wanted a way out."

A boyfriend, but no motive. Odd behavior by Lila, but not odd in the sense of giving away what she'd done. She hadn't sold his clothes or talked about him in the past tense. There was no evidence of blood or a fight. She'd gotten a lawyer immediately, but he was also a friend, and she was one, so even that choice wasn't suspect.

"If this is about getting out of a marriage, why take the risk and go after Aaron?" That didn't make sense to her.

"Men do it all the time."

"Yes, to protect their money and their reputation. They replace the old wife with the younger and newer version. Get rid of the responsibility of kids." She let her hands drop to her sides. Some of the tension inside her unwound. Charles wasn't yelling at her this time or demanding more. He sounded as stumped and flailing as she was. "None of that fits here."

"That leaves only a few explanations, and none are easy to tackle." Charles tapped his pen against his calendar desk blotter—the one from three years ago that he'd never bothered to replace. "What about a lie detector test?"

"Her attorney told me he didn't allow any of his clients to undergo them. Too suspect."

"Convenient." Charles grumbled something under his breath that sounded more like a string of profanity than an actual sentence. "Pete talked to one teacher here who had trouble with Aaron's shiny reputation but claimed it was *just a feeling.*"

"The woman who owns the agency Lila works at gave the same impression." That same *feeling* hit Ginny. Something about Aaron didn't sit right with her. People had sides and flaws, but so few people recognized or highlighted his. It was unnatural.

She worked with Pete and could name fifteen flaws without

thinking very hard, and she mostly liked him. That was the point. Seeing the full person wasn't about gossiping. Not always. Sometimes it was about how genuine the person was in revealing who they were. She believed, on that score, Aaron might be as closed off as his difficult-to-read wife.

Charles hummed. "Maybe he's not squeaky clean after all."

"No one is."

"Turn his life inside out, here and in North Carolina, and see if you find anything." He put down his pen and handed the file back to her. "In the meantime, put pressure on the boyfriend. He's lying, and water problem or not, the calls between them could mean a conspiracy. Get a warrant. It's possible whatever incriminates Lila is at his house."

Made sense to her. She'd actually suggested the same thing to Charles last night. Less than twenty hours later, it was his idea. What a shock.

But she stuck to the script and didn't challenge him. "Done."

She got to the door before he spoke again. "There's one possibility we're ignoring."

"Some sort of random crime?" She hated that option.

Charles nodded. "He stopped to help the wrong person, or walked in on something."

It was the nightmare scenario. The option that seemed impossible to solve because everything was unknown. "At four in the morning?"

"He was out that early on this one day—only this day—for a reason. Maybe someone called him out."

That was the problem. Not being able to explain why Aaron

made that choice poked at her. "If it's a random crime, we're screwed."

"No, because you're going to solve this while police and FBI, and the whole damn task force, are crawling all over our area looking for Karen Blue. Then we'll ride that good press."

There it was. The pressure passed from him over to her. "And solve the case."

His ever-present frown deepened. "Get it done before I have to concede and bring in other jurisdictions for help."

And now the launch of the full frontal threat. "Yes, sir."

"Because that would piss me off, Ginny." He stared past her, into the room behind her. The room where the desks were and the team sat. "Might even make me rethink the chain of command around here."

"I hear you." She heard the threat every time he made it.

"Then move it."

LILA OPENED THE door for the first time in days. Hiding behind it, she ushered Christina inside before slamming it shut on the chaos lurking outside.

She'd ignored the press line out front for as long as possible. The cameras and trucks. The crowd of field hockey parents holding signs and demanding she tell what she'd done to Aaron. If it weren't for the garage connected to the house, she'd have to run the gauntlet of fury every time she moved. Even with the barrier, they still surrounded her car and banged on the windows when she left the safety perimeter and crossed into the street.

Christina flipped her sunglasses to the top of her head and glared at Lila. "You don't need to do this."

"You're trying to run a business, and I'm a distraction." More of a liability. The brick thrown through the real estate office window last night proved that.

"People are so disappointing."

Lila grabbed the box containing the contents of her desk and gestured for Christina to come into the family room. "Thanks for bringing this over. I'm sorry I missed being there for the search. I just couldn't."

After unloading the box on the kitchen counter, she followed Christina to the couch. Even steamed and frustrated, she presented the perfect outward appearance in her navy-blue pantsuit and bright blue shirt. Everything about her said *I'm in charge, so get out of my way*, and smart people listened.

She dropped her oversize leather bag on the floor and crossed her legs. "It's everything CID didn't take."

"They took stuff?" Lila had been careful about what she left behind. Gum. Pens. Some leads on possible future clients.

Christina waved off the concern. "Your computer and notepads. Nothing big, as far as I could tell."

They fell into a comfortable silence. Lila made tea for both of them. They'd worked together long enough—shared stories about annoying clients and gossiped about other agents in the office—for her to know Christina's preferences. The quiet company suited Lila.

She handed a mug to Christina and sat down across from her. "I know all of this is a pain in the ass."

Christina shook her head. "Stop."

She meant it. Christina never said anything she didn't mean. She wasn't the type to placate or ignore nonsense.

Lila appreciated the concern, but her life and her mess had leeched out and now infected other people's welfare. "I'm really—"

"I mean it. Stop." Christina froze as she stared at Lila over the top of the mug. "Your time away from the office is temporary until the pressure is off."

On one level, they both knew this was the end. Her life would never be the same. It would never be easy to be the person who sided with her. "Yes, ma'am."

"Besides that, this is on Aaron, not you."

Not totally true. "People blame me. Some people think he's dead."

"People think a lot of things. None of that nonsense has anything to do with me."

Lila wrapped her hands around the mug and let the warmth seep into her skin. "I wish I could say that."

"Hey." Christina focused all of her attention on Lila. "You stay strong. You are one of the smartest women I know. Whatever happened, and what is coming at you, you have it handled."

A laugh bubbled out before Lila could stop it. "Is that your subtle way of asking if I did something to him?"

"We're not talking about that—or the call in."

Everything inside Lila stilled. "What call?"

"The one that morning." Christina cut off her response

with a flip of her hand. "I was up working because, as usual, I couldn't sleep. Someone had signed in from home to Dan's computer. Since he's been gone for a few months and since only the two of us knew his sign-in, I figured out it was you and tried to message you."

An electronic message meant a trail. Ginny could eventually figure out Christina sent it because she thought Lila was awake, not asleep as she claimed. That kind of back-and-forth chat at four in the morning was the sort of thing that could be traced if they knew to check it, and now they would.

Silence filled the room as Lila struggled for the right thing to say. Come up with an excuse or deny? She went back and forth, but the bigger issue was Ginny. She needed the right excuse to throw Ginny off once she found the message, and she would.

"The problem is fixed. I deleted Dan's computer from the system and erased the backup logs. All anyone looking at the office computer system will see is me being online, working. No attempts to communicate directly with you. No evidence of Dan's computer being used. Eliminating Dan's account is easy to explain since he left."

Still, it was a potential hole. Lila had to double-check the street cameras that morning, the ones the county generously showed online so people could watch traffic and the weather. Two had been out, and she'd planned her return home from the school based on that but had a contingency if one or more had been fixed. Dialing in to the office meant the traffic check would be on Dan's computer early that morning and not relate to her at all. Checking her computer or any of the computers actively in use wouldn't show a thing.

"Christina . . ." But Lila still wasn't sure what to say.

She shook her head. "It's forgotten."

That was a huge burden to ask someone to carry. "Okay, but—"

"Forgotten."

Chapter Thirty-six

TOBIAS WAS RIGHT. LILA DIDN'T FLINCH. GINNY REALIZED THAT as she watched Lila play with the glass in front of her. They'd put her in a room and left her alone, and she sat there, one leg crossed over the other, swinging back and forth in the air.

Ginny said they would wait for Tobias to arrive, but Lila said to go ahead and he could join them. An interesting choice, but Ginny didn't question her luck.

Minutes ticked by, and Ginny waited on Pete's report. She'd expected it an hour ago, and still nothing. But she needed Lila here. Out of the way, with or without Tobias.

When Ginny reentered the room, she took her sweet time sitting down and pretending to read through her file. She knew the contents by heart, but this wasn't about preparation.

After a few seconds she glanced up to find Lila staring at her. "Is there anything you want to say to me?"

Lila lifted the glass. "The water tastes funny."

Smooth as always. Not a hint of worry in her voice. No panic. Also, no sign of concern about her missing husband.

There was a game to play here, one that would make her life easier and dim the spotlight glaring on her, but Lila refused to join in. Her personality telegraphed a level of disconnectedness that Ginny hadn't seen before. She'd handled sociopaths. Dealt with people with a host of issues, toxicity, and illness. Lila didn't fit neatly into any box. She wore the emptiness inside her like a badge of honor.

Finding a road in proved almost impossible. Ginny had tried flipping the questions and throwing her off, and none of it worked.

She aimed for the one potential weakness in the shell Lila had created. "We're conducting a search of Ryan's house right now. I'm guessing something there will point to you and provide more than a hint of a relationship."

Lila held the unblinking stare. "Okay."

With anyone else, Ginny would view that answer one way. With Lila, Ginny had to ask. "Okay, what?"

Lila pushed the glass away from her. "Ryan and I have been sleeping together for months. We meet at out-of-the-way places, usually a few times a month."

An admission. Within seconds, Lila shifted from her usual nondenial denials to spilling the truth. Ginny's brain lagged behind the conversation then caught up in a whoosh. "You're in a relationship."

"We have sex."

Of course she'd make that distinction. "I'm guessing you see those as two different things."

Lila smiled. "They are."

"It feels like we're playing verbal gymnastics." Again . . . still . . . for every second since they'd met. They continued the dance they'd done from day one.

Lila sighed and shifted in her chair as if settling in for a long talk. "When I first started out in criminal defense, I worked for a small firm. When you do that, you sometimes get stuck taking on cases outside of your area of expertise."

Stalling. A new tactic, but still a tactic. "This has something to do with Ryan?"

"I ended up handling some divorce cases. Horrible work. People fighting over their kids like they're curtains. It's soul-sucking."

Ginny played along. "I've heard."

"One of the things I learned, mostly from another attorney in the office, but I found it to be true, is that people marry for different reasons. It sounds simple, but it's subtle."

"Explain it to me."

"Some marry for money. A lot of times those of us looking from the outside see it and call the wife arm candy or some other derogatory term. But, reality is, many times it's a mutual understanding between the parties."

More disconnection from any emotion or empathy. "The couple."

"They're parties to a transaction. Whether people marry for stability or money, to escape or for children, it's a deal made between the parties in that marriage. A deal only they know the terms to."

The conversation circled and swooped. Ginny got sucked in, fascinated even though she fought it. "You're using the word 'transaction.'"

"Because marriage is exactly that." Lila's foot fell to the floor, and she leaned forward, balancing her elbows on the table between them. "Absent abuse or addiction, the transaction terms are violated when one of the parties wants a new or different deal. The trophy wife gets older and doesn't want to sit and collect jewelry."

"You mean when she doesn't want to be a trophy anymore." Made sense. It could also explain Lila's ambivalence about her marriage from the start. She looked like a trophy wife, but nothing else about her fit the role.

"Exactly. She has a kid, gains a few pounds, and her priorities change. His don't, and he wants out so he can find new arm candy."

The back-and-forth cut off, and the reality of all she said caught up in Ginny's head. "That's not very romantic."

"Romance as a necessary piece of the marriage contract is a relatively modern idea."

They'd spun and talked and not gone anywhere. "You sound like a textbook. And I'm still not seeing what this has to do with Ryan."

"Aaron and I married for security and comfort."

Those were not the reasons Ginny would have picked. She wondered if Lila and Aaron had different reasons for marrying that maybe even Lila didn't understand.

"We came from strained backgrounds and wanted companionship that was uncomplicated."

Every word chipped away at what little motive existed in the case, which Ginny assumed was the point. "Are you saying you and Aaron don't have a romantic relationship? Like, no physical contact?"

"We have sex." Lila's voice vibrated with a lack of emotion. So hollow and void of life. "But I wouldn't leave Aaron for another man."

Ginny wasn't sure how to assess that comment. "That's your view, but Ryan may have been a threat to Aaron. He could have seen Ryan that way, even unexpectedly."

Lila's eyes narrowed, but the amusement never left her tone. "Does Ryan strike you as a threat?"

"Most people would panic at the idea of having their affair uncovered." That came straight from the playbook relating to usual cases. Problem was, there was nothing usual about this case or the woman in front of her.

Lila shook her head. "Not me."

"Then why not be honest with me and disclose the affair from the beginning?"

"Because there's a target on my back, and I'm not stupid enough to make it bigger."

A knock at the door interrupted Ginny's response. Pete stuck his head inside and gestured for her to come into the hall.

"That took forever," she said. The energy pounding off Pete wiped away her frustration at his bad timing. "What is it?" She kept talking, too invested to let him answer. "You found something."

"The boxes are coming in now, but I thought you'd want to see this." He handed her a thick file.

"What is it?"

Pete smiled. "Page through it."

Chapter Thirty-seven

LILA DRUMMED HER FINGERS ON THE CONFERENCE TABLE. She'd been stuck in this room for over an hour. Ginny had called and asked her to come in. The curiosity proved too hard to resist, but boredom gave way to anxiety. Being here when she wanted to be somewhere else started a churning deep inside her. The shadow of doubt moved over her, darkening inch by inch.

Her choices raced in her head. She could get up. She hadn't been arrested. They had no cause to keep her there, and Tobias was going to kill her for talking without him. But Ryan and the search warrant. That combination kept her in her seat.

What felt like hours later, the door opened and Ginny came in with a new folder in her hands, this one thicker and tucked under her arm like a precious gift.

Lila tried to ignore Ginny's lighter walk. The cloud of tension that usually flowed around her had lessened. That could not be good. "Did he find my clothing at Ryan's house? I rarely slept there, but I remember leaving a—"

Ginny cut off the conversation by dropping the file on the table with a smack. She pushed it over in front of Lila.

Tobias picked that moment to breeze in. He was out of breath but managed to come off as cool and fine with the idea of his client blabbing to law enforcement without him. He flashed Ginny a smile then glared at Lila.

She felt his displeasure to her toes. She didn't blame him. She'd kill a client if they did this to her.

"Where are we?" he asked as he sat down next to her.

Lila was too busy staring at the file. Her hand hovered over it, but her fingers refused to close around the edges. "What's this?"

"Ryan's file." Ginny pulled out the chair and sat down again. "On you."

On her. "What?"

Her life. Her.

Lila's mind shot to the rows and rows of books lining the shelves in Ryan's office. The ones about poisons and manners of death. Actual cases. Some would have her fingerprints because she'd used those volumes as her personal library, picking out the pieces to help her plan.

The file in front of her didn't look familiar.

Tobias pulled it closer to him. "You're saying this is a diary?"

That sounded wrong to Lila. "He hardly seems the type."

"It's research."

The lightness in Ginny's voice had Lila on edge. Her gaze bounced down to the unidentifiable cover then back to Ginny. "I don't understand."

"I think you do." Ginny looked at the file again. "It's background on your parents. Notes about your upbringing once you went to live with other relatives."

The shaking started in Lila's hands. The jangling of her watch as it hit against the table. She clamped her fingers together and moved them to her lap.

Tobias covered her hands with his. "Did he say why he had all of this intel?"

"It looks like he's writing a book. About Lila and her family. One that focuses on her dad and all that happened years ago." Ginny's gaze moved over Lila's face. Whatever she saw there had her eyebrow lifting. "You didn't know?"

"You're assuming," Tobias said.

"Educated guess, but you can see that it's the most obvious explanation for collecting that sizeable stack. Taking those notes about Lila's behavior and the things she said."

At Ginny's urging, Tobias opened the cover and paged through. His frown deepened with each sheet he turned.

The life drained out of Lila. She forced her body to still, redirecting her energy to lifting her hands. She pretended to look over Tobias's arm at the file. "I didn't know."

She lost sensation in her fingers. Papers passed by her in a blur.

Tobias glanced at her. "He has information in here on Aaron and your life now."

"It looks like he was following you, talking to people about you, when you weren't around."

The steady drum of Ginny's voice echoed in Lila's head. The words bounced off her, refusing to process. "I can read."

Ginny reached over, paging through the pile and pulling one sheet out. "There's even a diagnosis in there for you, though that might not be the right word since he isn't that sort of doctor."

"Let's not—"

Lila pulled the page closer, cutting off Tobias's argument. The note jumped out at her. *PTSD. Anxiety disorder. Possible attachment disorder and dissociative state.*

The meetings. The meals. The laughter. Time with him let her step outside her life and experience a taste of normality. A peek into how others lived.

Memories tumbled through her. The park. His office. That hotel in Syracuse. None of it was real. He'd used her. Lied to her. One more man who'd disappointed her.

A scream rumbled up inside her. It pushed against her chest and battered her throat. Every muscle ached and strained to keep it in.

"You were work to him, Lila," Ginny said.

Yeah, she got it. He viewed her as a case study. As a way to make money and prove whatever point he intended to make in a new book. It was all about tenure. His work. His research. Money or fame.

The message blared in Lila's head: he viewed her as some sort of crime statistic.

She'd never played the role of girlfriend and never wanted

a boyfriend. They didn't share a great love. She didn't even know what that meant, but they'd been clear their relationship operated on a different level. But she expected respect. She believed in comfort, in bed and out. Wanting and desire, listening and caring on a fundamental level of at least human decency.

It had all been a lie.

She talked over and around the unexpected body blow, refusing to let Ginny see any reaction. "And? I'm assuming you have some grand point in showing this to me."

"If he was watching you so closely with the idea of writing about you, making money off your life, I wonder what else he knows."

A headache thumped through Lila. She tried to find the right answer through the thoughts and worries swimming around in her brain. "I don't know where Aaron is."

Ginny smiled for the first time that afternoon. "But maybe Ryan does."

Chapter Thirty-eight

THE SCREAMING IN LILA'S HEAD WOULDN'T STOP. SHE COULD hear Ginny's taunting voice and see the panic in Tobias's face when she told him about Ryan's research. After the meeting, Tobias gave her a long lecture about talking to Ginny alone then stayed at the sheriff's office, trying to get some information about what else they'd pulled out of Ryan's house.

She wanted to march over and burn Ryan's office down. She called and used their emergency signal, but he didn't call back. Not that she could stay rational and focused if he did pick up.

Seeing the old newspaper clippings about her father and Amelia in that damn folder had set her off. He even had a copy of her name change paperwork, which was supposed to be sealed. He'd likely sweet-talked some clerk into giving it to him. She'd told him about how she could no longer be connected to her old name and old life but never suspected he would go hunting.

She'd told him so much. About the way her moods swung from furious to hollow after the policewoman told her about her mom. About the sucking pain that doubled her over when she realized that her mother would rather be dead than be her mom.

She thought they were sharing and she could trust him. They connected for sex, but she could talk to him. He listened. He didn't understand surviving dysfunction the way Aaron did because he hadn't lived through it, but Ryan didn't judge. He asked open-ended questions and let her talk.

Now she knew why.

The longer she stood in the middle of her family room, the louder the voices in her head became. A riot of shouting and banging. The worst parts of her life ran in fast-forward through her mind. Her father's voice. Aaron's sick laugh on the video. The way Ryan reassured her as he smiled at her across the coffee shop table.

Men using her. Lying to her. Screwing her. Desperate to break her.

Shutting her eyes and covering her ears didn't stop the fever pitch. The room spun, and rage crashed over her. It slithered up her body and danced in her throat. Darkened every inch of her until that scream trapped inside her clawed and fought to get out.

Unable to choke the fury back for one more second, she reached for the vase on the end of the mantel. Grabbed it with both hands and smashed it as hard as she could against the stone of the fireplace. Let out a pain-soaked yowl.

Her screeching echoed through the quiet house.

The satisfying *crack* rang in her ears.

Blue glass shattered, sending shards over the hardwood floor and bouncing under the couch and into the fireplace. Pieces pricked at her legs, and she felt a slashing low on her cheek.

She blinked, trying to focus. Forced her breath to slow and her body to keep from crumpling on a heap on the floor. When she did, she saw the fallout from the shower of glass. Pieces stuck everywhere. Some crunching under her feet.

Her body suddenly weighed too much. It was difficult to keep her eyes open and keep her head from bobbing. With careful steps, she walked over to the kitchen and out of the middle of the debris field. The glass crackled as she tried to maneuver around the worst of the mess and make it to that bar stool across the room.

A few minutes later, she sat at her kitchen counter recovering from the aftermath. To cut through the thoughts cramming her head, she flicked the switch and let someone else talk.

This is Nia Simms and Gone Missing, *the true crime podcast that discusses cases—big and small—in your neighborhood and around the country.*

After days glued to this stupid podcast, she heard that opening in her dreams. She'd roll over and Nia's deep voice would call to her. The line between real and nightmare shifted and blurred.

*Today is our weekly call-in show. Let's talk about the investiga-
tions and the three missing women. And since we're talking about
mysteries and missing neighbors, let me know if you have any
thoughts about Aaron Payne. Are the disappearances in our area
tied? Should the task force be reviewing all of these cases together? What do we need to know to bring these people home?*

Even on this podcast where Nia worked so hard to keep the
names in the news, three women missing, and Aaron's name
was the one in the spotlight. He sucked up all the energy in
the room, and he wasn't even there.

Nia did the initial hard work. She pushed the theory of the
connection among the three. She forced the issue, kept them
in the news and the public's mind, after they'd become voice-
less, hardly mentioned. But now she and the people who called
in broke into a frothing frenzy talking about the men who
might have perpetrated the violence. Their interest turned
into something feral and disconnected from the women as
people. Ignoring the loss to those families.

Karen Blue. Julie Levin. Yara James.

Lila vowed to remember their names.

The theories droned on. She listened as the calls morphed
into one big guessing game. Anyone talking about Aaron
talked about her. They made assumptions. Made her out to be
some pathetic loner who was happy some man had paid attention to her and who had killed her husband to keep the other
man's interest. All bullshit and maddening.

She slid her arm across the counter, unable to do much

else. She'd expended so much energy, her body now felt heavy and lifeless. An extra push and she touched the end of the remote. She brought it closer, ready to turn it off just as the next caller broke in.

"I know Aaron, and he's not the man everyone thinks he is."

A quick shot without any detail. Probably easy for most people to ignore. Not Lila.

The comment breathed life back into her exhausted body. She recognized that voice.

Chapter Thirty-nine

EXACTLY TWO HOURS AND A QUICK CLEANUP JOB LATER, LILA tracked Ryan down at his office. He'd ignored her repeated attempts to reach out, even the one through the college's main number.

By the time she got to his office door, she'd worked herself into a full-throttle rage. Anger poured through her. His notes and all those side comments he'd written ran through her mind like a movie.

She opened the door and walked in without knocking. The move caught Ryan off guard. He dropped the book in his hand as he spun away from the window to face her.

Nothing in his expression said *welcome*. She picked up a bit of *how dare you?* mixed with *oh shit* and decided he was half-right.

After a few seconds, he nodded his head in what she took was a gesture to shut the door. Keep all the secrets in and don't let the public see the mess. She'd grown up that way, and being with him threw her back into that mindset. The secrets and the scheming. But she closed it anyway.

He was the first to speak, and the harsh whisper of his tone

matched his stiffness. "What the hell are you thinking by coming here?"

"You didn't answer my call." She didn't bother to lower her
voice or rein it in. He'd lost the right to have her care about
his reputation when he dug into her past with abandon.

He bent down and retrieved the book, returning it with
care to its assigned space on the shelves. "The police searched
my damn house yesterday, Lila."

"CID."

"Does the precise name of the office really matter?"

His voice rose along with her indignation. Every cell inside her screamed to open his window and shout about his
betrayal to the quad. Let him regain his *favorite professor* tag
after that. "You don't get to be pissed off."

"Excuse me?"

He'd flipped the whole situation around and blamed her,
put her in the role of begging forgiveness. As if she didn't
have enough garbage to worry about right now.

Screw that shit. This offensive strike was meant to throw
her off balance. Little did he know that's where she lived now.
On the fringes, ready to fall into the abyss.

"The drama, the fake outrage—whatever this is—tone it
down. Your students aren't here to watch and applaud."

A muscle in his cheek twitched. "Your marriage bullshit has
turned my life upside down."

Maybe true. She needed to own a part of that, but she'd do
it in silence unless and until he explained the reams of papers
he had collected about her without warning. "Oh, really?"

"I have a job and a life, Lila." He pointed toward the closed window behind his desk. "Right now I have a meeting with the department chair and—"

"You used me."

He froze. A second later his arm fell to his side. "What are you talking about?"

But he knew. The sudden blank expression and slight up-tick of his voice gave him away.

She'd thought he was so different, but he wasn't. "The research. My life. My father. My mother's suicide."

His hand closed over the back of his chair. "I can explain."

Sure, now he wanted to explain. How convenient. "That you're a piece of shit? No need. I get that."

His fingers tightened. "Be careful."

"Of what?" When he didn't speak, she tried to spell it out. To make sure they were on the same plane. "Threats? Really, Ryan?"

He blew out a long breath and visibly regained control. Gone was the tight frown line on his forehead. His hand no longer held the leather in a suffocating clench. "Okay, let's calm down for a second."

Déjà vu slapped her across the face. The calming voice. The gaslighting. Aaron had used those tactics. He'd excelled at them. She hated the nonsense even more coming from Ryan because she'd expected better of him. "Now you want to pla-cate me?"

He reached over and closed the blinds, blocking out the

sun and plunging the room into shadow. "We shouldn't do this here."

He chose this battleground when he refused to respond to her. "Are you afraid I'm going to yell? Embarrass you?"

"The research isn't what you think it is. I'm sure you've blown this into something bigger, but—"

"Aaron said the same thing to me."

Ryan's head snapped back. "What? You're comparing me to your asshole husband?"

She would not be sidetracked. Not until he admitted his plan and where he thought she fit into it. "They. Found. Your. Notes."

"We started working together, and you had this background . . ." He winced. "There was no grand plan. It just happened."

"Sure it did." She felt hunted.

"It's what I do, Lila. I hear about cases, get interested, and dive in."

She didn't waste one second waiting for the apology that would never come. "Is that the entire explanation? Like having a big brain excuses you from being a jackass?"

"I'm writing a book. You knew that."

She grabbed on to the bookcase to keep from throwing things. "You left out the part where it's about my family."

"No." He held up one finger, like he might do to a child. "It's about the connection between upbringing and crime and—"

"I don't care." She didn't need a lecture. All she wanted—

craved, really—was a few minutes of honesty. "Admit the truth. Spell it out."

She let the quiet stretch between them. After a lifetime of filling in the blanks and letting things slide because that was easier than feeling anything, she could not let this go.

Ryan shifted his weight from foot to foot right before he started talking again. "It's background. This is not a big deal."

Funny, because it meant everything to her. "You lie with such ease that I wonder what other bullshit you've dusted off, packaged, and sold to me in some other form."

He shook his head. "Right back at ya, babe."

The return of the flippant tone meant they'd skipped from subterfuge—finally—to something real. "I told you about my upbringing. I never thought you'd have the balls to use it for a book."

"What about the rest? Like, the snooping we've never talked about?"

"What are you saying?"

"You wandering around my office." His gaze shifted to his bookshelves. "You think I don't remember? More than once you insisted on meeting me here. You studied my shelves, looked through my books. I thought you were paging through, burning time."

Her heartbeat thumped in her ears. "I was."

He pulled out one book. *The* book. The one with the case from years ago that had taught her how to rig carbon monoxide through the air-conditioning vent.

"What were you really doing? Maybe studying? Learning how to take care of Aaron once and for all?" Ryan asked when he clearly thought he knew the answer. "Learning about how to kill and hide the body?"

"You're unbelievable."

"Is it that outrageous?" He shoved his chair to the side and stepped up to the desk, right across from her. "I used you? Fine. Guilty. Maybe I did. The opportunity was right there, and I grabbed it."

"I'm an opportunity now?" Whatever pang of guilt she'd felt for tangentially implicating him by paging through a few books disappeared in a hailstorm of anger.

"But I've been wondering if you used me, too. The questions about my work. The interest in my field." With his fists balanced on the desk, he leaned forward, getting his face closer to hers. "You stalked me."

The ego . . . how had she missed it before?

"I answered the phone when you called about buying a house months ago. It's what I do, genius. I suck up to people for a commission." Months ago she didn't know Aaron was a monster. She wasn't looking for a way to stop him. That morphed over time.

What she'd had with Ryan had been real . . . for her. At least at the beginning. Then, when she needed a little expertise, the relationship turned out to be convenient. She'd thought it was happenstance, but now it seemed more like he'd been the one stalking her, going after her for the information he needed.

His eyes narrowed. "I looked at the books that grabbed your attention."

"Say it." Challenge rose in her voice. "Stop playing and make whatever accusation you're dying to make."

"I don't think I have to."

The knock came as he finished his sentence.

"Ignore it," she said. Because they were not done.

The door opened, and Ginny stepped inside with two sheriff's deputies Lila recognized from the same office where Ginny questioned her. They stood just behind her, on either side. As a team, they made a formidable one.

Ginny's gaze fell on Lila, and she shook her head. "What a surprise to find you here."

"Are you still following me?" It made sense. With Aaron missing and no new clues, they had to be desperate. But dragging her to the station again?

"Should I be?" Ginny shot back with her usual take-no-shit style.

"Lila is only here to ask about my notes. Thanks to you." Ryan's voice ratcheted down to a normal level as he spoke with Ginny, his affect calm and in control.

Ginny appeared less than impressed. "She admitted you're having an affair."

His gaze shot to Lila. "She did?"

Lila hadn't gotten to that point yet. If he'd responded to her, this wouldn't have been a shock. "You're not the only one with surprises you forgot to share."

"Nice of you to give me a heads-up." He looked at both women as he delivered the comment.

Ginny snorted. "Do I work for you now?"

"My point about Lila being here was to say nothing else is going on." He waved his hand in the air. "We were just talking."

For a man who handled twentysomethings with ease, his defensiveness came off as conspiracy fodder. He had to know that. Lila couldn't help but roll her eyes. "The panic in your voice suggests otherwise, so maybe tone it down."

"She's not wrong, but you can explain why everyone is where they are when we get back to my office." Ginny gestured for her underlings to step aside and for Ryan to step out of the office.

Not her. That thought ran through Lila's mind. She was here for Ryan, not her. Lila had no idea what that meant, but she appreciated the front-row seat to the action because it would save her from guessing what happened later. Nia and the podcast would know, but this time she'd know first.

Instead of moving forward, Ryan retreated closer to the window. "What are you talking about?"

"We have questions for you." Ginny stood there, in a face-off, not giving one thing away with her body language.

When she reached for Ryan's arm, he shrugged away from the hold. "No. You know what? I'm done. No more. I don't even know the guy. Ask someone else about Aaron Payne."

"We found his phone in your house." Ginny's gaze traveled

from Ryan to Lila then back again. "Aaron's phone. The one that went missing when he did."

Ryan's mouth dropped open. "What?"

"*What?*" Lila asked at the same time.

"We found it in your house." This time Ginny grabbed for Ryan's arm and held on. "So, no, you're not done with questions."

Chapter Forty

LILA MET TOBIAS AT THE SHERIFF'S OFFICE. SHE WASN'T ALLOWED near the room where Ginny had Ryan in for questioning . . . again. Tobias left to get some intel on what was happening and confirm that the phone was the only surprise they had to survive tonight.

Her fight with Ryan had come at the worst time. She'd just tipped off his memory of her paging through the books in his office then aimed him directly at Ginny. He might right now be scrambling to protect his ass by offering up hers. The move would be typical, not surprising.

Ryan had operated from an agenda the entire time, and she'd missed it. Her instincts had misfired. The last thing she needed or wanted was to have her upbringing split open for everyone to pick at and dissect. Reliving those empty years was not an option.

But a much bigger mess loomed. One she could not explain. Aaron's phone. Nothing about the location in which it was found made sense. Ryan never had it. Despite Ginny's assumptions, the two men never met, or if they did it was so secret they hid it from her. She couldn't figure out why that would ever happen.

A wayward thought. A little pinching at the back of her neck raised the possibility that the men had colluded without her knowing. They could have met. Might have fought. If Ryan was desperate enough to find fodder for his book, he could have reached out to Aaron for background. But the jump from there, which sounded tenuous at best, to the idea of Ryan helping Aaron disappear seemed too broad to bridge.

That last possibility, regardless of how remote it might be, made her stomach flip. Fighting one of them sucked. Going up against them both had her brain scrambling to come up with new options and plans.

But the Ryan-as-accomplice idea sounded so unlikely to her that she forced her mind not to focus on it. That left her back in the confusing mire. The cell should have been where she'd left it: in Aaron's jacket pocket. She flipped through each step of the plan in her mind. She'd struggled but gotten through them all.

Invisible noxious fumes. She'd expected a haze, but everything looked normal when she peeked in the room. All but Aaron's body, laid in a diagonal sprawl across the guest bed.

With a towel clamped tight against her mouth, she ran inside, deep into the stale, poisonous air, to the other side of the room. With every step, she held the cloth tighter against her closed mouth. The finicky window lock fought against her fin-

gers. *She tugged and pulled until her lungs burned with the need to inhale.*

A few seconds more, and the metal hinge opened with a snap. She shoved the window up, and cool air poured in from the dark backyard. She gulped in the freshness, wishing she'd thought ahead and bought a mask. The carbon monoxide canister had required enough subterfuge and lying. Angling it just the right way in the air vent and taping around it to protect the rest of the house had proven daunting.

She looked around the bed, anywhere but at Aaron's unmoving body. When she finally focused on his hair, she thought about the one time she'd joked that he'd soon need to color it to chase away the gray. His terse response still rang in her ears.

She looked at him now, quiet and still. The worries of gray hair far behind him. An arm stretched out to his side, with his shiny gold wedding band showing.

She waited for the inevitable shot of guilt, a dose she'd convinced herself she could tolerate for a lifetime if it meant freeing those girls. But no feelings of remorse or pain hit her. Seeing those videos, listening to the girls praise his body and touch themselves for his pleasure, had turned him from man to pure monster in her mind.

She'd slain that dragon. Stopped his grooming—all of it.

She hadn't let him touch her since that night, and she'd done everything to keep her hands off him. Now she reached over and felt for a pulse. The telltale thump she half expected was gone.

That left the cleanup. Dressing his body, which now amounted to nothing more than deadweight. Getting him on the blanket and dragging him out to the garage. Loading him into the back seat and hiding him on the floor. Having the phone and the videos ready for discovery.

Her back was slick with sweat from the fight with foul air and a window. Her muscles tightened and locked from the soreness, but she had to keep going. Daylight would break, and the car had to be in position long before then.

Time was running out.

Tobias walked toward her, all traces of his usual amusement gone from his face. "Ryan is insisting he's never met Aaron and has no idea how the phone got in his house."

That fit with what she knew, but to Lila what mattered was the information he wasn't spilling, though she feared the answer might be "yet." "What's Ginny saying?"

Tobias shot her a *what's wrong with you?* frown. "I'm not actually Ryan's attorney, so she's not telling me."

Lila ignored the sarcasm and watched the staff of the sheriff's office scurry around. For once they weren't focused on her and whispering in the loud way men often did when they wanted you to know what they *really* thought about you. Today they answered phones and a few circled in a back corner near the biggest glassed-in office. No one paid any attention to her. It was almost as if they forced themselves not to.

She shook her head. "I don't understand this. This thing with Aaron's phone makes no sense."

Tobias guided her around the corner from the main room

to the quieter hallway leading to the front doors. "Lila, you need to focus. It's looking like Ryan is involved in Aaron's disappearance, or at least met up with him close to the time when he died, which is a problem, since he never disclosed that."

"That can't be right."

Tobias leaned against the wall with his arms crossed over his chest. "You're that sure?"

"There's no tie between them." Every time she said or thought the words, she felt more confident in them being true. That original assumption of this being something other than "real" evidence of wrongdoing by Ryan sounded right to her.

Tobias shook his head. "Well, there's you. You're a pretty big link between them."

"Neither one of them would fight to the death over me." They'd proven that through their omissions and behaviors.

Tobias swore under his breath. "Is it possible you're selling yourself short?"

"I know both of them." He didn't. Tobias sided with her out of years of loyalty. He knew she held back and didn't fight her. He was her toughest critic and biggest cheerleader. "Neither would be bothered unless it was to get together and talk about how much I suck."

"Enough with that kind of talk."

She ignored his frown and the slap of his voice. "I'm serious. Something else is going on here."

"You have a theory. Tell me."

Not yet. She knew better. "It's not that simple."

Something sinister played out around her, which meant Aaron stood behind it. His rotting core guided this. She could only guess he'd been following the podcast. He'd love that sort of attention from the recent-college-graduate-turned-podcaster. But a bigger benefit existed, and it had nothing to do with a podcast. Getting back at her through Ryan was exactly Aaron's style. Forget about hitting her straight on. He'd try to disable her from behind.

Tobias dropped his voice even lower. "I think we should tell Ginny about the videos."

"Why now?"

"She has your boyfriend in for questioning. That likely means she's working on a theory where the two men fought or, worse, that you and Ryan set this up and plotted to kill Aaron."

That's what she would do in Ginny's position. Focus in on the couple aspect and make one of them break. Lila could see Ginny thinking through the same steps and coming to the same conclusion. "That's ridiculous. She's too smart for that."

"Is it? You've heard the story a million times. You wanted out of your sad marriage and enlisted your murder expert boyfriend to help make it happen."

Her head started to pound again. "There is not one piece of evidence that points to that scenario."

"It's what some will assume, and they'll say it enough that it becomes fact in people's minds. The shouts and cries for justice will steer the investigation right into you, not away."

Her chest heaved with the force of deep breaths. She ached

to sneak inside that room and hear what was happening. "I get that public opinion—"

"It's not a *maybe*, Lila. It's happening. We have to get in front of this."

"Destroy Aaron's reputation." That she could get behind.

"Is that such a terrible thing? The asshole was sleeping with students."

"And disclosing that I knew puts the spotlight solidly on me. It provides motive, which is something Ginny currently does not have." It might tip her hand too early. There were still things he didn't know. Unraveling yet to come.

"Ryan gives her motive."

"That's not true."

"True or not won't matter. We need to scatter Ginny's focus. Make it so she's running around and can't settle on one theory. Let the public do the work on Aaron."

"Okay, but one problem." A big one. "What if the public does the work on me instead?"

The main door swung open behind them and Jared marched in. He stared at his cell but looked up right before he ran into her.

"Did Ginny call you in?" Tobias asked.

"Yeah." Jared sat down next to her. "She said there's a witness."

Lila wouldn't describe Ryan that way. "They found Aaron's phone. I need to explain—"

Jared frowned. "The witness is a woman."

Chapter Forty-one

JARED SAT NEXT TO LILA, HIS ATTENTION FOCUSED ON A SPOT on the wall across from them. The white paint puckered over the stucco, right on the edge of peeling off. "The guy with the phone is your boyfriend."

"Jared . . ." She wasn't sure what to say. There was no easy way to explain that the small flicker of light Aaron once lit inside her had died. That she dreaded the banality of living with him and had grown to hate the grating sound of his voice. And that was the tolerable stuff, the day-to-day things she'd figured out how to live with even as her disdain blossomed.

He blinked a few times before turning his head to look at her. His gaze toured her face. "Did Aaron know about him?"

The tortured sound of his voice ripped through her. She'd never expected her relationship with Jared to take this turn.

He didn't wait for an answer. "Because it sounds like they had some sort of altercation."

She couldn't let his mind travel too far down that road. "There's no evidence of that."

"Aaron's phone was at this guy's house. How do you explain that?"

Every mention of the cell chipped away at her confidence. Ryan might be an asshole, but a killer? An accomplice of some sort? Her mind bucked at the thought of either. "I don't know, but—"

"And now this woman. I don't understand what's going on." Jared rested his elbows on his knees and dropped his head in his hands.

The click of practical heels came right before the answer. Ginny hovered over them with Tobias close to her side. They'd been secluded, having a conversation about the newest surprise in the case and why it was released to the public before either of the people closest to Aaron.

"We have a witness. Her name is Samantha Yorke." Ginny stared at Jared then moved on to Lila. "One of your husband's former students."

Jared's head shot up. "Does she know where Aaron is or something about his phone and Ryan?"

Ginny's emotions stayed even. "We're still talking with her."

"About what, though?"

"Jared." Lila winced, trying to find the right delivery. "On some level, you know. A teacher and his student. My guess is she's saying she's more than a student."

"Interesting how you jumped to that conclusion." Ginny's expression stayed flat. Lifeless. "Unfortunately, you're also correct. She says they had a relationship."

"He was her coach?" Jared sounded more confused by the second.

Ginny shook her head. "Not only that type of relationship. This was personal."

"No. No way." Jared's gaze flipped between the people around him, landing on no one in particular before focusing on Lila. "You can't believe that garbage."

Lila let her silence speak for her.

"This woman is lying. Maybe she's scared or, worse, looking to put herself in the middle of the investigation. That's a thing people do, right?" Jared's reasoning raced and shifted. The desperation to convince someone—anyone—vibrated in his voice.

"She has a video she sent him. It's very suggestive." Ginny's expression stayed blank, as if she weren't taking a position on all she'd heard. "She says Aaron pursued her, convinced her they were dating, and then dumped her after they had sex. She started college this fall, but this happened while she was in high school."

Jared's mouth dropped open. "What?"

"She's quite clear this wasn't a one-time thing. Apparently, there are other girls, some as young as fifteen," Ginny said. "It sounds like this is what Aaron does. Picks a girl and makes her feel special."

Lila choked back the bile racing up her throat. This was what she'd wanted—the truth out so the healing could begin, if that were even possible. The secrecy Band-Aid had to be ripped off so the hero worship would stop, but that didn't make the process any easier to watch.

Jared's focus shifted back to that spot on the wall. "I can't believe this."

"We're going to talk about that." Ginny looked at Lila. "First, you come with me." Ginny gave Jared a fleeting glance as they started to walk toward the room where all of the questioning had taken place so far. "I'll talk with you next."

Lila hadn't walked through the specifics of how to handle this topic with Tobias. Strategy mattered, but she didn't have time to map it out.

She slid into the seat across from Ginny and asked the question dancing in her head—the one she'd tried to answer but couldn't find the evidence to ferret out. "How many girls?"

"I don't know yet. Samantha gave us some names to verify. We're also checking in North Carolina, since he taught there as well." Ginny rolled a pen between her palms. "She said the one she knows personally still worships Aaron, but she's heard rumors about others."

Tobias left his position at the door and joined Lila on her side of the table. "There are many girls, but this is the first you're hearing about this?"

"Good question." Ginny glanced at Lila. "Is it the first *you're* hearing about this, Lila? And keep in mind you already played your hand out there with Jared. You didn't show one second of surprise in finding out about your husband's extracurricular activities."

"Call him Aaron. Hearing this news makes me want to forget he's my husband."

Tobias made a strangled sound. "This isn't—"

"You didn't answer the question," Ginny said at the same time.

"Yes." The blurt worked here. They could run around in circles or Lila could push them forward. She chose the latter.

"You knew what he was doing with his students?" If the news shocked Ginny, she hid it well. Her voice didn't even lift.

"Before? Of course not. I figured it out after." Lila tiptoed through the facts and picked out the ones that fit her narrative. "I found videos in the house."

Ginny shook her head. "You forget that we searched the house."

"Your people missed them." They didn't know to look *on* her or in a safety deposit box she kept in another name.

"More secrets, Lila? You understand that makes you complicit, right?"

Lila leaned back and crossed one leg over the other, trying to trick her nerves into calming down by acting calm. "I don't know where he is and had nothing to do with his students. We both know you know that."

"You keep saying you don't know his whereabouts, but I notice you never say that you didn't kill him."

Because she couldn't. Lying wasn't a problem for her. It didn't call up morality issues. She could lie with impunity if the situation called for it. But people like Ginny would expect her to feel sorry for making that choice, to do a performative dance of guilt and shame, and Lila felt neither.

"Shouldn't your focus be on Ms. Yorke right now?" Tobias asked. "Does she know what happened to Aaron?"

"She has guesses. She thinks he went too far with a student this time and a boyfriend or someone defending another one of his students killed him, but there's no evidence."

The room fell silent at an unexpected knock. The door opened, and Pete stepped inside but didn't come closer. He stood with his back against the door. He'd clearly been listening and wanted a closer look.

"The videos. Where are they?" Ginny asked.

"Here." Lila lifted her bag and pulled out an electronic device about the size of an e-reader.

Ginny looked at the screen as she searched for the "on" button. "They're on a notepad you carry with you?"

"Where was I supposed to put them?"

"Attitude, really?" Pete asked.

Tobias exhaled. "Tell them where you found the videos."

"The tablet was tucked into a small space between a beam and the ceiling in the family room." Now she'd lied. Head-on and big. "I did a full search after your people did."

"And yet you didn't report the existence of the videos or suggest we come back and look at the ceiling." Pete stepped to the table and glanced at the device over Ginny's shoulder.

"I'm telling you now."

The device clacked against the table as Ginny put it down without watching the videos or looking at any of the content. "Your story isn't very convincing."

"Lila." Tobias's voice rang out in the quiet room. "You can tell them the truth."

She thought back to all she'd told him and the bits of story she'd confided. This was the time to lay the groundwork and ensure the investigation would go deeper than one man. "There's a reason for my hesitation. I was trying to figure out if this mess with his students was bigger than Aaron."

"How so?" Pete asked.

"How did Brent not know?" There were other targets, and he might be clean, but something felt off about him to Lila. Call it a mutual mistrust club. "Teens talk. They brag. They get pissed off and want revenge. And, nothing? It doesn't make sense the gossip didn't get out."

"You think Brent and Aaron are in this together? Like it's some sort of pedophile ring?"

Tobias held up a hand to keep her from answering Pete's follow-up question. "No one is using that phrase. We don't know what's going on. That's the point."

"If that's true, you should have told us and let us investigate." Ginny moved the tablet to the side.

The condescending tone rang in Lila's ears. Ginny might be right, but the words, the delivery, hit Lila wrong. "Next time I find out my husband inappropriately touched his students I'll know the proper reporting etiquette."

Ginny didn't back down. "If most people found evidence

pointing to a school-wide problem, they'd immediately report it. That would be the most logical choice."

"You've made it pretty clear I'm the lead suspect in Aaron's disappearance." The only one, as far as Lila could tell.

"As a result, Lila worried you would see the videos and get the wrong idea," Tobias added with his usual smooth delivery.

Ginny kept her attention on Lila. "Which would be?"

"That I was angry he was sleeping around and killed him." Lila had to force the words out. Sleeping around sounded voluntary. The phrase absolved Aaron from blame, and she hated doing that.

Pete's eyebrow lifted. "You weren't?"

Ginny's elbows slid across the table as she leaned in. "Pete's right. These accusations hit close. They must stir up certain memories. Make you furious for being put in this position. Again."

"Hey." Tobias tapped the tip of his pen against the table. "Let's keep the focus on Aaron."

Ginny held Lila's gaze with an unblinking stare. "But Lila's father had a similar problem controlling himself around young girls. This is a pattern with the men in her life."

Faces blurred in her mind. An endless line of weak men. Some sick and some pathetic, and all whining about how they weren't responsible for their putrid actions. "You don't need to sugarcoat it. My father stalked and killed a child. What Aaron did . . . he . . ."

"Your father raped and murdered your best friend," Ginny shot back.

She'd answered these questions decades ago, and here she was again.

You had to know how he felt about Amelia. The way he looked at her. What exactly did he ask you to do to get her to come to your house that day?

Tobias tapped the pen harder. "We're off topic."

Ginny's hand inched across the table. "Some people thought you were in on it back then. I've read the notes in the case file. There's a theory that you helped lure Amelia for your dad. A sort of father-daughter kidnapping team."

New images swam in front of Lila. Her father rubbing Amelia's back. His insistence on taking them to the pond to swim. The way he watched for hours from the front seat of his car.

I need to know you can handle yourself in the water. I might even jump in and join you.

Pain wound deep in her gut. Disappointment. Surprise. Sitting in her kitchen back then, trying to work through exactly what the adults were asking when they talked about "inappropriate touching."

Her father barely paid attention to her, but Amelia was special. Lila recognized it, too. Sunny and sweet. She wore a big smile and her blond hair in that perfect ponytail.

"You have a child." Lila cleared her throat, hoping to even out her voice. When Ginny frowned, Lila rushed to get to the point. "It's not a secret. There was a spotlight on you in the paper when you got promoted to this job."

"You're investigating me?"

She refused to be knocked off her path. A deep, aching

part of her needed Ginny to understand. To hear her and get what it was like to be so alone that the cold inside never warmed. To walk around always one word away from bursting into a fine powder and getting carried off with the wind. "What would you do for your son?"

Ginny shrugged. "Anything, but I don't see—"

"Right." Just what Lila expected. "No hesitation."

Pete shrugged. "What does that prove?"

This was between her and Ginny, so she ignored the male voice. "Your son knows that security. He knows his parents love him, because I'm assuming your husband would give the same answer."

"We're definitely off topic now," Tobias mumbled.

Ginny lifted a hand as if to tell the men to shut up. Her gaze never left Lila's face. "Make your point."

"Your son understands how you would advocate for him. That you love him and support him. He's learning it by living it. You've shown him every day of his life, and he carries that security, whether he truly appreciates it yet or not. It's so deeply rooted that he'll have it forever. You will be there for him." Lila gulped in air, forced her body to breathe around the pain stabbing inside. "You know what I learned from my parents?"

Ginny's expression telegraphed that she was listening—totally engaged—but gave nothing away about what was happening inside her. "Tell me."

"Unconditional love is bullshit. A trap that lures you in, makes you comfortable, then snaps, breaking you in half. Like hope, it blinds and destroys. Leaves you limping and unprepared for what's coming right for you." She had never known a moment where it played out differently. "People think my father is a hideous monster, but he's really a narcissist, incapable of love. Evil, possibly, but too self-involved for anyone to be able to honestly assess him."

"And your mother?" Ginny's voice sounded softer now, more coaxing.

"She showed how much she loved me when she threw herself off a building instead of sticking around and fighting for me." Lila fought to swallow back the anxiety welling up inside her. "She picked death over me."

Ginny's eyes closed for a second as if she were absorbing the words as she heard them. "Depression can—"

"Stop. No lectures. Not on this topic." Lila wasn't interested in granting her mother absolution. "I know what depression is. I get that a kid can't see the difference between a mother's pain and her own, and that as an adult I need to understand mental illness and not take her choices personally."

"But?"

"But we still end up at the same place. My parents both had a choice to make about what mattered to them, and in neither case was I the answer." They left, and her life spiraled. They gave up and she was supposed to take it and be fine. Well, she'd never been fine or complete . . . or forgiving.

People thought silence meant the absence of noise, and sometimes it did, but other times it screamed so loudly she had to fight not to cover her ears.

Not one to stand still for long, Pete shifted. He held out for a few more seconds before talking again. "What does this have to do with Aaron and his students?"

"I didn't help my father groom and then kill Amelia. I was totally blindsided and confused by what happened." Lila spoke directly to Pete then switched back to Ginny. "The same is true with Aaron. I didn't know about whatever sick needs he had, and if I did, I wouldn't have helped him."

Ginny's gaze wandered over Lila's face, studying her. "But would you kill Aaron for doing the same thing that ripped your family apart?"

"Okay, wait." Tobias sat up straighter in his chair. "That's a big jump."

Pete snorted. "Is it?"

Ginny appeared to ignore both of them. "You couldn't punish your dad. You were young and vulnerable. But you're an adult now. You know the flaws in the justice system. You understand that some men lie and get away with it."

Lila nodded. "All true."

"You couldn't help Amelia, but you *could* punish Aaron."

Lila had been wary of Ginny's brain and instincts from the beginning. She always was the smartest person in the room, constantly watching and listening. While the men preened and fought for the mic at press conferences, she hung back. Glory and election wins didn't motivate her. Justice did.

Her concepts of right and wrong were naïve and simple. Lila wanted to poke holes in the logic and laugh, but Ginny had an air about her that demanded respect. Lila had given it to her from the beginning because she was the one person Lila feared in all of this.

Lila shot back with the only bullet she had—a mix of misinformation and subterfuge. "You're looking at this the wrong way. Knowing what we know now, it's clear Aaron hurt the very children he was tasked with protecting. That would have caused a lot of anger. Created suspects. Ones you never would have thought to look for because you've been focused on me."

"You sound like a lawyer," Pete said.

Lila didn't break eye contact with Ginny. "I am."

"And she's right." Tobias put his hand on Lila's thigh in a subtle gesture to rein it in. They'd used the unspoken communication during countless cases and in numerous meetings. The signal said *let me handle this one.* "You've pointed this investigation in one direction only, Ginny, and ended up missing Aaron's true nature and his crimes. I doubt people in this county are going to take that well."

"Is that supposed to be a threat of some kind?" Pete asked.

Ginny crossed her arms in front of her. "Or, Tobias, people might think Lila hid the evidence about Aaron's misdeeds to protect her comfortable lifestyle. Husband with a trust fund. Beautiful house. No pressure to work unless she wants to. Enjoys time with a hot professor on the side."

Pete whistled. "It's not a bad setup."

The openness that usually radiated from Tobias dried up. "Try suggesting any of that fantasy in the press, and I'll sue everyone in this building."

Ginny made a noncommittal sound before turning back to

Lila. "What was that big fight about? The one that happened a few weeks back that had Aaron sleeping at his brother's house?"

A good shift. Lila had to give her adversary credit for never taking the easy way out of a conversation. "I didn't like how much time he was devoting to the school."

"You, who likes her time alone, wanted more attention?" Ginny scoffed. "Nah. Don't think so."

"Even I have limits." And Aaron had found them.

THE QUESTIONING WENT round and round for another twenty minutes. By the time Ginny and Pete stepped into the hallway, Ginny needed a glass of wine and something to kill the headache spreading down her neck and through every limb.

Ginny tipped her head back against the wall and closed her eyes for a second. They stood just out of range of the main room and the view from Charles's office. She needed the quiet to mentally untangle the discussion. The part about Lila's upbringing and feelings on abandonment from her parents struck her as genuine. The most real thing Lila had ever said. Her voice had shaken and her eyes had turned glassy as she'd spilled the personal details. Every cell inside Ginny told her that Lila had revealed a bit of honest weakness in those moments.

She'd offered a confession wrapped in a therapy session. Nothing Ginny could use in court, but almost as if, on some level, Lila wanted her to know she killed Aaron for a valid reason. For the girls he'd gone after. For making Lila relive that horror and be unable to stop it. Not for the sex or the weird-ness or for any other reason, but for the girls.

"What the hell was that about back there?" Pete whispered the question, keeping it between them only for now.

Ginny didn't have the patience to discuss the concept of nuance with Pete. "Where is Samantha?"

"She's waiting to talk with you and the sexual assault spe-cialist." He glanced at his watch. "The specialist is on the way over."

The expert worked with all of the local units and had been almost exclusively attached to the state police during the Karen Blue investigation. Ginny needed her now. "We have to watch the videos frame by frame. If Samantha is right about other girls—"

"Seems convenient." Pete was already shaking his head. "No one at the school hinted at this."

Maybe . . . but maybe not. "Circle back to the one teacher who didn't give Aaron a glowing report and poke around. There might be something there."

Pete nodded. "Right."

"And you asked what the hell that was back in the room." Ginny pointed at the closed door that separated them from where Lila and Tobias sat. "That was motive. Tobias knows it. The really strange thing is Lila knows it, too, but offered up the videos anyway."

"Why would she do that?"

"I don't know yet." But Ginny silently vowed to find out.

Chapter Forty-two

JARED SAT IN A DAZE. LILA COULD SEE THE CONFUSION IN EV-
ery line of his body. He'd slumped down in one of the chairs
in the sheriff's office waiting area. Ginny warned that his
questioning would be next, but, for now, she left him out
there with her. Stewing and shaking his head.

He leaned down with his elbows resting on his thighs and
stared at the linoleum floor between his feet. "I don't understand."

Lila glanced at Tobias before trying to reason this through.
"Jared, listen to me."

"Girls." Jared shook his head but never lifted it.

Tobias shifted out of the way as two men walked through
the open area and into the main room where the employees
sat. He looked out of place here, as he did in most places. The
expensive suit and perfectly shined shoes. He was smart and
loaded and totally in control of his surroundings. Lila hoped
he would help her maneuver through the mess she'd made.

"His students. Girls on the team." Jared made a groaning
sound as he looked up. "How does Ginny know this woman is

telling the truth? She gets things wrong. Really wrong." The metal chair made a cracking sound when Jared sat back hard in it.

Lila hadn't seen that side of Ginny, and the idea intrigued her. "What do you mean?"

"She's asked me about you and your background. She suggested the existence of the trust fund proved motive, first for you and then for me, once she realized the money came to me if anything happened to Aaron."

"When was this conversation?" Tobias asked.

"A week ago. In the middle of asking if Aaron had life insurance and, if so, who would inherit it, she brought up how Aaron's trust would go to me if something happened to him." He shrugged. "I'm assuming she searched his bank accounts and found the trust."

Lila knew the answer to that one. She'd fed Ginny the information, hoping to derail her for a short time as Lila chased down confirmation for herself. Sounds as if that one plan went the way she intended.

"I'm assuming the insurance goes to you?" Tobias asked her.

"I don't think Aaron going missing has anything to do with money." It also wasn't much of a motive. Aaron didn't believe in insurance. He thought paying money now to receive a possible settlement later amounted to waste. He insisted her getting the house and having a law degree was protection enough against future surprises.

Little did he know she'd be the one leveling the surprises.

Tobias pushed away from the wall and came and sat with

them in the rickety chairs. "Asking about money is routine. Ginny would be incompetent not to, and she is anything but. Having a woman come forward and make the sort of allegations we're talking about here is the exact opposite of routine. Ginny can't ignore the claims."

"You think Aaron touched . . ." Jared looked around the room and dropped his voice after looking at the couple across from them. "That he . . ."

"With Samantha? Yes, I think so." Lila knew so, but softening the truth struck her as the decent thing to do in these circumstances. Jared had enough harsh reality in front of him to face without adding to the pile.

"But the things she's saying about Aaron are . . ." His gaze focused on Lila. "Jesus, I don't know how you're processing this."

"There is a video. You can hear Aaron's voice. He's talking to her, and it's . . . graphic." Pete dropped that bomb into the middle of the conversation as he walked up and stood behind Tobias's chair, hovering over them.

"Okay, but . . ." Jared's usual cool demeanor kept slipping. He stammered and seemed to lose his words. "Is the video real?"

His cluelessness or unwillingness to "get" it, whichever this was, proved too painful for Lila to let slide. Before she could try again, Tobias spoke up. "Jared, come on. There's a suggestion this is an ongoing thing for Aaron."

Suggestion? Thing? No. Too neutral. Lila couldn't tolerate downplaying his behavior, not now that it was finally out in the open. "You mean that he's screwing all of his female students."

Pete nodded. "Some, yes."

A flurry of activity started down the hall. Uniformed officers scurried around, and Ginny's voice rose over the din, talking about cars and a long drive. She turned the corner and came to a stop in the doorway in front of them.

Her gaze bounced around the room before landing on Pete. "We need to move out." She turned to Lila next. "Go home and we'll contact you."

Pete looked as confused as Lila felt. "Something is more important than this?"

"Yes," Ginny confirmed with a curt nod.

"Are you kidding me?" Jared stood up. "You drop this bombshell and then you—"

"We have Aaron's phone, which means we have his GPS."

Ginny's words cut through the noise in the office and the emotional floundering inside of Lila. "You found something."

"An address."

"Where?" Tobias asked.

"Go home and wait." Ginny motioned for Pete to follow her. A few steps and they were out the door and gone.

Chapter Forty-three

GINNY REFUSED TO THINK OF THE NERVOUSNESS BOUNCING around inside of her as excitement. It amounted to energy. The fuel she needed to tolerate the long drive and see whatever there was to see once she got to the end.

She rode with Pete and a sergeant Charles insisted on sending along. They spent the almost three-hour drive shifting between silence, mindless talk, and theories about their destination.

They'd turned from the highway, onto a two-lane road, to a dirt path full of potholes and divots, to what amounted to a gravel driveway in a densely wooded area, thick with untrimmed trees and overgrown shrubs. Finally landing at the large parcel, marked off with a high fence but with no visible structures from the road, did not ease the wariness pounding through her.

She got out of the car and greeted the local police with obligatory handshakes and words of assurance about working together. Police cars littered the thin path from the road, more than a quarter mile into the clearing. She looked up, her gaze following the long line of the trees that soared into the sky and covered any peek of blue or clouds above the crowns.

People talked around her. Officers spread out, taking careful steps as they moved around the exterior of what looked like a one-room cabin. Off to the left was a small shed, on the verge of toppling over. A barn with cracked and scarred wood looked like it may have been painted red at one time but now blended into the scenery in a dull brown.

There were closer places to home to bring his students. Motels and rental cabins around Cayuga Lake. This location, out of view, away from everything, struck her as a place someone would go if they couldn't afford to get caught.

She ignored the shiver that raced through her as she took a few steps closer to the three stairs leading to the cabin's porch.

Pete broke away from the officer he'd been talking to and met her at the front of the car. "This is in the middle of nowhere. Owen over there says he grew up in the area and went camping in and around Moose River Plains, which isn't too far, and even he didn't know there was anything back here. Said a spot near here was earmarked as a campground years ago but then a private party bought it."

"Interesting." Aaron liked camping and fishing, but Ginny doubted he used the property for either. The woods thrummed with an ominous vibe. Tree limbs twisted and entwined above and around her in shapes eerily reminiscent of outstretched arms. She tried to imagine campers running around, laughing, but the only sensation she picked up was fear.

"Owen said they did a quick check outside after you called and advised we were on the way. Didn't go into the buildings, but these three structures are the only ones they found. No other outbuildings that they could see."

"There's nothing around here for miles." The kind of place where a person could scream and not be heard. Run and not get away.

A chilling thought that refused to leave her mind. Truth was nothing about the area said fun and camping. This looked like miles of untamed trees and wilderness.

"It's creepy as hell." Pete shook his head. "Like a setting out of a horror movie. Without evidence, all we can guess is he used it for hunting."

"I don't think so." In her gut, she knew this location was a much bigger piece of the puzzle than that. "Who owns the property?"

"We're checking. Apparently, the records are a bit tangled. There's a corporation that leads to another one. It will take some time to trace the paperwork and tax records."

In other words, a place someone wanted to keep as a secret.

The local police chief joined them, along with some of his people. All men. Ginny didn't have time for a jurisdictional discussion or a debate about who was in charge. She plunged right in.

She nodded in the direction of the double doors, with their chipping paint, and the shiny chain keeping them shut. "What's in the barn?"

The chief shrugged. "We were waiting for you to go in."

"Open it up."

An officer appeared with a bolt cutter. He and Pete worked on the lock—one that looked much newer than the rest of the place. They had it off and bagged up for prints a second later. The doors creaked as they pulled them open. Then everyone froze.

Officers looked at one another. One took photos.

Ginny broke the silence. "Aaron's SUV."

"The license matches," Pete said.

Ginny could hear the police chief talking about forensics and cordoning off the area. She listened while she walked around the car, using her flashlight to cut through the darkness of the interior of the barn and look in the SUV's windows.

"See if we can get any tracks coming in or out," she said to the chief in an effort to reestablish jurisdictional boundaries. "Set a perimeter, then I need to know what's in every direction. Gather video from any business anywhere around here. We need to see cars coming in and around, going back as far as we can get it." She glanced at Pete. "Open the back of the SUV."

"Maybe there's another cabin nearby," Pete said.

Owen shook his head as he opened the back of the SUV. "Doubt it."

The smell hit her. The unmistakable scent of decomposing flesh. She didn't need to look inside to know what they'd found. "We have a body."

The blanket covered the person's face. Pete used the long

end of his small flashlight to peel back the corner of the material. She spied a hand and a thin gold wedding band.

She needed to wait for the official identification, but she knew. Aaron. It had to be. The body was strangely in good condition.

Sadness hit her first. The loss of life. The utter waste. Then she thought about the girls and the breach of trust, and a range of different sensations slammed into her. Anger. Disappointment. Relief that he was gone.

"Ma'am? Sir?" An unfamiliar voice called out to her from the cabin's front porch and the police chief walked toward the house in response.

Ginny lost track of everyone then. Her thoughts scattered. She couldn't take death in stride. It demanded at least a second of quiet contemplation, and the crowd made that tough. "Not now."

"Ginny." Coming out of the cabin, the chief jogged toward her. "You need to come in the cabin."

"Why?" She glanced up and saw the chief's pale face and the stress pulling at the corners of his mouth. An alarm flashed in her head. "What is it?"

"You need to see for yourself."

Chapter Forty-four

SHERIFF DEPUTIES USHERED LILA AND JARED BACK INTO THE office through a gauntlet of reporters. No one seemed to know what had happened, but they guessed something had. Clearly the word had gone out that the story was here in the sheriff's office and not at Lila's house.

Samantha. The podcast. Ryan's involvement. Aaron's phone. Lila had a million questions. They slammed into her head, and she fought to categorize them. To sort them out so she could handle them. And that was before half the office went rushing out of there in search of . . . something.

Hours later they were all back in the same place—Ginny's turf. Lila and Jared sat in a small conference room. Not the place where they'd been questioned. This one had comfortable chairs and a round table. Coffee and water on one side of the room and a wall of windows across the back. The glass walls gave them a view of the main room where the investigators and others sat. Rows of desks and computers. Personal photos and a wall that looked like a call sheet of some sort. Aaron's name was right there, under Ginny's.

Tobias stepped out for his usual round of recon. He could sweet-talk most people into getting the information he needed. This trip took longer, but she finally saw him around a corner, coming out of the big office at the end of the hall that belonged to the sheriff.

She sat on her hands, forcing her body to still and not jump on him when he walked into the room. "What did you find out?"

He closed the door behind him and took a seat at the table next to Lila. "Ginny is on the way back."

The flat tone of his voice put her on edge. "Tobias?"

"They found Aaron's car."

Jared had been sitting with his eyes closed. At that answer, he jackknifed to attention and leaned in. "Where?"

Geography didn't matter to her. She had bigger questions. Ones that might end in answers that kept her in this building far longer than she wanted. "Like abandoned or was he in it?"

"I don't have a lot of details. It sounds—"

His voice cut off, and Lila knew why. The sight of Ginny stalking down the main room with her raincoat open and flapping with each determined step proved impossible to ignore. She frowned as she dropped an envelope on a desk and kept marching. Right for their room.

"This is bad." Lila hadn't meant to say the words out loud. She thought she'd whispered until Ginny's gaze locked with hers coming through the doorway. "Your poker face needs work."

"I'm not trying to hide anything."

Ginny's voice carried a mix of exhaustion and an emotion Lila couldn't identify. Her shoulders slumped, and cloak of sadness seemed to be draped over her.

"So, what are we looking at?" Tobias asked, jumping them all to the deep end of the conversation.

"We used the GPS to locate Aaron's car." Ginny sat down. She had a thin file in her hands and placed it on the table in front of her but didn't open it. "It was parked in a barn at a cabin outside a small town called Logan's Gorge."

Jared snorted. "What?"

"Where's that?" Lila asked at the same time.

"North and remote. It's near the Canadian border but not too close to it to be on a well-traveled road. The closest thing you might know is the camping area, Moose River Plains."

Jared shook his head. "I don't understand."

A wince came and went on Ginny's face before she started talking again. "The SUV was on a wooded lot, and Aaron was in it. In the back, Jared." She laid her palms flat against the file. "It looks like he was stabbed, rolled up in a blanket, and left there until we found the body."

Stabbed. The word punched into Lila.

Not alive. Killed, and not by her.

Jared's mouth opened as he fell against the back of his chair, almost boneless. "He's dead?"

Ginny nodded. "Yes, I'm sorry."

"Stabbed?" That meant . . . Lila didn't know what the hell that meant.

With her original plan, she'd anticipated feeling nothing

when Aaron's body was found. The videos would show why. There would be corroboration. She had a plan for that, too, but it turned to dust when Aaron's body went missing.

Every day since, her thoughts had ping-ponged between believing he was alive and tormenting her with the idea of an accomplice who'd stepped in to make her pay. She feared being found out and not having her carefully constructed story stick. She worried the girls at school wouldn't get justice.

Knowing he was gone but in some violent way she hadn't expected left her reeling. Shock churned inside her. Someone had killed or stabbed him at some point, and it wasn't her, which left a wide-open field of terrifying possibilities. The sensation of being hunted and watched, dissected and terrorized, hit her full force.

"Are you familiar with a cabin in Logan's Gorge?" Ginny wrapped her fingers around the top edge of the file. "I know he likes hiking and tough trails. He might have rented it or—"

"Not there. We went to one about thirty miles from my house. Nowhere near Canada or whatever this moose thing is."

Jared shifted around in his chair and drew out his cell. His fingers shook as he pressed the buttons. When he turned the screen around for Ginny to see, it showed a map and pinpoints around the lake indicating her house, and Jared's, and the rental cabin.

Tobias cleared his throat. "Where is Logan's Gorge exactly?"

"Almost three hours away. The GPS on his phone suggests he'd been there recently. We're trying to access older records." Ginny lifted the edge of the file but didn't open it.

Lila tried to get a peek at what Ginny found so important that she kept it close. Held on to it. The movements could be nervous fidgeting, but that sort of uncontrolled response didn't fit with the Ginny she'd been verbally battling in the case so far.

"Why would he go there?" Jared's voice faded in and out as if he was having trouble breathing. "When?"

Ginny smoothed her hands over the file again and dragged them to her lap. "I was hoping one of you would know about the property."

"No." Lila could pass a lie detector on that answer.

Tobias watched Jared for a few extra seconds before turning back to Ginny. "Can you track the ownership?"

"We will." Ginny glanced into the open room behind her before continuing. "The information is pretty fluid. All of this is unfolding as we speak."

"Stabbed." Lila blurted the word out again. It rumbled around in her head, begging to get out, as the others talked.

Ginny let out a small sigh. "Yeah, it looks like the weapon came from the knife block in the cabin's kitchen."

"So someone who lives in or rents the cabin attacked Aaron?" That made less sense to Lila than Brent or another accomplice. "This is insane. Why would that happen?"

"When?" Jared delivered the word in a louder voice, as if his brain cells had jump-started and he'd come out swinging.

Ginny frowned at the question. "Excuse me?"

"Aaron disappeared nine days ago. Has he been in the SUV all this time?" Jared's voice rose with each word. By the time he got to the end, he sat up straight, demanding answers. Then his body fell. It looked like all the air rushed out of him, and he doubled over in his chair. "Shit. I can't take this."

Ginny stood up and reached for the door handle and called for help.

On instinct, Lila rushed to Jared. She dropped into the chair beside him and rubbed his back. Seeing him broken and struggling hit her as if she'd slammed full speed into a brick wall.

"Okay, breathe." She whispered the plea directly into his ear. After a few minutes, his breathing seemed to settle. "You okay?"

A harsh laugh without any amusement erupted from deep inside of Jared. "No."

Lila glanced up in time to see Ginny and Tobias exchange a look of concern.

"I'm fine." Jared waved off the concern. "No need to call an ambulance."

Ginny waited until Jared sat up again to answer. "There's a possibility his body was moved to the SUV recently."

Just when Lila thought her thoughts couldn't be any more scrambled, her brain proved her wrong. She couldn't decipher Ginny's cryptic response. "He was alive and hanging out at some random cabin while we were all looking for him?"

Tobias shrugged. "Maybe the person who stabbed him held him captive there."

"We're not sure." The more Ginny talked, the more drained she sounded.

"This is . . . I don't know what this is." Lila's mind took off on another race.

Who other than her would want him dead? An accomplice. A victim? A parent who knew what he'd done? All sounded reasonable, but she couldn't make the jump from there to the notes left at her house and office. Those were personal. Threatening. They suggested surveillance and a specific knowledge of her plans.

And they'd stopped.

It had been days since she'd gotten one, which might mean Aaron had been alive and leaving them and then something had happened to him. She couldn't exactly ask, since no one knew about the notes. Just her and the person who'd left them.

"There's something else you both need to know, and I'd prefer if you heard it from me." Ginny shifted to serious investigator mode. Some of the haze cleared from her eyes as she stood there, ready to drop the next piece of information that would blow their lives apart.

Lila had run out of tolerance for surprises. "What is it?"

"There was another body on the property."

Tobias's eyes narrowed. "When you say 'body,' you mean—"

"Aaron wasn't alone."

Not possible. Not possible. Not possible. "In the car?"

"Again, we're collecting information and trying to wade through the evidence, but no. The woman was in the cabin and . . ." Ginny didn't try to hide the calming breath she took. "She's dead."

Chapter Forty-five

LILA SAT SLOUCHED DOWN ON HER FAMILY ROOM COUCH WITH her head balanced against the back cushions. She thought about opening a bottle of wine, but in her current mood she might chug it, and she needed to stay rational and in control.

She and Tobias had spent the last few hours babysitting Jared. He moved sluggishly and kept mumbling to himself. They dragged him out of the sheriff's office and back to her house but it took effort. He demanded more answers and wanted to talk to Samantha and know about the cabin. He'd yell one minute then look near collapse the next.

He sat in the oversize chair next to her fireplace and didn't say a word. She and Tobias engaged in mindless chitchat, trying to give Jared time to find a mental equilibrium. He'd wanted to go home, but she didn't want him to be alone. Brent had called. Work people had called. A few others she didn't know had called. All were checking in on him. Cassie had called for her, and she'd said they'd talk later.

This time the call was for Tobias. He listened but didn't say much. She heard him mention Ginny and then saw all the color drain from his face.

He got off the call, and his cell dangled from his lifeless fingers.

"What's going on?" She didn't know how the news could get worse, but it looked like it had.

"They identified the woman in the cabin." Tobias finally seemed to focus. "It's Karen Blue."

GINNY HUNG UP the phone and turned back to the medical examiner. Her case had now run right into the task force's jurisdiction, which meant her time on this might be winding down. Never mind that she had all the intel on Aaron and Lila and everyone they knew in town. The task force was too visible and had support from the FBI, and that trumped her.

That was the only reason she stood in the morgue, running out of patience and wanting to be anywhere else. Despite years of wading into violence and death, this part always unsettled her. People became faceless bodies and a source of information at this point in the process.

Dr. Lori Timmons moved around the room like she owned it. As the medical examiner, she basically did. This was her domain.

As the doctor finished typing in notes, Ginny stood by a tray of personal belongings and picked up a small plastic bag. The thin silver bracelet in it had a charm with the number seventeen engraved on it. "Was Karen wearing this?"

Lori glanced over. "Yes."

"Maybe it was a birthday gift. I'll have to ask her parents about it when they come back." After the initial identification, Karen's parents had been numb and exhausted. Ginny had sent them for coffee and a short break before the rest of the investigative team descended and started asking about Aaron.

"Do we have an official time of death? . . . Unofficial would be fine." She just needed to know when Karen was killed in comparison to when Aaron went missing.

"Well, that's going to take a bit longer." Lori stood between the two tables now, one with Aaron's body on it and the other with Karen's. "The decomposition seemed off, and there wasn't a blood pool for him, which would be consistent with a stabbing death."

"Maybe someone moved the body."

Lori nodded. "Definitely. After they thawed it."

Wait . . . no. "Excuse me?"

The doctor pointed at Aaron's lifeless form. "My working theory is that he was killed then frozen then thawed then stabbed and put in the vehicle. Stabbing is not the cause of death. He was long dead before someone picked up the knife."

This case kept taking odd turns. But Ginny had not seen this one coming. "Thawed . . ."

"It's not going to sound any better if you repeat it." The doctor picked up a file and flipped through a few pages. "I had an accidental drowning case about a year ago, right when I took over the department. The body had been frozen, so I did quite a bit of research on this. To confirm these bodies had been frozen and thawed, I measured the activity of short-chain—"

"Whoa." Ginny held up a hand to stop what sounded like gibberish but was really quite important. "Adding a lot of science talk isn't going to clear this up. Your point is, you know someone killed these two and froze their bodies?"

"Yes." Lori lowered the file. "I collected samples from inside the standing freezer on the cabin's back patio, and they confirmed my theory. Both had been in there. Her under him."

"Any chance you found anything else in the freezer?"

"Sorry, no. No fingerprints or stray hairs or anything." Lori looked at Karen's body. "I'll check her stomach contents to try to backtrack and see if we can match that up and get an approximate time of death for Karen. We don't have clothes, but her body did give us some clues."

"Such as?"

The doctor held up a bag. "She had scrapes all over her torso and arms, and her feet were pretty ripped up. Scabbed over in places and new cuts in others. All of which suggests she ran through the woods naked, probably more than once. These needles support the running recently. They were on the bottom of one of her feet." Before Ginny could ask a question, the doctor took off with more information. "She has ligature marks on her neck that match the rope found in the cabin."

"Are there fibers, DNA—anything that points us toward a killer? The cabin was clean except for one set of prints on the rocking chair." Ginny pointed to Aaron. "His."

"For someone who ran through the woods and got punched and hit with something—maybe a piece of wood, though I'm not sure yet—her body is debris-free. She has broken finger-nails and defensive wounds, so she clearly fought back."

Good for you, Karen. "Did you get anything from those?"

"A speck of human tissue under one nail, which I hope will lead us somewhere. I'll put a rush on it."

"Any sign of sexual assault?"

"I can't rule it out or say it happened, but no bodily fluids."

In any other case, a defense attorney would be all over the lack of blood and DNA evidence, claiming contamination or some other thing that explained the trace levels pointing to Aaron here. That was the least of her worries right now.

"So you're saying the evidence suggests someone—and the only 'someone' evidence might be from Aaron—stripped her, fought her, chased her through the woods, maybe more than once, beat her, strangled her, killed her, froze her, and then at some point thawed her and placed her on the bed, tied up with the same rope he used to kill her."

"It's a lot, I know."

"But is the series of events right?"

Lori shrugged. "Strange, but I can only tell you what the evidence says. I'm working on the timing for you, but I can't promise, and I certainly can't answer the biggest question."

Ginny was impressed the doctor could narrow it down to only one question. "Which is?"

This time Lori sighed. "If Aaron killed her, then who killed him?"

Chapter Forty-six

"YOU WANT ME TO BELIEVE THAT MY BROTHER WENT TO A cabin in the middle of nowhere, where a missing woman happened to be, and he got stabbed while someone killed her." Jared sat up higher in the chair, no longer sprawling and looking half-asleep.

It sounded ridiculous when Jared spelled it out. The connections also stuck out as obvious. "You have the right pieces but maybe not the right order," Lila said.

"Did he walk in on some horrible scene at the wrong time?" The shock never left Jared's voice. "And GPS. If Aaron knew about the place, he wouldn't need that. He had a great memory for directions."

If the cabin had been down the block or next door or a cabin that belonged to someone he knew, maybe. The distance and the way he set off with that destination in mind after Lila tried to kill him suggested something bigger to her. "If he'd never been to the cabin, how would he have known to go there? And why?"

Jared made a strangled noise. "Maybe he thought he was helping Karen."

"Oh, please." The snort escaped her lips before she could stop it.

Both men stared at her, but Jared was the one to voice the confusion. "What?"

The words had come out more dismissive and more flippant than she intended, so she tried to backtrack. Now was not the time for this discussion. She doubted Jared could handle a real talk, heart-to-heart. "Nothing."

But Jared wouldn't let it go. He leaned forward in his chair. "Say it."

Tobias started to stand up. "Maybe we should take a break."

"Say. It." Jared made the demand through clenched teeth.

Tobias sat back down. "This is not the time. Trust me on this."

"Ignore him," Jared said. "Talk."

Fine. If he wanted her theories, a walk through the sordid truth, she'd drag him there. "He was screwing his students, Jared. That type of guy doesn't somehow uncover evidence about a missing woman that every law enforcement agency in the state has been searching for and missed, then without word to anyone run out there to be a hero."

"What exactly are you saying?"

How could he not get this? "Aaron is not a fucking hero. He's the villain in this story."

They'd stepped right into a heated argument. Before this,

they'd never raised their voices to each other. They'd listened and supported. Now they sat on the edges of their respective seats and yelled back and forth, not caring about the fallout that would come later.

"You never told me any of this before."

"How do I start that conversation, Jared? *Your beloved brother is a pedophile, but watch out, because he'll deny it*? I just found out and had my life turned upside down. I didn't know how to tell you."

Tobias reached out and touched her leg. "Lila."

Their sign to rein it in. She ignored it this time.

The explanation—the only one she could see—spilled out of her. "The likely answer is that he knew Karen was in that cabin. That he put her in that cabin. I don't know why he needed the GPS help to get back there, but he went on purpose."

Jared slowly stood up and faced her across the coffee table. "What the hell is wrong with you? He's your husband and you're willing to believe the worst about him."

This was his family. His brother. His gene pool. He'd been hit with so many shocks today, but he had to believe more were coming. "You know I'm not lying about what I saw and heard on those videos. So is it really such a big jump to go from him abusing young girls to killing women?"

"In your family? No," Jared shot back.

Tobias stood up this time. "Hey. That's too much."

The shot rammed right into her. Because that was the point. She'd married the one man she vowed never to get involved with—a man like her father, with his fetishes and weakness.

She tried to drop her voice from a yell. To keep it soothing even as the vicious words snapped and stung. "Knowing what I know and how Aaron lied to me and to all of us about who he really was and what he was capable of, it's not hard for me to imagine he killed Karen Blue. I don't know why he escalated, but no other explanation makes sense."

Jared looked horrified . . . by her. "I get that your upbringing sucked and your dad—"

"Don't switch the subject," Tobias said, breaking into Jared's sentence right as he was warming up for the big hit.

Lila felt it coming. A part of her welcomed it. In a way she'd brought them to this point. She'd forced the issue with Aaron. She'd hunted him. Planned and suffocated him. She'd just failed to finish the job. She had to wonder if Karen Blue would be alive if she'd moved faster. Been more thorough. "No, say it."

"Everyone has been telling me you did something to my brother. I've defended you. Insisted you wouldn't hurt Aaron." He pointed at her across the table. "All I'm asking is that you do the same honor for the man you married."

Her heartbeat thumped so loudly in her ears. She could almost hear the blood whoosh through her. "I can't."

He walked away from her then. Dodged the chair, taking the widest berth around her, and headed for the doorway. He stopped at the last minute and looked at her. "I don't know who or what you are."

A heavy, unseen weight pulled her arms down and pressed against her back. She'd never felt this tired. "That's exactly how I feel about Aaron."

"Keep it to yourself." When she didn't say anything, he continued with his voice growing deeper, more full of fury, with every word. "You hear me. Whatever sick shit is going through your head as you confuse Aaron with your father, do not say it out loud or to the press."

He marched down the hall toward the front door.

"Where are you going?" She had to stop him. He wasn't fit to drive.

The door slammed. Lila felt it vibrate through every inch of her. For the first time since battle lines were drawn, she and Jared stood on opposite sides.

She mourned that loss more than she mourned Aaron.

Chapter Forty-seven

THE NEXT DAY PLAYED OUT LIKE A NIGHTMARE. PEOPLE VISITED and more of the press gathered. Lila insisted to Cassie and Christina, even to Tobias, that she felt fine when she felt anything but. She threw up the coffee she'd used as a replacement breakfast. Counting back, it had been more than a day since she'd eaten anything. She couldn't imagine that would change anytime soon.

Jared ignored her calls. Ginny put her off, saying they were collecting information and forensics and she'd get back in touch.

When Ryan's name showed up on a text on her phone's screen, she answered without thinking. Ginny likely still tracked her calls and texts. Right now, lost in this haze of confusion and frustration, she didn't care.

Ryan: You ok?

Lila: no

Ryan: I heard about Karen Blue and the cabin. Do u think Aaron was involved?

She no longer trusted her instincts or him. This felt like

fishing, maybe for the police to clear his name by throwing her under a bus the size of Texas, or for a more selfish motive.

She spun her phone around in her hand as she mentally searched for the right thing to type. The bar stool at the kitchen counter squeaked under her as she shifted around. Seeing Ryan's name pop up on her phone used to make her smile. The day could be shit, but he'd ask some innocuous question about how she was and a light would flick on inside her.

Seeing his name now made her wary. Careful. Nothing sounded genuine, and that tiny light had extinguished.

Lila: Is this for the book?

Ryan: I care about u

Lila: I don't know.

Ryan: It's possible he knew Karen.

That's not what she meant. After months of being on the same wavelength, they were talking past each other.

Lila: Gotta go

Ryan: Call me. CID still doesn't believe someone planted the phone at my house.

Lila: Did you ever meet him?

Ryan: NO

Even this little bit of conversation was about him. She'd heard the university wanted to suspend him, but he'd brought in a lawyer and fought it. He was taking the rest of the semester off from teaching but would be there, on campus, strutting around as he finished his book. She guessed he'd also be willing to answer questions about her life. His fungible boundaries would likely allow for that.

After Ryan's texts, Cassie came over with a cake and words of encouragement. Still nothing from Jared, but Brent stopped by. She debated whether to let him in.

The first thing he did was hand her a stack of mail. "I thought you would want it before the press looked through it."

She didn't care anymore. The press dug through her life. She'd seen photos of her father plastered on the front page of the news. She'd dropped her birth name to keep people from connecting her to him, but now, thanks to Aaron, everyone would know about her past. Every last detail would get dredged up again.

She walked back to the kitchen, listening to Brent's footsteps as he followed her. "What are you doing here?"

"I owe you an apology."

Guilt and shame didn't matter to her unless he was confessing to letting Aaron get away with his hideous behavior. She walked around, battered and half out of it from lack of sleep. Her mind refused to turn off as it churned through anxiety that had her up and staring out the window, trying to puzzle through what the cabin and the stabbing meant.

She dropped the stack on the counter. "It's fine, Brent."

"I didn't know about the girls at school. I mean, I knew their names when Ginny asked. That's how it works as principal. I know students, but, with most, I didn't have a personal relationship. They weren't close enough for me to know about their private lives, and no one ever contacted me to point out a problem with Aaron." He shifted his weight as he talked to her. Failed to give her eye contact.

She tried not to read anything into his nervousness, but that didn't mean she intended to go easy on him. "You should have known."

He lifted his head and looked at her. "How? None of them complained."

"Okay." But people were yelling now. She knew from the news that parents wanted him fired. An emergency school board meeting had been scheduled to hear complaints and arguments. There was talk of a suspension and an outside investigation. All things she secretly craved, but she couldn't take comfort in a minute of it. Not when everything else— every other piece of Aaron's disappearance and death—was a question mark.

"Do you really think Aaron had something to do with Karen Blue?" he asked.

"He had enough of a connection to have been killed in close proximity to her." Ginny still hadn't filled in those blanks or talked about forensic evidence that connected the two of them. The only thing that was clear was that Karen likely hadn't killed Aaron, dumped him in the back of the SUV, and then gone back into the cabin to die.

Tobias told her that meant the spotlight remained on her. Ginny, the press, and most people in town thought she'd killed Aaron. The Karen Blue piece was still a mystery.

He cleared his throat. "I know I accused you—"

She refused to make it easy on him. "Yes?"

"People are saying . . ." He swallowed hard. "Some think if you did kill him, that was okay."

She wanted him to leave. It took all of her strength to stand there and not shout questions at him. "Why?"

"The girls."

"How many were there at school?"

He went back to staring at her floor. "So far, four."

The number was far too low. She knew with every cell inside her that Aaron had been playing that game for years. There was a line of victims out there. Many probably viewed themselves as former girlfriends and not as his prey, but she knew the truth. From the drawn look on Brent's face, he knew, too.

"My wife—"

"Ex."

"Right. Ex." He stumbled through his words. "She won't let me see our kids until I prove I wasn't involved with Aaron."

She was lucky to live in another state, but clearly the gossip had reached her. Lila hoped she did what she needed to do to protect those kids. "Smart."

"Come on. You can't believe that. I wasn't." He coughed. "Involved, I mean."

That counted as the least convincing denial she'd ever heard. But it didn't mean he was lying. More like his life had been flipped upside down. He'd gone from Aaron's fiercest advocate in the search to a significant target.

She didn't care.

"And I didn't kill him." When she said it now she believed it was the truth. She had no problem selling it.

"I should go."

"Yeah." She didn't beg him to stay. What few niceties she

used to manage with him since the whole case had unfolded were gone. It was a struggle not to shove him and shout at him. She still wasn't convinced he was innocent of anything.

Ten minutes after he left, she dragged her body back into the kitchen to make coffee. As the water warmed, her gaze fell on the stack of mail. She'd turned the bills and financial stuff to email delivery right before Aaron went missing. Her mail usually consisted of magazines she forgot to read and mailers she didn't want. A few days ago, she also received a death threat. She guessed that investigation was sitting on the corner of Ginny's desk, inactive.

She pushed the pieces around. A few letters that likely included more theories and hate. No thanks.

She was just about to turn away when she spied it. The familiar white unlined card. It rested white side up in the middle of the stack. She turned it over and threw it on the counter. Let it lie there.

I FIXED YOUR MESS. YOU'RE WELCOME.

She silently repeated the words in her head. None of the notes had been from Aaron. They'd been from his killer. The person knew what she'd done and wasn't finished with her.

Chapter Forty-eight

This is Nia Simms and Gone Missing, the true crime podcast that discusses cases—big and small—in your neighborhood and around the country. This week we're talking about Aaron Payne. Isn't everyone talking about Aaron Payne? He led this pristine life as a teacher. Devoted coach. The guy around town who would do anything for anyone.

Little did we know.

As more and more female students, current and former, come forward, we have a new picture of Aaron Payne. As a predator. As a pedophile. As a sick, twisted man who fooled everyone. His body being found with Karen Blue's only adds more questions to the growing stack.

The task force has switched its focus and police in several jurisdictions across New York State are looking into Aaron's activities and his past. Any information you have about that cabin or Aaron, call in and we'll talk about it. Law enforcement is listening, and, don't forget, we all want to bring Yara and Julie home.

In addition to talking about Aaron, I want to talk about another woman. Lila Ridgefield, Aaron's wife. People have very different views of her. Beautiful and dangerous. Mysterious and aloof. Introverted and misunderstood. Wealthy . . . but from where?

A lot of listeners saw her as a heartless killer, but now what we know about Aaron shines a different light on Lila. Was she one more victim? Try to imagine what she faced at home with a man who believed in violence and had no boundaries.

And that brings me to my point for the day . . . someone killed Aaron. I can't say I'm sorry about that, though I wish it had happened soon enough to save Karen. What if we were right all along and Lila did kill her husband? Makes sense, right? She lived in that house.

So, let's say Lila did kill him. She figured out she was married to a monster—one just like the monstrous father she escaped years before—and then she decided to do something about him. Not let him run or hide. Not give those students the burden of having to face their abuser in court and testify against him.

If Lila broke out and went rogue, if she became a vigilante, determined to do what law enforcement had failed to do, and stop her vicious husband . . . would that be so bad? Is Lila Ridgefield a killer or a vigilante hero, or maybe both? And when you answer, think about whether Lila's decision to kill Aaron makes you feel safer. About what your opinion might be if one of your kids or friends or loved ones was one of Aaron's victims.

Chapter Forty-nine

THE CROWDS OUTSIDE LILA'S HOUSE MORPHED FROM AN AN-
gry mob to a cheering squad virtually overnight. The reporters remained, and their ranks swelled. No one jeered or
lobbed threats at her from the safety of the street. Banners
and signs sprang up. One called her a hero. Another said, WE
BELIEVE IN YOU, and the newest thanked her for doing the
justice system's job.

She hated all of it.

When the doorbell rang, she only answered because Christina texted first to say she'd just pulled in the driveway and
needed to come in. Lila cracked the door wide enough to hear
a cheer and people calling her name. She ushered Christina
inside and slammed and locked the door behind her, blocking out the sounds that disturbed her silence.

"Wow." Christina's eyes went wide as she repeated the word
two more times. "It's wild out there."

"I think the word you're looking for is 'nightmare.'" Lila
rested her back against the door, determined to physically
and emotionally put a barrier between *them* and her.

"It's a good sign for you. People no longer believe you're evil."

Lila groaned instead of answering. She gestured for Christina to head into the family room.

"I guess all of this means you're even less likely to come back to work."

"I'm afraid so." The idea of burying herself in paperwork and negotiating deals sounded like a dream. But no, she wasn't ready to drag her butt around town, pretending to be okay. She'd never been the type to live a happy, carefree life, but she'd managed to eke it out and be fine. Solid and workable. She had things she liked to do and a job that kept her just busy enough.

Aaron's secret life blew a hole through what little balance she'd attained and rattled her security. She'd done and thought things over the last weeks she'd never believed would have been possible. He'd burned through the last of her humanity, leaving her hollow and empty. A shell of a person, without drive and with no clear vision on how to move forward.

"I refuse to feel sorry for him. I'm talking like a thinking, breathing real person. A mom with two girls under sixteen who now doesn't have to worry about her kids being preyed on at school."

"You do, and you will. Aaron being dead doesn't eradicate all evil in New York." If only, then maybe she could function again.

Christina snorted. "It helps me sleep better at night. That's the point."

"Tell Ginny that," Lila said.

"I did even better. I wrote the prosecutor and my congressman."

Lila froze. "You didn't."

She waited for Christina to laugh her comment off as a joke . . . but she didn't. Lila's amusement faded. Stunned respect took its place.

"Of course I did." Christina's bracelets jangled as she moved her hand around in the air. "Screw the people in charge who prioritize the rights of the pedophile over the rights of the kids to be secure and alive."

Lila rubbed her forehead, trying to fight off a building headache. "I've spent close to two months trying to wrap my head around the man he really was."

"Months?"

Lila closed her eyes at the slip. When she opened them again, she smiled. "I meant weeks."

"Did you?"

All those feelings welling inside her, the same ones she tried to tamp down—anger and frustration, disappointment and surprise, the lack of regret when she turned on that gas and watched Aaron drift off forever, how she felt nothing when his body was found but surprise that someone stabbed him—bubbled up and poured over. She tried not to think about the twisting and turning inside her or talk about it because she couldn't. But for that one moment, she let the words slip out.

"I thought I'd feel relieved," she whispered into the quiet room.

"He ripped your life apart." Christina sighed. "Blame him, not you."

Christina always knew the right thing to say.

Lila never put much stock in friendship, even female ones. The one thing she'd learned over the last few weeks was that she'd been wrong not to take the lifeline when some women reached out over the years. Some people did deserve her trust.

Chapter Fifty

ROLAND WANDERED INTO GINNY'S OFFICE JUST BEFORE EIGHT with Chinese food. The smell had her head snapping up and her stomach growling.

He didn't lecture her about her work hours or cause a fuss. He sat down across from her and started unloading the white containers.

"You retain your title as best husband in the world."

"Of course I do." He handed her a set of chopsticks. "And this is the part where I remind you that you—your work—is responsible for finding Karen and returning her to her parents. You did an amazing thing and have earned a night of rest. Everything else, all the other details, can wait."

He knew what ate at her, the failures that poked and tore at her. He always knew. "Finding her now, after all this time, doesn't feel as great as you think. It's little consolation to her family."

"Ginny, that's not true. You brought her home. You gave them closure."

She tried to open the carton, but her fingers tapped against the cardboard, not getting the leverage she needed to get the job done. "I was too late. We spun around in circles, looking for Aaron, thinking he was a victim, and—"

"You said the initial report is that Karen was killed before Aaron." He took the carton of chicken and broccoli from her and opened it before sitting it in front of her. "That means you couldn't have saved her if you were faster or smarter, neither of which you could have been. You worked this case hard from the beginning."

She dug around the broccoli with her chopsticks. "I doubt Charles will see it that way."

"He has a severe case of political nearsightedness. That's not new."

He was talking about the case a few years back. Another killer. One she'd figured out, but Charles and the man who held her job before her didn't listen to her theories. Her suspect was a wealthy businessman who gave money in elections. She got shouted down and, instead of rallying, played the good soldier and took the back seat, and a young wife died. Finding Karen's body brought all of those failure feelings rushing back.

Ginny glanced out at the main room outside of her glassed-in office and lowered her voice. "He's worked more hours making sure our office got credit for finding Karen than I've seen him work on any case ever."

"There's a reason he hired you. You're the one who gets in the muck and works." He winked at her. "Ah, there it is. Your first smile in days."

"Now I need to figure out who killed the killer." But a part of her knew. She'd sensed the truth since the first time she met Lila.

Circumstance put them on opposite sides in this case, but she'd been fascinated with Lila's façade from the beginning. Her indifference and total inability to fake caring about her husband's fate, even though that turned up the spotlight on her, caught Ginny by surprise. She didn't see Lila as vicious or psychotic. She saw a smart woman who'd been treading water her entire life and no one had bothered to throw her a life preserver.

"You will make sense of the case," Roland said then stopped when he saw the look on her face. "What's with the shrug?"

"Lila was involved. She either did it or acted with someone else—the boyfriend, maybe."

"So you dedicate time to tracking her and proving that—" Roland's voice cut off. "Another shrug."

Ginny knew because she'd given the spiel to countless members of law enforcement and her boss over the last twenty-four hours. "There's no forensic evidence that puts Lila or Ryan in that cabin. We should have found Lila's DNA in Aaron's car since they are married, but someone wiped it clean. Not even a stray hair."

"Maybe Aaron had a partner who turned on him."

The possibility kept kicking around in her head. It was one that let Lila off the hook, made her irrelevant in Aaron's disappearance, so every time Ginny went there her brain rebelled. "Possible. I'm looking into his brother and his best friend, the principal who never noticed Aaron was messing with students."

Roland rolled his eyes. He'd made his feelings about Brent not knowing known at home. To her husband, that omission made Brent partially responsible for what happened to the students. "Whatever the answer, you'll ferret it out."

They fell into a comfortable silence. The kind that comes with years of marriage and knowing every tick and bug the other person has.

After a few minutes of shifting food around in the container but not eating it, she put it down and looked at him. "What if there is a piece of me that doesn't feel the driving need to follow this case where I think it will go?"

"Interesting." He didn't pretend not to understand. He got that this case had her conflicted and questioning what she believed.

"I mean, I do intend to solve it, but . . ." A strangling sound crept up her throat. "I don't get to make the judgment calls. There's evidence or not, and I go by that, wherever it takes me."

One of his eyebrows lifted. "But?"

"If Lila did it, I sort of get it. Her father did this unspeakable thing, then to have her husband . . ." She shook her head. "Forget it."

She tried not to let her mind go there. How hard Lila's life was as a kid and what happened to her back then shouldn't change the direction of the evidence. But the background picked at Ginny. Some of the things Lila said about her mother and her thoughts on marriage. The eloquent way she spoke but how the picture she drew didn't always fit reality. It was as if she'd been broken as a teen and never healed, and something inside Ginny rose up, wanting to get her help.

He moved the containers in front of him to the side and leaned in a little closer, as if he were sharing a big secret. "If it's true you think she did it and can't prove it, then I guess the question is whether you can live with that ending."

That's the one scenario that kept playing and replaying in her head.

He smiled at her. "And I think you just answered that."

That's what scared her.

Chapter Fifty-one

THE WORLD DIDN'T LOOK ANY CLEARER TO GINNY THE NEXT morning. She'd spent a sleepless night mentally running through the evidence, trying to find the hole she'd missed. More importantly, making sure she didn't drop an obvious lead because it didn't fit with what she thought should happen to Lila in the end.

She had a lot of time to think because she'd been called back out to the cabin in the middle of nowhere. Driving there meant stopping for coffee. She'd need the caffeine to get through the ongoing search. The search Charles had told her she needed to attend because heaven forbid her face and their office not be all over the news one night this week.

Pete rolled in at his usual time, acting like this was a normal day. He wasn't the guy who voluntarily put in extra time. He always would if she asked, but she had to ask.

He joined her on the drive, running through various theories until she started humming to shut him out of her head. Hours later they arrived and now he leaned against the front of her car. "After this, shouldn't we bring Lila in again for questioning?"

She eyed him while she sipped on the last of her now-cold coffee. "What do you plan to ask her?"

His expression went blank. "I don't understand."

"You want to ask her if she killed her husband. We've asked that already." She'd tried it head-on and going at it from an angle. She done it with Lila alone, before Tobias arrived, then again with him there. Pete had witnessed most of it and knew how futile it had been.

"Yeah, but things have changed." He glanced around at the cars and people carefully walking the wooded property and taking in every detail.

"Not for her. If she killed her husband, she still goes to jail. The stakes are as high as ever."

His expression morphed into a frown. "You saw the news. Public opinion has changed. Hell, that podcast is pushing the theory of Lila as vigilante hero. Karen Blue's father came out and offered to testify on Lila's behalf if the prosecutor was *dumb enough* to charge her. The office is getting calls making us out to be the bad guys for going after her."

"And all of that suggests to you that we should press her harder?" They would keep at it, but his unrealistic comments had her mentally sighing. The naïve belief that politics and public opinion didn't play a role in prosecutions would be burned out of him over time. She'd learned that early. He still hadn't.

A member of the forensic team stuck her head out of the open front door and looked at Ginny. "We found something."

Their focus immediately switched to the lure of potential new evidence. They stepped into the small bedroom. The bed had been shoved aside, and the boards underneath it had been removed to expose an open space. A metal box about half the size of a shoebox balanced on the edge of the opening.

"Should we wait for—"

"No." She wasn't in the mood for Pete and his suggestions right now. "Open it."

The forensic analyst who alerted them opened the box. For a second all Ginny could see was her blue gloves as her fingers worked on the small hook before she peeked inside. A necklace. A hair tie. Socks. A bracelet. Other personal items that generally belonged to women.

Pete squatted down next to Ginny. "What is it?"

She'd seen this before when she'd worked on one of her first cases. A nurse who liked to "help" his older patients into the afterlife. So she knew. "Possibly trophies from his kills."

"I don't know much about jewelry but is that from three women?" Pete asked.

"It doesn't look like just one." A heaviness grew in Ginny's chest. "Which means there probably are more bodies out here."

Chapter Fifty-two

LILA WASN'T IN THE MOOD FOR MORE COMPANY. SHE AND TO-bias sat on opposite ends of the couch, not speaking. When the doorbell rang, Lila ignored it. When it rang a second time, Tobias grumbled and stood up.

"I'm not expecting anyone." She thought that was good enough reason not to move.

"You're a murder suspect. I'd rather not have SWAT knock a hole through your wall." Tobias delivered the dramatic reasoning to match his dramatic sigh as he headed for the door.

Lila recognized the other voice. She didn't run to welcome the unwanted visitor because a visit from Ginny was never good news.

"More questions?" Lila asked as soon as Ginny came into the room.

Ginny glanced back toward the now-closed front door. "You have quite a crowd of admirers out there."

"Someone likes me."

Tobias glared at Lila over Ginny's head. "Where are we in the investigation?"

Lila noticed a few things at once. The envelope in Ginny's hand and the way she dropped into the chair across from the couch, as if the muscles in her legs gave out. The exhaustion pulling around her eyes and her very serious expression.

None of that looked good.

"The forensic team took a long look at the cabin and surrounding area," Ginny said, launching into her talk without any of the usual banter or back-and-forth she did with Lila when they talked.

"Okay." Tobias nodded. "And?"

"Yara James wore a thin gold chain with a butterfly ornament on it. It was a gift from her godmother. It went missing when Yara did."

A sloshing started in Lila's stomach. A sort of rolling that built to a bucking. "You found it."

Ginny didn't acknowledge the comment as she looked back and forth between Lila and Tobias. "Julie Levin had this little plate with her name and a phone number on it. It fit on the laces of her hiking boots. Friends and family said she wore it as a precaution because she often went on long hikes by herself. She had it in case she got hurt or lost. She thought the tag would help anyone who found her."

Their jewelry. Their belongings.

"Oh God." Lila didn't recognize her own voice, but she knew she'd said the words.

Her muscles grew heavy as reality hit and her body collapsed. The news shouldn't have been a surprise. Once they found Karen's body, some form of *this* was inevitable, but her mind sputtered and shock shook through her. She felt flu-like and achy, barely able to sit there as the truth spilled out.

"Both of those items were found in the cabin. Those weren't the only items." Ginny stopped to clear her throat. "The FBI is tracking the other pieces to see if they match up with any missing persons cases."

More jewelry. Other women.

All those fishing and hunting trips when she welcomed the peace that came with having Aaron out of the house. He'd really been out there . . . doing what? Scouting women. Hurting them. Dragging them away to that cabin.

"I think I'm going to be sick." Lila doubled over in her chair with her hand over her mouth.

"I have photos of the contents of the box and was hoping you could look—"

"Maybe not now." Tobias slid closer to Lila, with his hand rubbing up and down her back.

She didn't want to be touched or comforted. She pulled away, trapping her body against the armrest as she struggled to breathe.

"No, it's okay." She had to force every image from her mind. Tangled and mashed bodies. Aaron's smirk. "Let me see the pictures."

Ginny hesitated for a few seconds before opening the envelope and dropping photos on the table. Each one showed a piece of jewelry or a personal item Lila had never seen. Nothing looked expensive. Just ordinary items that belonged to women who never expected *that* day to be their last day.

She'd hated Aaron for so many weeks. As she paged through the photos, only one thought ran through her head: *I didn't kill him soon enough.*

She separated out one and slid the others across the table to Ginny. "None of these."

Ginny's gaze hadn't wavered since she'd delivered her devastating news. She pointed at the one photo Lila separated out. "Is that familiar?"

Lila picked it up to get a closer look. A bracelet. Nothing fancy. A simple silver bracelet with an "A" charm on it and some scrapings on the back. "It's the letter. Aaron's mother's name was Anna."

"What are you saying?" Tobias asked as he looked at her.

Something. Nothing, really. It had to be a coincidence . . . but the moment she thought that, old doubts pricked at her. "I've never seen the bracelet, and the name is common, but . . ."

Ginny continued to watch her. "She was killed by a hunter."

"Yes. That's the story." Aaron and Jared told it. They'd profited from it by getting the trust.

Color returned to Ginny's face. She looked more invested, more animated than when she'd first walked in. "You're not sure the hunting story is true."

"I don't know what to believe. Aaron didn't seem capable of . . ." She swept her arm over the table. "Well, any of this, when we got married."

Was it that much of a reach to think he'd killed before they'd moved there? Back in North Carolina or when he was growing up?

"The FBI is bringing in ground-penetrating radar and other resources to survey the land around the cabin for additional bodies." Ginny gathered the photos and put them back in the envelope.

One question hit Lila and wouldn't retreat. "Did you figure out who owns the property?"

"Aaron."

An off-pitch humming started in Lila's ears. She inhaled a few times to make sure she wasn't screaming out loud. "How is that possible?"

"It looks like he bought it under a corporate name years ago. Used trust money to do it."

Tobias sat forward, right on the edge of the couch. "How did Jared not know that?"

"I intend to ask that question." Ginny's gaze switched from Tobias to Lila. "But I do wonder how you, as his wife, didn't."

"I had no idea. I have nothing to do with that trust." That was the truth. The money wasn't hers and never would be. Aaron had repeated that tidbit so many times during her marriage that she heard his mocking tone in her sleep.

"You have to admit that excuse sounds convenient."

Ginny was a smart woman, but this part she'd gotten dead wrong. "Honestly? Nothing about being married to Aaron Payne was convenient."

GINNY STAYED FOR another fifteen minutes. She walked through more questions and doubled back to some old favorites. Lila struggled to concentrate through all of it.

When Ginny finally left, Lila headed for the bathroom down the hall. She shut the door with a bang and turned on the faucet. For a few minutes, she stood there watching the water twirl toward the drain.

She bent over, intending to splash water on her face and revive her body before she broke down. She got as far as resting her elbows on the sink. Her head fell forward; the cold water trickled down the side of her hair and dripped onto her arm.

She felt nothing. Her mind protected her by going blissfully blank. She doubted she could conjure up a rational thought if she had to.

Aaron . . .

Her knees buckled, and her body slowly sank. Her butt hit the tile, and she turned around to lean her back against the cabinet. She could hear the running water but didn't have the energy to turn it off.

The buzzing started in her pocket. Her phone. More news or some reassurance from Christina. Either way, Lila ignored it. So few people knew her private cell number but she didn't want to speak with any of them. Not right now.

She'd married a twisted man. Slept with him. Vowed to stay with him. She'd missed every sign and skipped every opportunity to stop him.

This was Amelia all over again. Some piece of her missed seeing the worst in men.

Unable to keep her eyes open, she tipped her head back and rested it against the cabinet. Desperate to drift off to sleep but unable to because of the self-loathing running rampant through her, she just sat there. The cool tile numbed her, and the need to throw up passed, but she wasn't sure how she'd get up without help. All of her reserves were used up and dried out.

Her phone buzzed again, reminding her of the unread text. She reached for her cell and opened her eyes just long enough to read the screen.

We need to talk.

She was wide-awake now.

Chapter Fifty-three

GINNY STARED AT JARED ACROSS THE INTERROGATION ROOM table. He sat by himself, insisting he didn't need a lawyer. He had motive—the trust. He might have money, but they were talking about millions more as Aaron's heir. Ginny also suspected his feelings for Lila weren't quite as brotherly as he pretended. His rush to defend her seemed ingrained.

As they sat there, Pete and Charles watched from the other side of the two-way mirror. That added a level of pressure that only made her more determined. Jared had always been rock solid, said and did the right thing. She wanted to test him now.

"Your brother slept with students. The evidence suggests he hunted and killed Karen Blue. We now know the DNA under her fingernails is his. There's also evidence of other victims." When he opened his mouth to say something, she talked right over him. "You really expect me to believe all of this is news to you?"

"He's not . . ." Jared exhaled as he dropped his arms on the table and leaned on them.

"What, Jared?" He could deny, but the facts of Aaron's culpability were difficult to challenge. Witnesses to the school victims. Personal testimony by one of those victims. DNA and a deed that tied him to Karen's murder.

Jared slowly raised his head. "Other victims?"

"We found personal items and jewelry he likely took from other victims." She slipped the envelope with the photos out from the bottom of her file but didn't open it yet. She wanted his full attention. There weren't any fingerprints on any of the items and someone killed Aaron, so she needed more.

He blew out a long breath. Looked like he was fighting to keep from falling over. "I can't believe this."

The shock playing on his face reminded her of Lila. She went pale at the sight of the photos. The more Ginny had talked about bracelets and victims, the more hunted Lila had looked.

"The two of you were very close. You went hunting and hiking on weekends." The prime times for Aaron to stalk his victims. "You can see why it's hard for me to believe you didn't have at least a hint about what he was doing in his free time."

"Never," he shot back.

"He didn't talk about the girls at school?"

"No."

"A stray comment about going away for a few days." It was a small opening, and she hoped he'd take it.

He slapped his palm against the table with a whack. "That's not who he was."

The raised voice amounted to more emotion than he'd shown since Aaron went missing. She dug in a little more. "It is, Jared. We have the evidence. He owned the cabin."

He scoffed. "He's being set up."

"By who?"

"The person who killed him."

That piece stumped her every time. She wished Karen had taken Aaron out, gotten her revenge before she died, but the tests suggested otherwise. Karen died first, days before Aaron. They were still waiting on Aaron's cause of death.

"Tell me who, Jared. You're the one who insisted most people liked him." She pretended to flip through her notes. "Who would set him up?"

"That Ryan guy had his phone. He was sleeping with Lila. That sure as hell sounds like motive." Jared moved his hands around in the air. "Wasn't he some sort of killer expert?"

"He claims someone planted the phone at his house and he's never seen it before." His prints weren't on it, and Aaron's were. Ginny knew a criminal defense attorney would jump all over that evidentiary loophole.

"Of course." Jared's voice got louder. "Because he wouldn't lie about framing someone."

"There's an easier solution."

"Nothing about this is easy."

He sounded so much like Lila. That fact hit Ginny again and again while he talked.

"Let's say Aaron had an accomplice. Someone who helped him hunt and kill those women." This option made sense to her, except that she couldn't figure out a way to believe in Lila's absolution in all of this, and she didn't see Lila as a serial killer accomplice, so . . . . "Maybe someone who got tired of Aaron's antics and killed him. Someone who financially benefitted from his death."

Jared dropped back in his seat. "You're looking at me for this?"

He acted as if the idea had never crossed his mind. She couldn't decide if this was a case of rabid denial or something else. "You are the most likely candidate."

"Because we're blood related?"

Because no one else made sense. As far as the accomplice theory went, the two she could see were Brent and Jared. No one else got close enough or spent enough time with Aaron to make it work, but both of those men did.

She opened the envelope and pulled out the photograph that had given Lila pause. "Have you ever seen this bracelet?"

"No."

"You're sure?"

He gave the photograph another glance before shaking his head.

She tapped on the corner of the photo. "Take a longer look."

"I don't need to." But he did pick it up and study it, then threw it down again. "You clearly think I should see something."

"You mother's name was Anna." She tapped the edge of the photo. "'A' as in Anna."

His eyes narrowed. "That's a leap. How many words start with that letter?"

He wasn't wrong, but the possibility was too important to drop without at least poking around a bit. "Is it her bracelet?"

The theory carried horrific connotations, but she had to ask. Even the FBI agents had looked stumped when she'd told them the old story and shown them the photo of the bracelet. The idea that Aaron could have been killing that long, leaving bodies in his wake, shook them all.

"She's been dead for decades."

"But do you remember if she wore jewelry?" To be fair, she didn't know if her son could identify her jewelry, but then he wasn't a killer who collected trophies.

"What does all of this have to do with Aaron?"

"The bracelet was in with what we think are the souvenirs from Aaron's other kills."

"My mom was shot by a hunter, not hunted down by a killer in training who happened to be her son." Jared glanced at the mirror before looking back at her again. "You can look it up. It was all over the news back then. She was hanging the wash out on the line. It was set off from the house in a spot that got more direct sun, and this group mistook her for a buck they were tracking."

"And you and Aaron have the trust fund as a result of the accidental shooting."

Some of the shock faded from Jared's expression. "I'm going to ignore how you phrased that." His voice took on an angry edge. "Look, I was out of town when Aaron went missing."

"I'm aware of your alibi. That conference was an hour and a half away. Plenty of time to go back and forth and not miss a session." They'd checked traffic cameras for his car, but he could have used a rental they hadn't found, or borrowed a car.

"You're reaching, don't you think?" He shook his head. "Ask me about the date this woman went missing."

"You gave us your calendar going back two years." A fact that always intrigued her. Most people didn't give *more* information than was requested. "You were at a conference then, too."

He threw his hands up in the air. "Okay, well. That's your answer."

"Is it?"

"I don't get what you want from me here. A confession?" His emotions seemed to bounce as he moved around in his chair. He shifted from shocked to pissed off. "Are you asking Lila these questions?"

Now, that was interesting. He'd always come off as her strongest ally . . . until right then. "You think she killed your brother and then came up with an elaborate plan to frame him for the murder of a woman he didn't know?"

"I know she was having an affair with a serial killer expert. That is a fact and the rest of what you're asking is based on wild assumptions."

He sounded fully in control now, acting like she'd expect from a suspect. Shifting blame off of him to others he viewed as less likely to have alibis. "And?"

"She's the only person I know who hated Aaron."

There was nothing supportive or brotherly in his tone now. "Hated?"

"Did that strike you as a happy marriage?" He'd calmed down, and his voice stayed steady.

"Most people don't kill to get out of a marriage."

He nodded. "But some do."

THE INTERROGATION WENT on for another half hour before Ginny gave up for the day. She walked out of the room and into the adjoining one, where Charles stood. Pete had left to escort Jared out of the building.

Before she could say anything, Charles handed her a file. "The FBI found Yara James's body an hour ago. It was buried about twenty feet from the cabin, deep in a thicket."

"They know it's hers?" She opened the cover and saw the photos. Lights set up to spotlight the ground. Mud and earth dug up to reveal bones wrapped in a disintegrating cloth of some sort.

"Dr. Timmons has the medical records. Yara had knee surgery and an arm broken in two places from a skiing accident when she was younger. The doc said the injuries match the ones on the body. She's working on time of death."

"Was that body frozen, too?"

"I don't know. The official verification will come later."

She closed the file and said a little prayer for the unfathomable loss for Yara's family. "I fear Julie is not the only other victim out there."

"Probably, but we don't get much of a say anymore. The task

force is taking over. You can sit on it, prep them, but we both know we won't be lead."

"What?"

Charles plucked the file out of her hands. "We're dealing with multiple murders here, probably a serial killer case. The FBI is all over this."

"I get that, but someone still killed Aaron, and the evidence tying him to these women is not significant."

"So far, but Doc Timmons might find more on the new body."

"Yara James's body."

"No one cares about Aaron's death right now. They're more focused on his victims." He said it out loud. Didn't even try to hide it.

She couldn't understand the pressures he shouldered, but he did have a job to do, and he was ignoring it. "We should care."

He closed the door, shutting them inside the small space and outside of easy hearing range of anyone walking by. "The prosecutor is not going to crack down on the woman who everyone credits with stopping Aaron. Not without evidence that she's involved in the other killings."

"She didn't stop him—or maybe she did. We don't know who killed him." When Charles stared at her, Ginny tried again. "But if she did kill her husband, she just gets away with it?"

A part of her had assumed Lila would walk away. She'd tried to convince herself she'd be okay with that, and she still thought that was true. That didn't mean she'd sit back and watch it happen. She had a job, and she'd do it until the end. If Lila emerged as the victor, Ginny vowed she'd move on, because she refused to let the death of Aaron Payne become her life's obsession. But she'd exhaust every lead first.

He shrugged. "It's not a terrible solution. The important thing is we've found two of the missing women and have every reason to believe we'll find the third."

"Abandoning Aaron's murder now, before it's finished, sends a message to every victim and every perpetrator." She tried to imagine the county, filled with people already on edge, taking the law into their own hands. "We can't condone vigilante justice."

He winced. "Don't be dramatic."

"Excuse me?"

"And don't raise your voice to me." He didn't blink as he spoke. "We both know I gave you a chance here. Don't test me."

Fury raced through her, heating every inch and every cell. Denials and arguments shot up her throat, but she choked them back. She loved this job, which meant suffocating on all the things she wanted to say but couldn't.

She swallowed a few times before speaking again. She refused to be accused of yelling or listen to the whispers about her being an angry black woman. She would not give him or anyone the ammunition to get rid of her. The idea of him and Pete being in charge chilled her from the inside out. "We don't know if Aaron was set up, which I doubt, but he very well could have had an accomplice, and we haven't explored that yet. We're talking about a second killer."

"The official line will be that there is insufficient evidence to prove Lila Ridgefield killed her husband but, while we don't condone vigilante justice, the important thing is that a serial predator and active serial killer has been stopped and the victims' families can now find peace."

Political doublespeak. People were dead and he was feeding her a PR line. "Charles—"

"We'll be turning the evidence over to the task force tomorrow. The FBI will report directly to the governor's office from here on out." He held the file to his chest. "Everyone is happy with our contribution, and we're going to keep it that way."

"But the official line about Lila is their line, not ours." She tried for a direct hit to his ego. "You're in charge here, not them."

He sighed. "Go home to your husband, Ginny. You've earned a night off."

He fell back on his usual condescending attitude, which ratcheted up her anger. "Talking to me like that is bullshit, and you know it."

"For the sake of your job, I'm going to ignore that."

Chapter Fifty-four

THE DINER IN DRYDEN, ABOUT FIFTEEN MILES AWAY FROM Ithaca, sounded like the perfect meeting spot. It's not as if Lila could go anywhere in the area, the state, or most of the U.S. right now without being noticed. Aaron's face was all over the news. The serial killer high school teacher who liked to fondle his students. He'd gone from a missing person—*the poor man was killed by his cheating wife*—to the face of evil.

She'd become notorious. The woman who'd taken down her killer husband but refused to accept credit. Some saw her as a wounded victim who'd finally lashed out. Others saw her as a kick-ass vigilante heroine. Neither description was a comfortable fit.

In all the scenarios she'd run through in her head about Aaron being found, none had ended like this. She'd wanted him to pay. She'd hoped the car setup would point to suicide and she could blend into the background and fade way. None of that appeared possible now. This unwanted meeting proved that.

She dropped into the wooden chair with the deep red faux-leather seat and looked across the table at the person who'd requested they talk. "Samantha."

"Happy you found the place." Samantha played with a stack of sugar packets. Her chipped blue nail polish stood out against the pink paper.

In the videos, she'd worn heavy makeup and a tiny lace see-through bra. She came off as young and desperate to look older. Today, with her hair pulled back in a ponytail and a sweatshirt proclaiming the name of her college, she looked like what she was—a student. Pretty but able to easily slip into a crowd and hide among the other freshmen. Nothing so striking or so different about her that people would do a double take, except that her photo had been all over the news along with Aaron's.

She didn't resemble the brunette, more petite Karen Blue in any way. It was almost as if Aaron had a type he slept with and a type he killed.

More than a few people in the diner stared. So much for subtlety. Lila debated staring back, making them as uncomfortable as their gawking made her, but just then the waitress stepped up to the end of the table. The woman, about fifty with a pen tucked behind her ear and another in her hand, didn't even glance up from her notepad as she asked about their order.

"Just coffee," Lila said.

Samantha nodded. "Same."

Lila watched the woman walk away. She nodded at a few patrons before slipping through a door that Lila guessed led to the kitchen.

The dining room staring contest continued, though a bit more subdued now. One couple pretended to be taking a selfie, but Lila could tell the camera was aimed at her.

Her gaze returned to Samantha and the way she balanced the sugar packets, as if building a house. She'd called and asked for the meeting. Lila didn't see a reasonable way to say no, but she wished she had. "This is dangerous."

"Anyone watching will see a survivor meeting with the woman who helped save her." Samantha finally looked up. Her cold brown eyes flashed with anger. "It could be a heart-warming headline on that ridiculous podcast."

At least they agreed on that one thing, or mostly.

"The same podcast where you called in to cast doubt on Aaron being a decent person." Lila remembered hearing the familiar voice and freezing. So much rode on Samantha's behavior.

"You're the one who insists he wasn't."

And she was right, but the idea of having her freedom, her credibility, dependent on the romantic whims of a college student scared the crap out of Lila.

"Besides, a public meeting is better because it doesn't look like we're trying to hide anything. It's easily explained away that I wanted to meet the other woman at the center of this mess."

"It's interesting you view me, the wife, as the other woman."

Samantha waved her hand in front of her, knocking down the packet tower. "Cut the shit. We had a deal."

"Keep in character. No anger or people will talk." The last thing Lila needed was to have someone decide she was beating up on poor Samantha, and public opinion would swing against her once again.

Samantha leaned forward and tapped her fingernails on the table. "Are you worried someone will think you're not actually a vigilante hero?"

Click. Click. The tapping sound grated against Lila's nerves. She only had so much bandwidth and very little tolerance left. "You got what you wanted, Samantha."

"No, I didn't." Samantha practically shouted the phrase. When people at the tables near them looked at her, she dropped her voice to a whisper. "You promised me the spotlight. That I'd be the hero and get my revenge on your shitty husband. But you went too far and now you're the star. Everyone wants to interview *you*. Talk to *you*. Poor little you."

The snide comeback didn't ease Lila's anxiety.

Samantha had been a wild card from the beginning. A risk Lila almost didn't take. When she approached Samantha that day at her college weeks ago, she'd tried to make amends for Aaron targeting her. Samantha insisted he'd loved her . . . It was pure nonsense, but convincing a vulnerable eighteen-year-old who didn't even realize how vulnerable she'd been was not an easy task.

That led to the next phase. Samantha made it clear she wanted revenge, but she didn't have the videos. Lila had an answer for that. Her videos. Her testimony. Her teaming up with Samantha to bring Aaron down. Then she'd slink away and let Samantha take all the glory.

Little did Samantha know that Lila said she had one plan—ruin Aaron—when the plan really was to kill him. Ruin him, giving him no opportunity to launch a defense.

Aaron, being the piece of garbage he was, had made Samantha feel loved and special. He built up her confidence, convinced her she needed him, had sex with her, then found someone new.

Lila now understood that was his go-to play with the students. Separate them from their family and friends, lavish praise, offer them grades they didn't earn, conquer, then run away. It was a sick spin on enjoying the chase and getting bored as soon as he got what he wanted.

Samantha had said she thought others didn't turn Aaron in because they got what they needed—entrance into schools they didn't quite qualify for. Glowing recommendations and raised grade point averages. But Samantha was different. She'd thought she and Aaron had something real, and she didn't appreciate being dumped.

Lila capitalized on those hurt feelings. She knew, deep down, using Samantha for her own ends made her as shitty as Aaron. She had to hope that Samantha would come to see herself as a survivor . . . or that's what Lila told herself during the countless hours she stared at the ceiling of her bedroom, unable to sleep.

"That's what this meeting is about? You're not getting

enough of the spotlight." Lila had feared that would be an issue, since Samantha seemed to crave attention.

"I could ask you the same kind of questions. Is your decision to act like the hapless wife who had no choice but to off her husband real or is it payback for our affair?"

The word—"affair." So out of place in this situation. "You didn't have a relationship with Aaron. He used you. He groomed you. He had sex with you, scored the point, then moved on."

Samantha smiled. "You're jealous."

She didn't get it. How could she not get it? "Do you know what separates you from Karen Blue, the woman everyone is saying he killed?"

"Please share," Samantha shot back in a sarcastic tone.

"Almost nothing." Lila felt conflicted and frustrated, furious and disappointed. She aimed all of that at Aaron. He was the cause of this mess and pain. She didn't understand how Samantha could see what had happened any other way. "You survived. That's it. You were lucky to get away from him, and she wasn't."

"We both know that's crap." Samantha shifted in her chair. "Your boyfriend set Aaron up. He's not a killer."

"Come on, Samantha. You're smarter than this."

"You would say anything to—"

"Listen to the news. There was a press conference just a few hours ago." Lila could hear the exasperation in her voice as her patience expired. "Aaron secretly owned the cabin he used as his killing ground. The police found his DNA on her."

The amusement drained from Samantha's face. For a few seconds, she sat there. Lila hoped that meant she'd cut through the spurned teen romantic and wannabe star to the truth.

But then Samantha whispered, "So you're both killers."

The waitress picked that minute to return. She filled both of the coffee mugs and put two glasses of water and menus on the table. This time she glanced at both Lila and Samantha. Her gaze lingered as if she'd realized she had pseudo-celebrities of sorts at her table.

"Thanks," Lila mumbled then sighed in relief when the waitress scurried away.

"The plan was to incriminate him and then let me step into the spotlight and confirm it all." Samantha wrapped her hands around the mug as she relaxed in her seat. "But you killed him instead."

"I didn't kill him."

"I guess I'm just supposed to believe you." Samantha shook her head. "How did he get to this cabin?"

"I have no idea." Lila exhaled and decided to go for it. "A part of me hoped you'd done it, because at least that would explain it."

"Don't blame me for your mess."

"The point is you were not his girlfriend." Lila needed Samantha to hear that part. To get angry for being used and then get help, if she needed it. "You were one of his victims. I don't hate you or want to take your spotlight. I want you to realize that you deserve to be treated better. That what he did was sick and wrong and you get to be upset about that."

"Don't tell me how to feel." Samantha let go of her mug and leaned in closer. "I went into that relationship wanting it and wanting him."

The words should have hurt. Should have sliced and cut through her, but Lila felt nothing but sadness for Samantha and her mistaken belief that Aaron cared about anyone but himself. "And it was his job not to touch you. Ever."

"He said he was pretty unhappy at home." Samantha shrugged. "I guess you were, too, since you had that hot professor guy."

Lila refused to talk or think about Ryan. "I found you on your campus that day because I was worried about you."

Samantha snorted. "He never tried to hurt me."

The sadness turned into a churning ache deep in her stomach. Aaron had ruined and destroyed so many lives. "All he did was hurt you, Samantha. I know you don't see it yet, but I hope someday, with a counselor or on your own, you'll get it and be okay."

"I'm fine."

Lila gave up. Samantha wasn't ready to deal with the truth and might never be. "Okay."

"Don't judge me."

Once the defenses rose, Lila knew the battle was over. She couldn't get through. She'd never get through. If she couldn't save Samantha, at least she'd save herself. "I will push to make sure you get more credit for unraveling Aaron's private life."

"Because you owe me."

Lila stared at her untouched coffee. Thought about how a part of her would always worry that Samantha would sneak back into her life and threaten to expose the things she *thought* she knew. "I actually don't."

"Really? I wonder what that investigator would say if she knew how much you knew about Aaron's affairs before he was killed."

She sounded ready to strike.

That made two of them. "Be careful, Samantha."

Samantha rolled her eyes. "You're threatening me?"

"You're the one who thinks I already killed someone. Be smart and don't push me." Lila slipped her hand in her pocket and took out a small tape recorder. She held it up for Samantha to see.

Samantha froze in the act of lifting the mug for another sip. "What's that?"

"The recording of you where you talked about how much you wanted Aaron to pay for leaving you the way he did." Because she wasn't a novice. Lila had known what a wild card the teen victim of her husband might be and had taken precautions.

Samantha slowly lowered the mug to the table. "You recorded me?"

"Call it insurance. It's one copy of many." Lila put the recorder back in her pocket. "Have you studied the concept of mutually assured destruction in your history classes? Simply put, it's the idea that if one of us goes down, we both go down."

Samantha's mouth opened and closed twice before she said anything. "You're a bitch."

Lila signaled for the waitress to bring the check. "A bitch with evidence that points directly at you. Remember that before you run off to talk with anyone about me or what you think I've done."

"Mutually assured destruction," Samantha said in a faint voice.

"I will make sure you're seen as a hero, and you will keep quiet." Lila tried to conjure up an expression that passed for a smile. "That's the only deal you're going to get."

Chapter Fifty-five

"REALLY? YOU MET AT A DINER?"

Lila had a feeling Tobias would find out about her little trip in his car and tried to launch an offensive strike by telling him. "She called, and meeting privately seemed like it would raise more questions."

"How about not meeting at all? Or telling me so I could tell you not to meet?"

"She's a victim."

Tobias balanced on the bar stool, somehow managing to look at home teetering while wearing expensive dress shoes. "Is that the point here?"

Kind of, yeah.

She sighed at him. "Lawyers are the worst."

"Yes, we are, and you will listen."

It was a fair request. She'd promised not to act as her own attorney. She knew from watching others do exactly that how it almost always ended in disaster. In crisis, people needed good advice unclouded by emotion. While she hardly viewed herself as the overwrought type, Tobias would see things she couldn't.

"She wanted to talk. She's confused, and the news of Karen's murder threw her." That wasn't quite true, but suggesting anything else could backfire. Like it or not, she was stuck in this twisted mess with Samantha. "Seeing her seemed like the least I could do."

"You're being watched by the police."

"By everyone in the state, apparently." Stupid cell phones.

The doorbell rang. Her body had been trained to tense up at the sound. Ever since Aaron had gone missing, it went off and her insides curdled. A voice in her head shouted at her to run and keep running.

She groaned. "Now who?"

"Jared," Tobias said as he slid off the stool.

No, no, no.

"What?" She needed more energy to walk into that battle again. His shots had been so unexpected that she was still reeling from them. The idea of another round . . . "I can't."

Tobias walked right past her and headed for the front door. "He wanted to talk."

"No."

"I'm not giving you a choice," he said over his shoulder as he walked away from her. "You need him as an ally."

She heard the front door open. Without looking, she knew the press was crowded in as close as possible. Neighbors had complained. She complained. All the law enforcement folks had done was push the media back to the end of the driveway and into the public street.

Jared stepped just inside the family room, wearing a navy suit with his tie loosened. A casual look for him.

"Hey." He smiled when he saw her, but it didn't reach his eyes. He turned to Tobias. "Do you mind if we talk alone?"

Tobias laughed as he sat back down on the bar stool. "Actually, yes. Just pretend I'm not here."

"He's being protective." And she appreciated the gesture. Arguing with Jared was the last thing she wanted today—or ever.

Jared stepped up to the back of the couch but didn't make a move to sit down. His stop put them a good six feet apart, but she could see the way he avoided straight-on eye contact. How he stared at the area rug and hardwood floor as if they were the most interesting things in the world.

She took pity on him. "Jared—"

"I know I lost my temper and took all my frustration out on you," he said at the same time. "I said things—"

"It's fine." They talked over each other, verbally bumped into each other. The awkward, disjointed sentences eased some of the tension pounding through her.

"It is?" Jared asked.

Tobias openly watched them. "Really?"

She gestured for Jared to sit on the other end of the couch. Not close, but there, in comfort, so she could let him know this was as hard for her as it was for him. "I haven't figured out how to process all of this. The idea of Aaron in that cabin . . ."

"I still can't believe it." Jared shook his head as he let out a long exhale. "I mean, we were raised together. We did so much together. How could I miss the signs?"

Tobias left the bar stool and joined them. He sat in the chair across from them, ignoring the emotional uncertainty zipping around the room. "Did Ginny question you?"

"Oh yeah." Jared leaned back into the cushions. "She clearly doesn't believe I didn't know."

"She has to push, but I'm sure she knows. That's how it works sometimes," Tobias said. "I've read books about families who didn't know they lived with a killer father. I've had clients not see the type of person who slept next to them each night." He glanced at her. "And some friends and colleagues who suffered from the same blind spots."

Jared winced. "I'm afraid I wasn't at my best during the latest interrogation."

"Meaning?"

But Lila knew the answer to Tobias's question. She didn't need a big explanation or lengthy apology. Jared went to the same place anyone in his position might go. "He's saying he blamed me for Aaron's death."

"Ryan, actually. Well, more Ryan than you." Jared's wince didn't ease. "But yeah. I lashed out."

She got it. She understood. It's not as if she had the high ground here. She'd done things, horrible things. Things a better person might regret, but she didn't.

She reached her hand out and let it rest on the cushion between them. "It's fine."

Tobias laughed. "I think you should remove that word from your vocabulary. You clearly don't know what it means."

"He's not wrong," Jared said, already looking lighter and regaining some of his usual calm demeanor.

"My husband abused teens and killed women, all while I enjoyed some time alone and spent time with Ryan, thinking my marriage was just . . ." She stopped because the moment struck her as funny, and that hadn't happened in weeks. "Normally, I'd say 'fine' here."

Tobias rolled his eyes. "Uh-huh."

"But while all of that was happening and I was living my life, Aaron was hurting women. I listened to the press conference. DNA evidence. Yara James and Karen Blue both have been found on his top secret property." She couldn't figure out how to make her inaction, her not seeing the truth, okay. Missing the opportunity to stop the abuse . . . again. Being older and still not seeing it before it was too late was a sin that she couldn't find the right words to apologize for. "I didn't stop him."

"You didn't know," Tobias immediately shot back.

"Well." Jared rubbed a hand up and down his leg. "That brings me to the Brent news."

"What now?" She could hardly wait to hear what he'd accused her of without any proof. Talk about a wild card.

"He's been suspended from his job, pending an investigation." Jared stopped long enough to nod at her in affirmation. Whatever he saw on her face must have told her she needed it. "Apparently, there is a whisper campaign about how he knew what Aaron was doing with students and looked the other way, possibly took part in it."

"I don't know about the accomplice part." Tobias made a humming sound, the type that said he was mentally working through an idea. "That sounds like idle gossip."

Lila knew a bit about that. "It's someone else's turn. I'm tired of being the target."

"I got the impression they did a search of his home and office and found something problematic." Jared's hand clenched and unclenched where it lay on his thigh. "The school has an investigator on it. The state police are looking into it. I'm sure Ginny is poking around in the accusations."

"What did they find exactly?" she asked.

Jared winced. "The word is he had photos on his computer—"

She waved her hand, trying to bat the words away. "Oh, God. Enough."

Tobias whistled. "Unbelievable."

The news struck her as upsetting but not shocking. "Is it? I'm starting to think we can never really know what's going on in someone else's head."

"But murder?" Jared asked.

That's exactly what she was talking about. "Especially murder."

Chapter Fifty-six

THE NEXT DAY LILA STEPPED INTO GINNY'S OFFICE ON HER WAY back from a meeting with the sheriff and the prosecutor. Tobias was still with Charles, doing his schmooze thing in the hope of pulling a bit more information out of the guy. She took the opportunity to peek in on Ginny.

Before she got to the office door, she saw the board through the glass wall. Photos and newspaper headlines. Cards with notes about evidence. Her face. Aaron's. It was disconcerting to have her life splayed open and put on display. But the more she stood there, her gaze scanning every inch of information, the more she realized this wasn't her life. This was an exhibit. She played a role. A bit player in Aaron's horrible opera.

She stood in the doorway and waited until Ginny hung up the phone to announce her presence. "I've seen those boards on television and in defense attorneys' offices. Never been the subject of one, though."

Ginny's head shot up. Her gaze went from Lila to the board to the open office behind Lila. "You shouldn't be in here."

Story of her life.

She stopped just inside the door and stood there. She hoped the casual entrance would ease some of the rushing panic thrumming off Ginny. "I got a call from the prosecutor's office."

Ginny stopped looking around and shifting in her seat and frowned. "About what?"

"A courtesy call about the additional bodies that had been found in and around the cabin. Julie and Yara. Yara had been on the news, but Julie . . . I guess it was inevitable they'd find her, too."

"Really?"

"They also wanted Tobias to know the FBI was all over this case now." The initial panic at hearing that news had worn off the second the FBI made it clear Aaron's crimes, not her potential ones, were the focal point.

"That's not necessarily true."

Ginny didn't disappoint. She fought the good jurisdictional fight to the end.

The fact she'd read someone right for a change made Lila smile. She came fully into the room and sat down in the chair across from Ginny. "What is true, then?"

The tension wrapping around Ginny seemed to vanish. She leaned back in her chair as if she were no longer ready to usher Lila out of the room and away from her precious board. "I would love for you to answer that question. Honest answers, without any zigzagging, would be a nice change."

"I keep seeing their photos in the press." She nodded at the photo of the pretty woman on the far right side of the board. Brunette with blue eyes. "Julie."

Sighing in what sounded like resignation, Ginny stood up. She went to the board and pointed to photos as she spoke. "Here's Karen, and this one is Yara."

Both brunettes with long hair. Pretty and alive with energy. Smiling in the photos. So young, with so much ahead of them, and Aaron had snuffed it out. He thought he was entitled. That even their breath belonged to him.

Lila's gaze fell on a photo in the middle of the board. "That is the bracelet you asked me about before."

She hadn't been able to get it out of her head since the first time she saw it. The idea of Aaron keeping his mother's bracelet ticked off a suffocating sensation in her throat. Was it love or loss . . . or something far more sinister?

"Any more information on that?" Lila asked when Ginny didn't offer any explanation.

"No."

The firm response grabbed Lila's attention. "Is it possible Aaron put his trophies in with jewelry his mother owned? Is that a thing killers do? Like, he lost his mother and this is all somehow wrapped up with that abandonment?"

Ginny shrugged. "Possible."

That tone. Ginny had a theory, and Lila thought she wanted to say it. "But you don't think so."

"The killings might relate back to his mother in some way, but no, I don't think this was a storage issue." Ginny leaned against the far end of the board. "I also think he killed more than the three women you see on the board."

Lila had the same fear. A man like Aaron didn't just start killing in his midthirties. His personality hadn't changed during their marriage. Maybe he'd become more settled, but so had she. She couldn't pinpoint any sort of break, which meant he hadn't changed and his violent behavior likely extended well into the past.

She heard voices behind her. Men talking and phones ringing. There were only a few people in the main offices at those desks, but the noise never stopped. Activity buzzed around them.

She got up and moved closer to the board. To the one photo that kept calling her. "What's this bracelet?"

"It was Karen Blue's."

Lila looked at the photo. Saw the round charm. It ticked off a memory in her head . . . one she couldn't quite grab. "Seventeen."

"Have you seen it before?"

"No." Lila's gaze moved to the next photo as she tried to connect the pieces, but her mind wouldn't cooperate. "This is the cabin? I thought it would look different."

"How so?"

"I don't know. More rundown, maybe. Abandoned, like he rarely went there and never just to hang out." The wood was in good shape. A sturdy front porch and solid roof. Falling leaves had been removed from the steps leading to the front door. The cabin looked lived-in, not like women died there.

"It's a one-bedroom with a storm cellar."

Cellar. Lila had seen enough movies to know that sounded bad. "Is that where Karen was?"

"No. She was . . ." Ginny stopped herself. Her hesitation ticked on for a few seconds. "Tied to the bed."

The words slammed into Lila with the force of a bat to her midsection. Every muscle stretched and shook.

"Aaron, you piece of shit." She meant to think the words, not say them, but they came out in a low whisper.

Ginny didn't say anything, but Lila could feel her gaze. She watched and assessed, as she'd done from the beginning.

Lila was about to turn around and go find Tobias when a detail caught her eye. She pointed to the photograph. "This chair."

"Yes?"

A rocking chair, probably handmade. Thin spindles and large armrests. A place where someone could sit and rest their hands. "Was it in the house?"

"On the front porch." Ginny stepped closer. "Does it look familiar?"

"Maybe." Definitely. "It was on the porch, out in the middle of nowhere?"

Ginny nodded toward the other cabin photos. The long rocky driveway. The green lawn made of low shrubs at the bottom of the porch steps.

"The house sits in a clearing, but yes." Her eyes narrowed. "What are you thinking?"

That the matching chair was in her attic. It looked just like this one. Same age and same details. It meant something, but she didn't know what. "It just seems weird for a serial killer to have a rocking chair."

"Handmade. We think it's a family heirloom."

She knew that to be true. "What does Jared say?"

"No more than you do."

Lila filed the photo in the back of her mind. She'd venture into the attic again and look at the chair. With the information tucked away, she flipped into defensive mode. She'd come too far to backslide now. "You can't believe I had anything to do with the Karen or Julie—"

"No, but I think you knew more about your husband's extracurricular activities than you admit to."

Lila wasn't sure what that meant, but the serious, unblinking stare told her Ginny was not done. FBI or not. "I told you I'd found the videos with the students. I handed them over to you."

"I remember." Ginny folded her arms across her chest. "My point is that I think you found out a lot earlier than you're admitting and then killed him because of it."

Very good, except for one thing.

"I didn't stab him." Lila could make the claim without one ounce of worry about giving herself away. She still didn't know who had, but with the arrest and whispers about Brent, she guessed him. He'd tried to spook her, threatened her. If he was an accomplice, she hoped he never knew another minute of peace.

"That's not what killed Aaron."

Lila was sure she'd missed something. "What?"

"Forensics confirmed that he was dead before being stabbed." Ginny watched her. Her gaze dipped up and down Lila's body, as if waiting for her to blow it.

Lila forced her body to stay still. Her expression froze, and she did a countdown in her head until she could shift even an inch. She refused to give away her surprise.

She fought to swallow over the dryness in her mouth. "Who would stab a dead man?"

"No idea." Ginny practically glowed with satisfaction. She'd stumped Lila, and she knew it. "There were high levels of gas in his blood and liver."

"I don't get it." But she did understand that part. She'd put the gas there. The setup of the car as a suicide was supposed to do the rest to explain any adverse toxicology results.

"Murder often isn't a rational act. It can be messy. Emotional. Spur-of-the-moment or planned."

An alarm sounded in the back of her brain. Ginny could be lying or playing with the facts. Nothing she said made sense except the reasons for killing someone, and a few of those hit too close to the truth. "I feel like I'm back in law school."

"My point is that you may not have stabbed Aaron, but I still think you killed him."

Lila needed to know if that stemmed from common sense

and good instincts or from a new and so far undisclosed piece of evidence. She could only fight one of those options. "Why?"

Ginny shrugged. "You tell me."

"It's your job, not mine."

This time Ginny smiled. "I'd think you'd want to know who killed your husband."

"You'd be wrong." Because now she knew.

She killed him.

ABOUT FIVE MINUTES after Lila left her office, Pete wandered in. Ginny wasn't ready for a conversation about protocol or arguments about how she'd handled the case. She kept mentally running through Lila's reactions to the photos and the news about Aaron's actual cause of death.

Lila finally had flinched. Subtle, but Ginny saw it. Some part of the news and a few of those photos shocked her. Threw her off her usual steady game. Ginny needed to know why.

Pete lounged in the doorway. "I saw Lila in here. Is it okay for her to see the board?"

She knew he wasn't seeking the advice from a more experienced officer. This was Pete's way of letting her know he thought she'd screwed up. She wasn't interested in playing the game. "No."

"So . . . why invite her in? I don't get it."

"Look at this." Ginny grabbed the photographs of Karen's bracelet and the older one they thought might have belonged to Aaron's mother off the board.

"I ran a check. There are no photos of Aaron's mother

and no relatives to ask, so I couldn't track it at all. The newer bracelet is from a company that services jewelry stores, clothing stores. They're not expensive and can be found almost everywhere. It was a dead end."

But it wasn't. The pieces started coming together in the most horrible way.

"That's not my point. Do we have other bracelet photos?" She could get the bags out of the evidence locker, but the photos might be enough.

Pete slipped out of the room and was back in a few minutes with an envelope in hand. He opened it and spilled the photos on the desk, shifting through until he found alternative angles of the bracelets. "What are we looking for?"

She saw it now. Had no idea how she missed it before. "Seventeen."

"Right, but Karen's parents said they'd never seen the bracelet before. I've asked two friends, and they say the same thing. She never wore it, and no one remembers her having it."

"Right." Ginny picked up the clearer photos of the older bracelet. The one with the "A" charm on it. "What if the long scratch on the back of this charm isn't actually a scratch?"

"I want to be excited, but you've lost me."

She put the photos of the bracelets side by side and the truth jumped out. "What if that scratch is a number one? As in, number one and number seventeen."

"You mean victims?"

"Yes." The more she studied the two, the more convinced she became. The first would have been scratched into the back of the metal decades ago, when the Payne brothers were young, and probably with a knife. The engraving in the more recent one was done by a steadier hand. Possibly an older hand, one more comfortable with killing.

That meant there should be bracelets out there for Yara and Julie, too.

"Seventeen victims?" Pete shook his head.

"Possibly."

"Holy shit. Are we really going to stop working on this case and just turn it over?" He looked appalled by the idea.

So was she, but she hid the excitement that came with un-raveling a case better, thanks to years of practice. "There's a chain of command and—"

"You can't be serious."

"Let me finish." She gestured for Pete to come farther in-side her office, then shut the door behind him. "There's a chain of command, and we're going to ignore it."

A smile slowly crossed his lips. "I'm listening."

"Good, because we're not done with Lila Ridgefield or her dead husband."

Chapter Fifty-seven

THE NEXT MORNING, LILA MADE THE DRIVE SHE'D TRIED TO avoid. She borrowed Tobias's rental car while he was in the shower and left a note about running errands. With Ginny and her crew officially off the case, that meant she didn't have to worry about being followed. She was on her own. No matter how painful this trip might be, she was doing it. She had to.

That bracelet. It sent her mind spinning.

The drive took almost three hours, just like everyone said. She'd planned out the trip, looking for side roads and work-arounds. When she got to the point where she would have turned right onto the final dirt road before hitting the driveway to the cabin, she kept driving.

She could see the yellow caution tape flapping in the breeze. Of course today was the day the cooler, wetter weather had moved into this part of New York. A steady drizzle slowed her down. The woods would be muddy, but she was prepared with boots. Her backpack had supplies, some she hoped she wouldn't need.

As she whizzed by the entrance, she saw two local police

officers standing by their cruiser, drinking coffee. Their presence wasn't a surprise. The tiny town and the cabin had gotten a lot of attention on the news. While the interviewees didn't give an exact address, she knew where the cabin was. The map and aerial view on Ginny's board confirmed the location and the thick wooded area around it.

She drove for another quarter mile and took a right. She could only drive in a few feet, enough to hide her car from the road. That's all she needed.

With the car locked and her raincoat hood up, she grabbed her backpack and headed toward the cabin. She knew the bulk of the forensics at the cabin had been done. There was talk of digging up the land and looking for more bodies, but that required special equipment, and the latest podcast said that would arrive tomorrow. That gave her a window of one day. One shitty, rainy day.

Her boots slid in the mud as she walked. Sticks cracked beneath her feet, and fallen leaves and broken branches made the walking slick. She didn't follow a trail because there wasn't one. She walked until she hit the fence. Six feet and made of wood. Hard to climb but, she hoped, easy to break through. But not yet. She followed the fence deeper into the woods, blocking branches with her arm as she forged a path.

The mist clouded her vision and dampened her cheeks. The jacket she wore repelled the rain, but her hair slipped out and now-wet curls slipped over her forehead. The longer she walked, the more moss she saw. Over the ground and downed trees.

The tree crowns provided an umbrella of protection, keeping the light from seeping in. It wasn't even eleven in the morning, and the entire area was blanketed in a sort of dingy gray. It looked and felt more like late afternoon. The scent of pine and dirt filled her senses.

She kept her focus on the fence, trying to catch a glimpse of the cabin from this side. After she trudged and slipped for what felt like forever, she spied the roofline. A few more feet and she reached what would be the equivalent of the back of the cabin. Breaking through the fence here seemed smarter. Police could be roaming, and she didn't want to run into them.

The rain switched to a steady drizzle. No more mist. It came down now, the tiny pings echoing as the drops hit the ground.

She scanned the fence, looking for weakness. The damn thing had faded with the years, but the wood hadn't rotted. That meant breaking through the hard way. Of course.

She picked two boards and slammed the heavy heel of her hiking boot against what she thought looked like the most vulnerable spot. The wood bowed under the onslaught of kicks, cracking and moaning but not breaking. The repeated motion rubbed a spot clear on the ground. With the grass completely gone, she slipped in the mud, unable to get the traction she needed for more shots.

A scream of frustration rumbled up her throat, but she bit it back. Swearing, she opened the zipper of the backpack and grabbed a screwdriver and hammer. One look at the job, and she pocketed the screwdriver. This required hitting.

She smacked the vulnerable wood, putting her weight behind it, and watched it splinter. Clawing at it, kicking it some more, let her break off a long piece and make an opening.

One more board and she'd be through.

She repeated the process, this time holding on to the fence to keep from falling. She could not get injured. Not out here, where no one would hear her or find her.

With both boards gone and sweat rolling down her back, she slipped through the open slot and stepped into the small cleared area behind the cabin. Her gaze shot to the back of the building then over to the shed. A gnawing sensation started in her stomach. The smells and sounds of the woods on the other side of the fence reminded her of hikes around Cayuga Lake, of walking around the preserve with Ryan.

This side felt still. She glanced up, letting the rain hit her face, and tried to find the sky. She saw nothing but darkness. A twisting of branches and swaying of trees.

She listened for the sound of creatures scurrying under shrubs but heard nothing. It was as if death blanketed the property. Even though she stood outside, tension pressed in on her from every angle. Her throat felt tight, and her breathing grew labored.

Yellow tape surrounded the cabin and the shed. Another bit outlined a hole in the ground and the mound of mud beside it. It had once held a body. One of the women's graves.

Her stomach heaved. She covered her mouth with her gloved hand and tried to inhale through her nose. She could not get sick here. Not because of evidence. Because of respect.

She owed Julie, Yara, and Karen better. She had to see this through. Walk where they'd walked. Feel Aaron's malice, let it fuel her.

He was dead, and he deserved to be. She didn't need the reminder, but this suffocating burial ground gave her one. She doubted she'd ever forget this place.

She dropped the hammer and her backpack on the porch. She used her pocketknife to slice through the tape at the door, then, with one last look at the rocky driveway leading to the house and trees that muffled the screams, she stepped into the cabin.

Silence inundated her. The thick air clogged her throat.

The curtains had been pulled back on the windows, and light entered the space. The kitchen lined the far wall. To the left, the door to the bedroom. She could see the end of the mattress but, knowing that's where they'd found Karen, couldn't force her body to step inside.

To her right, a sitting area with a plaid sofa and an ottoman. The kind of furniture she'd seen in countless hunting cabins. Old, durable. Frayed. Nothing on the walls. Nothing personal.

Except for the rocking chair.

It sat in the middle of the room, as if it had been dragged inside. She studied it as she'd done with the one in her attic this morning. There it was. A carving on the one armrest—a circle with a bear on its hind legs, paws in the air. Not a coincidence. This was the same design. Same workmanship. A match to the one she'd stored since she'd met Aaron in North

Carolina years ago, but in better condition. This one hadn't been hidden away and allowed to rot.

Her senses leapt to life. A thundering started in her ears. She inhaled deep, openmouthed breaths to keep from dropping to the ground in an anxiety-induced haze. She didn't know what she'd expected to find or feel, but all she could call up was emptiness. An overriding, pummeling guilt that pushed against her shoulders, trying to slam her to the dusty floor.

"I wondered if you'd come."

She closed her eyes at the sound of the familiar voice. The one she'd hoped not to hear. She'd never wanted so badly to be wrong.

She turned around and saw him. Tall and sure, dressed in his hiking gear and wearing that expensive watch.

Holding her hammer.

"Jared."

Chapter Fifty-eight

"I TRACKED YOU. HELL, I'VE BEEN TRACKING YOU SINCE YOUR big fight with Aaron two months ago. Figured you'd get curious and drive out here one day." Jared whistled. "But today you seemed distracted. When you ran out of the sheriff's office, head down and all determined, I knew you'd found something because I know you."

They always said that. Today she hated to hear it. "You don't."

"I could see it in your expression."

That persistent, nagging memory. "They weren't coins."

The words seemed to dampen his enthusiasm. "What?"

"In your office drawer at home." Her mind went back to her break-in. Coins in the desk drawer and coins in a jar a few feet away. That didn't seem like the meticulous Jared she knew, but she didn't pick up on the strangeness then. She'd been too busy feeling crappy for snooping around his office.

"Right. Spare charms. You found them before I could toss them out of a car window somewhere far from here." He put his hand in his pocket and pulled out a bracelet just like the one in the photo on Ginny's board. "Number eighteen. I'm hoping we don't need it today, but that really depends on you."

The words shot right through her. The number. What it meant. What he had planned for her. What he really was.

Jared shook his head as his smile returned. "Those fucking videos started all of this."

The tone, so deep and flat. Lila felt her stomach fall. "What?"

"I told Aaron to destroy them. Hell, I told him to stop going after his students and just play with the women I found, but he refused to listen." He pocketed the bracelet and spun the hammer's handle around in his hand, looking as if he were born to wield it. "It's like how he was when he first saw you. He was obsessed, and I told him to back off, but no. Then when he found out about your background, he knew you were perfect for him."

The perfect cover for the secret life he led.

She tried to think of the right words, to stall until her brain could catch up and she could figure out what to do. "What are you doing here? Why follow me?"

He frowned at her. "We've been playing this game. The notes. The fights. Arguing about Aaron." He scoffed. "Hell, I almost came right out with it a few times. When I found you in my office? I thought you were trying to tell me you'd figured it out, but then I realized you felt guilty for being caught looking around."

"I thought Aaron might have hid something in your house."

"He did. I kept copies of the videos with the girls and some of the other evidence he collected to keep them in line. It was in the safe under my desk. Note my use of past tense." Jared winked at her.

So many questions bounced around in her head. She grabbed on to the one thought she could articulate. "You wrote the notes to me."

"Of course," he shot back. "I couldn't just let you kill Aaron and not pay a price." He shrugged. "I thought for sure you'd guess. The notes were my way of getting even and letting you know who was in charge." He tapped the hammer harder against the side of his leg. "Me. I'm in charge."

He could get close to her house without anyone questioning it. He came in and out of her life, her office, and her home. He was always just . . . there. Dependable and strong. No-nonsense and undemanding.

He'd stalked her. Scared her. The smile on his face said he'd enjoyed all of it.

Her mind fought back, determined not to let reality set in. She shifted, keeping him in front of her as she circled, putting her back to the kitchen area. A sturdy wall and no way to be surprised from behind. "Tell me what's going on, Jared."

But she knew. Every word, the feral look on his face. He'd come home to his killing ground.

Only one thing stood in his way—her.

"Aaron arrived at my house that night after your big fight, furious and mumbling. You'd been digging around in his stuff. You'd found him out." He sat on the arm of the couch, looking relaxed and acting as if they were talking about normal things on any other day. "He was sure you'd talk to the police and he wanted you dead. That night."

"Sounds like Aaron."

"I said no, of course. People always blame the husband, and I couldn't have that kind of spotlight so close to me before I had a chance to prepare."

"Of course," she repeated the thrown-away comment as she glanced around the room, looking for something that could fend off that hammer.

"He liked the chase. Always did. Never enjoyed the kill." Jared laughed. "Which really pissed Dad off. All that training and Aaron was a lost cause. He fucked. I killed."

She froze. "I don't understand."

He sighed like he was disappointed in her. "You do."

God, she did. A family enterprise. Aaron had been blamed for the killings, but that honor belonged to Jared, and to his dad before him. Aaron's sin was not forgivable but was also not murder.

"Explain it to me." Still stalling. Still thinking of a way out.

"I'll give you a hint." He put his foot on the rocker part of the rocking chair. "This one is mine. The one in your house belongs to Aaron."

Identical chairs.

He tapped the rocker and set it in motion. "They were on the porch growing up. He'd sit there and look over his property. Watch the games begin."

Games?

"When Dad died, we each took one. I brought mine here so I could sit outside and enjoy a nice evening. Get a little air."

He sounded so logical and calm, just as he always did. She'd expected that someone who lived this secret life would be unspooled, deranged. Talking in undecipherable rants. Nothing prepared her for how *normal* he looked. She had naïvely believed she'd be able to pick horror out of the crowd and stay away. But the opposite was true. He'd blended in and made her believe.

"See, Dad liked to hunt. Animals were for eating. They served a purpose. The other hunts, the ones with women, those were for fun. He took us along from the time I was eight or so to this farm in Pennsylvania."

The thought of the boys being dragged along . . . "Eight?"

"I still remember it. Fischer's Farm. It sat near a lake, and the school sometimes rented it out for events." He let out a harsh laugh. "At first I didn't understand what was happening. All these men and this naked woman. Then they would give her a head start and go. They'd sit and wait before scrambling after her. Then the game would begin."

The dizziness hit her, and she fought through it. She had to stay on her feet and focus. "You can't be serious."

"Those guys were really sick. The things they'd do once they caught the women?" He shook his head. "Shit, that was too much for me. I liked the hunt, but at the end of every hunt you do the humane thing."

She didn't want him to say the words, so she did. "Kill them."

"Now you get it. You put the animal down."

"Jared . . ."

He actually smiled at her. "Aaron didn't have the stomach for it. He liked to mess with girls, have sex with them. It was this weird *conquer them* thing he had. But you know that because you were his biggest prize."

She couldn't let her mind go there.

She reached into her pocket and brought out her pocketknife. Tucked it into her palm. "This is your cabin."

His gaze bounced to her fingers then back up to her face. "Now you're catching on."

"You bought it in his name."

"I like to think ahead. Have an exit strategy." He shrugged and his voice took on a joking tone, as if he were enjoying this.

The pieces came together in her head. "You kill them. He, what, finds them for you?"

"No." Jared made a face. "Come on. You're smarter than that."

"Apparently not."

He stood up and took a step toward her. "I made him come with me now and then. He wasn't into the stalking and hunting, but he'd do it if I ordered it."

Her panicked breath came in pants now. "Why would you do that?"

"To keep him in line. If I needed to. You know, just in case."

"In case what?"

"You." He pointed the hammer at her. "He thought it was

funny that he thrived on doing the very thing that broke you as a kid. All right under your nose."

"He was a twisted piece of garbage."

"Careful. That's my brother you're talking about." Jared chuckled. "But he could be reckless. Making him come here, having him move a body or help me dispose of one, kept him culpable. I could control where my DNA ended up and, if needed, use his."

"Frame your own brother."

"He was hardly innocent." He frowned at her. "I honestly thought you'd leave him. Either way, there was a chance that you'd turn him in, which had the potential to blow back on me, and I couldn't let that happen."

Memories flooded her brain. All the meals together. The talks. The things she'd told him. How they'd joked about being alike.

The idea that she'd been feeding him information all along, that no part of their relationship had been real, made her knees buckle. She fought to stay on her feet and concentrate. To stay outside of swinging range of that hammer.

"I installed some cameras of my own across the street from you and around your house. They came in handy today when I saw you walk past the media and all of your new fans at your house and get into Tobias's car." He leaned against the rocker. "The way you messed with the neighbor's alarm weeks ago in order to make him turn it off? Brilliant. I admit at first I didn't know what you were doing. The walks up and down the street. Sneaking into their yard at night." His smile fell.

"But then one morning Aaron's car left very early, and you were driving, and I knew you'd launched some sort of plan."

He'd watched. He's seen her plotting, working on strategy. He'd been there, at least through a lens, on that final morning.

"Oh, you were bundled up and wearing what looked like one of Aaron's suits, but I could make out your face. Good thing I'd already left my conference in a loaner car."

"That could have been traced back to you." It would have. Ginny would have figured that out with a little time.

"Not when you pay with cash and use a license stolen from a drunk guy in the bar." He shook his head, as if impressed by his own ingenuity. "I still had to break every speed limit to get back to Ithaca in time and take care of the scene before dawn." He snorted. "And getting his car off the school grounds without being seen?"

"How?"

"I could only take it a few blocks. Parked it in plain sight in a neighborhood, covered in a tarp for two days while I figured out a safe route back to the cabin." He pretended to drive. "But imagine my surprise when I found Aaron slumped over the wheel with the engine running and the tailpipe blocked."

Dead. She'd killed him, and Jared had found him. It all made sense now. He'd tracked her and watched her and stepped in to save Aaron. "But you were too late."

"I was." He nodded. "I tried to revive him, but you'd been very thorough. Good for you."

The singsongy sound of his voice made her sick. It chipped

away at her focus. Took her back there, made her relive the panic over the notes and her fear that Aaron was still alive.

She tried to focus. To hear every horrid detail. "But you stabbed him."

He made a *tsk-tsk*ing sound. "I have spent a good deal of the last few months protecting you. Telling Aaron not to fight back. Watching. The stabbing was one more example. It was meant to throw off the police."

"He was already dead."

He shrugged again, as if they were not talking about killing and defacing his own brother. "Honestly, things seemed to be collapsing because of Aaron's extracurricular activities, so I thought it was time to pull up stakes and move on. You going rogue just moved up my plans. But I needed it done my way. With the cabin being found and Aaron taking the blame. That meant adding your plan to mine, which I admit was not a perfect fit, but it looks like it worked out. Aaron will get the blame. I'll leave town in horror, change my name, and then start again."

"You mean go kill somewhere else."

"Well, I enjoy hunting. Getting them out here, letting them run. Offering a sliver of hope then taking it away." He whistled. "The panic is something else. I love the panic and the begging."

The complete disregard and absence of any concern or feelings had a ball of anxiety forming in her stomach. "Did your mom know what was happening?"

"When she figured out the reason for the weekend games and all the hush-hush stuff, Dad set up one last hunt." Jared waved his hand in the air, swinging that hammer close to her face. "Got the guys together. Made sure it would look like an accident."

His mother. Hunted and murdered.

Lila's stomach pitched and roiled. She swallowed back the bile, determined to hear every horrible word. "And the trust fund?"

"Rich people will pay a lot of money to do some crazy shit." This time he tapped the hammer against his thigh. "So that took care of Mom, and when Dad started to lose it, when he started to babble about some secrets, which luckily sounded so brazen no one believed him, I handled it."

What the hell? "You ran him down on the side of the road."

"I *handled* it." His voice grew angrier. "It's what I do. I clean up the mess, including yours."

"No."

"We're connected. I know you feel it. You talk about it all the time."

Her focus faltered, but she kept going. Waiting until the exact right time. "Brent?"

"Yeah, I started the rumors about his involvement." He laughed to himself. "Wait until the police find the kiddie porn on his computer."

A psychopath. He outlined his sick crimes with the same emotion he used when he spoke to her about stocks. Clear and no-nonsense.

"Do you feel anything?" She had to know, though she doubted he would be honest.

"Do *you*?" He tapped the hammer faster against his leg. "You killed your husband and seem fine with that."

"You're sick." She knew from Ryan's books that she should appeal to his humanity, if he had any, but the words slipped out.

"I'm exactly like you." He took that last step that put him right in front of her, only a few feet away. "Emotions other people feel—guilt, love, devotion—mean nothing to me. I've tried to have a relationship, do the dating thing. So fucking boring. I need more. Excitement. The race."

"The girls from school were blondes."

He frowned. "What?"

"Aaron liked young blondes. You hunted for brunettes." The difference in the women became so clear to her now. "Aaron didn't kill any of them."

"I said this already. He was a failure in that department. I found the women. I lured them to look at something by my car or grabbed them at the gas station. In a parking lot."

"Did they look like your mom?" Like her?

"Don't psychoanalyze me. I picked women who asked for it."

She thought about Karen and Yara and Julie. All young and going about their business until he destroyed them. "How?"

"They got my attention."

He stood close enough for her to see the flatness in his eyes. She'd always been protective of him, viewing him as lonely and a little sad. Someone shaped by horrible circumstances and the early loss of a mother.

Now she saw him as an empty shell. Not to be pitied, but to be put down. Eradicated.

Fear flooded through her. Instead of hiding from it, she used it. Let it fill her with a dark energy. "What now, Jared?"

"That's up to you." His gaze traveled over her face, wild but not unhinged. "We can move away, pretend to be horrified by Aaron's actions, and start over."

Every part of her recoiled. "Me with you? Like, married?"

"Not like that." He shook his head. "Haven't you been listening? I have needs. Times I'd want to be away, at my special place. Hunting." He smiled again. "You've said it a million times. We understand each other. We share a bond. Hell, it's why I did all of this."

The panic inside her rose with each word. His disconnection to reality whipped and battered her. "Did what?"

"Moved Aaron's body. Planted evidence on Ryan and Brent." He smiled. "Let you live after you killed my baby brother."

"You're demented if you think I'd go along with your killing spree."

"I hoped you would. It would make things easier."

"Never." She brought her arm up and swung the blade.

Chapter Fifty-nine

JARED CAUGHT THE KNIFE RIGHT BEFORE IT PLUNGED INTO HIS neck. Blood dripped from his fingers where they clenched around the sharp blade.

He made that awful *tsk-tsk*ing sound again. "Naughty girl."

He tugged, and Lila felt her arm pop up at the shoulder. She blinked hard against the race of tears and pain. A harsh gasp filled her ears, and she realized it came from her. When she focused on him again, he was closing the knife and throwing it into the bedroom. She heard it crash against something but couldn't see where. She was too busy focusing on the hammer he still held.

"You won't kill me. We've known—"

"Our history doesn't matter. If you make me hunt you, I will. And I will savor it." He swung the hammer and caught her in the side.

She doubled over as pain shot through her, from stomach to back. She kept her head up because she knew if she looked away he would slam the hammer into her brain.

Her side thumped under her fingers, and an ache screeched through her head. Anxiety and panic mixed and swelled inside her. But she stayed on her feet.

"You're going to bludgeon me, Jared?" She tried to ignored the pain and breathiness in her voice. "How will you explain that to the police?"

"You assume anyone will find your body."

The hammer was right there, in front of her face. She bolted around him. Shifted to her wounded side. But he caught her mid-run and looped an arm around her waist, tightening against the wound he'd inflicted until the breath left her lungs. He pulled her against his stomach and held her there, his breath gliding across the back of her neck.

"That was a mistake."

She'd always thought of him as a guy who sat at a desk. In shape but normal. What a joke. He possessed enough upper-body strength to clamp down on her and limit her options. All that running and conditioning. She knew that was part of his game. Part of the hunt.

She would not die like this, another victim of the Payne men.

"Let go!" She scratched at his arm. When he lifted the hammer again, she kicked out her legs, throwing him off balance. He shifted backward and yelled in her ear to stop.

His anger breathed life into hers, but she tamped it down. He wanted her to fight. He got off on the hunt and the fear.

She would not give him either.

She made her body go limp. "Okay."

"Okay?"

His mouth was right next to her ear. His body so close. But she would not panic. She would not give him that.

"Do it," she said, issuing her challenge.

He loosened his grip. "Your game won't work."

But it had. Her arms were still trapped in his, but she could move now. Lower her hand.

"I won't fight you."

He whispered against her ear. "That's not like you, dear sister. You fight everything."

She forced her body to stay still. Lure him in. "You act like I have anything to live for. You and your brother destroyed everything."

"Oh, come on. Let me enjoy this."

He barely held her now. The space between them widened.

And she pounced.

Her fingers wrapped around the screwdriver she had hidden in her pocket. She thrust her arm into the air, breaking the last of his hold. She spun around and aimed for his neck. He ducked just in time, and the end rammed into his cheek. Blood spurted, and he reeled back.

She kicked him in the stomach. Used all the pent-up anger and fear and stretched out like she had with the fence. He went down, and the hammer fell from his fingers and cracked against the floor. Before he could get up, she jumped on him, arms waving, straddling his hips.

She shifted and heard his sharp intake of breath. When she looked down, she saw his jaw drop open and felt his hands pull at hers. The screwdriver poked out of his stomach, and blood gurgled up from inside of him.

It all happened so fast. The kick and the plunge. She'd stabbed him.

She shoved the screwdriver deeper into his body. Moved it around, causing as much damage as possible. Ripping and tearing.

As his eyes turned glassy and his voice died out, she leaned down. With her face just inches from his, she watched the life seep out of him.

"I knew about you all along," she whispered.

His mouth moved, but no sound came out.

"About this cabin. About you, you sick piece of garbage." Her side screamed in pain, and her fingers ached from the grip on the screwdriver, but she kept going. She needed his last memory to be of her. "I followed Aaron here weeks ago and figured it out."

"No." His voice came out as a low whisper.

"I had to wait. Bide my time and plan. I couldn't just kill one of you. I needed to wipe out your polluted bloodline. Make sure every last male Payne was dead, and now I've killed you both." She pushed the tool even deeper and his hands slid off hers and fell to the floor.

"I fucking win."

"LILA!"

She could hear Pete's voice but didn't let go. Jared's body turned boneless and his head fell to the side. She watched his chest, but it no longer moved up and down. Still, she sat on top of him and dug that screwdriver as deep as she could inside of him.

Blood soaked his gray shirt and flooded the floor beneath him. She could smell it, feel the stickiness on her fingers, but she didn't unclench.

The room started to spin, and the stitch in her side begged for attention. She heard footsteps thundering up the outside steps. Pete was yelling directions, and someone said something about an ambulance.

No need. She'd taken care of him. She'd ended it.

Pete skidded into the room. He hesitated for a second before running over and kneeling next to her. "Okay, Lila. Let go."

She shook her head. "I can't."

Pete felt for Jared's pulse. "He's dead."

"He killed them all. Those women. It was Jared. He set up Aaron, but he killed them."

"We'll worry about who did what later. I need you to let go now so I can get you some help." Pete tried to loosen her grip.

So many questions crashed into her brain, and her vision blurred. "Why are you here?"

"Ginny told me to follow you."

She thought a car had been following her, but then she'd looked back and it wasn't there. "You took your time getting here."

He shook his head. "I lost you near the end of the drive."

None of that mattered now. She knew who and why. Everything she'd ever thought about Jared had been wrong. The bracelets. The charms he'd used as some sort of official body count of his depravity. He was more than damaged. He was evil.

She forced her mind to focus even as her stomach spun and twisted. "Tell Ginny I wasn't too late this time."

Then she gave in to the pain pulling and tugging at her and the cabin went dark.

Chapter Sixty

THE NEXT MORNING, CHARLES CALLED GINNY AND PETE INTO
his office. Made a show of it, too. Yelled their names across
the main room and slammed the door, trapping them inside.

He'd been on the phone since she'd arrived at work. Rubbing his hand through his hair, which was never a good sign.

He disconnected the call and fell into the chair. He eyed up
both of them before turning to her. "I told you to stand down.
That was an order."

Only he would think that catching a serial killer and a
teacher who'd abused kids in the same week was a feat that
demanded an explanation. He fought for his job and his reputation. Just once she wished he'd fight for the people on the
ground. The people who worked so hard to make him look
good to the voters.

She inhaled, waging an internal fight. She kept her voice
calm and tried to be reasonable. "You said the FBI was taking
over. That meant—"

"You heard what I said. You were to stop working on the

case." He leaned back in this chair. "Instead, you sent Pete out on surveillance."

She would make the same call today and next week and next year. "It's good I did."

Pete nodded in an uncharacteristic show of support. He wasn't exactly one to buck authority. "She's right. Something could have happened to Lila."

"We might never have known that Jared was the killer," she added.

Pete nodded again. "Exactly."

Silence sucked all of the oxygen out of the room. There was nothing comfortable about this quiet. It itched and burned.

"There's one major flaw in your joint and obviously practiced argument." He pointed at Pete but looked at Ginny. "He didn't stop Jared. He didn't kill him or save Lila. He got there after Jared was dead. She saved herself."

All true, but Ginny thought he was trying very hard to miss the point.

"I found her over Jared's body." Pete stood at attention, but he wasn't marching to orders this time. "It was obvious from the scene he was looking for Lila to be his next victim."

Charles shrugged. "So?"

"*So?*" She was surprised her head didn't explode.

Charles glared at Pete. "What happened to your belief that Lila killed her husband? That Ginny was too close to this case to properly assess it?"

Pete's eyes widened. "I didn't—"

"It's exactly what you said. You came running to me, refusing to make a formal complaint but trying to cover your own ass, just in case."

The weasel. Both of them. Scurrying around, whispering behind her back. But still.

She forced her anger down, like she always did. "None of that changes what happened in the cabin."

"Or that Ginny's instincts about this case not being over were right," Pete said.

Not that she forgave him based on that small show of support. She didn't. Disloyalty, picking Charles's whims over her instincts, would take a minute for her to process. Not now, but back at home. She'd talk to Roland, and then maybe— maybe—she'd remember how green Pete was and let it go.

"What did happen in that cabin? Do we know?" Charles leaned forward with his hands folded together. This was his serious, *I'm in charge* position. He used it whenever he wanted to yell. "It seems to me, once again, that we're taking Lila Ridgefield's word on everything. We have to because she'd been leading us around the whole case."

But he wasn't wrong about that. Getting there just after the altercation, not knowing what they'd said and fought about, picked at Ginny. "What are you suggesting?"

Charles focused on her. Frowned and sighed and gave her the full *I'm pissed* show. "I'm saying with or without Pete in that cabin, this case would have ended the same way. With more questions than answers. With two dead men and a woman the public views as a vigilante hero. She is untouchable."

Pete shrugged. "I can live with that."

"Oh, really?" Charles's voice grew even louder. "See, I gave an order. I had an understanding with the State police and FBI, and you two violated it."

And there it was. The real reason for all of this, for launching into the screed in front of the full office. "This lecture is because we made you look bad in front of your important friends?" she asked.

"I'm in charge, not you. Do you understand me?" He didn't give her time to answer. "Well?"

Pete exhaled. "Yes, sir."

"Yes," she said without rolling her eyes, which she thought was a huge triumph.

"You're both on leave. I don't want to see either of you for a week. Not a word to the press or that woman with the podcast. Prove to me you can follow orders, or you're fired." He looked down at his desk blotter and treated them to a shooing gesture. "Get out."

SHE WALKED OUT of the office and made it halfway to the coffee before Pete's voice stopped her.

"Ginny . . ."

She turned around and saw the panic on his face. The frown and the furrowed brow. Time to be the bigger person—again. "It's fine."

Pete swore under his breath and took a step closer to her. "It's not."

Actually, it wasn't. It might never be. "We have to work together, Pete. Political types will come and go. They don't wander out in the field or put their lives in danger. We do that. And I need to be able to trust you."

"You can."

She snorted. "It sure as hell doesn't feel like it."

"I messed up, but I get it now."

She doubted it. "What do you get?"

"Lila. Your reaction to her."

"Huh." She crossed her arms in front of her. "I don't understand what you're trying to tell me. Explain."

"Seeing her there, holding on to that screwdriver in a death grip . . . It was as if she thought if she let go, then Jared would rise from the dead and attack again."

Ginny could picture it. She hadn't been in the room but had no trouble reliving the moment with him.

"A piece of her probably did believe that." Pete's pained expression pushed her to elaborate. "Imagine being her and having your life destroyed by your father's betrayal. By him doing the worse thing imaginable. Then his actions steal your mother away, leaving your trust and sense of safety irreparably damaged. Your life gets flipped again by your husband and the one person you think you can trust—your brother-in-law—turns out to be the worst of them all."

He was wise enough to wince at the factual scenario she laid out. "What does that do to a person?"

"Beats them down. Without getting help, probably made them more vulnerable to snapping." That's what Ryan's notes had said. Lila had never dealt with the loss. She'd pushed it down, ignored it, and the PTSD had festered until her sense of what she needed and her reality skewed.

He whistled. "So, what happens now?"

"Nothing. I stay home for a few days and annoy my husband and son."

"No way." He scoffed. "Wait, you're serious? You're going to give up?"

With the trust gone, the last thing she wanted to do was share any part of her thinking with Pete. "You heard the boss."

"Since when do you follow orders?"

But she did. That was the point. In the past she'd paid for it. A millionaire's wife had paid for it. She'd approached this case a different way, which made walking away so difficult. "I'm not losing my job over Aaron and Jared Payne. I wouldn't lose it for Lila either."

"That's not what I thought you'd say."

"I've learned my lesson." She almost smiled. She could imagine her husband's reaction if she tried to sell that line to him.

"Nah." Pete shook his head. "You'll be watching the case."

"Of course." And a weeklong break would give her the opportunity to learn one last thing about Lila and her life before she let the case go.

Chapter Sixty-one

Eleven Days Later

GINNY MADE IT MORE THAN A WEEK BEFORE HEADING BACK TO Lila's house. She thought people should praise her for that. Lila's neighbor stalked across the lawn and met her before she reached the door. "You need to leave her alone."

The only thing that kept her from yelling was the possibility that Charles would find out about the visit and fire her. "I'm just here for a final wrap-up. No questions." She held up a hand in mock surrender. "I promise."

"If you want to help, clear them off the street." Cassie stared at the media vans and press congregating at the end of Lila's driveway.

They would move on soon, enraptured by some new horror, and leave Lila alone. But she could help the process along. "I'll see what I can do."

Cassie rolled her eyes and stomped away. "Yeah, sure."

When Ginny looked back at the house, she saw the front

door was open and Lila stood there. She couldn't remember a time during this whole mess where she'd stood on her front porch.

Ginny walked up the driveway toward Lila. The first thing she spied was the sign on the lawn. The next was the open curtains on the front windows.

"Visiting with my neighbors?" Lila sounded amused at the idea.

"You're moving?" Not what Ginny had intended her first question to be, but it worked.

"Being here is not exactly comforting."

Ginny smiled at the sarcasm in Lila's voice. "It's hard being a hero."

"Tell that to my cracked rib." Lila put her hand against her side.

"I heard about the injuries." Broken rib. Dislocated shoulder. Shock. It had all been in the medical report. "You okay?"

"It's one last gift from the Payne brothers." Lila stepped back and gestured for Ginny to go first. "Come in."

The house was so quiet. No podcast or music blaring. Boxes piled everywhere. Garbage bags filled and closed, waiting to go outside or be donated. Ginny wasn't sure of the contents, so she could only guess.

She waited until Lila stepped into the kitchen to talk again. "Are you worried about being able to sell the house after everything that's happened? It has quite a history."

Lila put a used coffee cup in the sink, likely the neighbor's.

She got a clean one out of the cabinet. "I was concerned at first, but apparently there is a thriving market for people who have an unhealthy interest in serial killers."

"That can't be true."

She refilled her mug. "We listed three days ago and Christina has received two offers so far, one from out of town."

"Damn."

"My life story is very lucrative, usually for other people." She held the pot up. "Coffee?"

Ginny nodded then held on to the mug to make pouring easier. "Meaning?"

"You didn't hear?" She set the pot down and turned to face Ginny again. "Ryan already got a new book deal."

"Son of a bitch."

"I've been using 'bastard,' but your words work, too." Lila cradled her mug. "A true-crime, forensic *I was part of this case* personal insights thing. Got a crap ton of money for it."

Bastard. "Unbelievable."

"Is it?"

"Maybe not." He'd seemed nice enough and said the right things. Liked to talk and clearly viewed himself as the most important person in the room . . . yeah, Ginny didn't get what Lila had seen in him. "I guess you're not together."

"No." Lila leaned back against the refrigerator. "He avoided criminal charges thanks to Jared's admission about planting the phone and ended up with exactly what he wanted—a front seat to a real crime."

The industry that had grown up around death had never sat right with Ginny. "That's bloodless."

"He insisted it was business and we could continue to sleep together."

Ginny saluted Lila with her mug. "Nice of him."

"My taste in men sucks."

"It really does." Ginny sat on one of the bar stools. Being there, talking like this, it would be easy to forget they operated on opposite sides of this case. Anyone walking in might see them as two friends gossiping. But that wasn't why she'd shown up today. She needed Lila to know. "You did okay in the end."

Lila stared at her over the top of her mug. "How do you figure that?"

"The trust fund."

"Aaron's trust went to Jared."

Ginny thought she saw a small smile come and go on Lila's mouth. Whatever game they'd been playing clearly was not done. Ginny threw down her last card. "Jared was Aaron's beneficiary, but no one mentioned that *you* were always listed as Jared's only beneficiary. Not Aaron. You."

"So it appears."

"Since Aaron died first, his trust went to Jared. As Jared's beneficiary, you get his estate plus whatever will go to him from Aaron."

"Yes." Lila set her mug down on the counter.

"Between the houses and Jared's other accounts and the

trust, we're talking about ten million dollars." Pete had wanted to run into Charles's office and show him after she'd told him the number, walked him through the assets.

Ginny knew better. This fact, even though it provided some pretty juicy motive, wouldn't matter. The search for more remains continued. Everyone—maybe even her—was fine with letting the case end this way. Pretty, with a bow but no real answers about who'd killed Aaron and why.

"It's closer to eleven million."

Ginny felt the emotions in the room shift. An odd sensation wound around them. Not really tension. More like a mutual understanding. "That's a nice payday."

Lila winced. "I worked hard for it."

She sure as hell had and somehow had still come out as the hero. "Convenient how it all worked out in the end. The money, I mean. Not the killings."

Lila shook her head. "Again, the Payne brothers were anything but convenient."

"True."

"What's your theory?" Lila smiled, and for the first time since they'd met it looked genuine. Warm. "You want to tell me, so say it."

Almost, but not yet. "Why not turn the brothers in as soon as you found out about them?"

"Maybe I did." She shrugged. "You don't know."

"Let's pretend you didn't. Let's pretend you found out about Aaron and waited."

"Is your theory that I knew about who both brothers really

were and what they were doing but withheld the information from the police so that I could plot their murders, one after the other, in order to maximize the benefit I'd receive?"

The way the scenario rolled off her tongue. She didn't stammer or laugh. She spelled it out as if it were true . . . and Ginny was pretty sure it was. "It's a good theory."

"I'd have to be a psychopath."

"Or very smart. A person with a law degree who knew how the pieces worked." But that was only part of it. Stopping there made her sound calculating and most concerned with the money, and Ginny didn't buy that. "A woman who was done with the sick men in her life and took them out before they could do more damage. And just happened to earn a big payday doing it."

"Interesting hypothetical." Lila's smile grew wider. "I especially like the last part."

"We both know it's true."

Lila played with the mug. Spun it around but didn't pick it up again. "Have any evidence to prove it?"

"You know I don't."

Lila let out a long breath. "Well, if it makes you feel better, I have Tobias working with the student victims to pay out settlements and get them help. They'll be taken care of once the estate settles."

Of course she did. Ginny should have seen that coming. The blood money would bother Lila.

"He's also reached out to the families of Karen, Julie, and Yara about setting up some sort of foundation in their honor."

Ginny ran a quick calculation in her head. "That doesn't sound like ten million dollars."

"About half." Lila glanced around the now near-empty family room area. "I don't need big houses and fancy watches, but it will be nice not to worry about how to pay the bills."

"Any chance you're going to spend some of your remaining share of the wealth on getting help?"

Lila's smile fell. "Like a gardener?"

"Ryan might be an ass, but that doesn't mean his diagnosis of you was all wrong." Ginny could see Lila's body shut down. She hadn't moved, but that shield she threw up whenever anyone dug into emotions or health went up and stayed there. "You don't have to be a victim."

"I'm a survivor."

That's how she would describe Lila, too. If anyone asked her about this case in the future, she would use that word. "True."

Some of the tension left Lila's shoulders. "That's good enough for me."

"Okay." Ginny got off the stool and set her untouched coffee on the counter, closer to Lila. "Then we're done here."

"You're leaving?"

"I came to say goodbye. To let you know that you won. The case as to who really killed Aaron will slowly fade then be closed, but I know the truth. We both do." Ginny remembered one more detail. "And the information you provided about Jared admitting to setting up Brent? The computer analysts are double-checking to make sure that's true, but you likely saved him from jail time for something he didn't do."

Lila studied Ginny for a few seconds. Let her gaze wander over her. "You should be sheriff, not Charles."

"I'm not a desk job type."

"You're a leader. The only one in this case I ever worried about."

"I'm assuming that's as close as you'll ever get to confessing to planning the Payne brothers' deaths."

"Hypothetically, yes."

Then she'd take that. She'd make it be enough. "Goodbye, Lila. I hope wherever you go you find whatever it is you're looking for."

"Honestly? I've given up on finding anything worth keeping."

"I hope that's not true." She started down the hall, mentally debating if she could tolerate this ending. If she could let that last string about Aaron's murder sit there without pulling it. And she decided what she'd told Roland days ago was right—she could.

Lila being in prison wouldn't make anyone safer, and they didn't have the proof to put her there anyway. A form of justice had been served, just not the type Ginny spent her life fighting for. Vigilante justice just invited more and eventually the innocent would be hurt, but this was one case not a lifetime statement.

She would never grieve for Aaron or Jared Payne. Not one

minute. She'd save that energy for their victims. For the survivors who had to figure out how to move on. For the next case.

"Ginny?"

"Yes?"

Lila hesitated for a few seconds before talking. "There's a place called Fischer's Farm in Pennsylvania. I think the Payne family killing started long ago, when Aaron and Jared were young, with their father and some very powerful men who looked the other way. Their mother might have been Jared's first victim, but she wasn't the family's first."

She didn't think. She knew. Ginny could see it on her face. "Jared told you that?"

"He learned how to kill from an expert."

More bodies. More death. Possibly more closure for families who deserved it. "You didn't share this information with the FBI?"

"I'm telling you. Someone needs to be there for those women. I think you're the right person." Lila's head fell to the side. "Consider this my penance."

"I thought you were innocent."

"I never said that." Lila walked back into the kitchen. "But finish it."

Chapter Sixty-two

This is Nia Simms and Gone Missing, *the true crime podcast that discusses cases—big and small—in your neighborhood and around the country. And, boy, do we have a lot to talk about today. Events have unfolded at lightning speed.*

Aaron Payne the serial teen girl abuser. Jared Payne the serial killer. A cabin in the middle of nowhere and a woman who stopped them both. The lines are open and . . .

Okay, I'm told we have a special caller. Folks, her identity has been checked and double-checked. This is Lila Ridgefield.

Lila?

I've followed your podcast. Thank you for keeping Karen, Yara, and Julie in the news.

Of course. I need to ask—

I wanted to say one thing first, if that's okay. You've called me a hero, and that's not true. The credit goes to your listeners who kept the pressure on. To the families of the missing women, who have to figure out how to survive such a horrible loss. To Samantha Yorke, for being so brave and coming forward. She exposed Aaron's true self and made it possible for other girls to get help.

Okay, let me ask—

And to Ginny Davis, the senior investigator in the Criminal Investigation Division of the Tompkins County Sheriff's Office. She understood this case from the beginning. She knew her theories were right and never gave up. She's exactly the type of person who should be in charge.

That's great. Now, Lila . . . Lila? Okay, listeners. It sounds as if we got cut off. I'll try to get her back on the line.

Lila hung up the phone. She'd covered every base and put the emphasis where it should be. Off the men who'd killed and on the women who'd made a difference.

No more talk about Aaron and Jared. Ever. She could leave town and start over. Erase her name and find a new life. Build something without a husband or father. Because she was in charge.

How long did it take to eliminate a family of monsters? Two months.

She won.

Acknowledgments

FIRST, APOLOGIES TO ITHACA, NEW YORK. YOU ARE STUNNING. I went to college nearby at Syracuse University. When it came time to figure out a setting for this book Ithaca jumped into my mind. The idea of setting something ugly in a place so bucolic appealed to me. But really, the story is from my imagination. It's me, not you.

The tiny spark of an idea for this book was born during a lunch with my editor, May Chen, at a writing conference. We'd worked together on romantic suspense novels for years. Our usual conversation about our current reads turned into a "what if I wrote something totally different . . ." discussion. So, when I finally figured out what my domestic suspense would look like, she was the first person we called. The only one, actually. Because if I were going to try a new genre, I wanted May and the entire HarperCollins group on my team. I am grateful they wanted that, too.

A huge thank you to my agent, Laura Bradford, for listening to me talk about this book and work through my desire to pivot to try new things. When I need support, you provide it.

When I need a kick, you gently deliver. Thank you for both . . . and for selling this book.

I happened to be on a writers' retreat with friends (read: tax deductible vacation) when I got the book offer. Thank you to Lauren Dane, Shannon Stacey, Jaci Burton, Vivian Arend, Angela James, Megan Hart, and Sarah Wendell for being there, for celebrating with me, and for talking me out of the *can I do this?* panic. Also, thank you to Jill Shalvis who provides weekly encouragement via text.

Thank you to everyone who has talked about this book, been excited about the book, reviewed it, and bought it. I am grateful and humbled.

And, as always, thanks to James. I couldn't have this career without you.

DARBY KANE is the pseudonym of a former trial attorney and current award-winning romantic suspense author. A native of Pennsylvania, Darby now lives in California and runs from the cold. When she's not writing, she can be found watching suspense, thrillers, and mysteries. Clearly, her interests are limited.